LAYER
UPON
LAYER

LAYER UPON LAYER

DEEDEE HORTON

Layer Upon Layer

Copyright © 2024 by David F Horton. All Rights Reserved.

No part of this publication may be reproduced, stored in a retrieval system or transmitted, in any form or by any means—electronic, mechanical, photocopying, recording or otherwise—without prior written permission from the publisher, except for the inclusion of brief quotations in a review.

This is a work of fiction. Unless otherwise indicated, all the names, characters, businesses, places, events, and incidents in this book are either the product of the author's imagination or used in a fictitious manner. Any resemblance to actual persons, living or dead, or actual events is purely coincidental or fictitious.

For information about this title or to order other books and/or electronic media, contact the publisher:

D2 Infinity Publishing
Layeruponlayer.com
Layeruponlayer@davidhorton.com

ISBNs:
979-8-9902091-1-4 (hardcover)
979-8-9902091-0-7 (softcover)
979-8-9902091-2-1 (eBook)

Printed in the United States of America

Interior design: 1106 Design
Cover design: Meenal Rahatkar of SimplyBe, a Hawke Media Company

In honor of two LCs,
two incredible impacts on my life.
You saw me.
You mentored me.
You set me free to pass it on.

CONTENTS

AUTHOR'S NOTE

BY DAVID HORTON,
THE AUTHOR'S HUSBAND

It is the greatest tragedy of my life that DeeDee is no longer with us to present *Layer Upon Layer* to her readers. This work was a six-year-long process of writing and combining two novels into one, which she called a "work of love." Her final of many edits was underway in preparation for publication when DeeDee developed seizures and was diagnosed with an aggressive brain tumor.

Early in treatment, DeeDee had rapid progression of her cancer and began hospice care, prioritizing what was most important to her: "slow, calm, quiet time together, enjoying each other, views of nature, and short walks." Amazingly, this came to pass due to the steadfast support of teammates and coaches from DeeDee's high school days, enabling us to share innumerable beautiful and loving moments during her end-of-life journey—a short nine-month journey in which we both experienced more love than we could ever have imagined in a lifetime.

With the time DeeDee had left, she knew she would not complete the editing of her novel but entrusted me to complete *Layer Upon Layer*—so long as I protected its "heart and soul." I believe I have done this, and she would be happy.

I know this novel's core well, having read it in all its many forms. To me, it is a "Barbie sports story," continuing the conversation about the female experience of living in a society dominated by ingrained, invisible male privilege. Sports are just the vehicle for sharing one woman's journey through the layers of cultural expectations and programming that trap her, wondering if there is a way out. Barbie might summarize it as one woman finding her answer to a vital question: *Should I be brainwashed, or should I be weird?*

Being "brainwashed" may seem more effortless and less painful, while being "weird" can seem daunting and lonely. Suppose that, instead of conforming, you are courageous like Samantha, our heroine, and remain true to yourself. You will likely be barraged by messages not to be too vocal or opinionated, or to make waves because it's more important for females to be "nice and liked," keeping it comfortable for others. And what if the people most important to you fail to see and celebrate YOU? Hopefully, along the way, you will encounter mentors who can illuminate the path to finding your hopes and dreams, reminding you of what is possible. Still, by remaining silent about the resulting hurt and anger, these feelings can turn inward and change into shame and unworthiness, keeping you from inner peace and self-acceptance.

Although DeeDee wrote her book primarily for women, as a male, I encourage boys and men to read this book and ponder Sam's many questions and observations. I am thankful to DeeDee for making me more aware of entrenched male privilege and more empathetic to the frequently silent pain and suffering it brings to women's lives. Hearing and seeing each other on our 32-year journey together allowed us to forge a deep and loving connection, unquestionably the greatest gift of my life. Exploring these issues with the people most important in your life may help bring the same gifts to you. I wish this for everyone.

Lastly, thank you for honoring DeeDee with the gift of your time to read *Layer Upon Layer*. If you have thoughts you would like to share or discuss, I would be honored to hear from you. Please email me at: david@layeruponlayer.com.

CHAPTER 1

SEPTEMBER 2006

I checked my phone for messages before leaving campus. There was one.

"Oh my God, Coach. I got the internship; I got one of only five spots! You're the first person I'm calling. I can't thank you enough for all your help with my essay, especially the interview prep time. I would've bombed that part without your help. I'm so excited, and I still can't believe it. Thank you, thank you—" The time for her message ran out.

Whitney's joy was evident in her volume and fast pace. Although I laughed at her unabashed delivery, I was touched by her appreciation. She was a senior, a team captain, and an incredible person on and off the court. The basketball component of my job at Kalispell College fueled my competitive spirit, but these moments off the court ignited my deeper purpose and passion each day.

The two-hour drive from Kalispell to Missoula was wide open. I strummed my fingers across the steering wheel in time with the music blaring from my radio and belted out the lyrics when Kanye's "Gold

Digger" came on. The following songs were upbeat, matching my excitement at Whitney's news. Unfortunately, the closer I got to the airport, the deeper my mood sank. My thoughts shifted from basketball to family dynamics. The term that came to mind was "force of nature," and the image was an earthquake. But unlike when an earthquake shook the Puget Sound of western Washington, leaving me unaffected in Montana, when it came to family, it seemed that geographic distance couldn't provide enough protection. Being in the path of destruction felt inevitable.

The airport wasn't busy, so I pulled up next to the curb by Arrivals to wait. After a few minutes, my mom walked through the sliding doors, pulling her small suitcase. I started to worry about my hair, my face, my clothes, and my body. I walked around to the back of the car to raise the trunk before getting her attention. I worried about what she saw when she looked at me.

"Hi, Mom. It's good to see you. You look great." She looked like she'd stepped straight off the pages of a Nordstrom catalog.

"It's good to see you too, honey."

I put her suitcase in the trunk, and we hugged. My shoulder-length brown hair, pulled back into a short ponytail, combined with my jeans and sweatshirt on my five-foot-eight frame, didn't give her anything about my appearance she could compliment.

She opened the passenger door and sat in the front seat. I held on to the door, looking toward the terminal's exit doors.

"Did Dad have a problem with his luggage, or did he stop at the bathroom?"

"No, he couldn't make it this time," she said, pulling the door from my grasp to shut it. That closing somehow felt like more than just a car door. I froze in place, this revelation causing a momentary paralysis. Was she joking? And what did she mean by "not this time"? As if he'd made it *any* time. Before getting into the car, I cast another glance toward the exit, wishing to see my dad standing there and hoping this was a prank.

As we pulled away, my mom started chatting like everything was normal. There was no mention of my dad, why he couldn't make it, or when the decision had been made. Not sharing this with me was a blow. Instead, my mom shared every possible detail about my sister Emily and her three kids. I love my niece and nephews, but the information felt like an overload at times like this. And Mom had pictures for every story, so even as I drove, she tried to keep either her phone or a printed picture in my line of vision.

"You're as bad as a teenager," I said with a chuckle. "There's not much difference between looking at pictures on your phone and texting while driving."

"Oh, sorry. I'm just excited to share. It seems like it's been so long since I've seen you or since you've seen Em and the kids."

After a brief silence, like my mom didn't know what to talk about if she wasn't talking about the grandkids, I asked a few questions focused on her—her job managing a dental office, activities with friends, her health, and exercise. Although her answers were detailed, all too soon, her conversation returned to the grandkids. Maybe if she got most of it out now, we could talk about other things the rest of the weekend. Twenty minutes from home, I found a natural break in the conversation.

"I'm surprised Dad didn't come. This was finally the trip that he was supposed to make." I tried to keep my words and tone neutral.

"Oh, Sam. Do you have to bring that up now?"

Her irritation shocked me. "If not now, when would be a better time?"

"This is a quick weekend, and I was looking forward to spending time with you and having fun. You know your dad is busy. I don't understand why you must turn everything your dad does and says into a federal offense."

I was stunned into an extended silence, but she said nothing to fill it. My mouth had turned into sandpaper, and I took a sip of water so I could speak.

"I wasn't trying to make it into a federal offense. I was looking forward to him finally making it here, seeing my house and the campus, and meeting Fitz and the team. Let me know if there is a good time to discuss this while you're here."

We were silent the rest of the drive. My mom followed me from the garage, through my tiny laundry room, and into the kitchen. "Everything looks just like I remembered," she said, her friendly tone returned.

"Let's take your stuff to the bedroom. It's late. Are you ready for bed, or would you like some tea first?"

"I may read for a bit, but you don't need to worry about me. I've got it from here. You can get ready for bed."

I hugged her goodnight.

Lying in bed, staring at the ceiling, my mind raced, but not with the usual things related to basketball and our team, the Cougars. Although I was happy to see my mom, and she seemed glad to see me, there was this lurking question: Was she excited to be here? She was supposedly here to see me, but in our four hours together, everything had been about my sister and her kids. When she visited Emily, did she go on and on about me, my job, where I lived? Did she think that what Emily did was better or more important?

Of course, there were two more significant questions: Why didn't my dad come? And would we ever talk about that? I pressed the heel of my hand against my eyes, trying to stop this mental gerbil wheel. I rolled onto my left side and tried to focus on my breathing, but before long, I shifted to my right side, my stomach, and then back to my left side.

The red numbers on my bedside clock glared into the darkness, chastising me for still being awake. Yet having my mom visit me was so much better than when I visited home. There, I was always surprised at how quickly we both seemed to be transported back to the roles we'd played while I was growing up, including the corresponding emotions.

For me, that was not feeling pretty enough, feminine enough, or outgoing enough. When I was with my parents, I was not enough.

As we pulled into the gym parking lot, I reviewed my schedule for the day with Mom. "We'll have the kids out on the track, then in the gym, and back in the classroom last. You're more than welcome to join us for any or all of that or—"

"Sam," she interrupted as I got out of the car, "don't worry about me. I'm going to enjoy myself."

"Okay," I said and waved goodbye as she drove out of the parking lot.

It was 9:40 a.m. As I walked across campus, the combination of sunshine and crisp fall air felt invigorating. All the outdoor seating areas were filled with chattering students excited about starting a new school year and enjoying the gorgeous fall weather.

As I opened the door to my office, I was startled to see Brian, known as Fitz to all of us. Tall and a little pudgy, he had thin brown hair and a beard. His usual campus attire—a Cougar basketball polo shirt with polyester pants hiked above his waist, made Fitz look older than his 49 years. His demeanor almost always exuded enthusiasm or compassion, instantly putting others at ease. "Fitz, what are you doing here this early?"

He was looking at my crowded bookshelves but straightened up and turned when I said his name. "Man, I'm not sure if I should be impressed or alarmed at how many psychology books you have in your collection. And it seems to grow by the month."

"Maybe it's grown because I'm trying to figure out how to work with my assistant coach." I tried to keep a serious look on my face, but it lasted for two seconds before I felt the edges of my mouth curl into a slight grin. Although this was our fourth year coaching together, from the beginning, it felt like I'd known him all my life. We had plenty of differences in personality and style, but at the core we were kindred spirits.

"Hey, before we get into basketball, how's it going with your parents?

"Well, just my mom. I gave her the car and she's exploring alone today, but we'll do something fun together tomorrow."

"I thought your dad was coming. I was looking forward to finally meeting him."

"I know. With the school year and his coaching, it's hard for him to get away." Even with a close friend, sometimes making an excuse to soften the sharp edges of reality felt better in the moment.

"Wait. Do I remember correctly—didn't you send them the plane tickets for this trip?"

"Yeah," I answered quietly, looking away.

Fitz took a deep breath in and slowly exhaled. "I'm sorry, Sam. I know how much you were looking forward to this, how much it meant to you." I looked him in the eyes to show I'd heard him, but I couldn't hold his gaze for long. The compassion on his face put a lump in my throat.

He grabbed a copy of the day's plan and handed it to me. I was more than happy to move on. "Think we'll have any pukers today?" I asked as we headed out to the track.

"Nope. This will be our first year without that 'special moment.' It will be our program's turning point—it's going to be a season of greatness."

This first track workout always revealed who'd spent time on conditioning during the summer. Afterward, the kids scrimmaged for an hour. Fitz and I watched from upstairs, looking for intangibles: which returners demonstrated leadership, how hard players worked when they were tired, whether any cliques were forming, and who would be our fiercest competitors. For our incoming freshmen and those hoping to be walk-ons, this was our first opportunity to see them in a new and challenging environment.

At the same time, Fitz and I also made a concerted effort to watch our returners with fresh eyes. We wanted them to know that they started each school year and season with a clean slate, a new chance to show their growth and improvement.

"Suzie, it's so good to see you again. You look great." Fitz stood to hug my mom.

"Thank you, Brian. It's good to see you, and Anne too. Thanks for inviting us for brunch before I leave. It was such a quick trip this time."

Our waitress brought a fresh pot of coffee. Once we placed our orders, my mom asked about Anne's work. Anne was a veterinarian, and it took only two minutes of hearing her speak about her job and patients to realize she was in the fortunate minority—someone whose career was their true passion. After a few touching animal stories, my mom asked about their kids, Stacey and Trevor. Both jumped in to share brief, proud updates.

Our food arrived, and the conversation slowed as we started to eat. Fitz and Anne asked us about our visit, then there was a brief pause. My mom rarely asked me about my coaching or team, so she was at a loss for any specific questions for Fitz.

Finally, he broke the silence. "Did Sam tell you we're going to our second wedding of a former player next weekend?"

"Is that right? Sam keeps attending former players' weddings but isn't close to her own." Her lighthearted laugh fell flat. "Maybe if she hadn't run off to Spain right after college."

I filled my mouth with hash browns, an excuse not to respond to her jab. Fitz jumped into the void. "I bet she learned more in those four years than she did in all her undergrad school and master's degree combined." His brown eyes lit up, and he beamed as he spoke from the heart.

My mom fell silent. She never asked questions about those years of my life. After college, I'd gotten a once-in-a-lifetime opportunity to play professional basketball in Madrid. The sticking point for my parents had been that it took me so far away, but those were some of the best years of my life, an unexpected blessing that revived my love for basketball and put me on the path to coaching.

During those years, I had repeatedly encouraged my parents to visit. My mom had always wanted to see Italy, and we could have made that trip together. It never happened, and from the time I came back to the States, we'd just danced around any conversation about that time in my life.

"Stacey's a senior this year, isn't she?" Mom asked. Brian and Anne both smiled and nodded. "Imagine your twenty-two-year-old daughter decides to move to Europe indefinitely for a job. Do you think you'd be supportive and feel excited?"

Fitz was a keen listener and sensitive to the unspoken words beneath what was said. "Well, of course, there would be a big part of me missing her. But yes, there would also be a part of me cheering her on and feeling proud of her independence and boldness."

My mom gave him a tight smile. "Well, it's probably different how dads feel about their daughters compared to moms. How do you think you'd feel, Anne?" It didn't take a rocket scientist to recognize an emotional button for my mom. Was it anger, hurt, resentment? Since my mom wouldn't speak honestly about her feelings, it left me guessing.

Anne replied, "I think my brain would say, 'Great for Stacey—go for it!' while my heart would say, 'I miss you so much. Why couldn't you have found something closer?'" After a brief pause, she added, "And then I'd be hoping it was Paris so I could visit." She smiled, which softened my mom's stone-like stance.

By the time we were back in the car, headed to the airport, my mom's mood had shifted entirely. "They sure are nice people," she said in a cheery tone.

"Yeah, they're great. I'm lucky to have Fitz as an assistant coach, and Anne has been so supportive too." I realized my mom had not asked a single question about my team, job, or the college during her entire visit.

Her next words came out slowly and deliberately, as if she were carefully considering each syllable before speaking. "Sometimes I worry because Brian and Anne are the only friends I've met or heard about. I worry you're lonely and won't ever meet a future husband." She laughed before she said, "I thought I might be meeting a boyfriend when the dinner reservations were for three."

I didn't say, "For three of us, because Dad was supposed to be here." Though I bristled inside, I laughed along with her supposed joke.

"My job keeps me so busy, and I'm surrounded by wonderful people. I cherish the time to myself when it happens because it's so rare." My parents saw my job as the same as my dad's high school coaching job. They had no idea of how much more it entailed than coaching high school students. If they'd shown more interest by asking questions rather than making assumptions, they'd know precisely how packed my schedule was.

"Your dad and I miss you. College, Spain, now Montana; we don't get to see you as much as we'd like. And we worry. If you ever have kids, you'll understand."

Oh God, let's not start down this path. Marriage talk was terrible enough.

"You know, Mom, I love what I do, who I do it with, and where I live. I'm happy and think that would be the top priority you'd want for me."

"Your dad and I want you to be happy, Sam. That's the most important thing . . ." She left that thought hanging in midair, like she had more to say.

"But—what?" My tone was short, my irritation close to the surface.

"What do you mean 'what'?"

"It sounded like you had more to say but were holding back for some reason."

"It just never gets easier, this job of being a parent. It's painful to watch your kids, adults now, make choices and then struggle through those choices when maybe we feel we could've prevented some of that struggle." She shook her head as if trying to clear out the cobwebs. "I don't . . . I'm probably not making any sense. Maybe the best way to describe it is that I still have that Mama Bear in me. I thought that feeling would disappear once you and Emily left the house."

I pulled up to the terminal, put the car in park, then turned to look directly at her. "Do you still have that Mama Bear feeling for Emily, too, or is it just me?" I left off the last part: ". . . because I'm not married."

"No. Of course, it's Emily too." She sounded incredulous, like my question was crazy. "It's just about different things. With Emily, it might be more around how she's raising her kids or her relationship with Jack."

Did my sister take in my mom's feedback about her choices as a mother or a wife without pushing back? I tried to keep the expression on my face neutral because I preferred her sharing her thoughts rather than talking behind my back. I nodded, showing that I'd heard her.

I popped the trunk and grabbed her suitcase. As we hugged goodbye, I said, "I wish you wouldn't worry so much—about either of us. You must tell that inner Mama Bear that she did her job well and that her cubs can fend for themselves now."

She pulled away as a tear slid down her cheek, but she still smiled.

"Put that energy from worrying toward something that makes you happy," I said.

"I hope you know how special you are to me, and how much I love you."

"I do, and I love you too. Thanks again for coming. Give Dad my love. I hope next time he'll be able to come with you." I watched her walk away, and she turned to wave before entering the sliding doors.

My driving time was usually productive—I could problem-solve and plan, but not now. My mind raced with thoughts about my mom's visit, things that had been said, and those that hadn't. There was also the monumental weight of my dad's absence and the lack of any honest discussion about it.

My thoughts homed in on the changes in my relationship with my mom. She'd never sided with me against my dad, but she had served as a supportive buffer throughout my middle and high school years. Now, I felt none of that. It felt like she shared the same judgment and disappointment I'd always felt from my dad. Maybe she'd just hidden it better than my father when I lived at home. Maybe she, too, had wanted me to be different from who I was, different than who I had become. I felt drained. I turned on the radio, found an oldies rock station, and turned it up loud. I hoped to drown out the thoughts in my head.

When I walked into the house, the blinking light on my phone caught my eye. Two messages. The first one was Fitz.

"Sam, I'm so sorry I wasn't a better conversationalist today at brunch. I should've done better at steering clear of family quicksand pits. I hope it didn't make the drive to the airport feel like two days instead of two hours. Anne already lectured me and punched me in the arm, so you won't need to." I heard his chuckle. "I'll see you tomorrow."

I pushed erase, and the second message started. It was Cassandra.

"Sam! Did you survive the weekend with your parents? Call me immediately when you get home. I want to hear all about it." Just like in high school, Cassandra liked to get right into it. Picturing her leaving that message and waiting for my return call made me smile. She'd have to wait a little longer because I needed a bike ride first to clear my head, an actual necessity.

Cassandra answered on the first ring. "God, I thought you'd never call. Did you do that on purpose, bitch?"

I laughed. "For being such a great writer, you sure have a way with the spoken word."

Now it was her turn to laugh.

"It's good to hear your voice. At least I know you survived your parents' weekend. My caller ID says you're calling from home, not prison or the loony bin."

"Well, it was just my mom, so I guess you could say I got off easy."

"Really?" Her tone became serious. "I thought your dad was finally coming this time."

"That was the plan, but something came up on their end. It was a shock when it was just my mom. But she changed the subject when I tried to talk about it. No explanation, no apology. Sweep it under the rug and pretend everything's okay." My voice was flat; my disappointment had drained my energy.

"I'm sorry, Sam. Besides that rocky start, did you have a nice time with your mom?" She sounded both cautious and hopeful.

"Yeah, for the most part. If I avoid topics like marriage, kids, my job, and why I'm living in Montana instead of closer to them in Washington . . . it's all good."

Cassandra snorted a half laugh. "Good God! Did you do a movie-fest this weekend?"

"That might've turned out better. No, mostly I heard about Emily and looked at hundreds of pictures of her kids. I'm sure that's what she does when she visits them too. Oh no, she couldn't. She didn't take any pictures."

Cassandra's laughter was restrained; we were skating around the edges of something sensitive and more personal. "We've talked about this before," she said, "but have you thought any more about writing your parents a letter? They continue to brush off your efforts by phone and in the last few in-person visits. And now, this happens. Maybe direct dialogue is too intimidating as a first step."

"I haven't started anything yet, but I'll think more about it. That's enough about my parents. How's work?"

Cassandra was a journalist for *The Seattle Times*. Because she couldn't always write and cover the stories that meant the most to her, she'd also started a blog where she could write from her heart. Women's rights were at the top of her list. She also wrote about minority rights and the rights of the LGBTQ community. She was still fighting to raise awareness, like when we met in high school.

She told me about a few of her recent interviews and projects, and I asked, "So when can I expect you to announce your candidacy for governor of Washington?"

"I think my viewpoints on social issues would get me more death threats than votes. But I'm always available for speaking engagements. When can I return to talk to the team again?"

Cassandra had a genuine interest in my work. She knew all the players on the team, whether she'd met them or not. She wanted to know the ins and outs of our team dynamics, both on and off the court.

We invited guest speakers to share their life lessons and keys to success each season. They were from various careers—a school principal, bank president, financial planner, doctor, and service member. Most were women. I believed our kids couldn't hear the message enough: they should dream big, allowing no limits to what they believed they could accomplish.

My job had never been about only what happened on the basketball court. I was their coach, of course, but I also had the opportunity to be a mentor to help prepare them for the world that, inevitably, was waiting for them on the other side of that diploma. I'd been lucky enough to find people who helped guide me. My job was my platform to pay that forward.

Our guest speakers were one layer of that work. In our second season, Cassandra gave a dynamic presentation about overcoming obstacles and using challenges and setbacks as growth opportunities. The kids talked about her and her talk long after her visit.

"I'm trying to space them out, so we don't have any repeats during a player's four-year career."

"I had no idea you saw me as so one-dimensional! I have more than one topic I can talk about."

I chuckled. "I have no doubt you do," I said. "But you can visit, see the team, and hang out anytime. You don't have to plan it around being a guest speaker."

"I know, and I just might take you up on it this year."

We chatted a few more minutes before hanging up. A minute later, I got a text from Cassandra: *I'm sorry your dad was a no-show this weekend.*

I plopped down on my couch, deflated. If the relationship with my dad stayed this way for the rest of our lives, would the pain continue to feel like this, or would it subside over time? Cassandra knew my problem with my dad, but I'd changed the subject as quickly as possible. If I'd shared how hurt I felt, I worried she'd be disappointed by my lack of backbone. I'd never liked disappointing others, especially someone I cared about.

Like in high school, when I felt an injustice, I internalized it, and thought I could prove my worth through my actions. Cassandra picked up the proverbial pen and sword and approached the issue head-on. Her approach seemed to get better results. I might need to adopt a new mantra for dealing with conflict: What would Cassandra do?

September 2006

To: Samantha Shuster
From: Laurie Collins

Dear Sam,

You are finishing your first full week with your team, and I
hope things are off to a great start. I just wanted you to know
that I'm thinking about you and looking forward to following
another great season online.

Keep in touch,
Ms. C

CHAPTER 2

SEPTEMBER 1986

"Where are you going this early?" my dad asked as I opened the front door.

"To the library. I need a few articles for my current events class." His eyebrows furrowed, and his eyes narrowed. Even without words, his skepticism and judgment were evident.

"On the third day of school?"

"Oh, honey," my mom chimed in. "You know Samantha doesn't have a procrastination bone in her body. That's why she's such a great student."

My mom's role as a mediator between my father and me seemed effortless.

I smiled. "Have a great day, Mom and Dad. I'll see you tonight."

Truthfully, though it bothered me that he was suspicious, Dad wasn't wrong. I wasn't headed to the library.

About a year earlier, I'd begun stopping by the middle school in the morning twice a week to see Ms. Collins, my former gym teacher. She had never been one of my coaches, but she knew more about basketball than anyone I'd ever met. She'd caught me after a home game the year before and congratulated me on how well my skills were progressing. It had been a grueling game. I felt like my basketball coach, Ernie Walters, had criticized every shot I'd taken. By the end, I could barely hold back tears. At that moment, hearing a compliment from someone I admired as much as Ms. Collins felt like a lifeline.

The following day, I'd gotten up early and slipped out without anyone noticing. Entering the middle school gym, I knew it was Ms. Collins practicing post moves at the far end because of the red tennis shoes and blue sweatsuit she wore daily to school and to every game. She was tall and big-boned, but she moved gracefully, making me think she'd probably been a great post player in her day. Her face lit up when she saw me approaching, and her easy, friendly smile told me her offer of morning coaching sessions had been sincere.

"Well, Sam Shuster! It's great to see you! What are you doing here?"

She invited me in, offered me a seat, and we talked for almost an hour—discussing skills I wanted to work on, players we both admired, and what it would take for me to play basketball at the next level. The time had gone by so quickly that I'd been startled to realize I had only fifteen minutes to return to the high school and my homeroom before the second bell.

I was gathering my jacket and backpack when Ms. Collins cleared her throat. "Sam, I realize I'm not your coach. I wouldn't want to step on Coach Walters's toes, but if you ever want to work on extra drills or get feedback on your play, I'm always here about an hour before classes start."

I couldn't help but smile. "Could I come by tomorrow?"

Starting the next day, I stopped by the middle school several times a week for the rest of the school year. Ms. Collins would help me with my form, give me drills to run, or just let me ask questions about how to improve.

I'd never mentioned my sessions with Ms. Collins to my parents. I knew I couldn't avoid the subject forever, but it never felt like the right time to bring it up, especially with Dad. Despite our shared passion for sports, he'd repeatedly sent the message that my drive and commitment were not the right balance. I was supposed to have outgrown that and turned into a "normal" teenage girl.

That morning, I found Ms. Collins in the storage closet with a clipboard, taking inventory of field hockey equipment.

"Hey, what a pleasant surprise! I wasn't sure if I'd see you these first couple of weeks." She stepped out and motioned toward her office. "How was your summer? Tell me all about volleyball!"

I let out a breath I didn't realize I'd been holding. "I think we're going to be good this year."

Volleyball was our high school's only girls' sports program with a winning record. Our coach, Kathy Nelson, was known within our league and throughout the state as a demanding coach who always got the best from her teams; they'd made it to the state tournament for the past eight years. The previous year, we finished third in the state, our program's highest finish. This year, as seniors, our goal was the state championship.

As we sat in Ms. C's office, I told her about the twice-a-day practices we'd been holding the last few weeks of summer and some of the feedback I'd gotten from Coach Nelson about improving my speed.

"Sounds like it's going to be a busy season. What days are game days?"

"Tuesdays and Thursdays," I said.

"Sam, you know I'm always happy to work with you, but don't forget that rest is also an important part of the training process. We can always wait until volleyball season is done."

I worried if Coach Nelson or my teammates found out about our basketball sessions, they'd question my commitment to volleyball. But basketball was my passion, and I knew I could balance both.

"I know. But if you don't mind, I'd like to start immediately."

"Okay." She smiled. "But you have to promise me you'll cancel any of our sessions if you're tired, assignments or tests are stacked up, or you're sick." A steely stare was her way of saying, "Don't make a promise you can't keep."

"I promise," I said, unable to mask my excitement about getting a basketball in my hands and working with her soon.

"Great! How about our usual time on Mondays and Wednesdays?"

"Perfect," I said, glancing at my watch and grabbing my backpack. "Thanks, Ms. Collins. I'll see you Wednesday."

Pulling into the back row of our high school parking lot, I glanced in the rearview mirror to check my face and hair. Not that it mattered. At school, I was invisible.

I liked my teams and sports. They had been my anchor since the sixth grade. I dreaded the social part of school—the cliques, the gossip. I never felt like I fit in. I kept hoping these feelings would decrease or disappear, but they didn't.

My psychology class was in the same hall as my dad's classroom. His history classes were popular, but I didn't know if it was because being the boys' basketball coach made him seem cool or if his students enjoyed how he taught the material. I'd never been his student, at least not in a formal classroom setting.

When I was younger, our time together felt like teacher and student, but our subject matter was basketball. I hung out in the gym watching his practices, traveled with him to weekend tournaments for his younger teams, joined him to scout opponents, and sat next to him on the couch, watching and dissecting games. But those days were long gone. I walked by his classroom without a sideways glance.

Third period was English. Mr. Morris stood in the hallway, greeting students. Although he was probably in his late forties and had been teaching for more than twenty years, he exuded the energy and interest in students of a first-year teacher.

Mr. Morris had us take out our notebooks. "We'll do a series of five-minute free writes based on specific prompts. The only requirement for this part is that you write something, *anything*, for those five minutes. Are we clear? Are there any questions?" He scanned the room for a raised hand, but the class was ready.

Once we'd finished, Mr. Morris had us pick two writings to share with a partner. My partner was Cassandra, a quiet senior I'd hardly interacted with during our three years of school together. I knew she was on the student newspaper, but only because I'd seen her name attached to several articles I'd read.

Cassandra read first, and it was apparent she was talented. In these quick, initial drafts, her writing already sounded polished. Her sentences were rhythmic, and her words were specific without being showy.

"You're an excellent writer," I said.

"Thanks," she said, dropping her eyes to her paper. "It's a different style than newspaper articles, but I enjoy all writing." She said this last part like it was embarrassing.

It was my turn to read. I felt awkward because I was a novice compared to her, and reading my words out loud sounded so different from the voice in my head. It felt intimidating, even just reading to one person sitting across from me. I might as well have been standing on stage in front of a thousand people, naked.

When I finished, Cassandra said, "I like that second one about Shakespeare." Her acknowledgment gave me a boost of confidence.

Mr. Morris rallied us back as a group. "I hope your feedback helped you pinpoint one of these drafts to develop." The bell rang. "Come back tomorrow ready to start revising."

Outside in the noisy, crowded hallway, my sister's voice caught my ear. It was distinct, and it didn't match her petite build. Her voice evoked the image of a large, self-assured bartender who sometimes needed that voice to control her intoxicated clientele. Emily's voice came in handy for her as a cheerleader, and I think she used it to draw attention to herself.

Emily was with three cheerleader friends, talking and laughing loud enough to draw attention. I had no doubt she saw me, but she stayed focused on her group without a hint of acknowledgment. How fitting. My feelings of not fitting in at school were a large-scale version of what it felt like within my own family.

I found a place where I could enjoy lunch in the fresh air and sunshine. Tables were set up outside the cafeteria, but they were full, and though it was only the third day of school, social cliques were already apparent. The most obvious were the "jocks," mainly the better players on the boys' football and basketball teams. Within that group, there was a further hierarchy of popularity and influence.

Female athletes had no comparable social group. If anything, the more committed, competitive, and accomplished a girl athlete was, the lower she fell on the social ladder. Most female athletes tried to blend into other social groups to avoid being stereotyped as an athlete. It never made sense to me: The thing that catapulted boys to the height of popularity made girls into outcasts. So my lunch today would be alone, like most days of the school year.

Wednesday hadn't arrived quickly enough. I was anxious to dive into my early morning workouts with Ms. Collins.

"You were so quiet I didn't hear you come in," Ms. Collins said as she walked toward me, a basketball in each arm.

It was five minutes before our official start time, and I'd just finished lacing up my basketball shoes and doing light stretching. I didn't want to waste a single precious minute, and I didn't want to be disrespectful of Ms. Collins's time.

"You ready?" Her excitement seemed to match my own. I smiled and nodded.

"We are going to work on post moves," she announced. "As a five-eight guard, I bet most of the guards matched up against you are smaller. Even if you already have a couple of moves, it's one more weapon for you—it's one more way to make yourself unguardable."

I watched as she positioned herself above the low block to show a good post-up position. She motioned for me to stand on the perimeter and pass the ball in to her.

"The other thing that makes this such a valuable move for you is that most guards don't work much, if at all, on post defense. How much time have you spent at practice learning to guard in the post?"

I realized it was close to none. Almost all our defensive breakdown drills were set up with guards defending guards on the perimeter while posts were defending each other inside. My hesitation must've signaled my answer.

"Exactly," she said. With that, she showed me the basics of our first post move. She emphasized body positioning, where to hold the ball once I'd caught the pass, and how to use a head and shoulder fake to get the defender leaning before pinning them with my drop step and power dribble.

"Okay. Your turn," she said as she took my spot as the passer. I tried to mimic what I'd just watched her do. I stood with a broad base and held my hands up as a target, waiting for her to pass the ball.

She corrected my starting position before making the first pass. I caught the ball, quickly looked to the middle, and stepped with my lower foot to make a power lay-in. I got my rebound as the ball came through the net and passed it back to her. She fed me again.

As I looked toward the middle, she said, "Freeze." I stopped.

"Look where the ball is," she said as she took three giant steps toward me. "When you have the ball lower, this is where pesky guards can reach down and slap away or tie up. But if you bring it up to your chin, grip it firmly with your elbows out, a defender can't knock it loose."

I brought the ball under my chin just as she described.

"Good. And the other thing is to sell your fake. The biggest mistake is to go so fast that the defender doesn't even have time to respond."

We repeated the drop step drill from the right and left blocks for twenty-five minutes. There were many starts and stops where she corrected or questioned me. Soon, I began catching my own mistakes. I could feel frustration building, as my movements alternated between feeling uncoordinated and mechanical. I liked learning something new, but I expected to be able to do it well immediately.

There was always a feeling of embarrassment when showing incompetence to an audience—even an audience of one. As much as I tried to ease my discomfort with the thought that I'd work on the new skill between now and the next session, it still felt like a public humiliation.

"How'd that feel today?"

"You mean other than feeling like I have two left hands and two left feet?" I tried to laugh it off like it didn't bother me, but my voice fell flat, and I avoided eye contact.

"Hey, go easy on yourself. This was your first time with these moves. If you feel like a klutz with butterfingers and like you're doing everything wrong, then you're learning and extending your comfort zone, which is uncomfortable. But embrace it!" Her enthusiasm contrasted with my mood, which I'm sure she could see, though I tried to mask it.

"Thank you, Ms. Collins. I'm probably not showing it, but I'm excited to start working out. And I appreciate your time with me." I still had a hard time looking her in the eyes. I couldn't shake the feeling that I may have disappointed her with my performance.

Ms. Collins put her arm across my shoulder as we walked toward the gym door.

"I know you well enough to know that today did not leave a good taste in your mouth. It's easier said than done, especially for a perfectionist like you, but one of the most important things you can learn is to be willing to put yourself out there, take risks that might make you feel foolish or inept in front of others, knowing that with repetition, you will master the new skill. It will help you to excel at the next level, because as good as you are, you still have so much potential that won't be realized until you embrace the idea of getting comfortable with being uncomfortable. I hope you'll think about this, because if you're willing, I'd like to work with you on that."

"Okay," I responded quietly.

"Okay?" she laughed. "I said for you to think about it. This isn't a mandate."

Standing in the open doorway and finally looking up to meet her eyes, I said, "If you think this is the best step for me to keep getting better and be ready for college, then I don't need to think about it. I trust you."

Thursday's volleyball practice felt good. Although school had just begun, our team had been practicing for a few weeks, and electricity hummed on the court even as we warmed up.

I always partnered with Lindsey, another senior and my only real friend. Our friendship had grown since our sophomore year. While Lindsey and I were both athletic, that was where the similarities ended. Our friendship surprised me, not only because of our opposing characteristics but also because of the tense relationship we both had with our fathers. Lindsey's dad was our basketball coach, and he didn't like that I was a stronger player than his daughter. His disappointment was evident, making it a shared burden between Lindsey and me.

My dad's disappointment was hidden. I'd lost count of the times he had compared me to Lindsey, but not for our athletic performances. Instead, it was about appearance, personality, and popularity. I'd heard him repeatedly ask my mom the same blunt question behind their closed bedroom door: "Why can't she be more like Lindsey?"

I wanted to be liked and accepted within my peer group, just like everybody else. But the very thing I turned to for escape, basketball, had moved me farther away from the sense of belonging I desired. The more significant pain, though, was feeling like I didn't belong within my family. Because I felt too uncomfortable to share my dad's sentiments with anyone, this was a pain I dealt with alone.

We worked on serves, serve receives, and offensive attacks from multiple positions. It was an efficient, spirited practice, and I was surprised when Coach Nelson blew her whistle and gathered us together.

"Great practice today, ladies. I loved the energy, the talk, and the focus. Are you excited about our first match next week?" she asked.

A cheer erupted from our small group as we clapped. Coach Nelson reminded us that our late summer practices were planned so we could charge out of the gate strong in our first official match on Tuesday.

On the way to the locker room, as if Lindsey could hear my thoughts, she said, "I think we're going to win it all this year. We were so close last year. I think that disappointment unites us and keeps us hungry. It just feels different."

I smiled at this acknowledged shared feeling about the direction our season was headed.

As I walked into the house, the first thing that hit me was the smell of spaghetti. The second thing was the noise—my mom working in the kitchen, my dad's news program blaring from the den, and my sister talking loud enough for both to hear her. No one heard me arrive, so I headed to my bedroom. I changed out of my practice gear and pulled on sweats.

"Mmm . . . smells great, Mom," I said as I entered the kitchen.

"I didn't hear you come in," she said with a smile, looking up from stirring the sauce. "I'll pop the bread in the oven now," she added. "Samantha's home," she yelled toward the den. "You want to put the salad and the dressings on the table? Then fill our water glasses, and we'll be ready to eat."

"Okay." I grabbed the salad bowl and the dressings. The dining room table was set as if we were having company. As I returned to the kitchen to fill the glasses with ice and water, I commented on how nice the table looked. "What's the special occasion?"

"We don't need a special occasion to enjoy dinner together as a family, do we?" Mom responded in jest. "But with the school year starting and your volleyball and your sister's cheerleading, these opportunities will be few and far between until late March. Bring the plates, please. I think it'll be easier to let everyone dish up here." The buzzer sounded, and she yelled to my dad and Emily as she pulled the garlic bread from the oven.

Seated at the table, we passed around the food. Emily's plate of spaghetti was tiny while her salad bowl was brimming, but no dressing, of course, and she refused any bread.

"Such discipline, Ems," my dad gushed and reached over to pat her arm. "I wish my guys had half the discipline you have." Both my parents looked at her and smiled.

The three of them dominated the dinner discussion. I listened as I continued to eat, enjoying their stories and my sense of ease while they talked, and I could be quiet. However, the mood changed when they shifted to the next night's home football game. What started as excited anticipation turned cold when they included me.

"Are you going to the game with us or friends?" my mom asked, dragging me into a conversation I'd hoped to avoid.

"Umm . . . I don't know yet," I said, keeping it vague. I had no intention of going to the game, but they didn't need to know that. "You know, spaghetti is my favorite. Thanks for such a nice dinner." I hoped to change the subject and get up to clear the table, ending family time.

My dad continued to probe. "What about your volleyball team—maybe a group of you going to the game together, a little team bonding?"

"We'll probably talk about it after practice tomorrow."

Emily continued adding details of her plans between the questions and pauses in conversation, but my dad stared at me. He was not going to let the subject drop. My social life, or lack thereof, had been a sore point for him throughout my high school years.

"You're not planning to go, are you?" he asked, interrupting Emily midstream. She stopped, my dad's tone indicating a new level of seriousness.

"I don't know," I said, choosing the honest route. "The gym should be pretty quiet on a Friday night, and I can't go through volleyball season without touching a basketball." I looked at my mom, hoping to gain her support.

I knew my dad would've been thrilled if he'd heard my words from one of his players. But it somehow seemed a very different story coming from his daughter.

"The reason it's not busy is because most *normal* people have social lives and friends. This is unbelievable!" He glared at my mom, though she hadn't spoken.

Nothing I could say would change his thoughts and feelings about me. I was struck by the irony that my sister's "discipline" at passing on bread and salad dressing drew my dad's praise, while my form of discipline and commitment drew scorn.

"I bet some of your teammates will make plans tomorrow, and it will all work out," my mom added with a sense of cheer I knew was an act. She had her own opinions and concerns, but when my dad took this edge with me, she donned the mask of peacemaker.

"Who's up for dessert?" Again, my mom's feigned happiness was evident. "I made the chocolate four-layer cake everybody loves."

As much as I loved chocolate, I was in no mood to sit around the table, feeling the heavy silence I somehow felt guilty for creating while disdain toward me simmered below the surface.

"I'll have an extra-large piece," my dad said.

"I want just a sliver—a true sliver, Mom. Like only a two-bite sliver," Emily said with a grimace, as if she was already berating herself for saying yes to dessert.

I jumped up from the table, grabbed my plates, and stacked them with my dad and sister's. "I'll help you with the dishes, Mom, while you serve the dessert."

"Thanks, honey. You can stack those on the counter. I'll load the dishwasher later."

"That's all right, Mom. I can finish this while you dish up."

"What size piece can I cut for you?" She already had my dad's extra-large piece and Emily's sliver on plates.

"You know, I think I'll pass for now. I'm still full of spaghetti; maybe I'll eat a small piece later."

My mom looked at me with mild concern, the crease between her eyebrows showing. "Sam, I hope this isn't because of your dad. His tone can sound gruff sometimes, but it's really his concern for your happiness."

"I know, Mom. I'm full and couldn't squeeze in another bite."

Although not the truth, I did not consider this lying. I put this answer into the category of "placating" and found it an easy way to keep the peace—on the outside.

"I'm going to work on homework, okay?"

"Okay. But hug me first."

I hugged and thanked her again for the delicious meal. I quickly left the kitchen so I wouldn't have to hear my dad's comments about me skipping dessert.

I sat on the edge of my bed, facing my closet doors. Staring at my Spud Webb basketball poster and goal cards taped to the closet, I thought: *Stay focused. Don't let Dad's comments distract you.*

My bookshelves, dresser, and desk had once been covered with soccer and basketball trophies, ribbons, and framed team photos. They'd been a source of pride and celebration, a shared accomplishment with my dad. However, early in middle school, there were subtle and not-so-subtle signals about needing to redecorate. I didn't understand it then, but I didn't resist as we took almost everything down and put it in the garage for storage. They had tried to persuade me to remove my goal cards, too, but that was one thing I refused to do.

In third grade, basketball became my true love and greatest passion. Even at that young age, I knew it was not enough to just play—I had to be the best. By the end of elementary school, I had printed my long-term basketball goals on large index cards and taped them to my closet doors. They were the first things I saw and read every morning.

- *I will graduate from high school with All-State honors*

- *I will receive a scholarship to play Division I basketball*

- *I will graduate from college with All-American honors*

- *I will make the Olympic team*

A fourth index card was added later, sometime in middle school.

- *I will dunk a basketball.*

The last card explained the Spud Webb poster on my wall. He could dunk despite being one of the shortest players in the NBA at only five foot seven. If he could do it, so could I. In middle school, I began doing exercises to help improve my jumping ability. In high school, I switched from soccer to volleyball, where jump training was a part of conditioning. It became a new stat I added to my record keeping. Maintaining diligent notes helped me stay focused on my long-term goals, even when my classmates avoided me.

It was one thing to choose between my big sports goals and having lots of friends. But feeling like I had to choose between excelling in sports and making my parents happy felt like a no-win situation. There was only one possible outcome—betrayal. But betraying whom?

September 2006

To: Laurie Collins
From: Samantha Shuster

Dear Ms. Collins,

I'm working on notes for the next basketball team meeting I'll lead, which brought you to mind. We've had our players reading Don Miguel Ruiz's *The Four Agreements*. I'll cover the Fourth Agreement: "Always do your best."

Of course, when I think about this Agreement, I realize it goes hand in hand with the fear of failure and not being perfect. These are two areas you've helped me with so much. I'm not a perfect student (did you catch that?!), so it's a lesson I continue to work on, but without your invaluable mentorship, I know those two fears would've held me back from my goals. You helped me to see failures as not permanent and not a source of shame and embarrassment. Instead, I needed to embrace them as a source of learning and growth. I am so grateful.

I hope it makes you smile today, knowing that I'm still embracing the significant life lesson you taught me so long ago and endeavoring to pass it on to my players. I will feel happy with my coaching accomplishments if I can share even a fraction of what you taught me. THANK YOU!

I hope you have a fabulous Friday and weekend.

Sam

CHAPTER 3

SEPTEMBER 2006

Fitz entered the office, singing an opera song loudly and off key. I turned to face him, eyes bugging out of my head in disbelief. He held the final note extra-long, then bowed at the waist.

"What . . . no standing ovation? No roses thrown at my feet?"

"Please. We need to introduce you to some new radio stations, so I don't have to hear that again."

He just shrugged and smiled. Sitting down, he pulled a folder from his coaching bag and handed me a paper.

"You may not like my singing, but I bet you'll like this." In bold print, it read, *The First Agreement: Always Be Impeccable with Your Word.*

"Now you're talking. It's like what we do with our kids. We put them in positions that play to their strengths so they can be successful. This is your strength, and one of many. Just not singing."

I glanced through quickly, because this lesson was repeated yearly. The typed notes that went into our players' notebooks summarized the material, but the discussion Fitz would lead, getting the kids to relate to the concept individually and as a team, was the most valuable component of his prepared mini-lesson.

After the track workout, Fitz and I walked behind the team to the weight room.

"You know, this is only our second day on the track, but it feels different compared to our last few starts to the school year. Am I imagining that?"

I thought for a second. "No, I sense it too. More like the kids have a bigger purpose than just surviving our torture."

"Yeah, and a shared purpose rather than simply surviving individually."

"Yeah—I like that. It'll be interesting to see if the seniors are doing something differently or if this reflects a different group mentality."

We finished our walk to the weight room in silence, both lost in our thoughts. The team was completing stretches, and a few had already grabbed their folders to record their weight and repetitions. Fitz and I moved around the room, checking their form and encouraging them.

A junior, Kelsey, was partnered with our senior point guard, Olivia. Their personalities were similar off the court. Both tended to be quiet, listening more than talking and observing more than initiating action. Once on the court, however, Olivia became a different person. She embraced her role as point guard, the leader on the court.

At the bench press, Olivia lifted first, effortlessly completing a set of twelve repetitions. "Good job, Olivia," I said as she settled the bar on the rack. "If that's your starting weight, that shows improved strength from last year."

"Thanks, Coach," she said as they switched positions.

"Um . . . maybe I'll try two-and-a-halves instead of the fives," Kelsey said.

Olivia quickly grabbed the two lighter plates. After only three lifts, Kelsey's pace slowed; it was taking more effort early. She did one more, then put the bar back on the rack. This wouldn't have been a red flag if Kelsey were a freshman. I said nothing but watched as they both completed all five sets. Kelsey's final set was with only the bar, and her arms appeared spent.

Whitney gathered the group into a tight circle once everyone was finished lifting. "Good job today. Remember, the harder we push ourselves now, the harder we'll fight down the stretch. We are going to be tougher than every team we play this year. Toughness!" The team repeated "Toughness!" right behind her.

"Okay," I said. "Make sure your lifting charts are filled out for today and put them in the file cabinet before leaving. Shooting workout in the gym—forwards and posts partner up, and guards work together."

Fitz and I watched from the corner of the gym. I was struck, again, by the different attitude and effort this early in the year. I attributed this to finally seeing the benefit of having more returners who knew what we wanted and could model those for our younger players. Neither of us spoke as we watched and made mental notes about things to work on with individual players.

Once they finished, Whitney brought the group together. We couldn't hear what she said, but everyone's eyes were on her as they listened. As the kids put the balls away, changed out of their basketball shoes, and put on their sweats, Fitz and I walked around the gym, ensuring each person heard a few encouraging words from one of us.

In the classroom, Fitz and I passed out the three-ring binders our players would add to throughout the year. Initially there was a lot to cover, but we tried to break it into bite-size pieces rather than one giant information dump.

"Now that the semester has started, you'll need to communicate with your professors about the dates we'll be gone so you can keep up with homework, quizzes, and tests. When you're organized and take the initiative to show that you take your class work seriously, most professors will work with you. Problems usually arise when student-athletes miss class on Thursday and Friday due to travel and then talk to the professor on Monday for an extension for missed work. You are student-athletes—but students first. The most important thing is that you graduate with your degree. That does not mean basketball is squeezed around your study time or when you feel like it. Both will require your total commitment. That's why time management is so important. We are here to help, but understand that it is ultimately your responsibility." I nodded toward Fitz.

He bounded to the front, all smiles and enthusiasm. "All right, gang, we saved the best for last—moi!" The kids laughed with him. Fitz had a larger-than-life personality, yet he never made it all about himself. Instead of hogging center stage, it was as if his gregariousness was an open invitation for all around him to be on the main stage with him, where his love and passion shined like a spotlight on every person.

Fitz held up a paperback copy of *The Four Agreements* (a self-help book with a system of behavior to help improve one's life) as he launched into his introduction. He briefly summarized the text and how it fit our team's code of conduct. Setting his book down on the front table, he handed out his typed copy of the First Agreement: "Be Impeccable with Your Word." Before getting around the room to each table, he asked, "What does the word 'impeccable' mean?"

This question started a discussion at each small table and then with the whole group. I watched for who talked, who was quiet, who listened, and who seemed disengaged. Body language spoke as much as the words verbalized. Fitz concluded, and the kids left the classroom talking with each other. Back in our office, I jotted a few notes about things to include in our small group workouts starting the following week.

Before Fitz left, I said, "Keep an eye on Kelsey. Something doesn't feel right. Today in the weight room she was lifting less than she had at the end of last year. Energy, personality, her weight—I'm not sure, but something seems a little different, and not necessarily in a good way."

"Some people have working lunches or even dinners. But here, we have working dessert," Fitz said, as we sat in our office. Although I couldn't see the cookies on the foil-wrapped plate, I could smell them. "That smells like extra workouts in my future, but it will be worth every bite. Thanks for bringing a treat."

We dove into the work, starting with recruiting before moving to the workout for the day. Just as we began discussing the team meeting, I heard the ping of a new email from my computer. I turned to look at my inbox and smiled. When I turned back around, Fitz was looking at me. "An email from Ms. Collins," I said, nodding.

Though Ms. Collins had never officially been my basketball coach, she was my role model for what a good coach could be and do. Years before, she taught me to believe in myself, even when others, including my father, didn't support me. She'd seen that my biggest obstacle was a fear of failure, and she'd been patient and steadfast in helping me build my confidence. She'd seen me more clearly than anyone, including my parents. When she found my email and reached out after I'd started coaching, I was so grateful to have her guidance back in my life.

As a coach, I frequently thought about this. One of the greatest challenges was figuring out how to fuse together what individual players needed while figuring out what the team needed as a whole. And that was just the basketball side of things. I felt even more strongly about figuring out what each player needed as a student and person and helping to challenge, guide, and support them beyond the basketball court.

"How is Ms. C doing?" Fitz asked.

"She's doing well. Still teaching and, of course, looking forward to watching our season unfold."

"It's almost time to have her return as a guest speaker," Fitz said. "Speaking of guest speakers—do we have our first one set up yet?"

"I have a few people to check with. Do you have any leads?"

"Yeah. I forgot to mention this. Anne met an interesting lady at her clinic last week who started a nonprofit using her farm and abandoned animals to help troubled kids. Anne was so impressed; she plans to visit her farm soon and is considering donating time to provide basic vet care. It made me think about passion, giving to others, and not allowing obstacles to get in the way of goals and dreams—all the things we share with our kids."

"That sounds great. Will you get her name and number?"

We'd finished our track workout, an hour of scrimmage and lifting, and the kids looked exhausted. I told the kids, "We've finished our first full week of school and basketball. Each week will get busier, with more demands, so it's important to get extra rest and stay on top of assignments and other schoolwork rather than letting it build into a mountain due tomorrow."

"Also, I want to remind you again about the importance of your decisions on your own time. What you do speaks about you and reflects on our team and the school. You'll hear me say this a hundred times: you're always sending a message, and it's either positive or negative. There's no such thing as a neutral message. So before you do something, ask yourself what message you'll be sending to others." I paused to let the silence reinforce that idea.

"This has been a great first week, so congratulations to all of you. Let's keep building on that. We have something special here."

Before they could get up, Whitney jumped in. "Let's bring everybody in for a huddle," she said.

As the team formed a small huddle, I opened the door in preparation for the group to leave. I peered down the hallway and saw a young man leaning against the wall, arms crossed over his chest, head tilted back against the wall, eyes closed. His body language communicated tight frustration. I wondered who he was waiting for.

Whitney shared plans for a team dinner at her house on Saturday. Then they finished with the group shout-out: "TOGETHER!"

Kelsey was the first to leave, obviously in a hurry. I started to turn back toward the classroom to say goodbye to each player, but a loud, deep voice caught my attention. I looked down the hallway.

"It's about time," the young man complained.

I heard a quiet "sorry" and realized his aggressiveness was aimed at Kelsey. He glanced past her and looked directly at me. Instead of saying hi or waving, he growled, "Let's go. I've been waiting," loud enough for me to hear. With that, he walked away briskly while Kelsey fumbled with her two bags, half jogging to keep up. Fitz was standing next to me. I hadn't heard him approach. I was transfixed.

"Who was that?" Fitz asked.

"A guy Kelsey left with."

Before we could say anything else, a group of four squeezed past us. "See you Monday," Fitz and I said in unison. I lowered my voice. "I didn't like what I saw with Kelsey and that guy. I'm worried this could be behind some of the behaviors we've been concerned about—the decrease in her weightlifting and always being in a hurry to leave practices and meetings."

"What did you see?"

I started to second-guess myself. "I don't know. It was a gut impression. I don't want to jump to conclusions."

"Hmm . . ." Fitz was deliberate with his response. "I wouldn't be so quick to dismiss your intuition."

I started our next team meeting with an emphasis on time management. Our message of staying ahead in their classes, proactively meeting with professors, and finding tutors, if needed, could not be repeated enough. Just like we would never allow them to go through the motions on the basketball court, we wanted them to know we had the same high expectations in the classroom.

I finished the serious part. "Okay. With that, I'll turn it over to Coach Fitz."

Fitz jumped out of his chair, bounded to the front of the class-room, and yelled, "An ass out of you and me!" It was certainly an attention-grabber. Our returners laughed while the new players sat there wide-eyed.

"What am I talking about . . . Kelsey?"

"Making assumptions," Kelsey answered, her tone flat.

"Bingo! You go, girl!"

Now, new players knew they could laugh at Fitz. He went around the room, giving each person a handout on our next Agreement.

"Before we get to our Third Agreement, a quick review. What were our first two? MJ," he called out, turning behind him to point to her. The kids behind him had probably thought they were off the hook, but he'd kept them on their toes.

"And no cheating," he said as he saw MJ flipping through old notes in her binder.

"Umm . . . don't take things personally."

"Three . . . two . . . ." Fitz started a countdown.

"Be careful with your words—use the right words," MJ rattled off quickly to beat Fitz's countdown.

Sitting in the back of the classroom, I silently chuckled. Suddenly, there was a time limit or, in her mind, a winner and a loser, and her competitive streak shone through. Maddie Jenkins, or MJ, was just a sophomore but our most competitive player. Part of her drive was likely due to growing up with three older brothers, but part was just her wiring. I loved and understood this entirely, but we'd had to work through it with the team a few times. That level of competitiveness was still something new and different for female athletes.

"Yes—that's it. Specifically, 'be impeccable with your word.' Good job," Fitz said.

"Our Third Agreement is 'Don't Make Assumptions.'" He'd finished handing out the copies and stood at the front of the room. Fitz elaborated with some stories and examples to illustrate his points. Then he led the conversation into how assumptions make a person feel, the impact of stereotypes and gossip, and the dangers of this kind of communication. I heard only bits and pieces of what was said, having become mentally distracted by a story that another player, Rachel, shared about someone assuming she was gay just because she was an athlete. Sometimes, I thought that the landscape for girls in sports had improved so much compared to when I was growing up, but then I was shocked back into reality by stories like this. They were a stark reminder that things had not progressed as much as I thought.

Fitz wrapped everything up, and our kids poured out of the classroom, talking and laughing. Fitz and I headed back to our office. We had just settled in when Whitney tapped on the partially opened door.

"Can I interrupt you guys for a minute?"

"Sure, come on in," Fitz answered. She stepped into the room but left the door open behind her.

"This will be quick. I wanted to tell you that our team get-together and dinner went well Saturday night. All our new players seem to be lightening up and feeling more comfortable around everybody, so that's good. Jamie is quite the character. You'll have to watch out for her," she laughed.

Jamie was a freshman point guard, who, if things went as planned, would learn a lot this year and be a solid backup for Olivia. By the following season, after Olivia graduated, she'd be ready to run the show.

"Did everyone make it?" I asked.

"Everyone but Kelsey," she answered. Nothing in her tone or body language signaled concern.

"That sounds great. Thanks for organizing and hosting," I said.

"Oh, sure. There will be many more get-togethers because this group seems to enjoy hanging out together."

"I'm happy to hear that."

"Anyway, I just wanted to give you guys an update. I've got to run to class." She waved goodbye, backing through the doorway.

"Thanks, Whit. See you tomorrow," I called after her. I got up to close the door as her footsteps faded down the hallway.

"So . . . Kelsey . . ." I let that sit while I repositioned my chair to face Fitz. "What are your thoughts on checking in with her?"

"Well . . . we've already got individual meetings scheduled. Let's try the more casual way first. If there's anything she's trying to keep secret, she's more likely to have her game face on in a more formal meeting," he said.

"Okay. I like that plan," I said, feeling like using our combined eyes, ears, and past experiences would help us avoid overreacting.

So much of the work Fitz and I did early in the school year was focused on building relationships with our kids to allow for changed team dynamics. Although we recruited for the same style of play—pressure defense and fast-paced offense— we shifted our coaching to maximize strengths and minimize weaknesses, making every year unique.

By communicating honestly and regularly, showing and expressing genuine interest, and being consistent in word and action—layer upon layer—we built the trusting relationships needed for a strong team foundation.

September 2006

To: Samantha Shuster
From: Laurie Collins

Dear Sam,

If anyone could do justice to Ruiz's Fourth Agreement, it's you. You're right that no one is the perfect student (nor is anyone the perfect teacher). But as someone who saw you overcome some incredible heartbreaks and setbacks, I hope you'll take it to heart when I tell you that I've never met anyone who so fully lived up to this Agreement. What it looked like to "do your best" changed dramatically for you during that last year of high school, and I was so proud of how you adapted to those circumstances. I'm sure you'll have great insight to share with your players.

By the way, if you're looking for a book to add to your off-season reading list, I'd recommend *The 17 Essential Qualities of a Team Player* by John Maxwell. It would make an excellent candidate for a team read next season. Even though I'm not coaching a team, many of the team concepts carry over into how I teach and work with other teachers. Your kids probably haven't realized this yet, but they will be amazed at how much they refer to your lessons and the books you read together, regardless of their chosen degrees and careers.

Ms. C

CHAPTER 4

SEPTEMBER 1986

Classes on Friday were a blur, with excitement, energy, and noise surrounding the first home football game of the season. An all-school pep rally was held in the gym during second period. The band blared so loudly you couldn't talk to the person next to you without shouting. My sister and the other cheerleaders did their part to rally the school spirit. Emily looked in her element, standing front and center, smiling, dancing, and showing off her petite frame. It always amazed me that we came from the same gene pool, because we were such opposites.

After the vice principal directed the first part of the assembly, the football coach took the microphone and called his offensive players to the gym floor. The star junior quarterback, Chris Daniels, drew all the attention as they simulated running a play. The coach yelled into the microphone that the team needed everyone at tonight's game. Then the band played the school fight song as the cheerleaders scurried onto the floor to bring the crowd to their feet.

I couldn't help but think about how different things were for male athletes. Even in the hallways, Chris had a swagger that required extra space, as if he were ten feet tall. Despite his monster ego, as both the quarterback of the football team and the leading scorer on the basketball team, he was respected and admired by his teammates. The arrogance he demonstrated would not last a day on a girls' team, and a female athlete would never induce the reverence Chris received from most of the student body. I was every bit the "star" athlete he was, and yet the very thing that made him a school hero, somehow made me someone to avoid.

When the assembly ended, I hustled through crowded halls, anxious to get to my English class to talk with Cassandra. We both arrived two minutes before the bell.

"Hi, Cassandra. What are your plans for the weekend?"

She laughed and said, "You're not going to believe this—I still don't. I've been assigned to be the sports writer for the school newspaper this year. My advisor thought this would be a good challenge and broaden my 'journalistic repertoire.'" She said this last phrase with air quotes and a mocking, pretentious tone, clearly quoting her advisor. "God. I know almost nothing about sports, which will become evident after I report on tonight's football game, and even more so after your first volleyball game—uh, match—next Tuesday!"

"You're such a good writer, and I'm sure it'll be easier than you're expecting. But I'd be more than happy to help you. Not the writing part; you don't need my help with that." I rolled my eyes. "I mean the sports portion. I'm a sports fanatic and could help with questions about the game itself, terminology, and things like that. We could meet at the library on Saturday morning if you'd like."

"Really?" Cassandra sounded excited.

"Of course."

"I'd love it if you'd be my sports coach! Instead of dreading it, I feel more excited about this now."

I woke up early Saturday morning and tried to sneak out of the house for a run in the neighborhood park. As I walked through the living room with a basketball in hand, my dad was sitting on the couch, watching TV.

He barely flicked his eyes toward me as he said, "Hey, it looks like you're heading to the park to work on your basketball skills. Shouldn't you be concentrating on volleyball?"

"Well, it looks like our volleyball team is going to be really strong this year, so it's more important for me to focus on basketball if I hope to be noticed by any college basketball programs."

My dad didn't ask any follow-up questions. Emily always made things so easy for him in conversation because she went into more detail than anyone cared to know, while I figured if he wanted to know more, he'd ask. I turned toward the front door. "Okay. Well, see you later, Dad."

With basketball in hand, I hurried to the neighborhood park, hiding my ball in the bushes by the basketball court. After a few light leg stretches, I jogged to the running trail that formed the park's perimeter. There were two hills about halfway around the trail. One was short and steep, the other longer with a gradual incline. I ran uphill and started the first of twelve hill sprints.

Although I was in good shape, conditioning for volleyball was very different from conditioning for basketball. Volleyball skills centered on shorter bursts of motion that mostly required anaerobic conditioning, while basketball required similar efforts in between running repeated wind sprints up and down the court. Getting in one or two running sessions most weeks during the volleyball season made transitioning into basketball practices much easier.

I remembered the first week of basketball practice in my sophomore year when two girls beat me in sprints. My sense of failure was compounded when Coach Walters made snide remarks about my apparent lack of commitment in front of the team. He said that I should've come into the season in better shape. Even though Lindsey finished behind me, I was the only one singled out. I hadn't come in second in any conditioning drill since.

Just thinking of Coach Walters and how he treated me changed how I ran and breathed, and I completed my final sprints as if I could outrun those lingering demons. My heart rate gradually slowed as I walked back to the basketball court, pulled the ball from the bushes, and started with my ball-handling drills. Transitioning to my shooting workout, I also included repetitions of the new post moves Ms. Collins taught me.

I walked through our front door just as Emily entered the kitchen. My sister was pretty, even with no makeup, messy brunette hair, and sloppy, mismatched clothes. She only gave me a sideways glance.

Within minutes, all four of us were eating breakfast at the dining room table and listening to my dad's play-by-play of the final three minutes of the previous night's football game. He couldn't make it to my match, but he had somehow managed to watch every second of the football game.

He started his extended football monologue, describing in excruciating detail every defensive play that gave our offense another chance to score.

"Dad, just get to the offense," Emily interrupted, excited, as if the game was going on right then and she didn't know the outcome.

I'd finished my cereal and wanted to shower, but I knew the "right" thing to do to keep the family peace was to stay and hear every detail.

"Okay, okay," he said, chuckling and looking at Emily. "So, we get the ball back. Chris and the offense run out onto the field to take over on our thirty-five-yard line. We have only three minutes and need a touchdown. Chris makes a few short passes where we pick up five or six yards. The clock stops when we get out of bounds and pick up the first down, so he's managing the clock like a pro. We're just over midfield, and the defense puts heavy pressure on Chris. He scrambles out of the pocket and heaves a pass, off the wrong foot, down the field for a twenty-five-yard pickup. It was amazing! His poise and awareness under pressure, his strength . . ."

I felt like I was listening to Chris's father retelling his son's phenomenal exploits, already making the game legendary after only a day.

"There's just over a minute left in the game. We have a couple of short completions but then a dropped pass. The game's final play had us starting on the twelve-yard line. Chris drops back, scans the field, and moves around a little, buying time for someone to get open. Not seeing anyone, he takes off himself, making a great move to get by one defender before falling across the goal line with three defenders hanging on him. He carried them the last three yards!" Emily practically bounced in her seat, clapping her hands together.

My dad continued, "Chris scored the winning touchdown on that final play of the game. It was all sheer will and determination—he would not be stopped. I love that about that kid." My dad finished his Chris reverie, and my mom made congratulatory comments. He'd just taken longer to describe the final three minutes of a football game and boast about Chris's leadership than he'd ever talked about any of my *whole* games.

"Wow. Sounds like a great game. I'm sorry I missed it," I said, hopefully concluding this topic. "Well, I have to go get ready. I'm meeting a friend at the library in about an hour." Cassandra and I had planned to meet and start her sports tutoring.

"Wait," my mom said, holding up a hand. "Did you tell your dad how great your volleyball team is looking this year?"

Emily quietly got up from the table, empty bowl in hand.

"Uh, yeah," I mumbled. Did my one sentence qualify? I gathered up my dishes. When I turned to the sink, Emily was leaving the kitchen.

My dad chimed in, "Yeah, it sounds like it will be a great season. I hope I can make it to the first match next week. It's at home, right?"

"Yes." I gave them both a tight smile. "Well, like I said, I'm meeting a friend at the library. Gotta get ready."

"Is it someone I know?" There was a little too much excitement in my mom's voice. I worried that she'd want Cassandra to come here, even stay for dinner, because she'd be so excited that there was something "normal" in my life.

"No, you don't know her."

My mom flashed me a smile. "I hope you know you could always invite her over here to work. I'd think it'd be a lot more comfortable than the library."

"Thanks, Mom. I'll keep it in mind for next time." I could not even imagine what she'd be like if I had a boyfriend.

Leaving to get ready, I heard my parents' muffled voices and paused. I couldn't hear the entire conversation, but he said, "If she wanted to share more about her long-range basketball plans, she would have. Why do I always need to play twenty questions with her?"

My dad's tone carried an edge of defensiveness. I thought he'd ask if he were interested, and he assumed I'd share if I wanted to. The result was no communication at all.

September 2006

To: Laurie Collins
From: Samantha Shuster

Hi Ms. Collins,

Thanks so much for your note of support on Monday. It has
been a great first week and this season started unlike any
other. (Knock on wood!) It took until the end of the week to
find the time to write a note to fill you in.

We are reaping the benefits of having so many returners,
and their leadership is impressive. It's like having several
additional assistant coaches, so our collective learning curve
has sped up. I'm excited, because we also have more athleticism and depth than ever before.

We had individual meetings with all our kids this week.
They turned in their first progress reports last Friday, so
classes and grades were the top items to discuss. We don't
have any red flags in this department, but it's not like that
frees us to focus on just basketball and team dynamics. There
are plenty of other issues:

- A returning junior was in tears about the financial stresses
  of being in an apartment instead of the dorms. She
  described being down to Top Ramen as her only food for
  breakfast, lunch, and dinner the last week of the month.
  When I asked her how much her new (LARGE!) shoulder
  tattoo had cost, she seemed confused at how the two
  are related. I guess I'll need to bring in a guest speaker
  to discuss money management.

- Our freshman point guard is still struggling with homesick-ness—another meeting filled with tears but for different reasons. I tried to reassure her that if she asked any of the returners on the team about their first few weeks of college, they'd probably describe the misery, the unhap-piness, and the feeling that they had made a significant mistake in their decision to play college basketball. But they'd also started to feel better when they did exactly what she was doing—talking about it, getting it out in the open. The best thing she could do was be patient with herself, lean on her teammates, and talk to someone who'd already been through it. I also reached out to our seniors and asked them to keep an eye out for her.

- A returning sophomore who is fiercely competitive (which I love and wish would rub off on her teammates!) is strug-gling with how her teammates receive her. This is still a topic I find disconcerting when it comes to female athlet-ics. I know firsthand what this is like, but I keep making the false assumption that this would be nonexistent given all the time since my high school days and the enormous increase in female participation in sports. It breaks my heart, not only for what this kid is experiencing but also for the bigger picture of what it says about how far we still must go in breaking specific gender "rules" and expectations.

So there you have it. Just when you thought basketball was at the top of the list for our daily work, you find out it probably doesn't make the Top 10 list! The many hats we wear . . . But I wouldn't have it any other way. Ultimately, I think those pieces make each season more memorable, our bonds much stronger, and the life lessons learned broader.

Now that I've probably bored you to tears with more detail than any sane person would like to know about our team, I hope that you'll fill me in on things with you. I hope that school is going well and you're enjoying classes. Are you still squeezing in a few fall hikes on the weekends, or has the weather changed enough that you can't get out?

Thanks again for thinking about us. Your support, mentorship, and friendship mean the world to me!

Warmest wishes,

Sam

CHAPTER 5

Fitz and I were in our office after the team meeting. As I stacked the handful of file folders I was carrying onto my desk, I turned and asked, "By the way—how is it that I've ended up with the Fourth Agreement every year?"

"You noticed that too? I think it's worked well, though. The final Agreement given by the head coach is a great way to end that unit."

"I don't know who you think you're fooling, but it's not me. I'm onto you and your ulterior motives." I tried to give him my evil-eye look, but it never worked. His goofy facial expressions always erased the small amount of acting ability I possessed.

He let out a loud belly laugh. "Are you kidding? If it were *really* fitting for you, it would have to be titled: Doing Your Best Isn't Good Enough Unless You Are the Best. Or how does this one grab you: There's the Best and Then Just All the Rest? And of course, my favorite of your mottos: Second Place Is Just First Place Loser!"

"Hey, shh . . ." I put my finger to my lips and peered outside the office door like I was checking for eavesdroppers. "I'm trying to keep that one top secret."

He let out another boom of laughter. "Coach, I think that cat was let out of the bag after the first game we lost in our first season together. No one wanted to ride back in your van. When we stopped to grab some food for the road, I had to take the team in while you sat in the van. . . . Is any of this ringing a bell?"

"Okay, okay, point made," I said, raising my hands. "Guilty as charged." Fitz stepped toward me and embraced me in a bear hug.

"I wouldn't have you any other way," he said. I could still feel the slight vibrations from his continued laughter.

"Thanks, Fitzy—I think," I said with an edge of sarcasm. He grabbed his bag, getting ready to leave. "So, you're still driving yourself tomorrow?" I asked. We had our coaches' conference for the season the next day.

"Yeah, if you're fine with that. I'm meeting up with a buddy, and I plan to stay overnight before heading home Sunday night."

"You know, I've got the meeting covered," I said, leaning back in my chair. "Don't feel like you must go. It would give you more time with your friend."

"I appreciate that, but I'll be there."

I grabbed an extra copy of the meeting agenda from my desk and handed it to him. "Okay. The unofficial start time is 11:00 a.m. to allow for a little socializing and meeting new coaches, and the official start time is when lunch is served at 11:30. We should be out of there at 2:30 since Jerry's pretty good about sticking to the schedule, which I like." Jerry was the most veteran coach in our conference, having been a coach at Carroll College for twenty-four years.

"Any new coaches this year?"

"One at Great Falls. Rob Jeffries? I don't know anything about him."

"Yet! This will be our first chance to start sizing up our competition."

I'd just gotten on the road after the conference and needed a distraction to take my mind off the day. Who better to talk to than Cassandra? "Hey, how are you, my friend?" I said after she'd answered on the first ring.

"Wow. What is it? Wait—let me guess. You met some incredible man, or you had a six-four post player call about transferring from the University of Washington to be closer to home and wondered if you had any room on your roster."

It took me a minute to recover from my burst of laughter so I could answer. "Oh, Cassandra. I knew you were the right person to call. I met an incredible man today, but not in the way you meant it."

"Ooh, give me all the details!"

"Today was our meeting with all the coaches in the conference. Great Falls has a new coach. He's young, inexperienced, and thinks coaching women is beneath him."

I heard Cassandra grumble. "Sounds about right."

"He said this job was temporary and something about paying his dues to get back to *real* coaching on the men's side." I sighed. "It made my blood boil."

Cassandra was aghast. "What did you say to him?!"

"Nothing, I was speechless! All I could do was excuse myself and go to the bathroom to breathe until I calmed down." I could still feel my shock and anger as I practically shouted all this into the phone.

It was my turn to listen to Cassandra's anger and disgust. "How did this guy even get hired? And if he's spouting stuff like this in front of the other coaches, imagine how he talks to his players. If it had been a racial difference instead of gender, he would've never spoken those words aloud. But because it's about women, it doesn't even cross his mind. He can't see it and doesn't hear the injustice in his words as he says them. That's misogyny, and it's still so pervasive, ingrained, and unquestioned; it's insidious . . ."

I could hear her passion and was moved by Cassandra's wholehearted commitment to fighting social injustice. "I'm sorry, Sam. I just have these buttons that immediately lead to my 'fervent soapbox diatribes,' as my mother always refers to them. That's why writing is better for me. It slows me down and forces me to take time to think before I put my '*radical*' ideas out there." She laughed at herself, and the intensity disappeared. I heard her breathe a couple of times before she continued. "See, Sam. That's where I need to learn from you."

"Learn what from me?" I asked with genuine bewilderment.

"How to think more before spewing words out of my big mouth."

I laughed, mostly because I could picture her face on the other end of the line.

"I love you, Cassandra. I think you're amazing, and I wish I could be more like you. I'm still learning from your example. And I'm lucky to have you as a friend."

"Where'd that come from? Is this some diversionary tactic?" We both laughed before she continued. In a softer, more relaxed voice, she said, "Thank you, Sam. I hope you know how much I cherish our friendship."

We wrapped up our conversation, and I let my window down partially for the cool, fresh air, then turned on the radio. U2's "Beautiful Day" was on, and I cranked up the volume, enjoying the rest of my drive home, mindless and relaxing.

I pulled three envelopes from my computer bag to take to the team room. One was for Kelsey. It had a quote I liked about dealing with difficult situations directly instead of pushing them away and hoping they'd disappear. I added a short note, reminding her I was there for her. I'd also written a quick note to Olivia, praising her play and leadership as our point guard, and to Ellen, commending her defense and rebounding.

It probably seemed old-fashioned in this era of technology and instant messages, but I still liked handwritten notes. Even when I complimented a kid repeatedly, it was often heard but quickly erased from their minds. Being able to read and reread handwritten notes containing compliments had sticking power.

Fitz was already in the classroom, preparing for the Monday morning meeting with our players. We greeted each player as they shuffled in and gathered around tables.

"Just a couple of things as we look ahead at this week. This is our final week of preseason workouts."

"No more track!" Steph hollered, producing instant cheers from her teammates.

"Well, hopefully," I responded. "Thursday will be the final timed mile and a half, and if you all make the time, *then* you'll be done with the track. If not, some of you may have morning appointments out there. Finally, on Friday, we have a guest speaker for our team meeting, after which we'll have pizzas delivered to celebrate the end of preseason."

They were happy about that plan. As they packed their bags and left the room, I caught Steph's attention. "Hey, I was hoping to catch you today."

"Oh yeah? That sounds a little ominous." She shot me a wary glance, waiting for the rest.

"Right before I came here, I had a phone call from a Mrs. Carlson from Oakmont Elementary. She sounds like a very nice lady and absolutely loves you."

"Oh, yeah . . . Mrs. Carlson's great," she said somewhat dismissively as we walked toward the door.

I stopped walking so I could look her in the eyes. "She shared that you'd been coming to her classroom to help students needing extra support. She appreciated your help but was especially touched by how much you've impacted one of the girls."

"Oh, she must be talking about Amy." A big smile spread across Steph's face.

I continued, "Amy has always been an outstanding student, but her parents divorced this summer. Mrs. Carlson said Amy had become withdrawn and had made minimal effort on her schoolwork until recently. She credited you as the main reason for the positive changes in Amy's behavior."

Steph appeared embarrassed by the praise. "It's only a couple of hours each week. I think Mrs. Carlson is giving me too much credit."

"Hey, don't downplay it. Mrs. Carlson thought this was an 'assignment' from the coaches and called to thank us. She was speechless when I said you did this on your own and this was the first I'd heard about it. She thinks you're an amazing young lady, and I completely agree with her."

Steph grinned sheepishly. She looked down as she said, "Thank you, Coach."

"I think it'd be great to get Amy to a game. I bet she'd love getting to see you play."

"Yeah, I'll have to give her a game schedule to share with her mom."

"Great!" I patted her shoulder. "Okay, get off to class, but I'm so glad I got to tell you how proud I am of you."

Nothing was more difficult than grabbing the team's undivided attention when food was in the room. The fact that it was Friday afternoon compounded the challenge.

"Real quick, before I lose you to the pizza," I shouted, and conversation slowly died out. "Fitz and I want you to know we couldn't be happier with your work this preseason. Yesterday's timed runs—it's the first time we've had everybody make their times before the season's official start. No early morning runners this year!" Whitney started a clap and cheer that was instantly picked up by the whole team.

"It's not just yesterday that has marked this group as different from past teams. Every week, Fitz and I have noted something—it might be the greater focus in the weight room, the intensity of the scrimmages, or the attention to detail at the skill workouts. Over and over, you've grabbed our attention in remarkable ways. So this is a congratulations on the end of one chapter in our season and a celebration as we prepare to start the next chapter Monday with our first official practice. We want you to keep building on what you've already been doing because we have something special here."

This time, Stephanie started the cheer by jumping out of her chair and yelling at the top of her lungs: "Frontier Conference Champions!" She jumped up and down like she was on a pogo stick. Whitney joined her, and then the cheers were deafening. Fitz and I watched, beaming with pride in who they were, and hoping for what they might accomplish together. They were an extraordinary group.

Surveying the remaining food, I said, "We've got leftovers, so pack up a couple of pieces to take with you." A few approached the front table and did just that, thanking us for dinner. I saw Kelsey starting to leave and went over to her. I put my arm around her shoulders and pulled her close so only we could hear.

"Hey, Kels. I wanted to compliment you on your attitude this afternoon. I know you've got some personal stuff going on, but seeing you so engaged with your teammates was nice. We've missed this, Kelsey." Kelsey nodded, and we continued walking into the hallway.

She looked at me for the first time. "Thanks, Coach."

I usually tackle the least enjoyable items on my to-do list first. It's better to get them done and then look forward to everything that follows. What did it say that today this dreaded task was calling my parents?

It had been three weeks since my mom's visit, and I hadn't talked with either of them since. Though I could rationalize that the phones work two ways and they hadn't called me, I felt obligated to call.

I turned my TV to a college football game, muted the volume, grabbed the phone, and dialed their number.

"Hello?" my mom answered.

"Hi, Mom. How are you?"

"Well, Samantha. It's so good to hear your voice. Just a sec, honey, let me get your father."

There was a loud clunk as she set the phone on the counter or desk. Then I heard her yell for my dad.

"He'll be right here. How are you? I'm sorry I haven't called since getting home. God, it's already been three weeks. I can't believe how fast the time flies."

I heard my dad's voice in the background, and they switched to speakerphone. "Your dad's here," Mom said. "We can both hear you now."

"Hi, Dad."

"Hi, Sam. Your mom had a great time visiting you. Sorry I couldn't make it, but it probably worked out better. Just special mother-daughter time together."

"We missed you, but hopefully next time . . ." I didn't get to finish because he was already talking again.

"Things have been so busy with school and preparing for the season. We've got so many guys that want to play; we just added a fourth team. We've had to interview and hire a C-team coach and try to schedule games, but it's tough because there aren't a lot of schools with C teams . . ."

Looking at my watch, it was 11:21 a.m. He continued to talk about basketball—his coaches' meetings, his players, who would be the toughest competition, and other things I only partially heard. My mind wandered. Would our relationship be any different today had I chosen a different career? Would he show interest and curiosity and ask questions if I had gone into something foreign to him, like law or architecture? Would that have made him proud of me? I'd picked coaching, something he knew so well. Was that why he didn't need to ask about my work? Maybe it wasn't me; perhaps it reflected my job choice.

I turned my attention back to the phone call as my dad reached his typical conclusion. Glancing at my watch, it was 12:07 p.m.

"It was nice talking with you, Sam, and thanks for calling. I've gotta run, but Mom wants to chat more."

"Okay, Dad. Glad you're doing well, and good luck this season."

There was no response, and then just my mom on the phone. "It's me now. I'm so glad your dad was home so you guys could talk," she continued.

"Yeah, me too, Mom. So, how are you doing?"

"Oh, pretty good . . ." That was all the prompting it took to get her talking about work, a neighbor she was helping because the guy's wife was in the hospital, and her efforts to get regular exercise. One topic seamlessly rolled into the next without extensive details until she got to Emily.

Then I heard about every detail of Emily's busy schedule and updates on her kids. Eventually, she paused and said, "I'm missing out on so much of their lives. I wish we lived closer so I could see them every day."

"I'm sure that's tough, and I bet they miss seeing you too."

"Have you talked with Em lately?"

"Not recently." I couldn't remember the last time.

"Just this past week, you came up in our conversation."

"Huh," I wasn't sure I wanted more information about that phone call.

"Your sister misses you."

Although I could've pointed out many signs to the contrary, I just let that one sit there.

"You know . . ." Uh-oh, that change in tone was not a good one.

"She was talking about how much she thinks her kids are missing out because they don't have cousins."

This was a new tack, bringing my sister into the picture to strengthen Mom's guilt trips. I closed my eyes and squeezed the bridge of my nose. What exactly did she want me to do with that information? Feel compelled to find a guy tomorrow, get pregnant, and give birth nine months from now, just so that my niece and nephews could have a more fulfilling childhood?

"It broke my heart. I hadn't thought about how she and the kids were affected. After that call, I couldn't get her comments out of my head. The only real conclusion I came to was that I must've been a horrible mother for you not to want kids of your own. Was I that horrible, Sam?"

I took a deep breath and answered as calmly as I could. "I'm not sure how you got to *that* conclusion. So many factors affect the decision—like first, I'm not married." I chuckled. "You were a great mom and still are a great mom. This has nothing to do with you."

She could've probed about those other factors if she honestly wanted to discuss my hopes and plans. But, again, she didn't, substituting emotional manipulation for honest communication. Was she interested in knowing me, or was our relationship just about meeting her needs and expectations?

October 2006

To: Laurie Collins
From: Samantha Shuster

Dear Ms. Collins,

It's been another busy week here.

One of my biggest concerns since day one has been one of our returning juniors. I've seen changes in her personality and attitude toward basketball and her teammates. I have a feeling it's stemming from a boyfriend, but she's remained secretive, even when Fitz and I tried to talk directly with her. I'm nervous about what this shift means for the team, but even more, I'm worried for her.

That's got me thinking more about why issues beyond the court are so important. Part of it is about team building, the commitment to a common goal.

But an even more important part is that I want to help my players build or bolster an inner strength I didn't have at their age. I don't want them to wait until they're almost forty to discover their voices, self-worth, and true identities. I'll feel successful as a coach and mentor if I can help them take even the first few steps on their journeys. That's the kind of mentor you were for me, so thank you for believing in me all those years when I had trouble believing in myself.

All my best,

Sam

CHAPTER 6

SEPTEMBER 1986

The library wasn't busy, and I found a large table in the back corner that would give Cassandra and me plenty of space to spread out, and where we could talk quietly without disturbing others. I'd just finished emptying my backpack when Cassandra walked up.

"Hey. Good spot," she said, glancing around and unloading her materials onto the table. "All right," she said, looking at me and rubbing her hands together in mock excitement. "Should we start with our English assignment or with my newspaper stories?"

"The sports section of the newspaper—definitely," I answered without hesitation.

"I was afraid you'd say that." She pulled out stacks of paper and sorted them into five sections.

"Football, volleyball, girls' soccer, slow pitch softball, and cross-country," she said, letting out a tired exhale. "And I don't know anything about any of them."

"You're the only writer covering all the fall sports?"

"Well, our school newspaper isn't that big, and honestly, I think football is the only sport they care if I cover. Reporting scores and outcomes for the other sports would be enough."

"Which one do you want to start with?"

"How about football," she said, sliding a large stack of papers toward me. She had photocopies of stat sheets and pages of scribbled notes where she'd interviewed the coach and a few players. She also had the rough draft of her article, with occasional empty boxes drawn in.

"This is great," I said once I'd read everything. "We'll fill in these holes, and it's done." Cassandra looked relieved.

We talked about football for the next thirty minutes, and I answered all her questions. We moved on to soccer and tennis. She took pages of notes as I described the rules, some of the challenges for players, and other nuances that couldn't be determined from a stat sheet. She finished her notes and asked, "If I bring a rough draft of these pieces on Monday morning, would you have time to read and make suggestions by Tuesday? I know it's a lot to ask."

"Of course. I'd be happy to."

"I appreciate all your help, and I better apologize now for any of my pissy attitude you may have to experience in this work together," she said with a half laugh and a half grimace.

"You don't need to thank me. I'm serious—this is fun. I've grown up playing and watching sports, and it's a passion." Other than Lindsey, there wasn't one other person I could imagine voicing these feelings to.

"Okay. Back to work. We saved the best for last," she said, pushing the pile of volleyball papers toward me.

So this is what it felt like to be "normal" . . . or closer to normal.

Even after not sleeping well Sunday night, I woke up ready to go Monday morning, looking forward to my basketball workout with Ms. Collins. I found her in her office and poked my head in to say I was there. When she joined me in the gym, I'd already taken my warm-up shots from close range.

"Looks good, Sam. That's the same form, arch, and backspin you want to see from every shot, anywhere on the floor." She held her hands up for me to pass her the ball, and I did.

We started with a catch-and-shoot from various spots around the perimeter. When we finished that set, she complimented me on always catching the ball in a position ready to shoot. I shot ten free throws, then she explained the next series of shots. Getting into a rhythm, all I heard was my shoes squeaking on the floor, the ball bouncing, and the beautiful sound of the ball swishing through the net on good shots. It was music to my ears.

After the next series, Ms. Collins said, "The shot fake is a simple move, but it's so effective for a great shooter like you. Defenders will run at you or even jump because they know you're money, and you must make them pay." She said this last part with a devilish grin.

"You need to remind yourself that you are unstoppable. Sometimes I don't think you enjoy that as much as you should," she added, now laughing. "But we'll work on that. Let's finish working on the new post moves we did last time."

She was pleasantly surprised at how smoothly I performed most of the moves.

"Somebody's been getting in some reps on the new moves we've been working on." I started to sit down against the wall to change my shoes, but Ms. Collins stopped me. "I want you to look at something in my office. You can change your shoes in there."

I grabbed my things, and we walked toward her office.

"I bet, as a little girl, you loved coloring books. And I bet you were good at it too . . . Am I right?" I laughed, first because her question seemed so out of the blue and second because she was right.

"Yep, I loved coloring books, especially when I'd get my new box of crayons right before the start of the school year. I don't know if I'd say I was good or not. It's not like I won a trophy or anything."

"Hmm . . . hold on to that thought. We'll come back to that."

She pointed to an oversize postcard inside her office—a replica of a painting. "This is one of my favorite artists, and this is about the only version of his works I'll ever be able to own."

She stared at it while I tried to take it in. I could tell it was a sailboat in rough waters, but I had to use my imagination because it did not have sharp details like a photograph would. "Now, what if I cover up all but this small square of his painting? How does it change?" She used her hand and a piece of paper to block a good portion of the image.

"Umm . . . it looks smaller. It looks plainer . . . it looks flat."

Still showing a small portion of the picture, she said, "This is what you're doing on the court. You only allow this tiny portion of your talent and passion to be displayed. What words did you use to describe it? Small, plain, flat?"

She removed her hand and paper so I could see the whole picture again and continued, "Instead of using the entire canvas, instead of using bold colors, instead of using wild brush strokes, like you are capable of, you are limiting yourself." She paused, but I kept my eyes glued to the picture.

"Because you don't want to make mistakes, and you want to do things the 'right' way, because you want to stay within the lines drawn by someone else, you don't allow yourself to flow, play in the moment, and stand out. You let yourself do only the things you've repeated so many times until the move is as close to perfection as possible instead of freeing your instincts to react." She blocked most of the picture again. "Your game looks like this." I stared, transfixed, more by her words than the image.

In a softer voice, but still gazing at the picture, Ms. Collins said, "It's about taking risks, overcoming your fear of maybe making a mistake, maybe not doing something perfectly," she removed her hand and the paper, "so your game can look like this."

Ms. Collins turned to look at me. "You've got something rare and special. My challenge to you is to play basketball with bold colors and wild brush strokes. I want you to play like there are no lines on the canvas predetermining what the final image should look like; it is not someone else's paint-by-number project. It's yours to create, and if you allow yourself to do that, every game will be your masterpiece."

I looked at the oversize postcard and slowly nodded. I got her message, and this was an idea that would keep popping up in my mind and lead to deeper insights over time.

"Remember when you said you didn't know if you were that good at coloring because you hadn't gotten a trophy?"

I nodded my silent answer.

"That's the same instinct. Stop looking outward for what goals and ambitions are realistic and acceptable. Look inward and trust that voice wholeheartedly."

She pulled open her desk drawer and pulled out a small package wrapped in brown paper. "I know you've got to get out of here if you'll make it before the bell. Just a little something for you." She handed me the package. "No need to open it now. I left you a note inside the cover that'll explain."

Holding the package to my chest, I grabbed my bag from the floor. "Thanks, Ms. C. I'll see you next week."

"Sam, come on in. Thanks for giving up your lunch period today to meet with me." Coach Nelson motioned me toward the green vinyl chair in her office and shut the door. "I ran into your friend Cassandra in the hall today. I'm so glad she's covering sports this year. Maybe our girls' teams will actually get some coverage." She walked around her desk, where her lunch was laid out, and sat opposite me. "Most times, it feels like everyone thinks football and boys' basketball are the only sports played at this school."

She chuckled a bit, which made me smile. I nodded and said, "It sure does feel that way."

She shook her head and stirred the bowl of oatmeal in front of her. "Grab your lunch stuff and dig in. We'll have to eat while we talk so you don't miss your lunchtime." She waited until I had my sandwich out of the bag. "So," she said, "we haven't had this conversation before because I've always known that basketball is your first love and your goal is to play college basketball." She paused to eat two more spoonfuls of oatmeal. "Have you thought at all about playing volleyball in college? Would you be open to the idea, or are you sure it'll be basketball?"

This was not a topic I'd expected when preparing for this meeting. I practically choked on a bite of my sandwich, chewed a few more times, and took a big gulp of water to help wash it down before responding. She had to be joking. "This is only my third year of playing volleyball. I'm not that good, and I don't understand the game and strategy that comes from years of playing a sport."

"Well, I can tell you that every coach in our league would differ with your assessment. I understand that you don't have the same comfort level with your general knowledge of volleyball that you do with basketball, but you're already an outstanding high school player. What college coaches see is a tremendous amount of potential. It's still early in the season, but I've already had two college coaches call and ask about you."

"What—community colleges?" It came out like a half snort, and I kept waiting for her to deliver the punch line for the joke.

"Hardly," she said with a smile. "A Division I and a Division II school. And I know I'll be getting more calls before the end of the season. That's why I need to know your thoughts about this. If you know you only want to play basketball, we shouldn't waste their time, and I'll be honest with them so they can focus on other recruits. But if there's even a sliver of interest on your part, you should talk with them, ask questions, get information about the school and the program, and you can factor all that in when making decisions about next year."

It was my turn to buy a little time by taking a few bites of my sandwich. I always struggled with thinking on my feet. I liked having time to let ideas sink in and explore possible short-term and long-term outcomes. Depending on what I was contemplating, I wanted feedback or information from others who could help, and I needed the time and space to think alone first.

I finally broke the silence. "I'm shocked, and I can't say the idea crossed my mind." Coach Nelson nodded but didn't reply. "I guess I'd say that I'd lean toward keeping all doors open." That was my cautious and practical side speaking. I wanted to attend college and knew I needed sports to pay the way.

Coach Nelson said, "Good. I'm glad you're at least open to the idea. Why don't you think about it? Maybe talk with your parents, and we can discuss this again later."

"Okay, thanks," I said. I was trying to think of whom, other than Coach Nelson, I could share this with and get feedback. I wouldn't ask any of my teammates, and I didn't feel like my parents could help me either. My mom didn't understand the sport or college scholarships well enough to help, and I certainly wouldn't ask my dad! His general view of girls' athletics was that it was a social thing, more like a sorority. Ms. Collins and Coach Nelson were the only people I could trust who understood enough to help.

Coach Nelson stood up and pointed to the clock. "Our lunchtime went fast."

As we left her office, she put her hand on my shoulder. "Sam, I don't want you to lose sleep over this. It is a compliment and something to feel good about. No big final decisions need to be made anytime soon, so keep the idea on the back burner, and we can talk more later."

"Thanks, Coach."

"I hope you feel comfortable discussing any of this with me, including basketball. I want you to know I'm here to help you in any way I can."

October 1986

Dear Sam,

One of my most supportive mentors was my high school English teacher. She shared advice with me that I've always carried in my heart, and I'd like to pass it on to you: Each of our lives is a book all our own. The important thing is to be your own author. Never give anyone else the power to write that story for you.

You get to share this chapter with this group of teammates and friends, but even within the same chapter, you'll each have different experiences and perspectives. And of course, your earlier and later chapters will all be very different.

When we face our biggest challenges, our most painful struggles, and our moments of utter despair with open eyes and honesty, we show that we have the courage and bravery needed to make every chapter in our story count.

Being authentic with ourselves and others is the greatest gift we can share. And, when we get to our concluding chapters, it will be with no regrets, only deep contentment and peace.

At our last meeting, I gave you a journal as a place to write and reflect on the challenges and struggles you will face as others try to define YOUR goals. Listen deeply to YOUR inner voice, and you will find YOUR best self.

Ms. C

CHAPTER 7

OCTOBER 2006

"Everyone on the baseline," I said as Fitz jogged over to turn off the horn.

Our practice had great energy, and there was a lot of talk on the floor, something we usually had to remind them about throughout practice. Fitz and I joked that in the vans or restaurants on road trips, we could never get them to shut up, but when we needed them communicating on the court, it often felt like pulling teeth. We also had a couple of groups struggling through our three-on-three defensive drills.

"We didn't quite get there this time but saw some good things. The talk was fantastic, and our containment on dribble penetration was better. But two groups didn't finish, so we've got some running to do."

Fitz set them up for sprints while I jotted down notes on the back of my practice plan.

Once they finished, most were bent over at the waist with hands on their knees, heaving deep breaths. Whit walked down the line saying, "Way to go," patting each player on the back. They slowly made their way to center court, where Whitney led the cool-down stretching.

I showed my notes to Fitz. The same four names were in the top three for all six sets of sprints: Rachel, MJ, Whitney, and Olivia. Kelsey's name was last for three of the six sets. Fitz touched her name and whispered, "That never would've happened last year."

"My thoughts exactly."

One by one, the team shuffled into the classroom for our team meeting. Once everyone was seated with binders out, I said, "We're going to keep this short today. First, looking at your calendar for the week, we've got our first scrimmage Thursday. I know you're excited to go against someone else, finally. Some other news about Thursday . . . Steph, why don't you share?"

She gave a sheepish grin. "My family will be here for the game, and my mom wants to have the team over to my apartment for a spaghetti dinner afterward. Coach gave the green light and promised to keep her postgame comments brief so dinner's not too late."

All the returners started clapping and cheering. Whitney then jumped in. "This is all cheering about Mrs. Powell's spaghetti, Coach, not about you keeping comments short after the game." She laughed, along with a handful of others.

As they left the classroom, I caught MJ's attention and had her stay behind. She hung back until everyone was gone.

"MJ," I said. "We wanted you to know that the way you practice and your competitiveness is exactly what we want from all your teammates. Even though you may feel like your teammates don't like it or are mad at you sometimes, try not to let it bother you. We need you to keep modeling competitive play instead of us trying to describe it for them. That way, your teammates know what it looks like."

Fitz jumped in. "We'll need you to be patient with your teammates during the learning process because it won't change overnight. We love how you play and need you to keep being you."

She said, "Thanks for telling me this. It helps to know that you see it and want me to keep playing aggressively. In high school, what made it harder to deal with, even more than how the other girls were, was that my coaches never acknowledged my drive. It left me wondering if the coaches wanted me to play hard or be more like the others. It was confusing."

After MJ left the classroom, Fitz and I headed to our office. "You know, I think this is the big topic we need to start focusing on for our team meetings—embracing competitiveness. We already heard some side comments in the individual meetings, and we're catching glimpses at practice now."

"Yeah, I agree," Fitz said. "Another big topic that goes hand in hand is the importance of open, honest communication. That came out clearly in MJ's observations."

"Well, there we go. With those themes, we have enough for the entire season's team meetings."

Preseason scrimmages were an opportunity to try different player combinations on the floor without worrying about winning the game. This allowed us to determine what groups worked well together, who stepped up in challenging situations, and to watch for any surprises from the incoming freshmen.

By the end of the scrimmage, we had played everyone and used everything we had practiced. Although the kids were excited about finally playing their first game—and winning—Fitz and I were most excited about having a game on tape to start dissecting the good, the bad, and the ugly.

"I'm a woman of my word," I stated in the locker room as everyone looked at me. "We have our first game under our belt, and we were delighted with the effort and the intensity. It's a great starting point from which to build. Now let's go enjoy a delicious spaghetti dinner at Steph's." Everyone erupted into cheers.

Fitz waited for me in the parking lot of Steph's apartment so we could walk into the dinner together. I almost ran right into Steph's dad, Larry, when I opened the front door.

"Hey, you look like you're about ready to run for it," Fitz teased him.

Larry laughed, and they shook hands. He embraced me in a big hug and said, "Well, you guys must be excited about this season, huh? The first scrimmage already looks like practically midseason play compared to last year!"

"Thanks, Larry. And yes, we are excited. We sure appreciate you and Carol making the trip for a scrimmage and hosting dinner," I said.

"We wouldn't miss it. It's practically like the countdown to Christmas, all the excitement about basketball season. It's not just the games, either. We love getting to know all of Steph's teammates. It's like a big extended family."

"You have an amazing daughter, and you should be so proud of her," Fitz said. Larry's smile was so big that it made his cheeks pinch into two small, pink spheres.

"We are pretty proud of her," he gushed. "And I hope you both know how much Steph loves playing for you. It sure makes Carol and me happy to know she's in a great place surrounded by all this love and support. Now, I've talked your ear off long enough." He motioned toward the kitchen. "Go find yourselves some food before the girls eat it all."

Fitz and I wound our way through a room packed with bodies carrying food-laden plates. "Carol," I called out as I entered the tiny kitchen. She had her back to me, stirring her spaghetti sauce.

"Coaches!" She turned with her arms wide and embraced Fitz and me in a group hug. "Congratulations! Your team looks fantastic, and it's just the first scrimmage."

It was my turn to brag about Steph. When I'd finished, Carol took a paper towel from the counter and dabbed her eyes. "You're not supposed to make me cry," she said, almost embarrassed. "You guys better grab your plates and dish up because some have already been back for seconds."

"You only have to tell me once," Fitz said, grabbing a plate.

"The salad stuff is on the table," Carol added.

I laughed, pointing at Fitz's now heaping plate. "I don't think he'll be able to fit any salad on that plate. Did you leave any for me?"

"Hey, I can eat salad anytime, but not Carol's amazing spaghetti!"

Fitz left and I gave Carol a conspiratorial look. "I think I'll do the same thing for the same reason," I said. "But don't tell him." Carol laughed.

Within an hour, things started to wind down. Across the room, I noticed Carol clearing the table. I jumped up and put my arm around her shoulder.

"Hey, Carol, the cook shouldn't have to clean up," I said.

"I don't want to leave this mess for Stephanie."

"Don't give it a second thought. All of us will pitch in and have this cleaned in no time. You guys have a long drive. Really . . ." I took the large black garbage bag she was using from her hand. "You focus on gathering what you need to take back with you and saying goodbye to Steph. We'll take care of this." Fitz and I mobilized the team to finish cleaning before we all filed back to our cars to head home.

"Did you happen to notice when Kelsey left?" Fitz asked as we walked out together.

"No, I didn't. It was so crowded; I guess it made hiding easy, huh?"

"I remember seeing her when we first walked in, but then I don't recall seeing her while we ate."

"Well, we planned to meet with her before practice tomorrow to discuss her poor performance at both practice and in the scrimmage.

We'll ask her about this too. You'll be ready an hour before practice tomorrow?"

"I'll be there."

Fitz walked in about ten minutes before we met with Kelsey and plopped down in his chair, facing me. "How many times did you watch the tape last night?" He had a crooked grin on his face.

"Three," I answered, a bit defensively. This transformed his grin into a full smile. "How about you?"

"Only once. Even that had me up past my bedtime." There was a light knock on the door. Instantly, the mood changed. "Kels! Come in and have a seat," he said.

Once we were all seated, I dove in. "I know Fitz and I have each mentioned some concerns we're having about your performance and commitment, but in the last few days, we've seen more examples that are just so out of character for you. When we had to do the extra sprinting after our three-on-three defensive drill, you came in last or second to last every set. Your play in our scrimmage yesterday was well below our expectations for you. It looked like you were going through the motions. That isn't the Kelsey we know. Can you explain what we're seeing?"

Her gaze remained locked on her backpack. The sound of the second hand on my basketball clock hanging on the wall thumped like a steady drumbeat.

Finally, Kelsey responded without looking up. "I guess I've been a little distracted."

"Distracted because of your classes? Your progress reports looked good," I said.

"No, my classes are fine."

"Is there something going on with your family?"

"It's nothing serious like that. It's just personal."

"I understand if you don't want to talk about it, but we must ask—are you safe? Is it health related?"

"It's not that. You don't need to worry about either of those."

"Okay. Well, that makes us feel better. And if you ever want to talk about it or need help with anything, I hope you know both of us are here for you," I said.

She nodded and mumbled a soft "thanks."

"We still need to address how this affects basketball. You have lost a starting position based on your effort level in practices and our scrimmage yesterday. You're a tremendous shooter and have the potential to play a big role this year, but not with the effort and attitude we've seen up to now. I hope you have the hunger and the drive to fight to get back in the starting five, but you need to understand it's not just given to you for past performance or your potential. You have to go out there and earn it every day at practice."

She remained bundled up, clutching her backpack in her lap, gazing downward.

"Then there's the non-basketball-related team time. Last night, at Steph's, how long were you there?"

This struck a chord because she instantly looked me in the eye. "Dinner last week, a game, and dinner this week. It's a lot, and it's always at night. We have lives, you know." This came out as a defiant outburst.

I took a breath before continuing. "Yes, we understand that you have lives away from basketball, and we want that. It's part of the whole college experience. But basketball is paying your way through college. Most students are working various part-time jobs to pay for school. Do you think they have a lot of free time?"

"No, but they get paid in real money and probably have a fixed schedule that allows for a social life at night and on the weekends. Our schedule adds so much stress to things . . ."

"Stressed about what? You already said your classes and grades are good. Is this about a boyfriend?"

"I don't want to talk about it anymore."

"Okay, Kels. But I hope you'll do some soul-searching over this next week. Your effort and attitude must improve, and the season is just starting. Our schedule will get even busier with games and travel. If basketball feels more like a stress or a burden rather than a challenging but fun experience, maybe changes must be made. And I'd prefer that decision come from you, after thinking about it, not from us."

The team was seated, facing the television screen where I'd paused the video on the first highlights I wanted to show them. "I want you to look at a few clips from last night's game focusing on great examples of competitiveness."

The segments I included were from various situations—diving after a loose ball, aggressively crashing the offensive boards, and a defensive block out that knocked the opponent to the ground. I pushed pause at the end and asked, "Did any of those look like dirty plays?"

The team shook their heads.

I continued, "Absolutely not. They are physical, aggressive plays. They show fierceness. This is competitiveness in action, not just words. How many of you think this is what it looks like at our practices?"

There were a few tentative glances around the room to see if anyone would raise their hand. "Does anyone have thoughts about *why* our practices don't look like that all the time, even in our full scrimmage situations?"

Rachel was the first to throw out an idea. "Um . . . maybe because we're afraid to hurt our teammates?"

"Did any of those plays we just watched result in an injury?" There was another chorus of noes. "Basketball is a contact sport. There's always the possibility of an injury in practice and games. The idea that if we don't go as hard against each other as we do against our opponents, then no one will get hurt is not the reality of our sport. There's a difference between being competitive and playing dirty. So . . . what else might be holding us back?"

In the silence that followed, I looked around the room at each of their faces. Whitney spoke up. "Maybe we worry that we might accidentally make somebody angry. Or that if we do well, it'll make our teammates look bad, and they'll be mad at us."

I nodded but didn't say anything, waiting to see if anyone else would jump in. Olivia surprised me by speaking next. "If we've had experiences like that in the past, maybe with our high school or AAU teams, we remember that. So even if it hasn't happened with this team, the negative experience is still there, and we don't want it to happen again."

There was so much to unpack from that nugget, but I reminded myself to stay on the main subject. "Interesting . . . how many of you have experienced that?" Every hand went up. They looked around the room at each other, seemingly surprised at the unanimous vote.

"Anyone want to share an example?" I asked.

Ellen described being given the silent treatment by some of her teammates. Steph told a story about being called "coach's pet" for what she felt was always giving her best effort.

"Here's the challenge for us going forward. We need to change our mindset about competitiveness: it's not, I can *either* be competitive, *or* teammates can like me. We can be both competitive and liked. Instead of all the worrying Whit described, we must embrace competitiveness every day, in every drill, at practice. Push each other, expect that from each other, and then celebrate the improvement coming from it."

I hoped we'd see a small amount of what we had discussed in the meeting play out on the court the next day. Progress started with baby steps and would require frequent reminders.

October 2006

Dear Steph,

*Thank you for opening your home and hosting such a won-
derful dinner for our team. Please pass my thanks on to your
parents for coming to support and generously feed us!*

*One of my mentors recently recommended a book about
how to build a successful team by a leadership coach named
John Maxwell. He shared a quote I'd like to pass on to you:
"Even when you've played the game of your life, it's the
feeling of teamwork that you'll remember. You'll forget the
plays, the shots, and the scores, but you'll never forget your
teammates."*

*I know from experience that he's right. Over time, you
forget the details of individual games. What stays with you is
the connection and community you develop with the women
who play alongside you.*

*Years from now, your teammates will have forgotten
whether we won or lost that preseason scrimmage, but they
will remember sitting in your apartment, laughing and bonding
over your mom's spaghetti. That's a true lifelong gift.*

Coach Sam

CHAPTER 8
OCTOBER 1986

Ms. Collins was surprised to see me with a folder in my hands rather than my basketball shoes.

"Good morning, Ms. Collins," I said. I cleared my throat. "I was hoping, um, that we could use this morning to talk instead of practice. I'm sorry to drop this on you at the last minute. Is that okay? I've got my shoes in the—"

Ms. Collins cut me off. "Of course. And, knowing you, this must be big stuff to talk about if it's replacing your court time." I shut the door to her office, and we sat facing each other. "So," she said, "what's going on?"

I told her about my lunch meeting with Coach Nelson and the idea of considering college volleyball. This was the first time I'd shared that with anyone. It left a funny aftertaste in my mouth, like black licorice, a flavor I disliked. I wasn't sure whether that was from me worrying that it sounded like bragging or the possibility that my basketball career might be ending.

"Wow!" She beamed. "How'd that make you feel?"

"Well . . ." I opened the journal she'd given me, where I'd written a page of notes.

She put her hand on top of the page. "We can get to that in a minute, but I want to know your initial impression."

"I laughed and told Coach Nelson I thought she was joking. When she said it wasn't a joke, I thought she must be talking about me playing at a community college."

Ms. C tipped her head back and let out a belly laugh. "Well, I want you to know what a compliment this is to you and your athletic abilities. Do you know what a small percentage of high school athletes get the opportunity to play at the next level? And here you are having to consider that option in two different sports. You could not receive a stronger confirmation of your athletic talent. Congratulations." She paused momentarily to let that sink in, then said, "You've had time to sleep on it. What do you think?"

I put the journal on her desk for her to see. "I started by writing down all the good, bad, and unknown things I could think of."

"Uh huh," she said, glancing over my columns of notes. "After doing that, did you find yourself more in one column than another?"

"Mostly the unknown. The more I thought about it, the more questions arose. It felt like a balloon expanding, realizing there were so many more questions than answers."

"I think that's a good place to be right now," she said. I looked at her, confused. "Because you haven't set your heart on a specific school for a specific degree, you can use this in your decision-making. Like colleges use the recruiting process to find student-athletes that will be a good fit for their school and program, you get to try to find the school and program that fits you best. And because you can choose two different sports, it'll give you many more options to investigate."

My frustration must've been apparent because, after a pause, she said, "That's a good thing."

Though I probably wasn't showing it, I was feeling better. She'd given me a fresh perspective by reminding me I had some control in this process.

"What did your parents think about this news?" Her question made me feel queasy.

"Umm . . . you know . . . I haven't told them about it."

Now it was Ms. Collins's turn to look confused. "Well, I'm sure you have good reasons, and from your notes, I can tell you're going about it thoughtfully and deliberately." I felt myself exhaling the pressure. I was worried she'd push me on why I hadn't told my parents, maybe even encourage me to get them involved earlier rather than later.

"As schools recruit you, one of the best ways to help in your decision is going on campus visits. Nothing can replace seeing a campus with your own eyes, meeting and spending time with the players who will be your teammates, and sitting in on classes. It'll give you a feel for whether that place could be your home for the next four to five years."

She waited to see if I had any questions, but I was still absorbing it all. "Back when I was coaching high school sports, the biggest mistake I saw players make was putting too much weight on external factors like where their parents wanted them to go or which school had the biggest name. Money can be an important consideration, but if the money is roughly the same between schools, your internal compass, especially based on a campus visit, will be your best guide."

I hadn't gotten that far in thinking about college decisions. I was still struggling with the question of volleyball versus basketball.

After a slight pause, Ms. Collins continued, "I know none of this was about whether you should choose volleyball or basketball, but I think it's helpful to see the whole and how the parts fit into it, like a puzzle. Just keep reminding yourself that you're recruiting them too. That helps in making a choice that sets you up for long-term happiness and success, regardless of which sport you choose."

"I hadn't thought about it like that, and I like that idea of me recruiting them."

She looked at the clock on the wall above her desk, and my eyes followed her gaze.

"I didn't realize it was so late," I said, stuffing my journal into my bag. "I need to head out. But the other thing I've been doing in my journal is brainstorming on the topic you brought up last time—about enjoyment, enjoying being able to dominate, about the artwork. What you said made me reflect on some of that. Maybe if we have time, I can show you next time. Unless that makes you feel more like a counselor than a coach."

"No, that's great, Sam. I'd love to see it. It's part of the mental game and every bit as important as physical skill."

"Thank you, Ms. Collins. I sure appreciate all of this. You've given me a lot to think about." Again, I felt at a loss for words to fully reflect my gratitude.

"I'm glad to do it. I'm happy for you. And I'm proud of you. This is such an exciting time, and you deserve it," she replied.

I left her office and headed to my car. Driving to the high school, I thought about how our conversation went versus how it would likely go with my parents. Ms. Collins was genuinely interested and curious. I felt like I could be open and share, a stark contrast with how I felt about communication at home.

Conversations with my dad never included questions about what I thought, wanted, or felt. Instead, it was a monologue. There wasn't room for me to have a voice, to be myself. And the more I thought about college, which sport I chose seemed less important than simply escaping.

Our volleyball team was cruising through league play. Our only loss had been against a much larger school. Though this loss was disappointing, it had been a competitive match, and I knew the experience we gained would be helpful in postseason play. We were as driven as Coach Nelson to win the state championship and practiced that way daily.

Lindsey stood next to me on the court, waiting for tonight's match to begin. She bumped my shoulder with hers several times and glanced at me sideways. "Are you ready?" she asked quietly.

I returned the shoulder nudge and said, "Absolutely!" She grinned at that. It was funny how different I felt before volleyball games compared to basketball games. With volleyball, I felt excited, lighthearted, and full of energy, while basketball felt heavier, more serious, and more intense.

Off to a fast and aggressive start, we opened a 6–0 lead before our opponent even got to serve. We won in three straight games, dominating the match in a no-nonsense manner.

My mom was waiting on the sideline when I walked off the court. She wrapped her arms around me in a tight hug. "Your team played so great, and you had an awesome game. I loved every minute of it."

"Thanks, Mom. It was a fun match. Everything was clicking. Did Dad make it?"

My mom sighed and said, "No, and he'll be just sick when he hears about what an amazing game you had."

I'm sure he will, I thought.

"Apparently, at school today, Chris asked your dad if he could talk with him about his college plans. Something about needing to decide which sport—I don't know. But because Chris had practice first and then needed to eat dinner, I don't think they could meet until about six thirty or so. Must've gone a little longer than expected because your dad said he'd meet me over here for the game."

My mom was still trying to explain away my dad's absence, lack of interest, and lack of support like she always did. My ears had tuned her out once I heard Chris Daniels's name. He wasn't even a senior this year, but he got more time and attention from my dad than I did. Chris was the son Dad never had, and apparently, having a daughter every bit Chris's equal in athletics couldn't fill that void for him. What about *my* void?

After dinner, I was loading the dishwasher when the phone rang. Emily answered on the first ring, always sure every phone call was for her.

"Sam, it's for you," she said, covering the mouthpiece with her hand. "It's a college coach."

Mom, Emily, and I stood frozen in place, staring at each other in silent disbelief.

Mom broke the silence. "Why don't you take it back in our bedroom? I'll hang up when you pick up and ensure your dad stays out of the room."

"Thanks, Mom."

I hurried to their bedroom, shutting the door behind me. I was still so shocked that I didn't have time to feel nervous.

"This is Sam," I said into the receiver, and I could hear the quiet click of the phone being hung up in the kitchen.

"Hi, Sam. This is Coach Gail Braxton. I'm the head volleyball coach at Sacramento State University . . ."

Ten minutes or ten hours later (I couldn't tell), I hung up the phone and sat on the edge of my parents' bed, replaying the conversation. They wanted me at their school and on their team next year. Coach Braxton was planning to come to watch one of our matches and hoped to set up a home visit together with my parents while she was in town.

Excitement pulsed through me like the nervous energy of pregame warm-ups. My mind raced. I wanted to share this with Coach Nelson and ask her questions about how the process would unfold and what I should do to prepare. Would she join us for the home visit?

A more immediate issue hit me: I had to discuss this with my parents right away. I headed to the den, not knowing what to expect. As I sat down, my mom was full of excitement.

"Well, who was that?" she asked, her eyes glued on me. My dad sat in his recliner, his eyes fixed on the TV.

"It was the volleyball coach at Sacramento State University." I figured I'd play it cool and just answer their questions, letting them guide the discussion. That way, I wouldn't sound boastful.

"What did you guys talk about? C'mon, Sam," Mom said, "spill the beans. This is exciting! I want to hear everything without having to play twenty questions."

"Well, she asked about our season and school. She has talked with Coach Nelson about me and mailed a packet of information for her to give me." I was starting to speak faster, my excitement coming through even though I wanted to downplay the whole thing. "And she said from—"

My mom held up a finger and interrupted me. "Just a second," she said quietly to me. "Mark, please turn the TV off and join our conversation. Sam is sharing about her phone call with a college volleyball coach." He walked across the room to turn off the television, then returned to his recliner, sitting as far away as possible.

My excitement was gone without me consciously trying to mask it. "She said that judging from game video and Coach Nelson's description of my athleticism, I'd be a good fit for her team." My dad's face was expressionless; he could've been listening to a weather report from China.

"Umm . . . she also talked about making a home visit and setting up a campus visit for me soon."

My mom's eyes widened. "Sam, that's fantastic! That means they're serious about you. How about that?" She looked at my dad to share the enthusiasm and signal that he could jump in with comments. He didn't.

"I hope it's okay, but I agreed to the date she threw out for the home visit. It's next Tuesday. She wants to see our match and meet at our house afterward."

"It's better than okay! It's great! I'm so happy for you and so proud of you. *We* are so proud of you," she added with emphasis. "I'll make a dessert for us when we get back here after your game."

"Thanks, Mom. I can help you. I don't want this to be more work for you."

She laughed. "Don't be ridiculous. It's not work, and I'm happy to do it. Besides, I look forward to meeting her and hearing about their program."

She looked at my dad again to see if he would say anything. After a brief pause, he said, "They must have quite the budget to plan travel at the last minute." He waited maybe three seconds and then asked my mom if he could turn the TV back on.

I sat stiffly in the passenger seat of Lindsey's car, my hands clutched in my lap and my stomach churning. I closed my eyes and took a deep breath before grabbing my backpack and opening the door.

"With any luck, my mom's brownies are just coming out of the oven. She was so excited you're coming today." Lindsey let out a small laugh and rolled her eyes a little.

I forced a smile. "That was sweet of her. Everything your mom bakes is wonderful." I closed the car door and looked at the Walters' neat white colonial.

Lindsey was halfway to the front door when she looked back and saw that I was still standing in the same spot. She walked back toward me. "Mom said she's glad it'll be a girl's night. Dad won't be home until late. He's got his monthly poker game tonight." Relief coursed through me; I felt my tense muscles start to unwind.

Such indirect acknowledgment was the closest we ever got to discussing how her dad treated me during the basketball season, and it was the only acknowledgment I'd gotten from anyone. It was just enough validation to ease some of my doubts. After three seasons without anyone else commenting on it, it was easy to start second-guessing my interpretation of the experience.

The one time I'd brought it up to my dad, it only made me feel worse. Halfway through my sophomore season, I was confused, frustrated, and angry about how Coach Walters treated me. I'd been holding it all inside but finally reached my breaking point. By exposing my feelings to Dad, I felt like I was rolling the dice and gambling with my entire future career.

I told him I didn't understand why Coach Walters treated me as if he hated me. I shared about one of our last games where, out of the blue, he'd told me, a five-eight guard, to guard the other team's six-one senior, all-conference post player. I was shocked; I'd never gotten repetitions at practice for post defense. But I embraced it as a challenge. I was feeling good at halftime, having guarded her the entire first half and holding her to only four points and no offensive rebounds.

Then I got benched the entire second half without a word of explanation from Coach Walters. The post player went off in the second half, scoring 18 points and grabbing 8 rebounds, and the other team killed us. He never said anything after the game or even at our next practice.

Then I told my dad that Coach Walters had me stand against the wall for nearly everything—drills, scrimmages—at three different practices in the past two weeks. I was called to join in only for the conditioning sprints. Essentially, he'd benched me at practice as well, again with no words of explanation.

I felt a sense of relief simply from telling someone what was happening instead of bottling it up. Then I saw the look on my dad's face—disgust. He did that thing with his eyes—closing them like a blink but leaving his lids closed for a few seconds—and shook his head slightly. The message was crystal clear—that Coach Walters was intense and had high standards. This was not what I'd hoped to hear. Dad said he should be coaching boys and couldn't figure out how he survived coaching girls because girls needed to talk about everything, including their feelings, and they needed everything explained. His tone dripped with disdain, whether for me or all females, I didn't know.

Staring straight ahead at the television, his final comment had been, "Don't be so sensitive, Sam." I'd gambled and lost. That was the last time I said anything to him or anyone else about what was happening in basketball.

"C'mon," Lindsey said, tugging my arm and walking backward toward the front door, "I need you to be the tiebreaker. Wait till you see the dress my mom wants me to wear. I told her it's homecoming, not the Miss America pageant!" She shook her head, her ponytail bobbing from side to side.

We dropped our bags in the front hallway as Lindsey launched into her plan for the night. "Okay," she said, "first, let's go up to my room. I'll try on the three dresses I got, and you help me decide. Then we can break the news to my mom and let her feed us brownies."

"I thought I heard you drive in," Lindsey's mom said, walking toward us from the kitchen. "Hi, Sam. It's so good to see you." She opened her arms to hug me.

"It's good to see you, too, Mrs. Walters."

"Do you two want to start with a treat? We can go in the kitchen—"

"Nope. First dresses, then dessert, Mom." Lindsey started up the stairs to her bedroom. "And you stay down here. I don't want you influencing Sam's opinion."

Mrs. Walters patted me on the shoulder and winked. "I'm so glad you're here, Sam."

"Gosh, Linds. You make this tough because they all looked so good on you."

We were standing at the end of Lindsey's bed, looking at all three dresses laid side by side. Lindsey had changed into sweats. Now she squinted at me and crossed her arms. "No way. You're not getting off that easy."

I continued to look at the dresses. Finally, I pointed to the burgundy dress. "I think this is my favorite," I said. "I like this color the best with your hair and the simplicity of the style."

A slow smile spread across her face. At first, I couldn't tell if she was laughing at my choice or happy with my selection. "That was my pick too," she said. "Guess which one my mom wanted?"

I pointed to the light pink one. It was a little frilly, lacy, and busier overall. Lindsey laughed. "Exactly." She pointed to the third dress on her bed. "You know, I think that blue dress would look great on you if you wanted to borrow it. There's still time to change your mind about going. You can buy tickets until next Friday." I smiled and shook my head. Lindsey frowned briefly before saying, "You don't feel like maybe you're missing out? Like you might look back later and wish you would've gone?"

My internal voice chimed in immediately with a flippant response: *Are you kidding me? Missing out? I can't wait to get out of here!* But that stayed inside because I knew her question was sincere.

"I guess I just don't look at my high school experience as this great thing, the pinnacle, where I should be trying to collect all these experiences and memories. I guess I see it more as the doorway to the next phase—college. Does that make sense?" Although I'd felt this way throughout high school, I'd never verbalized it. I found it funny that such intense feelings that were second nature to me, like feeling hungry or tired, could be so challenging to put into words.

"Yeah, I guess," Lindsey responded hesitantly, clearly struggling to understand how I felt.

"It's probably hard for you to understand what I'm describing because our two high school experiences have been like night and day. For you, it's lots of involvement—music, sports, and student government. Even though I'm involved in multiple sports, basketball is it for me. So the most important thing about my high school experience is to be good enough at basketball for it to pay for college and allow me to keep playing at the next level."

"You know, this whole thing about college—I don't think I'm as strong as you," she said, furrowing her brows. "The whole going away, not knowing anyone, basically starting over is intimidating."

I was shocked at her description; *strength* never would've been a word I'd use to describe myself. Lindsey, with her good looks, popularity, outgoing personality, and overall balance in life, embodied strength by my definition. The core of my decision was about ending my feelings of suffocation. It was about escaping and creating my true self outside the narrow confines I'd always felt. It was about nothing short of self-preservation.

Lindsey shrugged her shoulders and smiled. "C'mon. Let's break the news to my mom and dig into those brownies."

October 2006

To: Samantha Shuster
From: Laurie Collins

Dear Sam,

Thank you for the newsy letter. You could never bore me
with details about your team, practices, games, planning—any
of it. Through your stories and updates, I'm reminded of my
experiences so long ago as an athlete and a coach. Thank
you for sharing with me so I can live vicariously through you
and your teams.

That is exciting about the leadership coming from your
returning players. It's one of those "intangibles" that make
such a difference, especially when you hit bumps in the
road—and there are always bumps. Please don't underestimate your role in that leadership development, first
in the direct teaching and modeling of leadership skills,
but second, in creating an environment that encourages
using those skills. I've known plenty of coaches who talk
about the idea of leadership but then don't let their players lead on the court. The kids are left to try out those
skills elsewhere.

I must admit, I laughed out loud about your tattooed Top
Ramen kid. I would've loved to be a fly on the wall to watch
you control your facial expressions and hold back the laughter
I know you felt. I also laughed, picturing her telling a friend
about your conversation: "I'm talking with my coach about
rent issues and not having enough money for food, and out
of the blue, Coach starts talking about my tattoo?! I wonder

if she's losing her hearing or getting the start of dementia 'cuz that's just crazy." It still makes me chuckle.

I'm sorry to hear about some resistance to the strong competitiveness of one of your players. Sports are an in-your-face version of competitiveness (or lack thereof), but we see it in other parts of society too. Our culture still sends the message to girls about being ambitious—but not TOO ambitious—about being assertive—but not TOO assertive. It's still more important for females to be nice, liked by all, and blend in. So please, even though that won't change overnight, keep working on it!

My classes are going well; there is nothing new or exciting to report there. I expect my hike last weekend was the last one I'll get for a while. The weather has finally changed, so it's time to settle in for a few months of gray and rain.

Thanks for taking the time to send me such an informative update. I look forward to tracking your team's progress and success this season. I'm not a techie, but I'll try to figure out how to watch a few of your games online. Please know I don't expect regular updates because I know how busy you are. Enjoy your kids and enjoy the season.

Go Cougs!!

Ms. C

CHAPTER 9
NOVEMBER 2006

As I merged onto the highway, I checked my rearview mirror to make sure Fitz was still behind me. We were fifteen minutes into a three-hour ride, each driving a van full of players, on our way to our second scrimmage of the season.

In the mirror, I caught sight of Steph in the seat behind me, rummaging through her backpack. "Okay, everybody, take out your earbuds 'cuz we're gonna play a game," she announced.

Road trips brought out the entertainer in Stephanie. She could make it a safe and fun zone for all. I saw Olivia, probably our quietest kid off the court, turn sideways in her seat to see what kind of craziness Steph had up her sleeve.

"Ta-da!" Steph hollered. I glanced up and saw she was holding something above her head. "Mad Libs," she announced, sounding proud of herself.

I sensed no one else in the van knew what these were. When her surprise was met with silence, she jumped in with the first one.

"You'll see. I'll call out your name and tell you what part of speech to give. Don't think about it too long; shout out the first word that pops into your head."

"Olivia, a noun," Steph started.

"Car," Olivia answered immediately.

"Okay. MJ, verb, past tense."

"Chewed."

Steph finished going around the van, collecting different parts of speech, and then she was ready to read the final product. Her teammates laughed hard as she finished reading the resulting nonsense and begged her to start the next round. By the time we stopped for food, they had completed four, each a little better than the last.

Overall, I'd been happy with our play that day, showing some slight improvement from our first scrimmage. Fitz and I kept our postgame comments brief, knowing we'd spend more time at practice going over what we saw. Our immediate feedback focused on defense and rebounding.

When we stopped for our postgame meal, I held the glass door open for our players as they quietly shuffled into the diner, squinting under the bright fluorescent lights. As they passed me, it was an opportunity to compliment several of them on their individual play—good decision-making, excellent shooting, lockdown defensive work.

Each kid had the same response. They dropped their eyes to the ground, gave a sheepish grin, and murmured a meek thank you. Why did praise seem to be accepted with embarrassment and was so short-lived while a single criticism or failure could hang on forever? Even one bad half or criticism at practice could flush all the confidence and compliments received right down the toilet. I wished there was a way that could be reversed.

The preseason was now over, and the day of our first home game had arrived. From the opening tip, we dominated the game in a way our team had never done before. Our defense stymied our opponent, forcing five early turnovers and holding them scoreless for the first five minutes of the game.

Offensively, we looked sharp as well. Olivia knew when to push the pace and when to slow things down. Rachel's shooting was lights out. With her perfect form, she finished 12 for 16 from the floor, including 4 for 4 from three-point range.

After winning in such a calm and business-like manner, the whole team erupted in uncontrolled excitement when they reached the locker room. Fitz and I watched them, grinning for a minute or two before they all sat down, ready to listen.

"That was a dominant forty minutes of basketball, and you should feel excited and proud," I said. "Our defense held them scoreless for the first five-and-a-half minutes of the game." I paused for their clapping and then shared a few key stats.

Everyone huddled with hands extended into the middle of our circle. "Great win tonight, ladies. And it's not just the win itself. It's *how* we did it," I said and then nodded to Whit to finish.

"TEAM, on three. One, two, three!"

Fitz and I went to our office to put away our clipboards and stats before returning to the gym. The largest gathering was around Stephanie. Her parents, brother, sister, and grandparents had all made the trip. As I approached the group, I noticed a young girl and a woman I didn't recognize.

"Coach, I just introduced Amy to my family and wanted to introduce you too. Amy, this is Coach Sam. This is Amy and her mom, Mrs. Russell."

"Hi, Amy. It's nice to meet you. Thank you so much for coming to our game tonight," I said, extending my hand. With all of Steph's family looking on, Amy seemed embarrassed at being the center of attention. I greeted Mrs. Russell and then turned my attention back to Amy.

"So, how do you think Steph played tonight?"

"She was awesome!" Amy looked up at Stephanie with reverence, like she was meeting a celebrity.

Steph bent down to meet Amy at eye level. "Do you want to see our team room?" Amy nodded enthusiastically, and they walked away, with Steph's sister tagging along.

Mrs. Russell wasted no time sharing her appreciation with Stephanie's parents. "I'm sure you already know this, and you probably hear things like this all the time, but I want to tell you what an incredible daughter you have. She has made a tremendous difference in Amy's life in just a short time." Mrs. Russell paused, trying to contain her emotions. She described the changes with Amy at home and school since her recent divorce. I could see tears brimming at the edge of her eyes. "I can't thank you enough." Carol wrapped her in a warm hug.

I put my hand on Mrs. Russell's arm. "It was so nice meeting you and Amy. I hope we'll see you at more games this season."

Then I walked over to Jamie and her parents. "Hi, Mr. and Mrs. Wilcox," I said, shaking their hands. "It's great to see you. Thank you for making the long trip."

"Well, thank *you*," they replied, almost in unison.

"If it wasn't for you and Coach Fitz, I'm not sure Jamie would've made it this far. I'm sure you know, but the first month was tough. She was so homesick," Mrs. Wilcox explained. Mr. Wilcox had his arm around Jamie, giving her an extra squeeze.

"It must be tough to hear the pain and tears over the phone and feel helpless. Many parents give in to that and say, 'Come home.' But we're glad you didn't. We think Jamie's pretty special," I said. I thanked them again before leaving so they could enjoy some time together.

Other than losing in an exhibition game, we were undefeated heading into an early, nonconference tournament at Whitworth College. The long drive, hotel stay, and two games in two nights was a good challenge and gauge of our progress.

Fitz and I had parked both vans in front of the gym and waited for the kids to climb out with their bags. I gathered everyone together in the parking lot. "This is the time to mentally prepare for our game tonight. We'll watch the first half of this game because we'll be playing the winner. When you walk into the gym, enter as a group and find a section in the bleachers where you can all sit together. It would be best if you put cell phones away now. No texting and no phone calls. From this minute until the end of our game, the focus is only on basketball and our team."

Fitz took notes on Evergreen State College during the first half while I focused on UC Santa Cruz. Though we would get a copy of the game DVD, there was something about watching a team live that added a different perspective. At halftime, Santa Cruz was leading 37–31, but they did not execute in a way that made me confident to predict the game's outcome.

Back in the locker room, our team looked ready to go as I started speaking. "This is Whitworth's tournament, playing in front of their home crowd, and they want to win it. They can't control who they'll play in the second game, but they had their choice of three teams to play in this first game. They wanted to pick the team they felt would be the easiest to beat and make it to the championship game. They picked us. I want you to go out there, in front of their crowd, and show them that they were wrong—very, very wrong!"

I knew our team wanted to win, but all teams take the floor wanting to win. The common elements of championship teams were feistiness and fearless determination. Fitz and I had been working to build this competitive mindset since our first season together. We had made significant improvements each season, but with this team, I felt an inner urgency for it to happen now. I looked each of the starters in the eyes, hoping they'd see my fire and feel my confidence and belief in them. I nodded to Whitney, and she concluded with a team cheer. "COMPETE, on three!" she yelled, and the team erupted on her count.

As we entered the gym, the prior game was down to the final ten seconds, with Santa Cruz pulling out a close victory. Once both teams had filed off the court, our team jogged onto the court, starting pregame warm-ups.

Whitworth College won the tip and scored on their first possession. Immediately, they were in their full-court press. Olivia recognized it and called out our press break to her teammates. Wasting no time, we attacked their press with two crisp passes, giving us a three-on-two scoring opportunity.

We were aggressive on offense, but defensively we looked tentative. After four minutes with the score tied at eight, I called a timeout to refocus our defense. I held Olivia back as the other four walked onto the court. "Pick up their point guard as soon as she crosses half-court. Get into her; don't let her breathe."

Olivia did precisely that, and instantly, our defense turned up the heat. Whitworth's coach called off their press, subbed various players, and used a timeout, but nothing slowed our momentum. MJ and Kelsey played in the first half, and all seven players scored. Rachel led us with her lights-out shooting, scoring 14 points. We were up 20 points at halftime.

I had the team huddled around me as we prepared to take the floor for the second half. "We've been talking about competitiveness, but this is where you show it. Imagine the scoreboard being 0–0 and this next twenty minutes a whole new game. Keep the pressure on, and don't give them even a moment to think they are in this game."

Our high level of play continued from the very first play of the second half and remained strong, led by Rachel, our sharpshooter. Whitworth's level of play never matched the game's first four minutes, but they continued to play hard, and our team never let their guard down. We beat them by twenty-four, and I was happy with our consistently high focus and energy.

Standing with Fitz outside the classroom, looking at our final stat sheet, we could hear the excitement in our players' voices. Whitney's booming voice rose above everyone else's as she praised Rachel's shooting. Steph followed that up with something funny, but I couldn't make out her specific words, only her voice and then the laughter of her teammates.

Fitz opened the door and yelled, "That is what we're talking about! Do you know what most teams would've done in that second half? They would've lost their focus, let the other team cut into the lead and gain momentum, and then the game could go either way by the end. That's what average teams do." He paced back and forth in front of the room, his energy more like leading a pep rally. All eyes were glued on him.

"But you just proved that this team is not average. You played with a competitive fire for forty minutes against a strong team. That is the mark of a championship team!" Then he lowered his voice. "And we are so proud of you."

Rather than getting into specific stats, this seemed like an excellent way to end our talk. There would be plenty of time to share the details when we watched the tape, but right then, it was about recognizing and praising these intangibles missing in our past three seasons.

I reinforced Fitz's message and reminded them we needed to keep that competitive fire burning for our next game. "Our opponent for the championship game now knows what they're up against. So let's get some good food and rest in preparation to win this tournament," I added. With that, the kids changed quickly and ran out to our vans like a military unit preparing for their next battle.

We stopped at a diner a few blocks up from the hotel. The kids sat together at two large tables, while Fitz and I grabbed a booth nearby. Just as we finished our meals, Kelsey came over to our table.

"I finished eating and was wondering if I could return to the hotel?"

"No, Kels. Everyone is nearly done, so I'd like us to walk back together."

"Okay." Her response was muted, but I was glad there wasn't any arguing or eye-rolling. Instead of returning to where the team sat, she walked to the front and waited in the entryway. She immediately pulled out her cell phone.

"Kelsey and her phone are going to drive me nuts," I mumbled to Fitz.

October 2006

Dear Steph,

I am so proud of the initiative you're taking by volunteering in Mrs. Carlson's class. You have an extraordinary gift. You have a warm and genuine way of interacting with others, positively impacting all those students, especially Amy.

We become the people we are because of the support and mentorship we receive from others throughout our lives. It builds us up, layer upon layer, and allows us to do the same for others. You're offering those students a layer that will stay with them for the rest of their lives. Never underestimate the impact you're having.

Coach Sam

CHAPTER 10

OCTOBER 1986

I was lacing up my basketball shoes when Ms. Collins greeted me in the gym.

"I'm sorry to bring something up at the last minute again, but I was hoping we could stop early to discuss recruiting. A college coach called me last night."

"Sam, that's fantastic. I look forward to hearing about it. I was already planning a slight change for today anyway, so we'll do all three things," she said.

Our first twenty minutes was an efficient shooting workout, starting with repetitions of post moves from both blocks and then moving to perimeter shots. She had me finish with free throws; I made nine out of ten.

"Now for part two. Oh, this is going to be fun," she said. She jogged over to a box in the corner. When she came back, she had four racquet-balls in her hands. Tossing one to me, she asked, "Can you juggle?"

"No."

"Good. . . . And the answer is 'not yet.' This is our first failure challenge."

She demonstrated, making it look easy, and then explained the pattern and how to start. Over and over, I'd toss and catch, trying to repeat the pattern she'd demonstrated, but with no success. She had a sly grin, and I wanted to tell her I thought she was enjoying this way too much. Fortunately, I was anxious to share about the phone call, significantly reducing the frustration with my inability to juggle.

Finally, she let me off the hook. "Okay, enough juggling. I want to hear all about this recruitment call! How are you feeling about it?"

"Honestly, it hasn't sunk in yet. Now that it's real, I'll have to go back and study my list of pros and cons again."

"I'm sure Coach Nelson will be a big help, and I'm always here if I can help in any way."

"Thank you. I appreciate it."

As I changed my shoes and got ready to leave, Ms. Collins said, "Here's my quick message for you today—mistakes and failures are a must for you to grow, especially when starting something new. You know, like juggling. The important issue is not whether you failed. It's whether you let the first attempts and failures become your last. To be the best at something, you must be willing to try things outside your comfort zone. You must be willing to risk making mistakes and feeling embarrassed to grow and excel."

I nodded. "Okay. That wasn't too bad."

Ms. Collins tipped her head back and laughed. "That was nothing yet, Sam. And remember that word, *yet*. It's a biggie."

The last week before districts went by in a blur. When I was not at practice or a game, I thought a lot about the information I read from Sacramento State and the thought of playing volleyball in college. My feelings about this were all over the map. At practice or games, I felt more optimistic about the idea. Our team chemistry and success colored these thoughts with enthusiasm. The mental pictures I constructed were in bright and vivid colors, as if lit by a high-powered spotlight—probably thanks to the images in Coach Nelson's information packet. I could see and feel myself being a part of something new and different, and on my own, away from home.

But then, just as those images and feelings soared, there were other times they plummeted. During my morning basketball workouts with Ms. Collins, I was reminded of the passion for basketball that had burned inside me since second grade. It was so familiar, so comfortable, like an old pair of shoes, so worn in from countless hours that they had been perfectly molded to my feet; they no longer had any support, feeling more like slippers, but I couldn't part with them.

The idea of possibly not playing basketball after my senior season left me with an immobilizing despair. In contrast to the bright imagery of volleyball, my images of basketball were silent movies in slow motion, and the only colors were muted grays. It felt like a funeral—my own.

Meanwhile, all the talk and energy at school was about homecoming. If I'd thought Chris Daniels's ego had filled the hallway before, now it was on steroids. Usually, his arrogance and popularity filled me with disgust and resentment, but for the first time, it didn't bother me because I was finally being seen and acknowledged for my athletic abilities.

The idea that a Division I school would be interested in me lightened my spirits. It was as if a weight I didn't know I was carrying had been lifted off my shoulders, and I felt greater confidence. If volleyball coaches were interested in me, I'd surely have basketball opportunities too. In short, I had my ticket out of this place. Even Chris Daniels parading through the hallway couldn't squelch my excitement.

At home, my mom initiated the only discussion about Coach Braxton when she asked if I'd given any more thought to the campus visit. I repeated what Ms. Collins said about the importance of seeing schools with my own eyes. Mom agreed. The only thing Dad said was that I'd need to talk with Coach Walters, as I'd probably miss two practices.

Sitting at my desk, staring at my calculus homework, I was amazed at my dad's ability to turn something positive into something to be critical of. I didn't understand how events that should be celebrated ended up making me feel like I was walking on eggshells in my own home. What did my dad want me to do? Turn this opportunity down? And why was this so difficult to talk about openly?

My mind raced with these unanswered and unspoken questions until I heard a knock at my door. Mom pushed the door open just enough to poke her head in. "The phone's for you. It's another college coach." I was so lost in thought I hadn't heard the phone ring. "Do you want to take it in our bedroom?"

"Sure, Mom. Thanks."

After a thirty-minute conversation, I walked, zombie-like, back to my room, shut the door, and sat back at my desk. Excitement, nervousness, anxiety, fear, and fatigue washed over me in a jumbled mess. I closed my eyes and took a couple of deep breaths. After completing as much homework as I could, I walked to the TV room to say goodnight to my parents.

"How'd the phone conversation go? Who was it?" my mom asked.

"Her name is Coach Lori Stevens, and she's the head volleyball coach at Boise State. She saw me on game tape, and they're interested in me for their team. She'll attend the district tournament and hoped to schedule a home visit."

"Wow, Sam! That's great!" Mom's excitement sounded like a kid at Christmas. "Mark, did you hear that? Now it's Boise State."

Dad looked at me and said, "That's great, Sam." His facial expression and tone seemed softer and more sincere. That was all he said, but it was enough. It wasn't negative or sarcastic. I got up to leave before that could change.

My mom had made a great effort to create a warm and inviting environment for Coach Braxton's visit. A soft glow emanated from lamps and candles on the dining room buffet. The smell of cinnamon and baked apples filled the house; I felt like I was already eating a piece of warm apple pie.

With my parents close behind me, I opened the door to greet coaches Braxton and Nelson. Mom stepped next to me and put a hand on my shoulder. "Please, come in." She motioned with her other hand. "It's wonderful to meet you, Coach Braxton."

Coach Braxton reached out her hand to shake my mother's, then my father's. "Please, call me Gail. And thank you for opening your home to me and taking the time to meet. I know it's a weeknight, so I promise to keep things efficient." She had a friendly, easy smile; it made me feel like I'd known her for years. The corners of her eyes crinkled with her smile. Her skin was tan and she was a few inches taller than me, with a lean build.

As my mom bustled around, taking everyone's coats and offering coffee or tea and servings of apple cobbler, I stood frozen in the hallway. Coach Nelson turned and gave me a reassuring smile. I'd asked her to come, not knowing how things would go with my parents. Just seeing her gave me a much needed sense of relief.

My mom ushered everyone into the living room. When we were seated, the conversation started with our game, our season, and the upcoming tournaments. My dad stayed quiet throughout, just eating his dessert. Coach Braxton then shifted gears.

"As much as I'd like to continue talking about this, I better share some information about our school and program since I promised to leave by ten. I always discuss academics first, because that's the top priority." She described how players communicated with professors and coaches monitored attendance and grades, and had a mandatory study table for all first-year students and anyone below a 3.0 grade point average. And she proudly shared statistics on the 100 percent graduation rate for those who stayed in the program for four to five years.

She turned to look directly at me. "Have you thought about possible areas of academic interest?"

"I don't know, but I like psychology, so possibly a counselor or psychologist."

Before I could continue, Dad, who had barely said five words to this point, jumped in. "You don't want to be a psychologist. They're usually crazy themselves and went into that field to try to figure out what's wrong with them. You know Mr. Stanton, down the street? He's a psychologist." Like that proved his point. Even Mom, usually so good at cutting things off before they advanced too far, sat in stunned silence.

I tried to change the subject. "I also like writing, so I've wondered about journalism too. But really, I don't know for sure yet." I hoped I wasn't failing this part of the visit by not having a plan for my degree.

"You'd have a tough time making enough money in journalism to support yourself," my dad added in a quieter voice, almost like he was talking to himself.

Coach Braxton jumped in. "That is perfectly normal. Most incoming first-year students don't have a declared major, and it's common for students to change majors several times before finding the right fit. That's one of the exciting things about college. You're exposed to so many possibilities." She was trying to bring back some excitement to the room after my dad's comments and tone had deflated the energy. From there, she continued to share an overview, and Coach Nelson and my mom asked a few questions.

As Coach Braxton wrapped things up, she acknowledged she'd thrown a lot of information at me in our first discussion, and she wanted me to feel free to call if other questions came up later. "And the other thing we'd like is to set up a campus visit for you. We hoped to schedule that for the week right after the state tournament and before

Thanksgiving. It would require you to miss school on Friday, and you'd need to provide transportation to the airport. If you're still interested, I'll call with your flight information this weekend and review a detailed itinerary for your visit. She'll be in good hands," she added, giving my parents a reassuring smile. "She'll be with someone on the team or the coaching staff the entire time."

"That sounds wonderful, Gail, and we'll look at the calendar and talk about it this week," my mom said.

Coach Braxton shook hands goodbye with all of us and said she hoped to see me in Sacramento. Coach Nelson left right behind her, and my mom and I thanked her for joining us. My dad had already excused himself and was in the den.

I gave Mom a big hug. "Thanks for making the evening so nice and being so welcoming."

She said, "You're welcome. I'm so happy for you and so proud of you."

"Thanks, Mom," I said, then returned to my bedroom without saying goodnight to my dad.

Later that night, I could hear some of my parents' conversation across the hall. My mom was clearly upset; my dad told her I had no idea what I was getting myself into at that level. He asked what was wrong with me staying in town and playing both sports at the community college level. The last thing I heard before their door closed and the voices became indecipherable was my dad saying, ". . . it's good enough for Lindsey. . . ."

I wanted to tell him that I'd already spent four years with Lindsey, and in that time, unfortunately, her beauty and bubbly personality hadn't rubbed off on me. I didn't think another two years would make a difference and somehow transform me into her.

The bus ride to our final league game of the season took just over an hour, and the team was more animated than usual. Some excitement was about the game, but most revolved around homecoming weekend, which had everyone in a good mood. As I looked at each of my team-mates, I ran through a mental checklist of those with boyfriends.

I turned to Lindsey in the seat next to me. "Do you know if most of our team will be going to homecoming?"

"Oh yeah, everyone on varsity. We've already made plans to meet at the dance to get a team photo in our formals. We thought Coach Nelson would like that, seeing one picture in our uniforms and one where we're all dressed up." After a second, her smile faded. "Oh, Sam. I'm sorry. I didn't think before I said that. My mom says I do that all the time."

"Don't be silly, Linds. You don't need to apologize for anything. It's not your fault I'm not going. I know if it were up to you, I would be."

She smiled, and I could see the relief on her face. "Are you at least coming to the game?"

"With Emily on the homecoming court, I think my family would disown me if I didn't. They already think it's bad enough that I don't make it to every game to support her." I rolled my eyes.

Lindsey smirked and tapped her finger on her cheek. "Funny, I can't remember the last time I saw Emily at one of our volleyball games."

I laughed. "I'll be sure to bring it up. Right after I tell them I voted for you for homecoming queen, not Emily."

Lindsey gasped. "Sam!" Then she giggled. "Your secret is safe with me. And I'm honored. Anyway, I'm glad you're coming to the game. It's always fun."

"Yeah, but sometimes it feels like everyone thinks football is the only sport worth watching, right?"

"Yeah, I guess," Lindsey said, "but it's always been like that."

"But doesn't it bother you that someone like Chris Daniels can be so arrogant and strut around campus, and everybody acts like he's this perfect role model?"

"I don't know, I think that's just how it is with guys," Lindsey said, shrugging her shoulders.

I furrowed my brow and sat back in my seat. That was the problem; the guys were treated differently. If a great female athlete like Lindsey didn't see that as a problem, who would? Maybe my dad was right. Maybe I was just too sensitive.

I felt Lindsey's arm wrap around my shoulders. "Hey, no more talk about homecoming tonight, okay?"

She clearly didn't understand why I was upset. "Okay," I agreed.

We won our match in four games, but the ride home was quiet. Coach Nelson got everyone's attention when the bus pulled to the curb in front of our gym entrance. "First, let's congratulate our JV team on the big win tonight and capping off a great season by finishing 11–3." The whole bus erupted into cheers and applause. "Now we begin part two. Tomorrow's practice will be one hour, varsity only. We'll celebrate our JV team at the banquet, but let's give them one more cheer tonight."

Until then, I hadn't thought about this being the last game for our JV team and the fact that they had no more practices or games, no more time together. This reminded me of how close we were to the end of our season.

November 2006

Dear Olivia,

As you know, everyone recognizes a loud social leader, and that personality style has been seen as the gold standard for leadership for a long time.

More reserved leaders like yourself bring a lot to the table—things like being a great listener and, therefore, able to make strong connections with people; being observant and reflective so ideas shared come from deep thought.

Celebrate your own style of leadership. Don't try to be different from who you are.

Your quiet leadership is one of the reasons our team is having such a great season.

Coach Sam

CHAPTER 11

NOVEMBER 2006

Our first tournament was coming to an end. Fitz and I were down in the hotel lobby fifteen minutes early, waiting to drive the team to the gym for the championship game. When they stumbled out of the elevator, they were laughing uncontrollably.

"Wait till you hear this one," Steph started, as the group hurried over to us. "Alice went down the hall to the vending machine, and when she didn't come back right away, I went looking for her, afraid she got lost, being a freshman and all." Steph made an exaggerated facial expression. "Instead, I found her standing in front of the machine, holding three bags of peanut M&M's and looking confused." Steph imitated Alice's voice. "She said, 'I wasn't trying to get M&M's, and now I'm out of money.'"

"So I'm wondering how you make the same mistake three times, right? It's not that she had three different candies—she had three bags of M&M's." Steph knew how to pause and speak slowly for dramatic effect, comedic timing to perfection. "So she points to the thing she was trying to get, a packet of Advil. It was B14. I'm looking at the machine, still wondering how she ended up with M&M's. They aren't even close to each other in the machine. I asked her what she punched in, and this is the best . . ."

Back in acting mode, she played Alice's role for us. "She goes, 'I pushed B-1-4, but before I could even finish with the 4, the bag of M&M's was coming.' She's showing me on the keypad. Now it's my turn to look confused. 'You did the same thing three times?' I asked. 'Well, not exactly. I tried pushing the 1–4 a lot faster, but it still just took the 1.'" At this point, Stephanie was laughing so hard she was bent over.

"'I tried punching it faster,'" Steph repeated as she mimed the action in the air.

Our entire group was in hysterics, and Steph had tears sliding down her cheeks.

"You should've seen the look on her face when I showed her the 10+ button." We were all laughing.

"But hey, she's got lots of peanut M&M's to share with us now. And I think she's probably forgotten all about whatever it was she needed the Advil for."

As Steph finished her story, she put her arm around Alice's shoulders and pulled her in for a sideways hug.

"We love our freshmen. You know that, right?"

The team had their game faces on when we met for our pregame meeting. It didn't matter that only four teams were playing in this early season, nonconference tournament—we were here to win it. I loved the intensity I saw on every face.

We were dialed in from the opening tip, jumping to an early six-point lead. Offensively, we attacked their zone defense off the pass and the dribble. Patience, precision, and good spacing led us to wide-open shots. Rachel continued her hot streak, hitting four for four from three-point range, and Olivia also drained a couple of threes.

I subbed Ellen in for Heather with two minutes left in the half. As Heather jogged past, I gave her a high five. "Great job. Your post defense and rebounding were just what we needed."

With 1:11 on the clock, everyone on our bench gasped as Rachel fell in a heap. Her pain was evident as she lay on her side, clutching her knee. I was out of my chair and onto the court before the referee had motioned for me. When I reached Rachel, she was rocking side to side, moaning in pain with her eyes clenched shut. I knelt beside her and held her shoulders, trying to get her to hold still.

"Rachel, Rachel, I'm right here. Can you open your eyes and look at me?" She opened her eyes, and they were filled with a mix of fear and anguish, as well as tears. "Is it your knee?" I asked.

"Yes," she grunted through her clenched teeth.

"Okay. Let's slowly lie back so you're on your back. I'll hold you, slow . . . slow."

Just as she was positioned on her back, triggering another wave of pain, Whitworth's trainer knelt by her side, opposite me. As she asked Rachel a few questions, assessing her level of consciousness and shock, I stood up to see what her teammates were doing. They were standing a safe distance away, watching. I mouthed, "It's okay," and Fitz called them over to him.

Someone else joined the trainer to help, and I squeezed Rachel's hand and told her to hang in there. Once the trainers helped Rachel off the court, I walked back to the rest of the team. "Rachel's in good hands," I said. "We need to finish this final minute, then we can regroup at halftime."

Before heading back to our classroom with the first-half stats, we checked on Rachel, who already seemed more comfortable. She was in her sweats, and the trainer had placed ice bags around her knee, held in place with an ace bandage.

"Can we get you anything?" I asked, my hand resting on her shoulder.

"No thanks, Coach."

Before joining the team, I paused and asked Fitz: "You ready?"

He nodded. I took a deep breath, and we opened the door to a silent classroom.

"We are all concerned about Rachel," I said, "but for these next twenty minutes, we can do nothing to change the situation. She is being taken care of, and we must stay together and take care of the second half." A few of them nodded in agreement.

"We never know when an injury might happen. It's out of our control. How we respond in the face of this challenge is in our control. It's not about one player stepping up to fill Rachel's shoes but about each of you doing a little more. We need each of you to score two extra buckets and grab two extra rebounds. We can do this together. That's what championship teams do. Let's bring it in."

In the second half, our offense was a bit unsettled without Rachel, but luckily, our defensive intensity made it difficult for UC Santa Cruz to score. Olivia's leadership on both ends of the court was instrumental in preventing our opponents' attempt at a final run. Although they closed the gap to eight in the final minutes, we ended up winning by eleven points.

In the classroom, our kids were excited but far from celebratory. I didn't know whether that was due to the uncertainty around Rachel's injury or a sign that our beliefs and expectations about our success were changing. The more a team wins, the more it expects to win.

They were all seated by the time Fitz and I were standing in front of the class. "We'll keep it short because we must get out there in a minute for tournament awards, but that win showed a true competitive spirit. Rachel goes down, and we could've folded and used that as an excuse. But we didn't. We stayed focused, together, and kept fighting."

Fitz added, "We are so proud of your effort and how each person added a little more. It was a true team effort all the way. Let's head out there and pick up our trophy!"

Back in my office on Monday, I was shocked to see Kelsey at my door. "I'm sorry to drop in unexpectedly," she said apologetically. She must have seen my lunch spread out on my desk. "Should I come back later?"

"No, don't be silly. That's the great thing about peanut butter and jelly sandwiches—they don't go bad," I said. "How are things, Kels?" When she finally looked up at me, her eyes were filled with tears.

"Not very good." Her voice was quiet, as if she could control the tears by controlling the volume.

"What's not very good?"

"This will sound stupid, but it's about my boyfriend." Just saying the words out loud opened the floodgates, and the tears poured down her face.

I set my hand on her knee. "Oh, Kelsey . . . that doesn't sound stupid at all. I'm so sorry you're hurting."

God, I wished Fitz were here. There was something comforting about us working together during a crisis. I took a deep breath before asking, "Do you feel like talking about it? Is there something I can help with?"

Now that the tears were flowing, it seemed to free her to start talking. The flow of her words matched the flow of her tears.

"It's just I'm feeling so much pressure right now. He thinks basketball takes up all my time. And I feel like I'm doing the bare minimum, racing out of here after practices or meetings. But he doesn't understand. I love him, though, and things were so much better during the summer. Now, with games starting and our tournament this weekend, it seems like everything's changed." She finally paused for a second to wipe her nose and her cheeks.

"This weekend was hard. He kept calling me all different times, wanting me to talk for a long time. He was irritated if I didn't answer, saying he knew I wasn't at the gym, so why wasn't I answering? He even said other girls he knew liked him, and maybe *they'd* make better girlfriends because they'd make more time for him." Her crying became more vocal, and she could no longer talk through her sobs.

My head was spinning with initial thoughts about this guy—*what a creep! He's trying to control, manipulate, and threaten her.* She'd been reluctant to share for so long that I knew I needed to focus on listening. Internally, I was fuming, wanting to jump up and down on my desk to try to get her attention, yelling, "Where are *you* in this relationship? What about your voice, your needs, your goals? You've been shrinking in this relationship—how small will you have to become before you wake up and see this for what it is?"

Her crying lessened to intermittent sniffles as she stared at the ground.

"Kelsey, I'm so sorry you've been going through this pain and still hurting so much, but I'm glad you're talking about it. Sometimes, getting something big like this off your chest is the first step to working on it. I hope you know you don't need to go through hard things like this alone. You have so many people around you—your teammates and coaches for starters—who care about you and are here to listen and support you in any way. . . . Have you shared this with anyone on the team?"

She looked up. Her eyes were red-rimmed and glassy. "No. I didn't want any of you to think badly about him. He's really a nice guy."

Again, my racing mind got ahead of itself, visualizing worst-case scenarios. This behavior, this secrecy, this defending him, raised red flag after red flag. I tried to shift my focus away from my thoughts and more to my feelings, but those weren't much better. I felt compassion and sorrow for Kelsey's broken heart, but I also felt fear for her physical and emotional safety.

Kelsey pulled her cell phone from her sweatshirt pocket. "Oh God, Coach. I've gotta get to my one o'clock class. Thank you for listening. I do feel a little better." She stood up and grabbed her backpack from the floor.

"Good. I'm glad you came by today."

"Thanks, Coach," Kelsey said as I opened my office door for her. "I'll see you at practice." She stepped into the hallway and gave me a small smile over her shoulder.

"Hey, Kelsey?" She turned to look at me. "I'm here if you need me." She smiled again and gave me a small wave before hustling down the hallway.

I watched the last players leave the gym, happily chatting about their plans for Thanksgiving break. Just as I turned to pick up my water bottle, the door swung back open, and I heard Fitz shout, "Look who I found!"

I could hear Rachel before I saw her, the familiar clack of crutches echoing down the hallway. She smiled up at Fitz as she passed him and approached me, with Fitz following close behind.

"Rachel! How'd it go?" I asked.

Her face fell, and she let out a loud exhale. "It's my ACL, and the doctor says I'll need surgery. My season's done."

I pulled her close. "I'm sorry, Rachel." I could feel her body shaking as she gave in to the emotions she'd been fighting. I looked over her shoulder to Fitz and saw the heartbreak on his face.

"The season just started. It's going so well; this team is such a special group. Now, I don't get to be a part of it."

"Whoa!" I leaned back to look her in the eye. "I agree with you on the first part, but that last statement is untrue. You will still be a big part of this team this season. It will just be in a different role than what you started with." I knew how isolating injuries could be, and we would not let that happen to Rachel. "For now, just try to enjoy Thanksgiving with your family. If your parents have any questions, have them call me anytime."

"Thanks, Coach. This was my last stop before I headed out for the break."

"Good." I walked toward the gym door with her. "How about you swing by my office when you return to campus? In the meantime, rest, eat some good food, and know that the whole team is here for you if you need us."

Fitz zipped by us and opened the swinging door. "Yeah, and listen, use this to your advantage." He smirked. "Pumpkin pie tastes even better when your mom hand-delivers it to you on the couch."

We spoke when we were alone. "God," Fitz said, "I feel sick for Rachel. I know how hard she worked this summer on her conditioning and shooting. Now this," he added, sounding exhausted too.

"The only good thing," I said, "is that it happened so early in the season. She's only played three games, not counting scrimmages or our exhibition game. I'm 99 percent sure she'll be able to declare a medical redshirt this season. So at least she won't lose a year of eligibility."

Fitz looked at me with his crooked grin. "Well, look at you, Suzie Sunshine. You always amaze me with your ability to find the silver lining, even in our darkest hour."

"Our darkest hour, I wish. You know as well as I do— more challenges are coming."

"Oh—there you are! Now I recognize you much better, Peggy the Pessimist."

I laughed at him, and it felt good, a positive release for some of the tension I'd been feeling since Kelsey's visit.

"I have more to share. Kelsey came in earlier today and opened up about what's been happening," I started. I summarized my conversation with her, trying to leave my concerns out. I wanted to hear his initial reactions without my perspective coloring it.

"That explains a lot. It's a big first step for her. It gives us something to work with instead of playing a guessing game," he said.

"Happy Thanksgiving, Sam. I'm so glad that you're here." Anne wrapped me in a warm embrace.

Taking the first step into the house, the aroma of turkey made my mouth water. "Mmm! Anne, it smells so good in here. I know that's a lot of work, and I wish you would've let me bring more to help."

She smiled. "I've got it all covered. Hey, Brian told me Lauren Smith is coming out to talk to the team about her work with the animal sanctuary after the break."

"She is! We're excited to have her. Thanks for the connection. She's talking to the team about the passion and perseverance needed when you decide to take the road less taken in your career. I think they're going to get a lot out of it."

Anne nodded. "She's the perfect person for those topics. The amount of work she put into getting that farm up and running is impressive, and her work with those kids is so important."

Just then, Fitz came around the corner and greeted me with a hug. "We're in the back watching football. C'mon," he said, pulling on my arm.

"I'll be right behind you," I replied. I looked at Anne. "Isn't there something I can do to help you?"

"Nothing right now. I will put you to work when it's time," she said with a grin.

Fitz led me back to the TV room, where everyone rose to greet me. Fitz's son, Trevor, was the closest and hugged me first, followed by Stacey, his daughter.

"You remember Anne's dad, Paul," Fitz said.

"It's wonderful to see you again, Paul. Happy Thanksgiving," I said, giving him a big hug.

Paul took my hand and started toward the couch. "Come, sit next to me. We have lots of catching up to do."

Fitz, Trevor, and Stacey all resumed watching the game. Anne joined us, and the room filled with laughter, conversation, and commentary from the game on TV.

Paul asked me many questions, and not just about basketball. He remembered I loved reading and asked if I had any new book recommendations. He also asked personal questions about living on my own, and whether I was dating or interested in getting married one day. The way he asked seemed honest and curious, not judgmental or preachy. He also shared about himself and some of the challenges of being widowed and living on his own.

"It's already been six years, and I still think about her and miss her every day," he said. I listened as he described his regular social activities, but he said those didn't fill the absence he felt in his home and heart—a hole that couldn't be filled by anyone or anything. "It's probably a reflection of some deficit in my personality, like I'm too needy," he concluded, half joking.

I put my arm around him and said, "Oh, Paul. You look like you're doing a great job taking care of yourself and still getting out to socialize. That doesn't seem like neediness to me. It's more a reflection of your deep and lasting love with your wife."

I was touched that he felt he could confide in me, even about things that weren't happy. I also appreciated his questions and follow-up comments, showing he listened. We talked a little longer, then it was time to eat.

I felt joyful and calm throughout the scrumptious meal and friendly conversation. I realized that my visit with Paul made me feel heard and understood, so different from how visits with my parents felt. It was reciprocal and deeper. It was real. I wondered whether Anne felt that way with her dad—or maybe the parent-adult child relationship was never as real as those with friends.

When the dishes were loaded into the dishwasher, Fitz and Anne dished the dessert, and I delivered it. I stayed for another hour before excusing myself to head home.

"Everything was so delicious, Fitz. I can't thank you enough. I know you don't see your kids as often as you'd like, so I appreciate you including me with your family."

"Whether you like it or not, you're part of this family, warts and all," Fitz said.

Driving home, I felt filled to the brim, physically and emotionally, and I was genuinely grateful. Before bed, I sat at the desk in my study, thinking more about the day. The contrast in communication styles between my phone call with my parents today and my visit with Paul sparked more ideas.

I pulled the letter I'd started writing to my parents two months before from my files. I had some new thoughts to include. It wasn't ready to mail yet, but it was getting closer.

November 2006

Dear Kelsey,

I know our conversation the other day was a tough one. Being a student-athlete is difficult, and I appreciate your honesty about the pressures you face.

I hope you always remember that your teammates and coaches are here to support you. We may not have a solution, but we love and care for you and want to support you. You are not alone.

Coach Fitz and I would both like to be part of your support system. My door is always open if you want to talk about anything. I can't promise to have the answers, but I promise to listen.

Coach Sam

CHAPTER 12

OCTOBER 1986

Homecoming night was cold, and I stuffed my hands into my coat pockets as I climbed the metal stands. Behind me, referee whistles blew, announcing halftime. Ordinarily, that sound would've signaled a mad dash to the concession stands and bathrooms, but that night, everyone stayed in their seats, eyes glued on the field.

"Ladies and gentlemen, please welcome your 1986 homecoming court!" The tinny sound of the speakers rang in my ears.

One by one, the announcer called out their names. I craned my neck, looking for Lindsey, who looked gorgeous in her burgundy dress. Emily took the field in her cheerleading outfit. Of course, hoots and hollers erupted from every corner of the field when Chris's name was called. He jogged from the sidelines, wearing his football uniform and waving to the crowd.

When everyone had reached the field, the homecoming court paired off into couples, and the marching band played a romantic waltz. Everyone did well, considering the court had only two weeks to learn the waltz—not exactly television-worthy, but no one tripped or fell, so it went okay. From the cheers that ripped through the crowd, you'd have thought they'd just watched a professional performance.

The announcer continued. "Are you ready to meet this year's homecoming king and queen?" More cheering broke out, and a Mustang convertible slowly pulled onto the field. "Please give a round of applause for Chris Daniels and Lindsey Walters!" The crowd erupted in shouts and whistles again.

I smiled as our principal crowned Lindsey and handed her a huge bouquet of red roses. Then my eyes landed on my parents, standing on the sideline next to Lindsey's parents. My mom beamed and clapped her hands. My dad reached around her to shake hands with Coach Walters, and they stepped to the side, laughing and talking. My dad gave him a few hearty pounds on the back.

Lindsey looked beautiful, smiling and waving into the stands as the Mustang took a slow lap around the track surrounding the football field. I made my way down to the sideline and caught Lindsey's eye after she'd gotten out of the car. She smiled as I reached out to hug her.

"Congratulations, Queen! I wish they shared the vote totals because I bet it was unanimous." I could feel her laughing in my arms.

She stepped back and said, "You really need to do something about that competitive streak of yours. Try to keep it limited to just the gym floor, would ya?" Someone called her name, and she looked over her shoulder.

I laughed. "Hey, go greet your adoring subjects! I'll see you Monday."

She hugged me again. "Thanks, Sam."

As she turned and walked back into the crowd, I took a deep breath and looked for Emily. I found her with friends, all laughing and giggling. I rolled my shoulders back and walked toward her.

"Hey, Em." I got her attention despite the small group surrounding her. She looked up. "Great job with the dance."

She smiled. "Thanks, Sam." I gave her a small wave and then stepped back toward the stands as the football teams prepared for the second half.

After the game, the students raced out of the stadium to get ready for the homecoming dance. I followed a few feet behind my parents as they walked to the car. Mom was going on about how beautiful Lindsey looked and how much her dress suited her.

My dad nodded. "She looked stunning. Amazing to think she's a great athlete, but then can dress up and look so feminine too." He looked back at me.

I forced a smile. "She really did look beautiful."

I'd barely finished my sentence when he said, "Her dad must be so proud."

My mom swooped in to break the painful silence that followed. "Well, I'm just sorry I won't see them all in their formalwear. I'm sure Chris will look handsome in his tux."

My dad chuckled. "I'm sure I'd hardly recognize him. He'll look like a young man instead of a kid."

We reached the car, and I climbed into the back seat. My parents chatted happily in the front about Emily and her plans for the dance while I stared out the window and retreated into my thoughts.

Her dad must be so proud.

What things made parents proud of their kids? Was it a universal list? Was it different for moms versus dads? Was it different for sons versus daughters? Had he ever felt proud of me?

I knew my parents, even my dad, loved me, but maybe there were different levels of love, like loving your kids because you must or loving them because they made you look good . . . perhaps even loving your kids for being exactly who they were, even if they were different from you. Love didn't seem like a black-and-white emotion; it felt more like complicated layers of gray.

The next day I was back in the gym with Ms. Collins. I'd started my practice on the right baseline, making the first three shots but missing most of the rest. I'd shown my disgust at each miss by breathing loudly. After finishing only three for ten at the second spot, I felt like I was about to explode. I'd still hustled to the third spot, preparing to catch and shoot, but Ms. Collins's question stopped me in my tracks.

"Sam, what are you feeling right now?" she asked, walking toward me with the ball under her arm.

I looked at her with a quizzical expression. She shot back a look that said, "Don't play that game with me. You know exactly what I'm asking."

"Anger and frustration mostly, with a bit of embarrassment too."

"Good. That's a good first step: recognizing what you're feeling. The next one is figuring out what you will do about it. There's not much downtime in basketball, so you must change things up here immediately," she said, tapping her temple. "So how do you do that?"

It was not a rhetorical question.

"Umm . . . I focus on the next play? Don't dwell on the mistake; try to make up for it on the defensive end."

"I like that, and it'll help to an extent, but that same surge of anger that helped with defense will likely only hinder your offense. Let's say you miss another shot; you perpetuate the cycle. You need to disrupt that mental cycle on the offensive end." Again, she paused to let me think about that, putting myself in that situation to visualize and experience it.

"You are a 50 percent shooter from the floor in games. That statistic gives you two important pieces of information you must regularly remind yourself of. First, you are going to miss half the shots you take." She grinned slyly, like she was trying to hold back a laugh. "If you take twelve shots in a game, how many, on average, will you miss?"

"Six."

"If you take twenty shots in a game, how many, on average, will you miss?"

"Ten." I wouldn't say I liked how this math game was playing out.

"Of course, it's good to go into every shot believing you will make it. But the reality is, as a 50 percent shooter, you'll miss half your shots."

"The second point is that when you miss one, it means you have one coming to you. You miss two, then you have two makes coming. How many are coming to you if you start zero for your first seven shots?"

"Seven," I replied, grinning to myself now.

"Exactly! But you must keep shooting to get those seven. The absolute worst thing you could do is quit shooting. As we start again, I will be your inner voice, your self-talk. Turn yours off and listen to mine."

She commented after every shot during the catch-and-shoot drill. After shots were made, it was "Good follow-through," "Good rotation on the ball," "Good with your legs," and "Good arch." After a missed shot, she'd say, "I've got one coming." She continued that for the first three spots and told me to take over, but I had to verbalize it so she could hear it.

I started shooting, and it felt silly talking out loud. I made three in a row, and on the third, I hesitated about what to say about the shot.

"You don't hesitate with the misses, so you can't with the makes. It's got to be automatic. When nothing specific stands out because it all felt good, say, 'Yes!' Celebrate it."

I finished my ten shots at the last spot and said "yes" on every make. When I did, Ms. Collins echoed my "yes" with a louder one of her own. I could feel the smile on my face even as I shot the last two and tried to stay focused.

"I think I saw a smile. Oh my God, she's even showing signs of having fun while playing basketball." Her teasing made me smile even more. "I know you love basketball, and there is nothing wrong with showing that sense of love and joy. You do it in volleyball . . ." She left that thought hanging in the air, unfinished. Her timer went off.

"Okay. My time is up. Your turn—you told me you had some news to share?"

"I talked with the coach from Sacramento State and told her I wanted to visit the campus. She'll be sending me an itinerary."

"Fantastic! Bring it in; I'd love to see it. So how has all this gone at home?"

We both knew that when she said "at home," she referred to my dad. Even with Ms. Collins and Coach Nelson, I was careful about what I said about my dad. I didn't want them to see him in a negative light.

"He hasn't said much, at least to me. I overheard a few comments to my mom where it sounded like he was worried that I didn't know what I was getting myself into, that the Division I level would be too dog-eat-dog for me."

"What?" she said incredulously. "Sam, you have the rare combination of great athleticism and incredible work ethic. You can play, even excel, at whatever level you choose, including Division I. Don't let anybody tell you otherwise." All the lighthearted clowning around from earlier was gone. I held her gaze momentarily, wanting her strength of conviction to wash over me.

October 2006

To: Samantha Shuster
From: Laurie Collins

Dear Sam,

Congratulations on an incredible tournament. Some coaches downplay early success, saying they don't want to peak too early in the season. But there is nothing like the confidence a team gains from actual wins compared to losses, which pushes the coach to reinforce positives like effort and improvement to build morale. I'll take the wins anytime! :)

I was sorry to hear about Rachel's injury. It's always heartbreaking to see a player's season end that way.

If it's possible, I'd love to get periodic game tapes. Mostly, it would be for the enjoyment of watching your team play and improve throughout the season, but if you have an interest, I could study a game for you as an outside set of eyes and give you a scouting report as if I were preparing to play your team.

If you'd be interested in that, you would provide an old lady with some fun. Especially with Christmas break just around the corner, I'll be out of school for an extended time. And as you know, the hiking is not so great this time of year.

I looked back at this email, and what started as a short note of congratulations has turned into a long-winded letter. I just wanted you to know how happy I am for you and your team. Keep up the great work!

Ms. C

CHAPTER 13
NOVEMBER 2006

It was an hour before our Monday practice. Fitz and I were in the office when Steph knocked on the door.

"Hi, Coach. I just wanted to see if we had any leftover T-shirts from camps. Amy will be at the game Wednesday, and I was hoping to give her one."

"That's a great idea. We have a box in the storage area, so let's look after practice," I said.

As Steph hurried away, we could hear her greet Kelsey in the hallway. Fitz and I looked at each other, encouraged that Kelsey might be the one taking the initiative to talk with us rather than us chasing her down. Kelsey tapped on the door, but it was just to get our attention since it was already cracked.

"Do you guys have a minute?" she asked tentatively.

"Come in, Kels." I thought she looked paler than usual, and her mouth was pinched into a tight line. She did not look at either of us. "What's going on?" I asked.

"Umm . . . my bag with all my gear is in the locker room . . . cause . . . um . . . I need to quit." Her voice was so quiet I wasn't sure I'd heard right. A hundred questions whirled through my mind, rendering me speechless. *Where do I even start? Which one do I ask first?*

"I don't understand, Kelsey. What's going on?" I asked, working hard to keep my voice even.

"I'm quitting. I'm sorry I couldn't at least finish the season, but I can't do this anymore." She dropped her chin to her chest again as she answered.

"Is something happening within the team that we should be aware of? Something we can work through together?" Fitz asked.

"No, this isn't about anybody on the team."

"Is this about your playing time or a different role?" Fitz asked.

"No."

"Is there something going on with your family?" Fitz was being so much more patient than I was feeling.

"No, my parents are fine." Kelsey kept her eyes down and picked at her cuticles.

"We're not playing a game of twenty questions. You come in here and drop a bombshell; you need to explain what's going on." My tone was direct.

After an extended pause where Fitz and I let her simmer in silence, she finally answered, "Things have just changed for me."

"Last week, you shared with me about your boyfriend. Is that the change you mean?" My irritation was boiling just below the surface. Suddenly, our office felt like a sauna. I took off my jacket.

Kelsey nodded but said nothing.

Fitz jumped in. "I guess I'm a little lost. I'm not sure I understand how your boyfriend could be related to you quitting, especially after the season has started. Some of your teammates have boyfriends, and they're still playing. Does he live somewhere else, and you want to move? Are you going to be dropping out of school too?"

"No, I'll still go to school here. He's a student here too." She stopped as emotions started to seep through her stoic façade.

"Well, I'm relieved to hear that because our top priority for you—for everyone on the team—is to graduate with your degree. But that still doesn't explain the basketball side of things," I said, trying to give her time to gather herself so she could answer.

"It's just that everything about basketball is taking up so much time. Our practices go into the evenings, and games are at night. We travel and are gone for days . . . social things with the team, weightlifting . . ." Her mumbling trailed off, tears sliding down her cheeks.

"Weightlifting?" Fitz cut in, looking baffled.

Kelsey's response was a whisper. "It makes my muscles too big, and we don't get options to do a different style of lifting more for tone."

At this point, I felt so irritated with her responses that I decided to go a different direction.

"Have you told your parents? What did they think?"

"No."

"When are you planning on telling them?"

A muffled "I don't know," was her answer.

"What about paying for school? If you quit, you'll be forfeiting your scholarship starting next semester. Did you think about that?"

She shook her head, no.

"Have you shared your plan with your teammates? What do we tell them, especially now, after learning that Rachel's season is done due to her injury?" It hadn't been my intent, but the questions continued to roll off my tongue in a way that probably made her feel like she was being interrogated in a courtroom.

In her stunned silence, Fitz tried to soften the edges. "Maybe there are some other aspects you want to consider before making such a drastic change. If you need to skip today's practice to give yourself more time to think through some of these issues Coach brought up, that's fine. We can sit down again tomorrow."

"I've made my decision." She stood up and was through the door in the blink of an eye. All Fitz and I could do was stare at each other, wide-eyed and speechless.

With practice looming, we'd need more time to strategize what to do. We grabbed our practice plans and whistles to head to the gym. Fitz put his hand on the door handle but paused before opening it. "I don't think that's her final decision. My gut says she'll be back here, apologizing and asking to stay part of the team."

"Well, you've got a much nicer gut than mine. Mine is telling me to go strangle the boyfriend."

Fitz chuckled. "Yeah, he sounds like a real prize."

Without time to wrap my head around what had happened with Kelsey, I opted not to mention it at practice that day. But by the next day, I knew I shouldn't keep her teammates in the dark any longer. At Tuesday's practice, we shared the news that Kelsey had left the team. Her teammates seemed as shocked as we had been.

We had very little time to make team adjustments before our next game, and it showed. At times, we played well. At other times, it looked like our first game. Although we won Wednesday's game, 'survived' was probably a more accurate description.

In the locker room, I could see in their faces and body language that they weren't happy about the game. To a certain extent, I liked that; it showed that they expected more from themselves and each other. Winning wasn't good enough; they wanted to dominate. We tried to focus on the positive things in our postgame talk in hopes that we could maintain their belief in what we were doing while making changes that had been forced upon us.

Fitz and I left the locker room so they could change and then talk with family and friends in the gym. Back in the gym, the group that immediately caught my eye was Steph and her big family, standing with Amy and her mom. I walked over to say hi. Steph had already given the T-shirt to Amy, who was wearing it over her sweatshirt.

"Hey, Amy, I like your shirt. It looks great. Perfect for our number one fan," I said.

Amy beamed.

As Steph bent down to whisper something in Amy's ear, Mrs. Russell whispered to me. "Thank you for the T-shirt. She loves it, and I'm sure she'll want to sleep in it every night and wear it to school every day." We both smiled.

Steph's mom joined us, putting an arm around Amy's mom. "Coach Sam, it looks like we've got a future Cougar on our hands here!" she said, nodding toward Amy, who blushed.

I smiled. "I sure hope so, Carol. I can't start recruiting her yet, but in the meantime," I pointed at Steph, "she's got the best coach I know."

November 2006

To: Laurie Collins
From: Samantha Shuster

Dear Ms. Collins,

I hope you had a lovely Thanksgiving. (Are you one of those "Black Friday" shoppers who line up to shop at 2:00 a.m.?!) Our kids had a couple of days off, and I joined Fitz and his family for a wonderful afternoon, and of course, ate way too much.

Thank you again for your earlier email of congratulations and your generous offer. Your feedback about what you see from our team would be invaluable, and I'm always open to suggestions on better ways to utilize our talents. I'll mail you the two games from our recent tournament, but now, without Rachel, our offense especially will look very different.

We've also lost another one of our juniors. She's been struggling all season with drama related to a boyfriend, but she came by my office earlier in the week to turn in her gear and tell us she was quitting the team. It broke my heart for both her and her teammates. I worry for her and hope she'll come to me if she needs help. All I can do is leave that door open.

Among the things I'm most thankful for is your support and friendship!

Sam

CHAPTER 14
DECEMBER 2006

We were heading into our first two conference games undefeated, yet I felt far less confident about where we were than I had at the beginning of the season. Obviously, losing Rachel and Kelsey had impacted our play, but a troublesome team dynamic also lurked below the surface.

I knew growth was not a linear process; it could move forward and backward. I also understood that it was normal to revert to old behavior patterns in times of great stress and difficulty. But seeing these two concepts in action simultaneously, right before we started our conference games, made it something we needed to address sooner rather than later.

In the first half of our team meeting, we watched game film. Then I shifted the topic to a James Baldwin quote on the whiteboard: *Not everything that is faced can be changed. But nothing can be changed until it's faced.*

"I'd like you to take a few minutes to talk about the meaning of this quote. Think about specific examples; they don't have to be basketball related."

Conversations began filling the room. After a few minutes, I took the floor again. "Let's share with the whole group now. How did you interpret this quote? What kinds of examples could you think of that fit with its meaning?"

Whitney's hand shot up and I nodded at her.

"Most people don't like to deal with conflict, and the bigger it is, or the more personal it is, the harder it is to have that conversation. The most common approach, or maybe the most comfortable, is to try to forget about it and push it off to the background to deal with later, hoping it will disappear."

"Good. Does anyone want to add to that? Were there any specific examples you discussed?" I waited, but it remained quiet. "How many of you feel that way when dealing with conflict with someone else or having a difficult conversation?"

Everyone raised a hand. I raised my hand and said, "Me too." I nodded and scanned the room to include each of them.

"Me three," Fitz announced as if it were something to be proud of. Many looked surprised, like they couldn't believe that dealing with conflict made *us* uncomfortable.

"It's not surprising to see everyone raise their hands. I can honestly say that I have never known anyone who likes conflict."

"You haven't lived with my brother." Steph's one-liner was meant for her table, but everyone heard her, and we laughed.

"I believe part of the angst about dealing with conflict is its negative connotation, and yet it's impossible to have a real relationship with anyone without having conflict. It's normal, natural, and necessary, so it is important to learn to deal with these difficult situations, whether with people at work or with family and friends." I pointed to the quote on the board for emphasis and said, "Nothing will change unless it's dealt with. We have something within our team that needs to change, so we will face it together."

I scanned the room and noticed kids shifting uncomfortably in their chairs and stealing glances at each other.

"Anytime we learn something new, we must expand our comfort zone. This makes us temporarily uncomfortable. Then, when we hit a setback, our natural tendency is to slip back into old habits, which are more comfortable." I paused to let that idea sink in. "We've been working hard this season to not only accept but also expect a high level of competitiveness at every practice. But since we lost Rachel and Kelsey, we're pulling inward instead of expanding. We've slipped back into our comfort zone."

In the back of the room, MJ sat quietly, staring at her hands in her lap. To my right, I saw Steph lean back in her chair and furrow her eyebrows. To my left, Whitney folded her arms and cocked her head to one side.

"The ripple effect from shrinking back to our comfort zones has created division within the team. Whether or not you intend to send a message to us about our overall team goals, your actions speak loud and clear. If a team goal or mission matters here," I tapped my heart, "we can overcome our differences. The opposite is also true. If a team goal or mission is unimportant, personal differences become the focal point and cause for divisions."

As I turned toward the board to write, Fitz jumped in. "I know you guys realize there will always be some people you like less than others, but you must still be able to work together and get along. But a team is something different. What we're trying to accomplish together is larger. We have big goals and limited time to accomplish them, and each of you plays a vital role."

Fitz's voice was passionate, and I felt goosebumps on my arms. I knew exactly what he was saying, and I felt the power of it coursing through my veins. I'd finished writing my notes on the board and turned to face our kids.

"The problem we are talking about is like a three-headed monster." I pointed to the list I'd written. "The first is the lack of competitiveness. The second is the commitment to our team goals. And the third is the division within our team. Two and three are different than the first. We need to decide and make a commitment to them today. We can keep working on embracing competitiveness, but if we can't come together about the last two, we're stuck. So I'm going to ask you," I tapped the whiteboard with my marker next to the second point, "have our goals changed from the beginning of the season? Do we need to modify them because we've lost two players?"

I watched the kids. Some stared at the floor; others glanced tentatively around the room.

Stephanie broke the silence. "No, our goals haven't changed. At least they haven't for me, and I hope they haven't for anyone else here."

I loved how she said it—definitively, as a statement, not a question. She was not testing the waters but challenging her teammates' commitment. Not surprisingly, the three seniors immediately chimed in their support. The rest of the team followed suit.

"We're glad to hear that. *We*," I motioned between Fitz and myself, "still believe in this team and what we can accomplish this season, but our belief doesn't matter as much as yours. Just because we have this shared commitment to our team goals doesn't mean there will be no personality differences or disagreements. There will be times when we get irritated with each other. That conflict will still be there. It's normal. But we can see it from a different perspective. We can deal with it constructively."

Fitz let a moment pass before he said, "You know, I think that in sports, we often look at the men's game as something more important and something to take seriously. Meanwhile, women's athletics are often trivialized and seen as more for fun—a social outlet." He added a tone of derision to the words 'fun' and 'social outlet.' There are many positive lessons we can learn from the guys in athletics. They are highly confident and intensely competitive."

I saw heads nod and smiled to myself at how Fitz used the term "we," including himself as part of our group.

Fitz continued. "But I also think there are many positives the men could learn from us, and those things are often neglected in how we define sports and even success more broadly. I think female athletes more often play for each other. They place a higher value on the relationships built through the team. Teamwork comes from building and valuing those trusted relationships with your teammates. Those bonds are unbreakable when you play for each other and lose yourself and your personal goals in the bigger picture of how the team is doing collectively."

Whitney and Oliva smiled and pointed at each other. In the back, Heather bumped MJ with her shoulder. Fitz smiled at each of our players.

I said, "While we continue to grow and improve in the areas of competitiveness and confidence, let's not lose sight of the importance of our shared commitments and bonds." I finished by returning to Baldwin's quote. I felt like our message had struck a chord. As the last players flowed out into the hallway, I looked at Fitz and let out a deep breath. He rubbed a hand across his forehead and looked up at the ceiling.

"Nothing like having a 'come to Jesus' moment when we haven't even started conference games yet," I said. "It's one thing for them to listen and verbally back up the leaders, but tomorrow will be the true test."

We passed that test with flying colors. Starting in our pregame warm-ups, we had more energy and talk than the prior week.

The way we played in the first half had a combative, us-against-the-world feel. Our defense had remained solid despite the loss of Kelsey and Rachel. Every time we got a stop, we relished it, which energized us to want another, making our appetite for defensive stops seem insatiable. We held the other team to 22 points in the first half.

The real surprise came on the offensive end. Our movement was more aggressive, and the offensive flow incorporated all five on the court in a way we hadn't seen since Rachel's injury. The play from both Olivia and Stephanie stood out. Olivia was the floor general, pushing the pace at the right times and running set plays when we needed them. Steph's play highlighted three-point shooting, a side of her game we rarely saw. In the first half she was three for four shooting threes; she looked unstoppable.

When things click so well in the first half, I dread the half-time break for fear of losing focus and momentum. I didn't need to worry. Our team was out to send a loud and clear message. I was unsure whom the message was for, maybe for themselves. We sustained the excellence of the first half and won 79–48.

Fitz waited for me before entering the team room. He was still studying the final stat sheet as I approached.

"It's been awfully quiet in there," he whispered.

"Well, I know just the person who can liven things up," I said, smiling at him.

"Your wish is my command." With that, he burst through the door and used his biggest gym voice to say, "You just held a team under 50 points. Why don't I hear some screamin' back here?" That was all it took to get the voices of all twelve players to join in cheering at the top of their lungs, laughing the whole time.

"This was a total team effort," I said. "Even those who didn't play tonight had an impact. I loved hearing all the cheers when Olivia and Whitney took those charges. I loved seeing the wave go down the bench every time we hit a three. Everybody was locked in tonight, and you could feel it. That was a great win." I looked every player in the face and let the wave of excitement pass through me too.

I waited until late Sunday morning to call my parents, enough time to enjoy my coffee and the newspaper in the peaceful quiet of my home.

I was surprised when my dad answered.

"Hi, Dad."

My mom chimed in. "Hi, Sam. I'm here too."

"Hi, Mom. Good timing to get you both together."

"Yeah. I don't know how that happened. We've barely been at home together unless you count from midnight to six in the morning," Mom joked.

"Are things hectic now with your season underway, Dad?"

It was early in the conversation to get him talking about his team, but it didn't make that much difference. I appreciated how much he loved coaching and his kids; it always came through in his stories. I just wished he would allow me to share my passion for my team with him.

"Why don't you tell us about your team," my mom said twenty-five minutes later.

"We just played our first two conference games and won both. Did you get a chance to see them online?"

My mom started to reply, but my dad cut her off.

"You know, it was hard to watch. The person filming kept zooming in on wherever the ball was. I had to stop watching. Do you get any of Gonzaga's games out there? You should see how they do it . . ." he was off on another extended monologue. Although it started with how much easier it was to watch Gonzaga's games based on the camera angle, it quickly expanded to the entire men's basketball program.

The shock of such an absurd comparison jolted me upright on the couch. We were a women's basketball team with no money and an unknown coach at a small college. But that unknown coach was his daughter, and I had hoped he would have more interest and pride in our team. Did these conversations strike my mom as odd as they did me?

"Huh . . . I'll have to check them out," I said when my dad finally finished.

"Well, I better run, Sam, but thanks for calling. I want to leave you and your mom enough time for some girl talk. Oh, and congratulations on the two conference wins. Even though I couldn't watch, I checked out the results."

My mom jumped in without skipping a beat. "We're thinking about going to Emily's for the few days around Christmas that your dad has off from basketball," she said.

"Really? Dad has never wanted to do that before."

"I know. But Emily pushed when they were here for Thanksgiving. She said how much the kids would love to have grandma and grandpa at their house, with the tree and decorations and the Santa visit," my mom said with a chuckle. "And, of course, Emily knows how to get her way with your dad."

When I finally hung up, I felt antsy. I aimlessly paced around the house, then stepped outside for a walk. The fresh air would do me some good, and if I couldn't clear my head from the myriad of thoughts racing through my brain, maybe I could freeze them.

Were these phone conversations all part of a bigger plan to influence me to move closer to their home in Washington? Did they realize that never asking questions about my life or showing interest might become a constant, painful reminder of how distant I was from them? Their guilt trips and shaming had been more apparent when I was young, but at almost forty, they continued coming in various forms. They were subtler but still filled with messages of disappointment.

The parental toolbox may change as kids turn into adults. When we're young, the tools are hammers, chisels, and sandpaper, contouring us into the image they want. Later, when we become adults, they use paint and paintbrushes to cover up what they don't want to see.

I'd been walking briskly, breathing deeply, and allowing my thoughts to shift from venting to reflection. These reflections naturally expanded into my role as a coach. This was not the first time I realized that some characteristics I hoped to model and teach were not necessarily ones I lived out in all parts of my life. I could proactively send messages to my kids about strength, confidence, independence, self-worth, and the importance of listening to their voices. I could be assertive and outspoken on their behalf. Yet when it came to my relationship with my parents, I still struggled to hear my own inner voice. It remained a constant battle between being the nice, obedient pleaser instilled in me and rewarded at a young age and being the strong independent woman I wanted to model for my players.

Did that make me a hypocrite? Why hadn't I spoken up on the phone? How could I ever expect communication with my parents to change if I didn't address it? I was reminded of the James Baldwin quote: *Nothing can be changed until it's faced.* Was I encouraging my players to do something I was not doing in my own life?

I didn't have a clear answer, but my questions had given me a deeper understanding of the lessons I tried to teach. I remembered my internal struggles against limitations first imposed by my parents with the best intentions. Once internalized, those limitations could become a self-fulfilling prophecy or, if challenged, create a lifelong battle to reclaim our interiors for ourselves. I wanted more for our kids. I wanted them to have the awareness and courage to begin this battle now, instead of waiting until middle age like I had.

I reached my door and stepped into the warmth of the entryway. I peeled off my gloves, coat, and hat, toed off my boots, and headed straight for my desk. I pulled up the file with my rough draft letter to my parents and read through it. I added a few more thoughts, appreciative that the writing process, unlike speaking, allowed me to edit and revise. But I'd need to take the next step and mail it at some point.

Finals week was always tough on the team as they tried to balance studying for exams and preparing for our last game before Christmas break. That game was against Lewis-Clark College, the top team in our conference.

Both teams played hard and executed well, and the score went back and forth in the first half. During the final ten minutes of the second half, however, Lewis-Clark started building a lead as their size, depth, and talent began to make the difference. Despite that, our kids played with a sense of purpose and mission. In the end, they could get the score no closer than eight points.

After the game, Fitz and I walked into a silent locker room. Most of the kids had their heads down. The loss was hitting them hard.

"I need everybody's eyes up," I said, waiting for everyone's attention. "I can honestly say that in all the games I've been a part of, as a coach or player, I can count on one hand the games we lost that I still felt good about. This is one of those games. Though the score says we lost, I think this game was the best forty minutes of basketball we've played this season, including the tournament we won."

I paused, hoping these comments would sink in.

"They played just a little better than us *tonight*, just enough to win *tonight*. If we continue to play that hard and that well against every opponent, by the end of the season, it could easily come down to us against them for the top position in the conference."

I started to see some hope, some life, in their eyes.

December 2006

To: Sam Shuster
From: Laurie Collins

Dear Sam,

I am happily spending my off hours watching your team. I watched both games online (I feel so high-tech!) and one of the games you mailed me.

I'm not finished yet, but I wanted to share some initial observations. Remember, this comes from the perspective of a coach preparing to play your team, looking at how we might try to disrupt your offense and take away your main strength. Think of this like an opposing coach's scouting report.

Your team likes to get out in transition and create early offense through your fast break. Nearly every time, the ball goes up the right side. So we'd focus on two things:

Picking up your point guard as soon as she gets the outlet pass, forcing her to the left, and

Denying the right wing, so you can't start your offense the way you want to.

I like your fast break and transition offense. Your kids do a great job of looking for the initial quick attack and, when necessary, flowing into your secondary scoring options without having to stop and reset. One modification might be adding an attack on the left side, slightly different from what you run on the right. You've got the speed, wing players who can shoot and drive, and a point guard who is a very competent floor general, so that style fits your personnel.

That's just one option, and I'm sure you and Fitz, knowing your team's strengths, may go in a completely different direction. I'll keep you posted as I watch more of the game tapes you sent.

I know your team is working through the loss of two leading players, and I can see that when watching more recent games online. That transition may seem significant to you, but as an outsider, it looks like only a minor tweak being made. Also, your kids seem to play without fear of making mistakes. Sometimes, when coaches have a policy that one turnover or bad shot results in being subbed out of the game, kids hold back and play in a controlled and robotic manner.

All of this is to say that I really like how your team plays on both ends of the court, and I'm looking forward to reviewing more DVDs I might get from you as the season progresses. (How is that for subtle?)

I know seasons can be difficult, with ups and downs, but always remember how lucky your kids are to have you as their coach. Enjoy every day and every moment with them.

Ms. C

CHAPTER 15
NOVEMBER 1986

Our volleyball team continued its march toward district playoffs.

"Oh my gosh, Sam," my mom gushed, embracing me in a tight hug. I looked over her shoulder at Cassandra, who was smiling and stifling a giggle. "Every time I think I've seen your team play its best volleyball, you come out and play even better! And—"

"Mom . . . Mom . . ." I had to interrupt, fearing she might continue for another five minutes.

We'd just won two more matches, maybe our most decisive of the season. My mom was ready to celebrate, but I wasn't. Not yet. We needed to maintain laser focus; we had two more matches to win that weekend to make it to districts.

A little calmer, my mom suddenly registered that I wasn't alone. She let out a little gasp. "I'm so sorry, how rude of me. I'm Suzie Shuster."

"Mom, this is my friend Cassandra," I said.

My mom smiled and clasped her hands together in front of her heart. "Cassandra! It's so nice to meet you finally! I've heard so much about you!"

"It's nice to meet you too, Mrs. Shuster."

"Cassandra's here to cover the game for the school newspaper," I said.

Mom's face lit up. "Well, isn't that wonderful!" She started asking Cassandra question after question about the article, the newspaper, her classes, her family, and her plans after graduation. She was launching into another question when a woman dressed in black sweats walked up to us.

"Hi, Mrs. Shuster. I hope you don't mind; Coach Nelson pointed you out. I'm Lori Stevens, the head volleyball coach at Boise State." She shook my mom's hand, then turned to me. "Hi, Sam." She shook my hand too. "It's nice to meet you in person. Congratulations on two great wins today. I enjoyed seeing your team play. Very impressive, as is your play."

"Thank you," I said.

"My flight back to Boise is late Sunday afternoon, and I was hoping we could set up a time to meet while I'm in town. Maybe breakfast on Sunday morning?"

Mom looked to me for my preference.

"Sunday morning would be great." I could feel my heart pounding in my chest.

Coach Stevens asked my mom: "Is there a quiet place nearby to eat breakfast and talk?" We were interrupted by Coach Nelson calling for the team to load up on the bus. I looked anxiously at Coach Stevens.

"It's okay, Sam. It would be best not to miss your ride back with the team. I'm sure your mom and I can work out the details."

Mom smiled and nodded. "Absolutely." She put her hand on my shoulder. "We'll get it sorted out, Sam. I'll see you at home." She stepped around me and hugged Cassandra like they'd known each other forever.

"It was so nice meeting you, Cassandra. I keep telling Sam to invite you for dinner, so I hope to see you again soon?"

Cassandra smiled patiently. "That would be great. It was so nice to meet you, Mrs. Shuster."

I reached out to shake Coach Stevens's hand. "Thank you for coming tonight. I'm excited to talk on Sunday."

"Same. Best of luck tomorrow, Sam."

I hugged Mom, thanked her for coming, and Cassandra and I walked toward the doors to the parking lot. Cassandra was quietly squealing beside me. She grabbed my arm the second the gym doors closed behind us. "Sam! A college coach came to see you play. That's so cool!"

I stopped. "Cassandra, please don't say anything about this to anyone."

She frowned in confusion. "Okay . . . but why not? This is so exciting!"

I knew some other girls, especially the ones who'd focused solely on volleyball for the past four years, might feel disappointed or resentful that a coach wanted to meet with me. Our team's cohesion was so important right now with us this close to reaching the state championship. This season had been so special. I didn't want anything disrupting that.

I saw the last of my teammates climbing into the bus. How could I explain all that to Cassandra in just a few seconds?

"It's . . . just complicated. I promise I'll explain soon. But for now, please don't mention it to anyone."

Cassandra frowned and shrugged her shoulders. "Of course. Your secret's safe with me."

The next night, we won our first three games by being focused and controlling our possessions. Our third game was near perfect, with a serving ace to win 15–3. It felt like we were firing on all cylinders, all six players moving in unison, reading each other and adjusting intuitively. It felt good. We seemed strong and unified, not arrogant, but prepared and confident. Although we all felt electrified by how we'd won, we couldn't celebrate yet. We still had one match left.

As I slapped hands with the last player on the other team, I glanced up into the bleachers, looking for my parents. I saw Mom in the stands. She waved at me and gave me two thumbs up. I smiled but kept scanning for my dad. I finally spotted him sitting next to Lindsey's dad. I wondered if he'd even seen any of our match, then chided myself —at least he was here.

We went to the locker room without saying a word. Coach Nelson gave each of us a high five, smiling from ear to ear. For the first time since the end of the match, we cheered and clapped, the sounds reverberating off the locker room walls.

"That was absolutely amazing," Coach Nelson said. "In all my years of coaching, I can't remember a higher level of play, especially the play in that third game." I could feel her pride in my bones. "Do you want to know the most amazing thing about that game? Luck had nothing to do with it! You didn't just have an out-of-body experience and play an out-of-your-mind game that could never be replicated. When we communicate, take care of fundamentals, and stick to our game plan, it doesn't matter who is on the other side of the net—we can beat anybody."

We let out more loud whoops, and someone behind me shouted, "Three down, one to go!"

As she was about to leave, Coach Nelson added, "Remember this feeling, ladies."

After changing out of my uniform and slipping into my travel sweats, I was anxious to talk with my parents. Mom greeted me first with a tight hug and her mile-a-minute description of some great plays our team had made. When she let go of me, my dad patted my shoulder several times and said, "Congratulations on the win. You guys played well. Your team has improved since I saw you earlier in the season."

"Thanks, Dad. I appreciate you coming." I meant it, probably more than he could imagine.

Mom started talking about the match again, but I kept glancing at my dad, silently imploring more words from him. I knew he didn't know much about volleyball, but I was still hoping for more excitement and maybe some questions about the match. Instead, he just hitched up his pants and sat back down in the bleachers.

When the championship match began, our play slumped. We were down 0–5 in the first game when Coach Nelson called time out. She reminded us we didn't need to play above ourselves or make spectacular plays to win. We needed to play together, focus on the fundamentals, and serve well. We needed to play one point at a time, and we needed to believe.

We lost the first game, won the second, lost the third, and had to play extra points to win the fourth, 17–15. We were headed for a fifth and decisive game.

Even in this final game, we never played with consistency or established any rhythm. The whole match had a clunky, disjointed feel to it, but there was no quit in our team. Though it wasn't pretty, we managed to squeak out a 15–12 victory, making us the district champs. As we hugged each other and jumped for joy, it felt like it was more from relief than celebration.

As we posed for team pictures, beaming with the effortless smiles of the victor, it felt like we were standing in front of a packed stadium of fans celebrating with us. Once pictures were done, the photographer asked for a photo with just the seniors. Wendy, Lindsey, and I lined up against the brick wall. Lindsey's placement in the middle struck me as so fitting. She connected Wendy and me—just as she was my connector to the rest of our volleyball and basketball teams.

At that moment, I felt intense gratitude for Lindsey and how she helped me bridge the social divide with my teammates. She understood my challenges and shared my competitive drive. It was great to have someone on the team who understood me. Her acceptance had given me confidence and made me feel genuinely connected with my team. Even if it only lasted the season, it made a huge difference in my enjoyment. Before meeting Cassandra this year, Lindsey had been my only friend in high school.

After photos, we were directed back to our seats on the court as they prepared to announce the all-tournament team. Six players were selected, one for each position. Lindsey and I were named the two middle blockers. We hugged each other with a genuine sense of joy, celebrating each other's success.

My parents caught up with me just before we exited the gym and headed toward the locker room for our postgame talk. "Congratulations, Sam! A championship and all-tournament team!" my mom gushed. I felt a little embarrassed with my teammates around, as this visit was supposed to happen after our locker room talk.

"Thanks, Mom. We'll be right out." The coaches, who were usually the last to enter the locker room, walked past me.

"I know, I know. But we need to leave and just wanted to see you quickly before we go."

"Oh, okay." I was surprised; she always stayed after games. She glanced at my dad with a hint of a grimace, which let me know who wanted to get on the road.

After our postgame talk, I lingered near the gym door. My parents had left. I didn't see anyone else to talk to until I turned and saw Coach Stevens leaning against the far wall, her bag slung over her shoulder. She smiled, waved, and came over.

"Sam, congratulations." Her tone was exuberant and genuine. She reached out to shake my hand.

"Thank you. We didn't finish as well as we would've liked, but we'll take the ugly win."

"That happens to even the best teams at the highest levels. But your team showed a lot of resilience. Anybody can play well when everything is going their way."

I liked her candor. I nodded and said, "Yeah, that's what Coach Nelson told us after the game. I hadn't thought about it like that. Honestly, I prefer the wins where we execute everything well and dominate the other team."

She surprised me with a belly laugh, head tipped back and mouth wide open. People paused to look at her, wondering what was so funny. "Oh, sorry," she said as her laughter calmed. "I love that response. It shows me you're a competitor and what high standards you have, even in how you win."

I was struck by how much insight she'd gained from a few words. I wondered if that was a unique talent of coaches. I'd seen Coach Nelson and Ms. Collins do it too. I always tried to think before speaking, but this was a reminder that if I let my guard down, I'd reveal information about myself—thoughts, feelings, things I'd rather keep to myself.

"Well, I won't keep you. We'll have more of a chance to visit tomorrow morning. I just wanted to congratulate you. I enjoyed watching your team play."

"I appreciate you coming to the tournament."

"I'll see you tomorrow," she said, waving as she left to find Coach Nelson.

I turned and took in my teammates celebrating with their families and each other. I was acutely aware of how special this team and this season were. I'd been part of many teams throughout high school, and none had anywhere near this level of camaraderie. For me, it was a rare and treasured gift.

December 2006

To: Laurie Collins
From: Samantha Shuster

Dear Ms. C,

I loved your email and read it several times. I appreciate your time watching games, thinking about them, and sharing your insights. I can't thank you enough!

I appreciate your thoughts about our transition offense. You've given me a lot to think about, and I'm excited to brainstorm some ideas with Fitz about how we might add an attack up the left side with a slightly different look. I think this would be something we could add to the arsenal more quickly than in previous seasons. I will keep you posted on that. Better yet, I'll send you more game tapes throughout the season so you can see it with your own eyes.

Your scouting report reminds me how important it is to have "outside" eyes share observations about our team. I've always felt more comfortable being great at a few things than mediocre at many things. (Does that speak to my continual work as a recovering perfectionist?!) However, if that perfectionism goes unchecked, it can unintentionally hold our team back. I remember someone who recognized unfulfilled potential in me due to fear of taking risks and making mistakes . . . I still think of those important lessons you taught me. Thank you for continuing to shine a light on areas for growth and improvement. It will help me as a coach and as a person.

Our next team read is *How to Be Like Mike* by Pat Williams. It's funny how so many players roll their eyes when we describe reading a book together, but when we meet with seniors after the season for feedback about our program, the book reading has been named a highlight by nearly every player.

Thanks again for all your time and thoughts. I hope your last few school days go well and you enjoy your Christmas break.

Take care,

Sam

CHAPTER 16

My house, which normally felt spacious, now felt like a tiny studio apartment filled with the bodies and loud voices of the entire team. Hosting our pre-Christmas team dinner was one of my favorite parts of the season, a chance to bring everyone together one last time before they scattered for the holiday.

Fitz and I waited until they had dished up and were seated before venturing into the kitchen to get our dinner. It became quieter as the players ate; the only sounds we heard for the next ten minutes were "mmm" and "this is so good."

As the kids filed into my kitchen to load their dishes into the dishwasher, I handed each one a copy of my favorite chocolate chip cookie recipe. I'd written each player's name next to their assigned ingredient.

"We could tell you all enjoyed your meal, and now we're going to make dessert together. Grab your ingredient from the counter, then take a seat at the dining room table." Once everyone was seated with their ingredients in front of them, I put a large mixing bowl in the middle of the table and asked Whit to read the recipe directions in order. "When she calls your ingredient, add it to the bowl."

Just as Heather was about to add the final ingredient, a bag of chocolate chips, I stopped her. "Wait. There's one more ingredient." I saw the kids glancing up and down the table, looking confused. I handed Jamie a container of cinnamon. "Just put a dash, a little sprinkle, into the dough." All eyes were on Jamie. She gently shook the container twice, adding just a hint of cinnamon.

"Good. Let's stir that in and add the chocolate chips," I said. I set two baking sheets on the table and had them scoop small balls of dough onto them.

Once the cookie sheets were in the oven, Fitz asked, "Okay, so here's the million-dollar question. What are some similarities between the process of making cookie dough and the dynamics of our team?"

They sat quietly for a moment before Steph got the ball rolling. "For the cookies to turn out, you need every ingredient. If you left out just one, they might not puff up the right amount, be too dry, or something else that makes them not turn out right."

Whitney chimed in. "Yeah, and how each ingredient is important and necessary, regardless of the amount. So two-and-a-half cups of flour aren't more important than only one teaspoon of baking soda."

"Good. Now extend that more specifically to *this* team," Fitz said.

Olivia spoke next. "Well, everybody's role here is equally important and needed. It doesn't matter if someone scores zero points or plays zero minutes in a game; being fully committed to the team and doing their best at their role makes a big difference."

All nodded in agreement.

MJ leaned her elbows on the table and said, "Yeah, and even if it's hard to have a role as a practice player, for instance, it's helpful to remember that you can't have a team with just five players. Every person is important, but the people who play more must ensure they send that message too. You know, make practice players feel appreciated. Think about Rachel. When she comes back, she won't be able to practice. But she'll still be an important part of our team. It's our job to make sure she knows that." I smiled and nodded, wishing Rachel could have been with us to hear this.

"That's a great example, MJ," I said. "She'll continue to play an important role within our team, though it's different from the one she started with. Recognizing that shows great empathy, the ability to put yourself in someone else's shoes, and to try to see, feel, and understand a situation from their perspective. That's an important characteristic of thoughtful people who make great friends, teammates, and leaders."

When the timer sounded, I pulled the cookies out and set them aside to cool. Then I grabbed paper plates and a plate of cookies I'd baked that morning. Fitz helped me pass them out.

"This is the first part of our taste comparison. I made these earlier, following the same recipe minus the special ingredient. Jamie, what was your late addition?"

She leaned around Olivia to look at me. "Cinnamon?"

"Yep, a couple of shakes of cinnamon. Okay, start with these while your cookies with the special ingredient cool." They ate slowly and deliberately rather than devouring the cookies in one or two bites. They looked more like thoughtful wine tasters than kids eating cookies around a dining room table.

"Okay. Hold on to that taste, and I'll bring out the ones you made," I said. I returned with the baking pan and a spatula. "Now for cookie number two." They ate these in silence.

"So, what did you notice . . . other than one being hotter?" I asked.

Steph said, "It's subtle, especially tasting them so close together, but I think our batch tastes better. It's not even like it tastes like cinnamon, but it makes the chocolate chip and brown sugar flavors stand out."

"Wow! Your future career might be a professional food taster," Fitz exclaimed.

"That's a real job?" Alice asked, looking around the table at her teammates. "I'd like that career."

Steph laughed and said, "I can see it now. In our programs, which list our declared major, Alice's will change from 'undecided' to 'professional food taster.'"

When the laughter quieted, Whitney said, "I'm thinking more about Steph describing how the subtle taste of cinnamon strengthened the other flavors in the cookie dough and how it relates to our team. The dash of cinnamon was practically immeasurable, but it added so much. Just like when we talked about how all roles are equally important." She looked around the table at her teammates, who were focused on her. "But when Steph said you couldn't taste the cinnamon directly, that's like our team stats. So many things happen on the court that go uncredited—like setting a good screen or blocking out when you don't get the rebound. The cinnamon makes other things stand out and doesn't need any credit." What had started as a half grin turned into a full smile.

"Ohh . . . that's good," Steph said. "Every team needs a dash of cinnamon."

"And what that dash of cinnamon is could change from game to game or month to month," Heather added.

Whit continued, "Yeah, and I think we should acknowledge it as something to take pride in. Maybe we could make an award acknowledging the player who is contributing the most to those intangibles," Whit looked at Fitz and me. "You know, like how some teams give a Nail Award for the person who practiced and played tough as nails? This would be ours—the Cinnamon Award."

"That's a good idea. Maybe we can work on the details with the captains. Be thinking about it," I said, nodding to each of them. "A couple of final thoughts. We appreciate everyone taking this activity seriously, staying focused on the bigger message, and sharing great insights. And we hope you'll remember some of these messages about being a good teammate and leadership. There are no small or inconsequential roles on a championship team. And never underestimate the impact you can have on those around you, even with something seemingly small like a smile or a hello." I looked around the table and made eye contact with each of them. "Now, who wants some ice cream with these amazing cookies?"

The kids laughed and walked into the kitchen. They visited quietly in twos and threes as they dished up and found a place to sit. Fitz and I waited until the end to bring out our team gifts. It had become a tradition to present our team book to all the players as a Christmas gift. This year, it was *How to Be Like MIKE* by Pat Williams. Each book was wrapped, and we'd written their names and our season dates on the inside flaps.

As we passed them out, Fitz said, "Michael Jordan was not some freak of nature who had these gifts. His game was developed over time, with countless hours of hard work, many setbacks and obstacles, and a relentless drive to be the best."

I chimed in, "Though this is about a star basketball player, it's about so much more. It shares insights into what made him so special and how those traits apply well beyond sports. It also looks at how he had to learn and grow as a leader before the Bulls became champions. We can learn a lot from studying how the great ones became great. Take time with your families this week but come back ready to discuss the first three chapters." I saw a few heads nod as several players started flipping through their copies.

Fitz jumped in. "But hey, we're not done yet! Santa's brought you all one more gift!" His laughter boomed through the room. We had T-shirts lightly wrapped in tissue paper. Fitz and I handed them out. "Okay, you can open them," Fitz said.

Fitz and I had designed a team shirt with B14 printed in large block print on one sleeve. Giggles rippled through the whole team, but Steph was the first to speak. She stood up and held her shirt so the sleeve was most visible. "Hey, Professional Food Taster, you've got a tough choice about your future career: a food taster or a vending machine repair person."

Alice grinned and turned red as Whit wrapped an arm around her shoulders, and rounds of laughter started all over again. It was the perfect ending to our last evening together before they left for Christmas at home.

"Let me help you clean up this mess," Fitz said, collecting plates.

"Be sure to thank Anne for the delicious dinner and for coming over to get things going in the oven. Let's put the rest of these cookies in a bag. I want you to give these to Paul, my co-Cookie Monster."

Fitz laughed. "He'll love that. You're still joining us for Christmas Eve dinner, right?"

"Yep. Speaking of Paul, I'm looking forward to seeing him again. He's such a delight. He shows interest, asks questions, listens, and is willing to share openly about himself. Anne's lucky."

We stood in the kitchen in weighted silence. Fitz cleared his throat. "How are your parents, by the way?"

"Oh, about the same." I turned back toward the sink, trying to find a way to change the subject. Fitz let the silence hang, but I knew he wouldn't let me off that easily. "I've been working on a letter to them, hoping it might serve as the impetus to start having some difficult conversations. I'm hoping we can be honest with each other and begin to have a real relationship."

Fitz leaned against my fridge and crossed his arms. "I think it's courageous of you to take the first step like that. It's not easy sharing our truth with someone, especially if it goes against a pattern that's existed for so long. You know, Anne's relationship with her dad hasn't always been an easy one. After her mom passed away a few years ago, they finally opened themselves up to some difficult conversations. But they've had to work at it."

I faced him and leaned against the counter behind me. "I'm sorry to hear that it took her mom's passing to bring them together, but I'm glad they're being honest with each other."

Fitz nodded. "We can get complacent, always thinking we have more time —until we don't. I think that's what they both realized after her mom passed. Holding on to painful memories from our past keeps us from seeing and knowing each other in the present. It keeps us from healing and moving forward. But the first step can be scary. I'm proud of you for finding a way to share your truth with your parents," he said, then hugged me.

"Man, how did we get from the laughter and hugs with our kids to this dark, heavy topic?" I asked and laughed.

"Sorry. I should've known better than to ask a question about family relationships. Even when they're positive, complex layers always lie below the surface."

I took a deep breath and nodded. We fell into an easy silence, clearing the garbage and packaging the leftovers. When we were done, I handed Fitz a bag of cookies and walked him to the front door. He pulled his coat from the back of a chair, and we hugged each other goodnight.

Alone again, my thoughts went back to my relationship with Dad. Fitz's words about how complacent we become ran through my head. I tried to imagine how I'd feel if I found out my dad had passed away suddenly. Did my dad ever have sleepless nights, thinking about the relationship we could have had or wondering how we could improve it? Did he think about our relationship at all? I made a cup of tea and climbed into bed with a book, hoping to clear my mind. I read for an hour and a half before turning off the light.

In the darkness, my thoughts shifted back to the conversation with Fitz about family relationships. What is it within us that cries out to be heard, understood, and known, especially by our parents? How could parents possibly think their twenty-, thirty-, or forty-year-old child was the same person as the child they'd raised so many years ago? When do we lose our curiosity about others who are close to us? Why is it that we can show more interest and respect by asking questions and listening to strangers than we can with our own family? Despite the complicated, unanswered questions, I drifted into a deep sleep.

I woke up Christmas morning feeling rested, a rarity during the basketball season. Dinner with Fitz's family was always full of good food, great conversation, and laughter. I smiled to myself.

Then, with a deep sigh, I rolled out of bed. The morning's first task was to call my parents to wish them a Merry Christmas.

The sound of their voicemail greeting took me by surprise. I looked at the clock—only 9:00 a.m. I'd mentally prepared myself, so I tried again a few minutes later, thinking maybe they'd both slept in. No answer this time either. They must have gone to Emily's and never thought to update me.

Instead, I dove into work—planning practices, watching game tape, and verifying travel plans for the upcoming tournament. A knock on my front door startled me. The clock on my computer said 2:00 p.m., but I couldn't imagine who would drop by Christmas Day. I opened the door and there was Steph, her face a contorted swirl of emotions, none of them good.

"Hey, Steph. Come in," I said. I glanced toward her car to see if anyone was with her and realized she was alone. I tried to hide my concern that she'd made the four-hour drive from home in this condition.

"Here, let me take your coat, and we can sit on the couch. Can I get you something to drink?"

Without saying a word, Steph's face crumpled, her body collapsed against mine, and she began to sob. I wrapped my arms around her in a tight embrace. Although I didn't know the cause of her pain, it was all I could do to fight back tears, feeling her heaving sobs. I'd seen Stephanie excited and happy; I'd seen her frustrated and angry; but I'd never seen her so devastated.

Steph continued to lean against me, her face against my shoulder, when I heard her mumble, "My parents kicked me out."

I was speechless. My mind raced through scenarios that could lead to that response—coming home drunk, staying out all night without calling, having a heated argument. Nothing I could imagine warranted Larry and Carol's action, so I just held her and waited. She slowly pulled away from me and stood alone, her eyes on the floor.

"My parents threw me out. They disowned me," she said. Her voice was hoarse from crying.

I put my hand on her shoulder, hoping she could feel my support. "Steph. Whatever happened, whatever is going on, you will not be alone through this." Her slumped shoulders started to shake, and she began to silently cry again.

"Here, why don't you come sit on the couch," I said, steering her. "How about something warm to drink? Cocoa, tea, coffee?"

"Cocoa sounds good. Thank you." It took effort for her to get the words out.

When I returned to the living room with two mugs of hot chocolate, Steph was lying on her side with her knees pulled up. I set her cup on the coffee table and sat in the chair next to the couch. I'd taken a few sips before Steph sat up and reached for her mug.

She spoke her first sentence with the cup at her mouth like she wanted to spill her words into the cup, cover the top with her hand, and not let them out. "I told my parents I'm gay."

I wanted to take a deep breath to calm myself but was acutely aware that any sound or movement might be misinterpreted at such an emotional point. I didn't move; I didn't make a sound. I waited for her to look up. When she did, I met her gaze directly.

"Can you tell me about it?"

She held my gaze a moment, looked down into her cup, and took another long sip of cocoa before starting to talk. "I told my mom the first night I got home. I thought she might take the news better than my dad. It didn't work out that way." Her breath came out as if she'd been kicked in the gut. Tears fell down her cheeks. After a moment, she took a breath and went on.

"My mom said she was sure I wasn't gay and listed reasons to explain my feelings—I hadn't dated enough, I was still too young to know, I hadn't met the right guy. She didn't sound mad, so I tried to explain again. I said I'd known for sure that I was gay since sophomore year in high school. I'd tried to explain it away, ignore it, and even deny it. I reminded her I'd had boyfriends in high school, because I didn't want it to be true either. I hadn't known a single gay person then, but I knew myself." Slumped on the couch, staring straight ahead, she paused to take another sip of hot chocolate.

"That's when she got angry. She said a bunch of things, but the last was how it must be her fault. She should've made me wear dresses more often and not let me get as involved in sports. She warned me to think long and hard about sharing this with my dad. If I chose not to, we'd forget the conversation ever happened. But if I told him, there'd be no taking it back. Then she went into her bedroom and shut the door."

My eyes widened and my heart broke for her. I knew, as painful as the talk with her mom had been, things must have gotten even worse. I told Steph how sorry I was, and she continued.

"I got up early the next morning to talk with my parents while my brother and sister were still sleeping. My dad looked too angry to talk, and my mom asked how I could do this to them after all they'd done for me growing up. When my dad finally spoke, he accused me of choosing this lifestyle to rebel. I said it wasn't a choice; I had no reason to rebel against them. It had nothing to do with them. My dad got up to leave but gave me twenty-four hours to change my mind. He told me not to speak of this to my grandparents or siblings and that we'd meet again the next morning. He said if I had a brain in my head, I wouldn't test them and would not want to hear their ultimatum."

Steph had arrived at my doorstep looking emotionally spent. Now, after retelling and reliving this devastating interaction with her parents, she seemed drained of her very essence.

"When we met this morning, I repeated what I'd said yesterday—that I was gay, that I loved them, and that it had nothing to do with them. Basically, they told me I was no longer a member of their family; I was no longer their daughter. They didn't want me to call or try to have contact with any of them. I was no longer welcome in their home."

She put her mug on the table, pulled her knees into her chest, and wrapped her arms around her legs. "I asked about my grandma and grandpa, and they said not to say a word, because it would destroy them. They asked if I wanted that on my conscience too. Then they declared I must not have a conscience anymore, given my 'decisions.' They didn't know me and didn't want to know me. Then they gave me fifteen minutes to pack and get out."

This was a breaking point all over again. She collapsed onto her side, curled into a fetal position, and began sobbing again. I fought back my own tears. I wanted to be strong for Steph in that moment. There would be plenty of time to share tears later.

I was grabbing a blanket for her when the phone rang. I ignored it. The message machine came on, and we could both hear it. My niece and nephews were wishing me a Merry Christmas. As I draped the blanket over her, she said, "Don't you need to get that?"

"No, I can call them back a little later. Would you be more comfortable going into the guest bedroom?"

"I'm fine here, Coach, if I'm not in your way."

"You are not in my way. If you feel like resting, I'll be getting a few things done in my office. And if you feel like talking, just let me know, and I'll be right back out here."

"Okay. Thank you for listening to me and dealing with all this personal stuff, and on Christmas Day, no less."

I spread my arm out, pointing across the entire room. "I think you'd agree that it doesn't look like you're interrupting any holiday festivities."

This brought the first hint of a smile. I put my hand on Steph's shoulder. "I'm glad you trusted me enough to know that you can share whatever is going on in your life and that I'll always be here for you."

I went into my study. My laptop was open and papers were spread every-where. I'd been in the middle of something, but I couldn't remember what. I could only think about Steph and what she was going through. I plopped down in my chair, exhausted. I let my head fall back and closed my eyes.

I'd coached gay kids. I'd had gay teammates in college and on my overseas teams. But it was something we never talked about. I'd always considered myself open-minded and supportive of gay rights, and yet I had no idea what to say to Steph, how to say it, how I could best help her. I had a lot to learn to put my beliefs fully into action.

Over the next hour and a half, I didn't get much accomplished. Twice, I poked my head into the living room to see if Steph was awake, but she seemed to be getting some much-needed sleep. I went to the kitchen. As I pulled a container of beef stew and dinner rolls from the fridge, Steph staggered into the room.

"I was trying to be quiet. Did I wake you up?"

"No, it wasn't that. How long did I sleep?"

"A couple of hours. I'm sure you needed it. It won't take me long to get this heated up. Why don't you have a seat at the table, and I'll get you something to drink." I added, "I want you to know that it's okay if you don't want to talk about it. But I was wondering about the timing of telling your parents. Why now?"

After swallowing a bite of stew, she gave a flat chuckle. "Oh God, pretty stupid, wasn't it?"

"No. I was just wondering why you picked this time—Christmas, home for just a few days. I'm sure you had a reason."

"Yeah, I had thought about it, but it didn't go as planned." She put her spoon down and folded her hands in her lap, keeping her eyes on the table.

Then she shrugged and said, "I guess I started thinking about it a year ago when my girlfriend's grandmother passed away. She was so close to her grandma. She would go live with her every summer. It's been over a year, but she still cries over her loss, and much of her pain comes from feeling like her grandma died without truly knowing her. Seeing her grief and knowing there was nothing she could do about it now got me thinking more about my situation. My parents *should* live into old age, but there are no guarantees."

Her face remained emotionless, and her gaze had not wavered from the bowl of stew in front of her. "I've known for a long time but worried about telling them. I thought with my accomplishments—earning a full-ride scholarship to college, playing as a freshman, and doing well in my classes—their pride in me would outweigh any negative feelings they might have. I thought it might be easier now, in college, not living at home with them. You know, maybe out-of-sight, out-of-mind until they adjusted." Her mask of stoicism was starting to give way. Tears welled up and spilled over her cheeks. She didn't try to wipe them away. "I thought I could finally quit hiding, quit acting, quit feeling like I'm lying. I thought they'd still see me as the same daughter they've always loved, but they don't. They no longer love me, and now I don't have a family."

This concluding thought was the final crack in her armor. Her chin fell to her chest, and she sobbed. Crouching to her level, I hugged her until she stopped crying.

"You know, Steph, I think your parents need time." I gave her arms a gentle squeeze and sat back in my chair. "Your news was likely a big shock, and perhaps their initial response was more disbelief, so they didn't know how to respond. Not that it makes it right or any less painful for you." Trying to find the right words and tone felt like walking into an unfamiliar room in the dark, feeling for walls or other obstacles, trying to find the light switch. I wanted to be reassuring without giving false platitudes that might minimize her feelings.

"Yeah . . . maybe . . . I hope."

"Have you shared what you've been going through with anyone other than your girlfriend? What's her name, by the way?"

"Nikki. No, she's the only one I've talked to about it."

I felt a pang in my heart, picturing her holding all this inside and dealing with all the questions, concerns, and emotions on her own. "You are surrounded by love and support from your teammates, Fitz, and me. However long it may take your parents, we are all here and can remind you how many people care about you."

Steph nodded but then said, "What if my teammates respond the same way my parents did? What if none of them want to be my roommate on road trips? What if our interactions change if they find out because now they feel weird around me?"

Her trust had been shaken to the core. If her parents could respond with such venom, why would she think that others would react any differently? Her emotional wounds, so raw and vulnerable, broke my heart all over again.

"You're right, and we don't know how each of them will respond. I'd like to believe that they would all rally around you, showing you their love and being by your side for however long it takes. But we don't know for sure. I do know that I am here with you and always will be. I also feel confident that Fitz will be with you."

A half grin curled the ends of her mouth. "I can't get rid of him even with this, huh?" She looked up just enough for me to see her face briefly, and we smiled. Relief washed over me at seeing and hearing that quick glimpse of her humor.

She stood up. "I should probably go, Coach. God, I've been here all day. Sorry for just dropping in and dumping all this personal crap on you. Thank you for everything—letting me crash here, feeding me, and listening to me."

I stood up and pulled her into a hug. "No thanks necessary, Steph. You're always welcome here, no matter what is going on in your life." As we stepped back, I could see tears in her eyes again. "I also want you to know I will not share this with anyone unless you've said it's okay. You have control of when, how, and to whom it's told. Okay?"

"Okay. You can certainly tell Coach Fitz. I know you guys always talk and work together on everything for the team. I'd feel comfortable talking with him about it too. But I don't know yet about the rest of the team. I'll have to think about that."

We started walking toward the front door, and as she reached for the door handle, I said, "You're more than welcome to stay here, Steph. I hate for you to be by yourself."

"Thanks, Coach, but I'm fine. I feel like climbing into my bed and sleeping straight through until morning. I'm exhausted."

I thought about the difference between physical and emotional exhaustion. Physical exhaustion could be quickly remedied through sleep, food, and rest, while emotional exhaustion operated on a different timetable.

I hugged her goodbye and reminded her to call or come over if she was struggling or didn't want to be alone. I watched her back out of my driveway, then busied myself, clearing the table and cleaning up the kitchen. I tried studying a game video but couldn't stay focused for long so I decided work could wait.

I got on the computer to start reading about my most pressing concerns related to Stephanie. An hour into some initial research, I realized it was a good thing I hadn't known some of this before Steph left my house. I would've made her stay. The one glaring statistic I couldn't erase from my mind was a higher rate of depression and suicide.

As I tossed and turned in bed that night, Steph's words replayed continuously: *My parents don't love me anymore. I'm not the daughter they wanted.* That thought cycle was finally interrupted by one phrase: unconditional versus conditional love.

There seemed to be many conditions required to earn "unconditional" parental love. At the core of all those conditions was how we, as their child of any age, reflected on them as parents. It was about image, what others thought, and meeting their needs and goals. Thinking about what Steph was experiencing through this lens, I didn't know whether to feel sorrow that she had to learn this reality or feel some happiness that she'd made it this long before reaching this harsh realization. The layers of love are deep and complicated.

My last thought before falling asleep was that I needed to stop procrastinating and making excuses. It was time to mail the letter to my parents.

December 2006

To: Laurie Collins
From: Samantha Shuster

Dear Ms. C,

I hope you had a wonderful Christmas and enjoyed the break
from school. We're just about to hit the road for a tournament in San Diego.

There have been so many positive things going on with
our team, but unfortunately, we've had some devastating
ones too. One of our kids, Stephanie, showed up at my house
on Christmas Day, sobbing, distraught because her parents
kicked her out of the house. She told them she was gay, and
their response was to disown her.

My heart was utterly broken for her, and I'm trying to
learn as much as I can about how to help her through this. I
feel out of my league when it comes to knowing what to do.
Unfortunately, my research only scared the bejeezus out
of me. Stats on depression, homelessness, and increased
rates of suicide scream to me about getting a professional
counselor involved. But at this point, Steph wants to keep
things private. Given how her parents responded, I can't
blame her. We're planning to take it one day at a time, and
hopefully, Fitz and I will be enough support for now.

Steph is one of the most amazing young adults I've ever
had the pleasure to know. My feelings swing from deep pain
for her to a tsunami of anger toward her parents for doing this
to her. I worry that my emotional response and my inability
to remain neutral will interfere with my ability to help her

through this crisis. So far, I've been able to keep repeating messages of strength, love, and support, reminding her that she is not alone. But it's taking all my self-control to hide my feelings about her parents. I hope I've done the right thing by not pushing her to see a professional counselor.

I'm sorry for unloading such a depressing story on you. Thanks for listening and caring. I appreciate your friendship!

Happy New Year (almost!),

Sam

CHAPTER 17

NOVEMBER 1986

My alarm clock jolted me awake from a deep sleep. I needed to prepare for my breakfast meeting with Coach Stevens, so I quickly showered and dressed. As I was getting ready, I heard my parents talking down the hallway.

"Mark, how could you decide this now? Don't you think the coach expects you to be there too?"

"It's not like my being there affects what is said. I'm sure she'll give you a packet, and we can look at it together later tonight. I lost too much time between the drive and the two games yesterday. She's a coach; I'm sure she'll understand."

My mom responded, but her words were muffled. However, my dad's following comment was crystal clear. "I met the coach yesterday, and we talked a bit. What else is there for me to say? I'm not the one she's trying to recruit." Then I heard the front door open and close.

I began writing questions for Coach Stevens: How long had she been at Boise State? What had their record been? What would happen to players on scholarship if Coach Stevens left and there was a new coach? How many seniors would she lose that year?

I hesitated at that last question, worried it might sound like I thought I'd be good enough as a first-year player to take the spot of a graduating senior. I was scratching out the last question when my mom cracked open my door. "You almost ready to head out? It's just you and me this morning. Your dad had something come up."

I was initially concerned about my dad not attending the meeting with Coach Stevens, but I quickly realized his absence might be good. Mom and I could relax more without worrying about him making some blunt or inappropriate comment. "Okay," I said, not wanting to share those thoughts.

"I'm sorry," she said, sighing and entering the room. "I just found out this morning. He feels like he has too much to do for school and the start of basketball tomorrow since he didn't get much done yesterday. But we were so happy to be there to see you win the championship."

"That's all right, I understand. Are you sure you have the time? You were also there both days, and you must have things you need to get done."

She bent down behind my chair to hug me. With her arms wrapped around my neck and shoulders and the side of her face pressed against the top of my head, she said, "You are always so thoughtful. I have the time and absolutely wouldn't miss it."

Later that morning, I was back at my desk trying to process everything Coach Stevens had told us during our breakfast meeting. She'd offered me a spot on their team and a full scholarship. She also wanted me to come to Boise for a campus visit. That was exciting! Yet I felt a mixture of pleasure and dread churning in my stomach. It was all about the timeline. I'd have to commit to a volleyball team by mid-January, just about the time college basketball coaches began recruiting.

My mom waited until we were out of the parking lot and on the freeway before saying anything. I could tell she was excited because she spoke faster than usual, her words tumbling over one another. She ticked off several things that had impressed her before she paused and reached over to tap my leg.

"I'm sorry. I should be letting you talk first. You know how I get when I'm excited about something." She glanced sideways at me with a sheepish grin. "Please, I want to hear your thoughts and impressions."

"Well, I liked Coach Braxton and Coach Stevens, and I think visits to their schools would be essential to see the differences between their teams and campuses."

"You sound hesitant. What else are you thinking about?"

I took a deep breath. "Part of it is the difference in the timing of scholarship offers for volleyball and basketball. You know I've always loved basketball. It seems risky to give up a sure thing, a volleyball scholarship, without knowing if I might be offered a basketball scholarship."

Mom uttered a soft "uh-huh" in acknowledgment.

I added quietly: "And visiting Boise means I'll have to miss another two basketball practices. I'm not looking forward to talking with Coach Walters about it."

"Oh honey," she said, gripping the steering wheel and shaking her head. "He'll be fine with it. He must know this is an incredible opportunity for you, and you don't have much control over the timing. I bet he'll be happy for you."

She gave him way much more credit than he deserved regarding how understanding and happy he'd be for me. We rode silently for a while before she turned and glanced at me. "What if the sports were reversed in terms of the timing? Would you feel the same anxiety if Coach Braxton and Coach Stevens were talking basketball?"

"No. I'd take the visits and pick the one I liked best. I wouldn't think twice about it. Basketball has always been a 'known' to me."

She nodded. "So tomorrow, you'll talk with Coach Walters about missing basketball so we can get back to Coach Stevens?"

"Yes, I'll see him at the gym."

As soon as practice ended, I hurried to the door to the secondary gym, looking for Coach Walters. He was standing outside the gym door, watching my dad's practice through the small window.

"Coach Walters," I said. "Can I talk with you for a minute?"

He barely gave me a sideways glance. He kept watching the activity in the gym as he responded, "Yeah, but it's got to be quick. Coach Fox and Coach Stokes should be here any minute."

"Okay, thanks. I just wanted to let you know, as early as possible, that two schools are recruiting me for volleyball and have set up dates for campus visits. Unfortunately, it means I'll need to miss a couple of practices. They know I play basketball and did their best to minimize my absences, but it couldn't be avoided."

The only response I could see from his side profile was his clenched jaw. I felt my stomach tighten. "I wrote down the dates so you could put them in your calendar, and I'll be sure to remind you as we get closer." I held out the piece of paper. He swiped it out of my hand, still not making eye contact. Before he could respond, Coach Stokes cracked the door, saw us, and tried to excuse himself.

"Sorry, I didn't know you were meeting. I'll wait in the gym," he said.

"No, don't go. Sam was informing me that, in addition to missing the whole first week of basketball practice for a volleyball tournament, she now has additional dates she'll miss because she's going to visit colleges for volleyball." I stared down at the floor, wishing I could disappear.

"This is good for you to see so that if you decide to become a head coach, you'll have a better understanding of what you are up against when it comes to coaching girls and getting any kind of commitment from them."

Although he was speaking to Coach Stokes, I could feel him looking at me, daring me to challenge anything he'd just said. I flicked my eyes up to meet his. The look on his face matched his icy tone. I wanted to tell him that throughout volleyball season I'd put in extra time to keep up my basketball skills—running, shooting, ball handling, and working out twice a week with Ms. Collins. But I didn't say a word, fearing he'd think I was making excuses and being disrespectful. Coach Stokes stayed out of it as well.

"Do you have any other practices you'll need to miss? Maybe for a haircut or a babysitting job—something important like that?" Coach Walters asked.

"I'm sorry," was all I could mutter as I dropped my eyes to the ground.

He made a show of wadding up the paper I'd given him and throwing it into the trash can in the corner. "Seems like your commitment is elsewhere. Maybe you should reconsider even turning out for basketball this year. Remember, those who miss practices don't play in the games." With that, he stormed into the gym. I looked at Coach Stokes, but he just turned to follow Coach Walters.

I stood there stunned, unable to move. The balls bouncing and loud voices from the practice were muted, as if I were hearing things from underwater. I'd expected Coach Walters to be abrupt and cold; I had not anticipated his anger.

By the time I got home, I had stopped feeling so shell-shocked. I must not have looked better, though, because Mom met me in the entry, appearing concerned.

"Are you all right?" she asked. "You look very pale, honey." She placed the back of her hand on my forehead.

"I'm fine, Mom, just a little tired after practice."

"I worry about you and the schedule you keep. You can only push your body so much before it tells you you'd better slow down."

I dropped my two bags on the floor and wrapped my arms around her in a hug. "I'm fine, Mom," I repeated.

Our last volleyball practice before the state tournament was intense. At the end, we huddled together and put our hands in the middle to make our final cheer. There was a quiet sense of closure; this was our seniors' final practice in our home gym. I'm sure Coach Nelson also felt some of that, and she made a point of pulling Wendy, Lindsey, and me off to the side after dismissing everyone else.

"Remember, we still have the biggest and best part of our journey in front of us."

The three of us walked into the locker room, Lindsey in the middle, her arms draped over Wendy and me. It struck me how everything, big and small, would be our last together—last team dinner, road trip, huddle, and game. I had to keep telling myself to ensure these "lasts" were our best, in order to turn my emotions into a competitive drive rather than a prolonged and somber goodbye.

I was ready for bed at 10:30 p.m. when I finally got to talk with my dad. I walked into the den to say goodnight as he headed for bed. When he reached me, his two hands went to my shoulders, and he bent his forehead to be near the side of my head without making any other physical contact. It wouldn't seem so strange if that were how he hugged Emily, but because I got my unique form of a hug, it was hard not to wonder if he forced himself to do this out of parental obligation rather than love and affection.

"Hey, good luck this weekend. I'm sorry I won't be there, but your mom's cheering for both of us," he said.

"Thanks, and I hope your practices keep going well."

He was out of the room before I'd finished that sentence. My mom stood up from the couch and gave me a big hug. I wanted to ask her if her hugs were for the two of them too.

"I won't be there for your first match on Thursday, but I plan to be there for the next five." I smiled. It would take six matches to reach Saturday night's championship game. There was no question for her that we'd make it all the way.

"It's going to be great, Mom, and I'm glad you'll be there."

Walking into the gym on the tournament's first day, it felt as if our team was enveloped in a protective bubble. Others could see and cheer for us, but we saw and heard nothing but our teammates and coaches. It was a surreal blend—a competitive fury on the court while floating on a cloud, united as a team off the court. Time seemed to slow as we moved from the hotel to the gym and back to the hotel to watch and play. At the same time, everything felt like it was passing too quickly.

My mom was right. We marched through this magical time, securing a place in Saturday's championship game. Dominating our opponent in three straight games in four out of five matches, we became like a force of nature. Our play embodied power, beauty, and grace, pulsating deep within us.

It came down to the night's final match, determining who would go home state champions. I could feel the energy buzzing through my teammates as Coach Nelson reminded us to continue playing smart and as a team.

"That's what's gotten you this far," she said. "Hold on to it."

After one last hands-in cheer, the team turned to take our positions on the court, but Coach Nelson called for her seniors to stay behind. She bent forward, hands on her thighs, and looked each of us in the eye. "Win or lose," she said, nodding toward the court, "I want to thank you for making this one of the most memorable seasons I've ever participated in. The leadership the three of you have consistently shown, both on and off the court, has been remarkable. So before you head out there, I want each of you to know how special I think you are, not only as volleyball players but also as people. You have tremendously impacted your teammates, our program, and me. It has been an honor to be your coach." She stood up and hugged each of us before sending us onto the floor for the final match of our high school careers.

We played with an edge, like we were disrespected underdogs. Leaving no question in anyone's mind who the best team was, we won the championship match: 15–12, 15–11, 15–10. The celebration began as the six of us on the court crashed into each other as we jumped, hugged, and shouted. We were quickly joined by our teammates, followed by our coaches.

We held the first-place trophy high overhead as cameras flashed, snapping pictures. We returned to the sideline chairs just as the announcer began naming the all-tournament team. As Lindsey's name was called, loud cheers and claps erupted from our bench and crowd. She walked up to the table, accepted the small trophy, then took her place next to the other players honored. I saw my mom with Mrs. Walters, standing and clapping as they celebrated.

Then I heard my name and the words "tournament MVP." My world stood still momentarily as my brain processed what was happening. I'd been named first-team all-league for volleyball and basketball; but it had never felt like this! I took my place in the line on the court, my heart racing. I met Lindsey's eyes. She beamed and gave a thumbs up. It felt incredible, and sharing the stage with her at that moment made it even more special.

December 2006

To: Samantha Shuster
From: Laurie Collins

Dear Sam,

Oh … I am so sorry about what Stephanie is going through.
Even though we've never met, my heart absolutely breaks
for her. I apologize for such a short note. So many thoughts
and emotions are now swirling through my head and heart.
It would be better for me to feel more settled so I can write
something coherent to you, but I wanted you to know I got
your email. I'm thinking about both of you.

I'll write back soon. In the meantime, I wish you the best
of luck in San Diego.

Ms. C

CHAPTER 18

We'd left Montana in the dead of winter, and the team wasted no time getting out of the hotel and soaking up the San Diego sunshine. Between the buzz of city life and the warm temperatures, they were much more animated than usual, and they all seemed to be talking at once.

When we told them it was time to get ready, all that silliness disappeared—replaced with mission-like focus. We kept the film session short, then Fitz took over with his book talk.

"You read Chapter 4, 'The Fight'; Chapter 5, 'The Promise'; and Chapter 6, 'The Champion of the Whole World.' So, what did you learn from Michael Jordan's example that we can apply to our team collectively?"

Whit started. "The part that stood out to me was his competitiveness, not just in games, but every day at practice. His teammates didn't always like it, but they respected him and had to try to match his level of play every day, which made each of them better, individually, and then, of course, as a team." Whit paused and glanced around the table at her teammates. "I think it stood out because that's been something we've been trying to work on, being more consistently aggressive in our practices. It was a good reminder."

"I couldn't have said it better myself," Fitz said, high-fiving Whit. "We've talked about how competitive fury is accepted and embraced by male athletes, whereas females, and this is a generalization, struggle more with separating competitive anger from personal anger. Our goal," Fitz pointed to me, "is to see you practice and play with a physical intensity and competitiveness every day, making it as natural as breathing."

Fitz paused, and Whitney jumped in. "We all know who the most competitive person on our team is, especially at practice. And it hasn't always gone over well with us as her teammates. But I want to thank MJ," she turned to look directly at Maddie, who looked taken aback, "for being brave enough to show this side of her personality and for being patient with all of us since we haven't always embraced it wholeheartedly. I know you're not only making me a better basketball player but also making the team better, so hopefully, we can do a better job of following your lead. In short—don't change, MJ."

I was blown away by Whit's directness and sincerity. The rest of the team started clapping, slowly at first with just a few people, but quickly followed by the entire group.

When the cheers died down, and the sentiment still hung in the air, Fitz said, "MJ, I can't tell you how happy I am that you get to hear this from your teammates. It's not easy going against the grain. It can feel lonely when who you are as a basketball player and teammate is not accepted by those closest to you—your team."

Fitz's words instantly made my mind shift to Steph, but I did not let my gaze follow. If it was a lonely feeling not to be accepted by teammates, did we even have a word for that feeling of rejection from one's parents?

"You have shown tremendous strength and persistence. Things that would make *this* MJ very proud," he said, holding up Michael Jordan's book.

"And Whit," Fitz continued, "you've also shown us an amazing thing that would add chapters to Jordan's book. When a pink elephant is in the room, it's easier to pretend it doesn't exist, hoping it will go away on its own. It happens in families, with friendships, in the workplace, and on teams. That's magnified if, by calling something out, you must admit that you've made a mistake, were wrong, or need to apologize." As I scanned the room, all eyes were on Fitz.

"Thank you to both MJ and Whit, for modeling, in both their words and actions, how to deal with difficult situations with integrity and compassion. That's an invaluable team lesson and a life lesson," I said.

As our meeting broke up, the team left as one group, quieter and more unified than when they arrived. Fitz and I looked at each other with amazement. We sat back down in our chairs.

"Can you believe that?" I asked.

"No, I'm still speechless. We can spend all week planning team-building experiences, and then, out of the blue, one of the kids creates a learning and bonding moment infinitely better than anything we have planned."

Steph walked back into the room before I could respond to his comment.

"Am I interrupting?"

"Not at all, Steph. Come have a seat with us," I said.

She'd had a good practice earlier, but she'd been quiet the rest of the time. I wondered if her teammates noticed.

Steph looked at Fitz. "I'm sure Coach Sam told you about what's happening with me, but I just wanted to tell you myself. I didn't want you to think I didn't trust you or that I didn't want to talk about it with you."

"I didn't feel that way at all. Like Coach Sam, I'm here for you anytime and about anything. I always will be."

Steph nodded but kept her eyes on the table when she spoke next. Her voice was so soft we both leaned forward to hear. "A lot of the comments about MJ and Whit made me think of my situation, especially about how it takes strength and courage to speak honestly about a difficult situation, and most people take the easier way out by ignoring it. . . . I didn't know if you thought it would be better if I were honest with the team. You know, if I didn't avoid the pink elephant in the room?"

Fitz and I immediately shook our heads. Fitz said, "No, no, no, Steph. These two things are not comparable."

I jumped up from my chair and sat next to her. I had to touch her to convey my concern. Every time I saw her, my first instinct was to envelop her in a hug. It was as if pain, anguish, self-doubt, and shame had been injected into her by her parents' disapproval. I didn't think I had any words that could ease her pain, but I wanted her to feel love and acceptance.

"You did not avoid the pink elephant," Fitz said. "You showed incredible courage by coming out to your parents. You should only share with your teammates because you want to. If, when, and how are all things for you, and only you, to decide."

"I agree with Fitz about the courage it took to speak openly and honestly with your parents. I know this is something you had thought about and felt for a long time before you came out to your family. You found your authentic self and had the courage to share that. I know it doesn't feel like it right now, but you have offered your parents the most precious gift—the chance for them to truly know you. There's nothing more valuable than that."

Tears streamed down her cheeks and onto the table. She made no effort to wipe them away.

"And you know something else?" Fitz said. "What's coming out as anger is most likely masking their shock. But remember, that's on them; it's about their expectations, not about you."

"What if they don't change their minds?"

"There's no way to know how long it might take. It might take more time for one of your parents and less for the other. Or they might not change their minds. Like Coach said, you offered them the greatest possible gift, but ultimately, it will be up to them to accept it." Fitz's tone was full of compassion.

Steph stood up to leave. Her tears had stopped, but her eyes were red rimmed and puffy. Fitz and I simultaneously stood to hug her; it became a group hug.

"I'm still the same daughter they loved before." Steph's muffled voice was pure heartbreak.

I patted her back. "Yes, you are. You absolutely are, and don't you forget it." Even as I said it, I realized it didn't answer her real question— why her parents were doing this.

"You are still the amazing basketball player, teammate, student, and leader you were before sharing with your parents. You are still the amazing person you have always been," Fitz said.

As she thanked us for listening and understanding, I reminded her, "We are both here for you and always will be. You are not alone."

I pulled my car into the driveway and sat quietly for a minute, trying to gather some energy to unload my bag and head in.

We'd won both of our games in San Diego, but more important, we'd made significant strides in *how* we played with our changed lineups. Our team showed the same level of aggressiveness and confidence on the court as when Rachel was our leading scorer.

Steph played with a bottomless reserve of energy. Competing against other teams seemed to be a pressure relief valve, an outlet for her stored anger, frustration, and hurt. I think she could've played all forty minutes of both games without a sub. It was like an affirmation, proving to herself, her coaches, and her teammates that she was still a great basketball player. I hoped the ongoing challenges on the court would help her remember she was a great person too.

The sound of my phone shook me from my thoughts. When I saw it was Cassandra, I picked up right away.

"I wanted to catch you before you headed out on a hot New Year's Eve date."

I laughed. "Umm . . . I'm sorry. You must have the wrong number."

I'd been looking forward to catching up with her. As she told me about Christmas, her mom, her husband, and projects at work, I grabbed my bag from the trunk and headed inside.

"Okay, enough about me," she giggled, "tell me all about you! How's the team?"

"I know this won't surprise you, but you'll love this story about Whit . . ." I shared what Whit said at the table when our team discussed the Michael Jordan book, our two wins, and the strides the team had made.

I saved what happened to Steph for last. Even though it was a long story, starting with Christmas Day when Steph showed up at my house, Cassandra never interrupted. I finished with my concern that I should set her up with an actual counselor.

Cassandra let out a deep breath. "Oh, Sam. I am so sorry for Stephanie," she said. She shared stories about friends she had and people she'd met through her work in the LGBTQ community that were painfully similar to Steph's.

"Here's the thing, though. Everyone said they got through hard times because one person, whether a family member, friend, or colleague at work, had supported them through the early dark tunnel. Then, with time, they found wider support and maybe even professional help. You're the perfect person for Stephanie because she trusts and respects you, and you're giving her nonjudgmental support. Listen, I've got a ton of resources if you'd like me to send them to you."

"Please, send me everything you have. I don't want Steph to limp along, barely surviving—she deserves to thrive."

After finishing dinner, I decided to call my parents to wish them a Happy New Year. Their phone rang three times before my mom answered.

"Hi, Mom. Happy New Year."

"Hi, Sam. It's good to hear your voice. Happy New Year to you too."

"Did you and Dad go out and celebrate last night?"

She laughed. "No. We were asleep by eleven and missed the neighbors shooting off fireworks."

"I'm sorry I didn't get to talk with you on Christmas. Did you have fun at Emily's?"

"It was great. Even your dad agreed it should become our new tradition, at least while the kids are still young. They seemed to have more fun celebrating Christmas in their own home, and I can't say I missed all that cooking. It was good getting away for a few days during basketball season." She chuckled.

"How's Dad's season going?"

"I'll let him tell you. You know how much he loves to talk about his team. You two have always had that in common, haven't you? Hold on a second." I heard her call for my dad.

I wanted to laugh and say, "Are you kidding me?" Yes, my dad and I were both coaches, but if I loved talking about my team, they'd never know it because I never got the chance.

"Hey, Sam, Happy New Year." My dad's voice sounded far away, and I knew my mom had switched to speakerphone.

"Thanks, Dad, and the same to you. I'm glad you had such a nice Christmas at Emily's."

"Yeah, we liked celebrating over there. But we had to get back for basketball . . ." and he was off. I closed my eyes and listened—practices, plays, meetings, and games. He didn't need any questions to prompt him into lengthy storytelling.

Eventually, I found a pause in the conversation. "Well, good luck with your games. It sounds like you have the makings for a good run at state this year."

"Thanks. Maybe if we make it, you can come to see us play. It's a pretty good group, and we're getting better each week."

"Yeah, maybe," I responded, knowing that could never happen. Our conference games would just be finishing about the time of his state tournament, and if we made it to postconference play, we'd still be playing. Maybe *he* could come to see *our* team play for the first time in four years.

In the end, like countless times before, I didn't say anything. I kept my thoughts and feelings locked up tightly inside. I didn't question. I didn't challenge. I didn't share an opposing opinion. The message I'd received since I was young was that I shouldn't be too vocal, opinionated, or make waves—because people don't like that. It was far more important for girls to be nice and liked.

"Well, keep me updated, Dad!"

My mom's voice returned, and I could tell she'd switched off the speakerphone. "Oh, he's already off and running, but if there's good news, he won't be able to keep it to himself! Anyway, tell me all about your New Year's! Did you go out? Any resolutions? Maybe going on more dates?" She laughed like she was joking, but I couldn't even fake a laugh. She knew I'd never been the party type; we were still in the middle of basketball season, and I'd never appreciated comments about my dating life.

I slumped back on the couch, defeated. Nearly every phone call with my parents ended this way. We shared a few more superficial comments before saying goodbye. I finished with, "I love you, Mom."

It was not reciprocated. Instead, my mom said, "Thanks for calling, Sam." I heard a click followed by three beeping sounds before my phone went utterly quiet. I just sat there in stunned silence.

I'd heard and read about father-son dynamics, especially fathers wanting their sons to go further and accomplish more than they had. Those fathers took pride in their sons' ambition and success and in having built a sturdy foundation for the next generation.

Was there a parallel dynamic between mothers and daughters? Surely, women of earlier generations, including my mom, who didn't have the same educational opportunities or financial freedom to pursue their interests, would celebrate their daughters doing something different. Yet it seemed the contrary. Mom had always supported my pursuit of sports in high school, but everything seemed to change when sports remained my focus after college. Rather than taking pride in a daughter forging her own path and trying to break from the confines of rigid gender roles, my mom's pride had instead shifted to the daughter who'd made traditional choices—marriage and motherhood. If a daughter's life took a different direction, does it create jealousy or resentment rather than pride? Maybe she thought deep down that since she'd had to put her life goals on hold to be a wife and mother, so should her daughters?

This wasn't the kind of psychology I'd studied, but it was one that personally affected me. It seemed so complicated, so layered in dense tangles of unmet needs and unspoken expectations that connect each generation with a sticky but invisible thread, like a spider's web. And, like a spider's web, it was hard to break free.

That may have attracted me to sports psychology, which seemed more straightforward than family psychology. In sports psychology, issues are acknowledged and discussed directly and honestly, and goals are set to improve. With families, so much stays in the dark. The same patterns get repeated, handed down like part of our DNA, and healing never occurs.

I thought about the letter I had mailed them before leaving for San Diego. I hoped they were ready to start an honest discussion and begin the healing process.

We'd just finished practice, and it had been a good one. Whether working on our offense or defense, there was a level of cohesion among our starting five that was stronger and more consistent than we'd ever seen before. I loved it.

Though it wasn't on our practice plan, I'd decided to finish with a fun shooting game they all loved. It was a close finish, with Steph and MJ barely beating Olivia and Alice. Although they weren't required to run, Steph and MJ joined their teammates in the final conditioning sprints.

After practice, most of the kids stayed around to get extra shots. Fitz was passing to Heather, who was working on her post moves. Steph and MJ were at one hoop, shooting free throws. I saw Whit checking her phone on the other side of the gym and then tucking it back into her bag before starting to shoot. I walked over to where she was practicing and began rebounding for her as she took perimeter shots.

"Hey, have you heard from Rachel lately?" I asked, passing her the ball.

She caught it, cocked her head, and grinned. She tucked the ball under her arm. "Coach, are you psychic?"

I laughed. "Maybe. Why?"

She came over and spoke quietly, "Between you and me, Rachel's on her way over. She wants to surprise everyone though, so don't say anything. And act surprised, okay?"

"You got it. Top secret." A big smile spread across her face as she continued shooting.

"Does that mean you've been staying in touch with her?" I asked.

She took another shot and nodded. "Heather, Olivia, and I did a conference call with her a few days ago to discuss the Jordan chapters. She's been keeping up with our team reading."

I passed her the ball again. "I'm so happy to hear that. You can't imagine the difference that probably made in her spirits. I'm sure it's been hard for her being away from the team."

She took another shot. "I think she wants to be here for the last couple of team meetings and activities before classes start again."

"That's great. I can't wait to see her."

Then I moved to another hoop to rebound for Stephanie, but she'd just finished shooting, so I talked to her as she sat in the bleachers to change her shoes.

"Is Amy's mom bringing her to the next home game?"

She pressed her lips together. "I think so, but I'm not sure. I'm . . . I'm kind of worried her mom is going to ask where my family is. I'm worried *everyone* is going to start asking where my family is."

I had no easy answers. Since her parents rarely missed home games, someone would likely ask about their absence. I also knew that every time she had to try answering such questions, it would be another painful reminder—death by a thousand cuts.

"You can just say that they couldn't make it, and you don't need to feel pressured to share any more information than you're comfortable with."

Steph nodded, but her pained expression revealed doubt. I heard the gym door squeal, followed by whooping and shouting. I looked behind me. There was Rachel, barely through the door, surrounded by smiling teammates.

I turned to Steph, but she was already on the move, a huge grin on her face. "Well, look who finally decided to show up to practice, Coach!" she shouted loud enough for everyone in the gym to hear. As she passed me, she ducked her head and whispered, "Thanks for listening, Coach." Then she jogged across the gym to join her teammates.

December 2006

To: Laurie Collins
From: Samantha Shuster

Dear Ms. C,

I'm back from San Diego, where we played two great games, winning both and finally seeing some consistency from our changed lineup. Fitz and I like the changes we've made with our offense. Thank you again for the time you've spent watching our games and sharing your ideas.

I devoured the John Maxwell book you recommended. I've already passed my copy on to Fitz. In fact, I enjoyed it so much that I picked up Maxwell's book, The 21 Indispensable Qualities of a Leader, to read on the flights to and from California. I know you'd like it if you haven't read it. There was one section that made me think of you. Maxwell describes how there are "givers" and "takers," whether in the work arena or in general. It instantly made me think of you, the definition of a "giver." Your knowledge, support, and belief in me have been pillars of strength and growth for me going all the way back to high school.

I can't thank you enough for all that you've given me. Your role has evolved from teacher and coach to mentor and faithful friend. I hope you always know how much I appreciate you.

Sam

CHAPTER 19
NOVEMBER 1986

Our Monday morning assembly was being held to highlight our successful volleyball season and kick off the winter sports, primarily boys' basketball. I'd never been so excited about an assembly.

Rather than sitting with our first-period classes, the volleyball team met in Coach Nelson's office then sat together in the bleachers. Our principal made a few opening remarks and asked everyone to stand while our band played the national anthem. Mr. Burns, our athletic director, shared a few general comments about all our sports programs and how well they represented our school. There was some brief, uninspired clapping, and then he called on Coach Nelson.

With humor and passion, she briefly described some highlights of our season, capped off by winning the state championship. She also announced that Lindsey and I were named to the all-tournament team. As she called out each team member's name, we walked onto the court and formed a line behind her. She held the large championship trophy above her head, saying it was the first of its kind for the volleyball program and the first for any of the girls' sports at our school. The band started playing the school's fight song, and the start of some clapping showed that the student body was beginning to pay attention.

We took seats while Mr. Burns moved on to winter sports, explaining that teams started practices the previous week. He mentioned the girls' basketball, swim, dive, and wrestling teams before announcing my dad, who needed no introduction.

As Dad charged forward and took the microphone, his varsity team jogged behind him and formed three lines at half court. He bellowed for everyone to get on their feet and start cheering. It was as if the entire student body had gulped a six-pack of Mountain Dew and was electrified by the caffeine surge. My dad motioned to the bandleader, and as they started playing, his team began a combination half-court shooting and lay-in drill. It was as if it all had been choreographed and rehearsed because as the band struck their final note, Chris Daniels finished the drill with an emphatic slam dunk. The entire gym erupted into cheers.

I couldn't stomach the show any longer. The boys' basketball team had not yet played a game but had somehow upstaged our state-champion volleyball team. Seeing my teammates' lack of response to the vast difference in coverage received by boys' and girls' sports brought back the same gnawing questions I'd asked myself many times before. *Why am I the only one who sees this? Why am I the only one who feels it's an injustice? Am I being too sensitive?*

This volleyball season had been the most incredible experience of my life, but our seemingly unbreakable bond was already being broken. I was back on my own, an outsider looking in.

As the assembly ended, I walked out of the gym with glazed eyes. When I entered the hallway, Cassandra was waiting for me, an irritated look plastered across her face.

"What was all that about?" she asked. "You guys are state champions, and they barely mentioned it."

"You are the only person who commented on it, including my volleyball teammates."

"Really?" She crinkled her eyebrows and nose, showing her disbelief. "I know how I felt watching that assembly. I can't imagine what it must feel like for your team and coaches."

Cassandra's recognition bolstered my spirits the rest of the day—until basketball practice.

Coach Walters blew his whistle to begin practice. He'd not acknowledged Lindsey or me at all. I wasn't expecting, or even wanting, congratulations for our volleyball performance, but I was surprised by his contempt. I was glad his daughter played volleyball too; I couldn't imagine how he'd have acted if she didn't.

Although we'd missed the first week of practice on account of volleyball, most of the warm-up drills for the first thirty minutes focused on fundamentals. Lindsey and I executed them like we'd been there from day one. When we ran our conditioning sprints, I came in first every time. But nothing changed in Coach Walters's mood or demeanor.

Following a quick water break, we transitioned to a new offensive drill he'd taught during our absence. "Lindsey, Sam, get out here," he hollered. The only information Lindsey and I had to guide us was the name of the drill, "transition attack." After only two passes, Coach Walters blew his whistle, stopping the drill.

"No! No!" he yelled. "That's not what we're doing!" His face was flushed, his jaw clenched. I glanced at my teammates standing along the baseline, hoping someone would whisper or motion some directions to us, but they simply stood and stared at Coach Walters.

Lindsey started to say, "If we just watched one or two times through—"

Her dad cut her off. "Lindsey, watch while you both run suicides along the side. Kristi! Anne! Take their spots."

Without a word, Lindsey and I started doing sprints along the court's side. We watched as the new group ran through the new drill he'd introduced the week before. It was simple enough to understand. We kept running, waiting for another chance to get in the drill, but it never came.

Back in the locker room, Lindsey and I sat by ourselves in the back row, staring straight ahead in a stupor. Lindsey shook her head. "God, it feels so different, doesn't it?" She sounded tired, deflated, flat.

Although I felt the same way, I tried to remain positive. "Yeah, but you can't compare our first basketball practice to winning the state volleyball championship."

"You don't need to defend him. What he did to us today was so unfair. Was his goal to humiliate us in front of the team?" I looked at Lindsey. Her elbows rested on her knees while she stared into the middle distance. She could usually find the positive in bad situations, but occasionally, despair poked through her armor. When it did, it always came from the same source—her dad and basketball.

My heart ached for her. Having her dad as our coach, and more generally having coaches as dads, was challenging. I wanted to tell her I could relate to the pain she was feeling, that it was something we shared, but I didn't trust that I had the words to convey what I truly felt.

Instead, I said, "Hey, let's make a pact with each other right now."

She nodded in silent agreement.

"First, we will make this basketball season fun, no matter what. Second, we will not allow your dad . . . or any of the coaches, to get us down. If anything negative gets thrown at us, we'll counter that with something positive. And third, and most important, we won't let anything that happens this season get in the way of our friendship."

Lindsey looked back at me and said, "I like it."

I smiled and held up my right hand in a fist with just my pinky finger extended. "Pinky shake?"

"Yeah, pinky shake," she said. We crossed right pinkies and held on for a second. She finally let herself smile, and I hoped it released some of her sadness and anger.

When Ms. Collins saw me approach her office door, she jumped out of her chair and greeted me with a big hug. "Congratulations! State champions and MVP of the tournament—you must still be floating on cloud nine!"

"It was fantastic! I didn't want the weekend to end."

"You will always have those memories. You share something so special with a group; it stays with you." Her tone sounded almost reverent, like talking about this brought back memories from her playing or coaching days. I waited to see if she'd share personal stories, but she didn't elaborate.

"So, no rest for the weary. You've already switched gears and jumped headfirst into basketball now, huh?"

"Yeah. I've practiced two days now, but I'm already behind in a few new drills and plays."

"When is your first game?"

"Monday. I've got a copy of the schedule for you right here," I said, unzipping my bag to grab it. She glanced at it briefly before pinning it to her bulletin board.

"Why don't we focus on shooting today—get a rhythm, lots of reps."

That sounded good to me. The feel of the ball leaving my fingers with every shot and the sound of the net swishing felt like home. After finishing with free throws, Ms. Collins said, "That looked great, Sam. How'd it feel?"

"It felt good. I think that's just what I needed."

She stood next to me while I changed shoes. "This weekend is my first campus visit for volleyball," I said as I stood up.

"You must feel like a yo-yo, alternating between volleyball and basketball. Remind me, which school is your first visit?"

"Sacramento State. The first weekend of December will be Boise State." I hoisted my bag over my shoulder. "Then no more yo-yo," I said, smiling at her.

"This must all be exciting for you but probably stressful too."

I nodded.

"If anyone can balance the back and forth of two sports, plus school and travel, I'm looking at her." Ms. Collins put her arm around my shoulder and squeezed me.

"I hope so. I guess we'll find out after this weekend."

Thursday, I reminded Coach Walters that I would miss Friday's practice. He barely acknowledged me. The last couple of practices had felt better. Lindsey and I were now familiar with the new drills, and we could lead the way throughout practice. Despite that, our practices lacked team chemistry—they felt lifeless. I wanted to use volleyball as a model for our basketball team to emulate this season, but I also knew that Lindsey and I had a huge obstacle to overcome—her father.

December 2006

To: Laurie Collins
From: Samantha Shuster

Dear Ms. Collins,

This is a quick email to end the week because I had you on my mind this afternoon.

I've got two posters hanging in my office. One is a Michael Jordan quote. The other one is a poster of the painting you used to have hanging in your office—the scene with the sailboat.

I'm not sure if you'll remember this, but once during my senior year, you used that painting to remind me how stifling perfection can be. You encouraged me to be bold with my colors and wild with my brush strokes, to take risks and chances, to live and grow outside the lines instead of being confined to the lines someone else created for me.

I remember that conversation every time I look at the image of the sailboat, but I've added another mantra to contemplate as well: "Sam, you've got to be willing to rock the boat."

Thank you for being the first person in my life to remind me that coloring outside the lines and rocking the boat are things to be proud of. Those moments with you were true lifelines at a time when I wasn't always sure I'd make it to shore. I still carry them with me on days when the seas around me feel choppy.

Sam

CHAPTER 20
JANUARY 2007

It felt good to play a home game again, this time against Montana Tech. A larger crowd of students than normal cheered us on, probably excited about being back on campus after Christmas break. Even with that, the absence of Steph's family left a gaping hole in the bleachers, and I worried how it might affect her play.

I should've known better. Steph channeled her pain into a controlled rage on the court. She played even better than she had in San Diego. Her teammates, unaware of the source of her possessed performance, fed off her energy. We put on a clinic for anyone who knew basketball and a spectacular show for the rest of the fans.

The final score was 93–41, setting a program record for points scored in a game. That was despite calling off our press early and trying to control our fast breaks by executing offense instead. In the locker room following the game, Fitz and I kept our comments brief; there were only so many ways to say, "Great game." Much to our surprise, Rachel asked if she could say something.

"I haven't seen the team play for a while, so I might be able to see the differences better than any of you since you see each other daily. What I saw out there was like night and day compared to the team I saw a month ago. We've never played like that. I don't even think the number one team in our conference ever looked that dominant." Her teammates stared at her expectantly, hanging on her every word.

"I thought it would be painful to sit and watch the games and feel so helpless. But it was a treat. It was amazing. Whatever you've been doing—keep it up!" Rachel half shouted the last part, and the team exploded with cheers. They all jumped up and tried to hug her at the same time. Fitz and I slipped out the door and let them enjoy their special moment together.

Out in the gym, I answered a few questions for our local paper. By the time I was done, our players had started to trickle back onto the floor. I glanced around and saw Steph talking with Amy and her mom. Amy had a look of awe on her face. I hoped they would talk about Steph's performance instead of where her parents were.

I returned to the office, where Fitz was already seated at his desk, staring at the final stat sheet and shaking his head. I knew the feeling—disbelief. Games like that didn't happen often.

"And how 'bout Rachel sharing?" I asked. "I didn't think anything could get better than that game. Then, out of nowhere, she manages to top it."

The following day, I was putting away files as Fitz sorted through the thick stack of mail piled on a corner of my desk.

"Whoa, Coachie! Congratulations! Why didn't you say anything about this?" I only half looked in his direction, continuing to clear our workspace.

"What are you talking about?"

"What do you mean, 'what'? You don't think being inducted into your high school Hall of Fame is a big deal?"

As I stepped closer, he handed me the paper he was holding. I didn't need to reread it. I'd shoved it between some junk mail for a reason. I glanced at it, put it back in the envelope, and tossed it onto my desk. He sat still, waiting for me to say something. Finally, I broke the silence by asking, "Should we start with reviewing film before planning practice?"

"You're not going to say anything else about the Hall of Fame induction? I know you've always been humble, but come on. Not many people get this kind of award. I wish your high school were closer because I'd love to attend the ceremony."

"Well, it's not close, and I probably won't be going," I said. I pulled the game tape out of my bag, ending the conversation, and he didn't mention it again.

Before the next practice, I made a copy of our practice plan for Rachel. I knew she was busy with physical therapy, but we wanted to keep her connected to her teammates on a day-to-day basis as much as possible. We had her running the clock and keeping records of team drills at practices.

After practice, we watched game film of our upcoming opponent. Then Fitz led a talk on the final chapters of our team read. Today's focus was on leadership, and Fitz got many of the kids involved in sharing, either from the book or from their personal experiences and observations. Fitz concluded, emphasizing that they would have future opportunities to be leaders and inspire others.

As the team filed out of the classroom, chatting and laughing with each other, Steph stopped at the front desk to check in with us. "I was thinking about your idea of meeting with me regularly," she said. "Would Monday and Thursday work, say around one thirty?"

I'd asked Steph to pick a few weekdays to check in with us. Initially, I'd wanted us to meet daily, but Fitz convinced me that was too much.

"That'll work great, and afternoons should mean that Fitz can make it most days," I answered. "We're past the scheduled time today, but we could certainly do it now if you want to talk. No pressure. I want you to know it's an option."

She smiled. "No. Thursday will be fine."

Fitz and I packed up for the day, and he stopped just as we left the office. "Sam," he said. Fitz rarely used my actual name, which got my attention. "I'm sorry about pushing you on your Hall of Fame induction."

I stood and hugged him before responding. "Fitzy. You don't need to apologize. You know my high school years, especially my basketball experiences, were far from positive memories. Luckily, I had college and postcollege years that more than made up for that disappointment. I won't regret sitting this one out."

He gave me a nod. "Whether you go or not, it's a big accomplishment. Congratulations."

As soon as Steph appeared in the doorway, Fitz jumped from his chair and bowed down to her.

I laughed and said, "Come in, Steph. Don't let him scare you away."

Fitz straightened up and said, "You played an outstanding game last night, Steph. And it wasn't just the scoring; you did everything. It also energized your teammates."

She grinned and took a seat. It struck me again how infrequently we saw her smile these days. It used to happen constantly, and now it felt as rare as a seventy-degree day in February.

I said, "As great as you played last night, it's not like it will be a one-time occurrence. I believe you're capable of making that a nightly performance. Maybe not the 36 points every game, but the rebounds, steals, assists, outstanding defense, and overall leadership. That's what you're capable of regularly."

Had that game happened before her parents kicked her out, those words would have been a strong wind billowing her sails. She would've been proud, confident, and eager to go out and do it again. Today, her only response was a half grin, a slight nod, and a quiet thank you.

I waited a moment before continuing. "I saw you with Amy and her mom after the game. How'd that go?"

"It was good to see her again. She's happy to be with her mom after the holidays with her dad."

I waited to see if she'd share more. When she didn't, I asked the million-dollar question. "Did they ask about your family?"

"Yeah. I just said they couldn't make it, then changed the subject." Her eyes shifted down, and her face became flat and expressionless, like her voice. "I don't know how long that answer will suffice, depending on how many more games they come to."

"Remember, one day at a time, Steph," Fitz said in a soothing voice. "That sounds easy, but it's a challenge, especially in stressful times."

"You know what's weird about all this? I've lived for years, keeping things secret from everyone. Because it was a secret, I never had to give a second thought about how I interacted with people, about conversations, about anything. Now that I've told my family, the people closest to me, they disowned me, and I still feel this need to be secretive with others. Maybe I should've been honest with some of my teammates first, like testing the waters or practicing how best to share it. Better yet, why didn't I just keep it a secret? Things were so much better and easier before, and all for what? I'm still in disguise." In a defeated voice, she added, "Things were fine. They were better than fine. My family was great. And I ruined it—all for nothing. I wish I could take it all back."

Every fiber in my being wanted to console her and push away her fears and pain with reassuring words like "things will get better" or "your parents will come around." But I fought those urges, knowing they were trite and potentially hurtful, minimizing her feelings.

"You know, Steph, though it may not feel like it now, I still believe what you did was incredibly brave and loving," I said.

Fitz added, "When you said things were so much better and easier before, I might agree with easier. But I would differ with you on the better part. It's not a real relationship when we can't be honest and authentic. You've offered your parents the gift of a real relationship with you. It will be up to them to embrace it, which may take some time."

There was more silence. Then Steph said, "I sent them a Happy New Year's card to say I love you." She unzipped her backpack and pulled out an envelope, holding it up for us to see. "It came back," she said. Someone had drawn an X through the address and written *Return to Sender*.

"I'm sorry, Steph," I said. Words seemed so inadequate for all she was going through.

"Could you make me a copy of last night's game? Maybe they'll be more likely to open it if I send that. I'll even mark *DVD* on the outside of the envelope." The glimmer of hope in her voice practically broke my heart.

"Of course, Steph. We can have it ready for you today at practice."

"Great, thanks. I should probably go," she said, glancing at the clock.

I stood to hug her and said, "Two things I want you to try to think about and remind yourself of regularly: patience and compassion. For you and your parents. Okay?"

She nodded. "Okay."

I called Cassandra Friday evening, half expecting to leave a message. She answered after the first ring.

"I'm glad you called. I've been thinking about you, and especially Stephanie. How's she doing?"

"I think she's doing okay. Thanks for the information you sent. Reading and learning more about what she's going through and how I might help has been helpful. Hey, on a lighter note, you'll love this story about your favorite, Whit," I said.

At the end of practice that day, Whit had asked to make an important announcement. She'd reminded everyone about the Cinnamon Award we'd discussed weeks before at my house, which I explained to Cassandra. "Whit called Rachel up in front of everyone, and as Rachel leaned on her crutches and blushed, she thanked Rachel for her positive energy and support from the bench," I explained. "You might feel like your contribution is small," Whit had said, "but we all feel the tremendous difference you've made. So I'd like to present you with the first Cinnamon Award. Thank you for being our secret ingredient."

I could practically feel Cassandra's smile on the other end of the line when I'd finished the story. "Aww, Sam. I love that kid! That's amazing!"

"I know. I could tell it meant a lot to Rachel. It's powerful, the impact of praise from your teammates rather than just the coaching staff."

"Oh my God! I almost forgot! Congratulations on your Hall of Fame induction! It's well deserved, but that doesn't always mean those things are acknowledged. I think it's great!"

I chuckled. She didn't follow sports any closer today than she had when I'd met her, but that never stopped her from being my biggest cheerleader.

"Thanks, Cassandra. How'd you hear?"

"They asked me to emcee the event. I was a little surprised, given the stir I caused way back when. Plus, if they've paid any attention to my work in Seattle, they'd know I've only become more vocal and more radical." She exaggerated "vocal" and "radical" like they were bad words.

"They have no idea what surprises are ahead of them, huh?" I joked.

"I bet I'll have to turn in a script of my speech beforehand. And they'll probably make sure they have control of the microphone, just in case I start to ad-lib." She laughed. "No, but seriously, it'll be great to see you."

"Oh, well . . . I doubt I'll make it."

"What? You're kidding, right?"

"No, I'm serious. April is a busy month for recruiting. That weekend, there's an important tournament we always go to, and there's a chance we could have recruits making campus visits during that time." I paused. There was silence on her end. "Are you there?" I thought maybe the call had dropped.

"Yeah, I'm still here. Sorry, I was just thrown a little. It hadn't crossed my mind that you might not attend."

After another brief silence, Cassandra continued, "Have you talked about this with your parents yet? I'm sure they're thrilled for you. Have you told them you might not be coming?"

"I haven't talked with them since I found out. I just got the letter in the mail earlier this week. They probably don't know yet."

"Well . . ." It was unusual to hear Cassandra hesitate.

"What?" I pushed her.

"Your dad knows. He was notified because one of his former players is being inducted, and they contacted various coaches to take part."

It was my turn to be speechless. My dad knew and hadn't picked up the phone. Neither had my mom. Then I thought about which of my coaches had been invited. I couldn't picture Coach Walters getting up on stage and saying anything positive about me.

"I'm sorry, Sam. I hadn't thought all this through before bringing it up. I was just excited for you and about being there to celebrate this honor with you."

"Oh, you don't need to apologize. I appreciate your excitement for me, and you'll be a great presenter, but I don't know if it will be something we can do together. Do you remember which of my dad's players is being inducted? Was it someone from our time at school?"

"Yeah. It's Chris Daniels." Her tone was flat. She knew that this would only add to my negative feelings and memories. "I guess this probably adds another strike against the possibility of you coming. First, standing up there with your douchebag coach, then watching your dad heap endless praise on Chris."

I burst out laughing. Cassandra had always managed to walk that tightrope of being somewhat critical of my dad without pushing it so far that I'd jump in to defend him.

"Well, it's understandable. Chris was the son and basketball star my dad always wanted."

"Your dad had a basketball star. He just never saw it." The warmth in her voice touched a nerve. She was probably the only one who knew the depth of the pain those high school years caused me.

"Thank you. This doesn't rear its ugly head often, but when it does, I try to remind myself that it's ancient history and to let it go."

"Well, the past has a funny way of sticking around with us in the present, for good and bad."

That night, I sat at my desk checking emails, hoping to get ahead before the crush of the following week. I had several new emails, but one immediately jumped out at me. It was from Ms. C. I hadn't heard from her since her quick email the day after Christmas, though I'd sent her a couple more. It was unlike her, but I chalked it up to a busy holiday season.

I opened her email first. When I finished reading through the first time, I caught myself exhaling deeply, like I'd been holding my breath. I stared at my computer screen, then read through slowly three more times, pausing after each paragraph to let the words sink in.

January 2007

To: Samantha Shuster
From: Laurie Collins

Dear Sam,

I am so sorry for my last email, which probably seemed short
and cryptic, and the long delay before sending this one. It's
perhaps hard to understand, but I'll try to explain and hope
it makes more sense.

You are the perfect person to help Stephanie through
such a traumatic experience. You've built a trusting relationship with her, which is why she came to you on Christmas Day
with this horrible news. She not only shared her heartbreak
at her parents' response but also risked sharing with you the
same news that provoked such an extreme reaction from
her parents. That is trust.

I can understand why you might feel like you're in over
your head with someone who might need professional counseling. But I think that initially, your concern and support are
far more critical to Stephanie than anything else. A counselor
would be a neutral person being paid to listen and help,
while you are a significant person in her life. She respects
you. Hearing your words and seeing in your actions that
she is still the same person to you will bolster her defenses,
especially against self-doubt and self-destructive thoughts.
She is fortunate to have you in her life. She was before this,
but she REALLY is now.

Part of why I feel so confident telling you this, and why
this email took longer to write, is I speak from personal

experience. Reading your email describing what happened to Stephanie felt like a kick in the gut, leaving me winded and trying to catch my breath.

When you were in high school and we were working together, you asked once why I didn't coach the high school team. I knew you meant it as a compliment and took it that way, but it was also a painful reminder of a hurtful experience.

I had been a high school coach for several years and loved it. And then I wasn't. It was taken from me, and I didn't put up much of a fight. A player on my team, who was unhappy with her playing time, made up a story about me to her parents, and they went to the principal and athletic director, demanding I be fired. The girl claimed that she felt uncomfortable when I hugged her and that I acted inappropriately in the locker room around the team. The unspoken words were *because she's gay*. I'd never told any of my teaching colleagues about my partner. Like most gay people at the time, I kept my personal life entirely private.

Nonetheless, with this complaint and the fact that I was single, taught PE, and coached basketball, my principal and athletic director thought the best way to handle it was for me to step down immediately, claiming a health issue, and allow the JV coach to take over for the rest of the season. I did finish the school year teaching but moved after that and gave up coaching. Losing the opportunity to coach left a big hole in my life, and how it was done made me start wearing a personal coat of armor. I kept most people at a distance and stopped being completely honest with others.

Even today, I've only shared this story with a handful of my closest friends. The risk in wearing all that armor, being dishonest for the sake of others, is that it's toxic for the person living it. We can't truly accept and love ourselves when we hide or deny a core part of our identity. We can never feel whole. It's not something that happens overnight; instead, it's a slow, insidious drowning—think of the frog in the pot of water that doesn't recognize the increase in temperature until it's too late. With you guiding and supporting Stephanie daily, hopefully, she won't experience that slow drowning in isolation, secrecy, and shame.

Throughout my struggles, I've read a lot and been to counseling. One of the ideas that resonated the most is that we all have two different parts to ourselves—the inner and the outer. The outer self is what our parents and family, peers, house of worship, and culture tell us to do and be, and we work hard to please all these external forces. Then there is our inner self, true nature, essence, and soul. It is who we are at our deepest core.

The daily challenge is to decide which self we will be. Do we conform to others' expectations to make them happy and comfortable, or do we stay true to ourselves? Unfortunately, these two selves can feel like opposites, so far apart that they'll never cross paths. But when the inner and the outer selves align, we are in harmony with ourselves. The key is that we have a choice—and recognizing that we have this choice is empowering. It may seem like a baby step, but it's the first step toward self-acceptance—a gift of love from you to yourself.

It is excruciating to think that today, with all our progress, many people still must go through this same painful experience. I do know that you and Fitz will help Stephanie tremendously, and please also know that if there is any way I can help, I'd be happy to do it.

My heart goes out to Stephanie and to you. These will not be easy times, and you may be looking at weeks and months of difficult days ahead. I believe she will overcome this adversity with your strength and compassion to guide and support her. I'm also confident that having you in her life will help her be able to join the two parts of herself at some point in the future.

Your friend,

Ms. C

CHAPTER 21
NOVEMBER 1986

My campus visit at Sacramento State was terrific. My mom picked me up at the airport Sunday afternoon. She only had to ask about my weekend, and I talked her ear off on the entire drive home to Olympia. The team, coaches, facilities, campus, and energy—all of it felt like standing on the edge of freedom. That feeling was the only part I'd left out in describing it to my mom.

It was not until we exited the freeway that it hit me—I had done all the talking, and it was all about me. I'm not sure if it was embarrassment or critical self-judgment that washed over me.

"Oh my God, Mom. I'm sorry. Why didn't you say something to stop me from blabbing on and on?"

"Are you kidding? I loved hearing every word. My only regret is that I was driving, so I couldn't see your face as you shared all this. I'm so proud of you."

We pulled into the driveway a few minutes later. As she cut the engine, I said, "Can you give Dad the nutshell version of my weekend?

Emily probably doesn't even know I was gone, and Dad will be satisfied with a three-sentence story. Maybe after I visit Boise, we can all talk longer when we compare schools."

The expression on her face was a mixture of pain and sorrow. "I hope you know your dad is happy for you. I know he gets so wrapped up in his classroom and team stuff that it can feel like we don't exist, but that couldn't be further from the truth. I think he's struggling with the idea that you are a senior and will leave us soon. He's proud of you."

I just smiled and nodded.

During my Monday classes, I was distracted and thinking about that night's game, our first of the season. When we took the court for our pregame warm-ups, I was so excited that even our half-court drills felt too constraining. Adrenaline surged through me. But when Coach Walters announced the starters, he didn't say my name! Lindsey shot me a look, her brow drawn and lips pursed. Everyone froze; no one said a word. A few minutes later, the starters took the court, leaving me on the bench.

As the game started, questions raced through my mind. Was I going to sit out the whole game or just the first quarter? Was he doing this because he was mad about my college visits and missing practices? Why didn't he tell me beforehand so I could be prepared?

The first quarter ended with us down 14–4. During the break between quarters, I tried taking deep breaths to clear my mind so I'd be ready when my time came. But when the game resumed, I still wasn't playing. I made eye contact with both assistant coaches, but each quickly looked away.

We went to the locker room at half, down 24–11. Neither the coaches nor my teammates said anything or asked why I wasn't playing. They all acted as if everything was normal. I assumed Lindsey felt the same frustration and confusion I did, but she didn't make eye contact or offer a whispered word of support. Surrounded by my team and coaches, I felt alone. When Coach Walters finished his half-time talk, he said the same five starters would start the second half.

Two-and-a-half minutes into the third quarter we'd fallen even further behind when Coach Walters yelled my name. His only comment was to name the player I was subbing for. I hurried to the scorer's table before he could change his mind.

All my pent-up nervousness, energy, and anger finally had an outlet. With that anger—fueled by a feeling that I was being mistreated, with no control over something important to me—I dominated nearly every possession for the rest of the game. Defensively, I got steals and rebounds, took a charge, and even blocked a shot, trying to get a stop every time the other team had the ball. I attacked off the dribble offensively, practically daring the defensive player to try to stop me. I hit open shots and crashed the offensive boards for putbacks, but it wasn't enough. We lost by five points. Walking through the line to slap hands with the other team, I felt only anger.

In the locker room, Coach Walters said we were a young team with much to learn, but we'd had a promising start. He finished by telling us to be patient with the offense, it would come, and to focus on playing defense like we did in the second half of the game. I couldn't read whether my teammates were angry with Coach Walters, disappointed by the loss, or just apathetic.

The short bus ride home was silent. Mentally, I rehearsed possible questions for Coach Walters about my playing time. Unfortunately, I couldn't imagine a positive response or picture myself being able to ask.

At home, I headed straight to my bedroom. Mom walked out of my parents' bedroom and shut the door behind her. She knew me well enough not to stick around the gym to visit after losing a game, but my spirits weren't any better now.

"Hey, honey," she spoke softly. "I'm sorry about such a close loss. You sure played well, though."

I mumbled thanks without meeting her gaze.

"Why did you sit out the whole first half?" she asked cautiously, like she was feeling her way through a dark room.

"I don't know. All I know is I need to run. Otherwise, I won't sleep tonight."

With that, I laced up my running shoes and was out the front door in minutes.

At practice the next day, Coach Walters finished by reminding us that any player who misses practice might also miss at least the first half of the next game. Sitting in front of the team was awkward, knowing that his comment was directed at me. I wondered if my teammates knew why I had missed practices.

Once Lindsey and I had our sweats on, she looked at me to see if I was ready to walk out to our cars together.

"I'm ready." She turned to start walking, and I said, "Hey, wait."

She faced me, and I held up my free hand in the form of our pinky shake.

"Remember, we made a deal. Nothing gets in the way of us having fun this season," I said, smiling and waiting for her to shake.

"Deal," she said, latching her pinky around mine and smiling back.

The next morning, it was hard getting out of bed. I'd had a broken night's sleep, thinking about the playing time I'd be missing due to my campus visits for volleyball. I stood in the kitchen, eating breakfast in a sleepy haze, when my dad walked in. "Good morning, Sam," he said cheerfully.

"Congratulations on your game last night," I said, my mouth full of Grape-Nuts. I'd seen the game because Cassandra had asked me to sit through the boys' game with her and explain the plays.

"I was happy with our performance because it's only our first game. Always helps to have good senior leadership and a player like Chris."

A pang shot through my body. I'd grown accustomed to the difference in how my peers saw Chris's and my athletic accomplishments. But from my dad? Swallowing the lump in my throat, I reminded myself of the only plausible explanation—I wasn't good enough yet. "Yet," Ms. Collins's favorite word, was the critical part that drove me.

Once I'd regained my composure, I said, "I was impressed with your defense and how much you could change it on the fly. It took the other team completely out of rhythm."

My dad looked at me then and smiled. "Yeah, I was getting a kick out of the other coach burning through his timeouts so early. He was frustrated." At least we still had basketball to discuss, even if it was only about his team and players. He tilted his head like he was suddenly looking at me for the first time.

"You look ready to leave early this morning. What are you working on? Something for class?"

I paused for a moment, weighing how to respond. Dad was so proud of Chris's dedication. Did he even realize how dedicated I was? Maybe if he knew how hard I was working . . .

"I'm meeting Ms. Collins at the middle school for an hour workout on shooting and ball handling. We do it a couple of times a week."

His smile disappeared, and a crease formed between his eyebrows. "How long have you been doing this?"

"A little while," I responded tentatively.

"Did your volleyball coach know about this? Does your mom know about this?"

Any hopefulness I'd been feeling was now gone, deflated. My tone was flat as I answered him. "Coach Nelson knew. I don't know about Mom. I've got to go."

I didn't have the time or energy to listen to his many reasons why I should not do this. He would turn this into a federal offense and twist it into a source of shame rather than pride. I was sorry I'd opened my mouth.

Cassandra beat me to the library this time. Although it was nearly empty, when she saw me, she stood up and waved her arm as if trying to make herself visible within a crowd. I laughed as I made my way to the table.

"Hi! No time for small talk. Sit. Read." Cassandra pushed several printed pages my way.

"Okay, okay." I laughed. I could feel her eyes focused on me like lasers as I read. I tried to keep my facial expression neutral, not showing my shock.

Cassandra had written a letter to the editor of our school newspaper. She'd laid out a strong critique comparing the treatment of girls' and boys' sports at our school. She didn't sugarcoat it. Words like *injustice*, *inequality*, and *sexism* leaped off the page.

I purposely slowed down on the last page, giving myself time to think about my response. How could I tell her there was no way it would be published in the school paper?

Cassandra was watching me intently and probably noticed when my eyes quit scanning the page. Before I could look up, she asked, "What do you think?"

I met her gaze and said, "You are an amazing writer. But . . ."

"But what?"

"But I don't know if you can print these things." I didn't know exactly how to express my concerns and reluctance. There wasn't anything she'd written that I disagreed with.

Inside, I was filled with respect for her. But on the outside, I felt more comfortable downplaying these issues, though they'd weighed heavily on me for years. Broaching issues like equal treatment for boy and girl athletes or similar coverage for their respective teams felt too dangerous.

"What do you mean? It's not like I made this stuff up or blamed specific people for what's happening. I'm not encouraging people to quit going to games or riot in the streets."

She looked as if she honestly couldn't understand my concern.

"No, I know. I agree with everything you've written. I can't help thinking that some people will feel offended or attacked. It's powerful—maybe too powerful." I knew I wasn't making much sense.

"It's a letter to the editor, not investigative journalism. It's an opinion from a concerned observer that will hopefully increase awareness. That's not exactly revolutionary, Sam."

I paused, trying to come up with the words to accurately reflect my angst. Cassandra waited impatiently. I finally broke the silence. "Can I make a copy of it? Let me reread it and sleep on it. Maybe I'll be able to give you better feedback after thinking more about it. Maybe give a copy to Coach Nelson? She's in the middle of all this. What about Mr. Morris? He knows about writing and editing and would be more like a neutral party. He's a guy, but he's not involved in sports and won't take it personally. Maybe see what they think?"

Even if it was never published, I wanted a copy for myself because Cassandra had captured in words much of what I felt I'd been living since middle school.

Eventually, she nodded her head. "Okay. I'll share it with them, but only to see if they have any suggestions to make it stronger. I don't want to soften the message. We must bring this to people's attention. It seems obvious now, but before this year, I hadn't thought about how and why our sports teams are treated so differently. But now that I see it, it's shocking. When others are made aware, I think many will react similarly, and that's how change happens."

That was one of the things I admired about Cassandra. She wasn't afraid to raise issues, ask questions, and take her concerns to the higher-ups. She was fearless about stirring things up.

"That's a good idea." I was already relieved that she wouldn't send it to the paper the next day. Besides, she'd be able to get a better assessment from others.

We were quiet for a bit, and I let my gaze drift out the window. The two trees in my view had lost their leaves, and the thin branches swayed from sporadic wind gusts. The rain had picked up outside, and the thrumming sounds on the roof filled our silence.

Cassandra's internal fire shined a light on a side of my personality I wished were different. I always felt uncomfortable expressing my negative thoughts or feelings for fear of making someone angry or disappointed. I let that fear control me more than I wanted to, and it often became like a self-imposed prison sentence. Was this something she'd learned and developed, or was it innate? Maybe if I spent more time with Cassandra, it would rub off on me.

After a few minutes, she broke the silence. "You know, you said you were amazed at how I put those thoughts into words and how I'm willing to say things people don't want to hear. But honestly, I'm amazed at how you've been able to stay silent for so long. I'm new to sports, but this has been your life."

"I guess when you feel like you're the only one feeling a certain way, and it goes on for so long, it makes you question yourself. You figure there must be something wrong with you. I must be the one who is wrong in my interpretation and expectations; otherwise, more people, especially adults, would be doing or saying something."

"I can see what you're saying," Cassandra replied. "While boys and girls in the artsy crowd or band group at school get more similar treatment, it's different for you. The more confident and successful a star male athlete is, the more everyone respects him. But when you do the same thing as a standout female athlete, you end up farther outside the peer circle. It certainly isn't your personality. If anything, you're too nice and too humble." She said this last part with concern, as if it pained her to say it.

"Thanks . . . I think," I said, but she was already on to her next point.

"Chris struts around like he owns the school, but you're invisible, or even worse, shunned. Seeing that double standard must make it ten times harder for you. God, I don't know how you've put up with it this long. I would've exploded from rage a long time ago."

I was touched. She recognized and acknowledged something that had plagued me, and she felt outrage on my behalf.

"I wish I had an ounce of your feisty attitude because my situation would probably be different; it would be better."

"Different, yes, but I don't know about better. Having a big mouth doesn't always make situations better. Coach Nelson has never said anything about this?"

I shook my head.

With a bit of hesitation, dropping her voice to a whisper, she asked, "What about your parents—especially your dad? He's at the school. He sees the same thing we see every day."

I felt tears welling up in my eyes and started to blink rapidly to keep them from advancing. I shook my head again but said nothing. I had to hesitate before speaking to prevent the dam from breaking, unleashing a torrent of backed-up emotions. Cassandra's insightful observations hit too close to home and too close to my heart.

She sat for a minute before speaking. When she did, I appreciated that she didn't probe further into that exposed wound. "I wish we would've met earlier because then we could've teamed up to do something about this."

I smiled at her, feeling both gratitude and admiration for her can-do spirit. "I wish we had met earlier because you're a great friend, Cassandra."

December 2006

Dear Whitney,

Someone once told me that you should never request a letter of recommendation from someone unwilling to show you what they'd written about you, and I'm passing that advice on to you. Enclosed is a copy of the letters I've submitted to the MBA programs you've applied to. I hope it will be evident to the admissions committees and you that I think they'd be lucky to have you.

If you'll indulge me, I'll share another life lesson I've learned. Some of the skills that make me successful weren't directly taught in my college classes—things like listening to other people, working cooperatively, setting goals, and having a high level of commitment to make those goals a reality. You have developed these invaluable skills in spades.

Your leadership growth has been a true joy to witness. Carry those qualities with you, regardless of your career path. They will serve you and everyone lucky enough to be around you.

Coach Sam

CHAPTER 22
JANUARY 2007

I was shocked by Ms. C's revelation. The idea that a person I so respected and appreciated had to experience that hurtful and hateful treatment broke my heart.

It took me a long time to fall asleep that night. I covered the clock on my nightstand so I wouldn't be distracted by the time. The darkness of the room and my thick comforter enveloped me as my thoughts tumbled all over each other. I thought about Ms. C; I thought about Steph; I thought about Kelsey; I thought about former teammates of mine who might never have shared their authentic selves out of fear. Last, I thought about my younger self and the hole in my heart created by the feeling of rejection from within my family. Pain so deeply rooted can persist, solidifying its presence within us. It can become like carrying a bag of cement everywhere we go. Perhaps comprehending the source of our pain and summoning the courage to share our experience with others can allow us to leave behind that container of cement. Maybe by sharing our true selves with others, we shine a light that can guide us along a path from confusion and anger to understanding and happiness.

I wondered how different things might have been, especially my junior and senior years of high school, had I known about Ms. C's experiences. Would it have sped up my learning curve for what I was going through and feeling? Maybe when the outer selves of those you admire and respect look so strong, competent, and perfect, we wonder why we can't be more like them.

Would our personal growth benefit more from mentors, teachers, coaches, and parents honestly sharing their fears and struggles and how they deal with them rather than only showing a glossed exterior? Could we learn greater compassion for ourselves and others by embracing honest communication and acknowledging that everyone goes through struggles? Shouldn't we all be taught in youth that failures are inevitable if we set high goals, take risks, and push ourselves? If we allow ourselves to be close to others and be known, there will be disappointment, anger, and hurt accompanying the joy and celebrations. Can these lessons be talked about and taught?

I wondered if Steph looked up to me like I'd looked up to Ms. C. Did she falsely assume I had life figured out or that my life had been smooth because she saw how I handled situations now? That might only serve to create loops of destructive self-talk and self-doubt. I felt like a fake, giving off one impression as I tried to teach our kids about basketball and life, but not living out the same lessons in my own life. Do as I say, not as I do.

I needed to rethink what I shared with Steph about my own experiences. To share did not mean making my situation comparable to hers, but it could serve as a parallel, a lesson from my unguarded heart to hers.

I wanted the courage of those who speak and live their truth to become contagious. Ms. C showed her bravery by sharing her heartbreak, her low point, and how she learned from it. She let me see her inner self. I needed to find the strength to do the same. If we choose to be in our lives over performing in our lives, if we elect to belong over fitting in, if we pick loving ourselves over pleasing others, then the ripple effect on those around us could have transformative power.

Steph stuck her head in our office door to announce her arrival for her regular check-in with Fitz and me. "I'm a little early. Do you want me to come back later?"

"No, come in, Steph," I said.

Fitz spun around in his desk chair and motioned her through the door. We discussed Saturday's game, complimenting her again on her outstanding play.

"Steph the Stat Stuffer," Fitz said, clapping his hands.

Steph gave him a small smile. "Hey, do you remember Lauren? The guest speaker who runs the animal sanctuary?"

I nodded. "Of course. She's doing amazing work out there."

Steph shifted in her seat. "I was kinda thinking I'd like to go there. Not to work or get paid. I've just been thinking how cool it is that taking care of the animals is helping kids heal from trauma."

I nodded and waited for her to go on.

Steph took a deep breath and then went on. "I guess . . . I don't know," she stuttered. "Maybe I could help there, and it might also help me to process things. I don't know if you'd call it counseling, but that kind of idea."

I looked at Fitz, who was squinting at his computer screen and scribbling on a Post-it note. He turned and handed the note to Steph. "I think it's a great idea. And I'm sure Lauren would appreciate the help. That's her number. Give her a call."

Steph smiled as she reached for the paper. "Thanks, Coach. I'll call her this afternoon."

"Hey, speaking of volunteering," I said, "I also meant to ask about your new class schedule this semester. Are you still able to help in Amy's classroom?"

"Yeah, but only one day a week instead of two. I'm glad, though. I've enjoyed it." She picked up her backpack from the floor but paused once she had it in her lap.

"I also wanted to thank both of you for this idea of regularly scheduled meetings. I know I resisted at first, but it's been helpful. Instead of worrying about useless things, I think about going to Lauren's place or more constructive activities. I remind myself that I'll see you guys, which helps. Thank you for taking the extra time."

Steph stood up to leave.

"I'm glad you feel that way, Steph," I said. "And please remember, you don't have to wait for a Monday or Thursday. If you need anything, we're here for you."

When she was gone, I whispered, "Do we need to be concerned about her asking about Lauren's place? She specifically mentioned how the animals help troubled kids."

"I didn't get that sense from her. If anything, I saw all that conversation as very positive. We didn't have to ask questions to get her to share. She brought it up. She's planning and thinking about what will help her. I think it was all good."

"Okay," I said, hoping his optimism would rub off on me.

Friday morning, I'd been crossing so many things off my to-do list that I lost track of time until my stomach started growling. I still wanted to watch game tape but could do that while eating. I opened my door to head to the classroom and was shocked to see Kelsey standing there, hand raised, ready to knock.

"Kels. What a surprise. Do you want to come in?"

"Sure, please." She sounded hesitant and timid.

I shut the door behind us, and we both sat down. Kelsey didn't start talking immediately, but I waited and gave her space.

"Sorry I didn't call first . . . I . . . um. . . ." She shifted uncomfortably in her seat. "Um . . . I wanted to apologize . . . for quitting. I made a mistake."

Her eyes shifted between the floor and me. I nodded but remained quiet.

"I'd like . . . I was hoping I could come back . . . be on the team again . . . starting now? I wouldn't get any scholarship money; it's not about that. I miss the team and basketball." Her eyes were pleading.

Now it was my turn to look for the right words. "Gosh, Kels. This is a surprise. I'm sorry to hear that you feel like you made a mistake. Unfortunately, having you come back on the team won't work now."

Her chin dropped to her chest.

"We all make mistakes, and hopefully, we learn from them. It sounds like, by recognizing your mistake and apologizing, this was a lesson for you—a painful one."

I paused to see if she'd try to argue her point or get up to leave since she hadn't gotten the desired answer. She did neither, so I went on. "Even when we own up to our mistakes and apologize to the people we've affected, there can still be consequences. I know you didn't intentionally set out to hurt your teammates or negatively impact the team, but that's what happened. We've already worked through that setback and disappointment, and it would be too disruptive to the team now for you to show up out of the blue. Your situation is very different than a player returning after an injury."

"I know," she mumbled, still looking down.

"And honestly, it wouldn't be fair or respectful of your teammates' commitment to let you quit, have a month-long Christmas break, only to return six weeks later. Commitment doesn't work that way." I kept my voice neutral, but my message was direct.

"What about next year?"

"Well, I think that's something we could talk about later this spring."

"Could I apologize to the team?"

"I think that would be something later for the spring too."

"Is there anything I can do now to show the team I'm sorry?"

"I think the best thing you can do is to honestly reflect on what happened. Think about what led up to your decision and how that decision affected other people. You need to ask yourself if being back on the team is what you want and what you're willing to sacrifice and fully commit to. Use this time to ensure you are confident in your decision. Then your apology will mean more to the team because it will be sincere."

She looked up at me, her eyes full of hurt. "If I'd been more specific about why I'm sorry, would your answer have been different? I know I didn't handle things well with Jared and that he wasn't good for me. I can tell you more about that."

"No, Kels. This is about doing what's best for the team right now. But I'm glad that you came in to talk with me." I waited to see if she had anything else she needed to say. When she didn't, I went on. "Right now, focus on your courses. You'll need to make sure you're academically eligible next season. That's another way to show your commitment."

"Okay." She stood up to leave, and I stood up with her.

"I'm sorry I couldn't give you the answer you wanted. But I'm so glad to see you. I'm glad to know you're still here at school. Take some time to think about what you want. I hope I see you in the spring."

That brought a slight smile to her face. She looked at me directly and said, "You will."

It was 11:30 p.m. when the team vans pulled into the school parking lot. We'd cruised through our game that night, winning 83–50, but it had been a long trip, and most of the kids had fallen asleep on the ride home. I watched as players slumped out of the vans and headed for their cars.

Steph was the last player out of my van, and I pulled her aside to catch a private moment. I handed her a brown paper bag from our campus bookstore. In the semidarkness, she peered inside, struggling to figure out what was there.

"It's a journal. I know that writing can be a helpful way to sort through things during an especially stressful time. I know you've got a lot on your mind and in your heart right now." She gave me a tight smile and nodded. "Try it and see if you like it. I hope you find it helpful, maybe comforting in some small way. But you might not, and that's okay too."

"Thank you, Coach. I appreciate you thinking about me." She shifted her bag from one shoulder to the other. "I was going to wait until our next meeting, but I wanted to tell you I talked to Lauren the other day. She said she'd love to have me come out on Sundays. She's low on volunteers during the winter."

"Steph, that's great news! That's probably going to trigger some reflection too. I remember Lauren said something like, 'We can let our guard down around animals.'"

After a pause, Steph asked quietly, "Have you or Coach Fitz talked to her? I mean, about what's going on with me?"

"No, that's not our information to share. You decide when, with whom, how, or if at all."

"Okay. That's good," she said with a small exhale of relief. "I just don't want people to think negatively about my parents, you know, because they don't know them. My parents are good people." With all Steph was experiencing, her first concern was what Lauren might think about her parents.

"I know that, and you know that. They're just struggling right now." I leaned forward to hug her. "And you are a tremendous person too. Don't ever forget that."

She gave a slight nod. "See you tomorrow, Coach. And thanks again." She lifted the bag.

I gave her a wave and watched her jog toward her car.

January 2007

To: Kelsey Jones
From: Samantha Shuster

Dear Kelsey,

I send my best wishes to you as you start a new semester.
Make sure to keep your grades up! I'm thinking about you
and hoping you are doing well.

Coach Sam

CHAPTER 23

DECEMBER 1986

Before the next varsity game began, Lindsey and I sat in the bleachers watching the JV game. I asked about her classes, student government, and her boyfriend. She answered, but mostly with the usual brief, detached responses. I thought about how different things had become since we started basketball again. We remained friends, but we weren't communicating like we did during volleyball season. We sat for the rest of the half in a cautious silence, our self-preservation mode.

Everything about our season had gotten worse since Coach Walters started benching me without any explanation to the team. Our practices had become flat. Lindsey and I were the only players who talked while we were on the court, and even that was probably only about 10 percent of the time. The coaches and their whistles dominated the other 90 percent. Our teammates played with glazed-over looks in their eyes and a numb, robotic rhythm.

After the JV game finished, Lindsey and I walked behind our teammates, heading to the locker room to prepare for our game. I nudged her and slowed my pace to allow a little distance from the rest of the team. "Is it just me, or does our team seem comatose today? At this rate, by the end of the season, we may need stretchers to carry them on and off the court."

She let herself half smile and said, "Yeah, maybe we'll invent a new form of basketball that's played on gurneys."

We took the floor for pregame warm-ups, and I watched Lindsey come to life. Although it was a home game, we had no band, no cheerleaders, and no reporters or photographers from the local paper. Once the game started, though, nothing mattered as I became consumed with a fierce drive to win.

About two minutes into the game, on a dead ball, the horn blared. I didn't glance over to the bench; I usually didn't sub out. I was getting into position to inbound the ball from the sideline when I heard my name. Jill was jogging toward me and calling my name. I was stunned. I just told her the number of the player I was guarding and hustled to the bench. When I sat beside Coach Walters, he said, "Your girl got an offensive rebound. If you can't keep her off the boards, you won't play."

"Okay," I responded. I told myself he was using me to send a message about the importance of blocking out and rebounding. I could do that when I was back in.

He put me back in after two minutes of game time. I immediately lost myself in the flow up and down the court, defending and then trying to score. I got a steal and started a fast break, scoring on what turned into a two-on-one with Lindsey. It was a good momentum boost for our team, but I got subbed out again at the next dead ball. I sat down on the bench next to Coach Walters.

"What kind of pass was that? If you're going to be that careless with the ball, you won't play."

I hadn't made a turnover, so I wasn't sure which pass he was referring to. But I answered with "Okay." He put me back into the game with fifty seconds left in the first quarter.

The second quarter unfolded just like the first. I was arbitrarily pulled out again and chewed out for reasons that made no sense. At timeouts or halftime, he never once addressed the team about his concerns. To make things even more confusing, these "mistakes" apparently only mattered if I committed them.

We lost the game. Coach Walters didn't have much to share in his postgame talk. After he and the coaches left, the locker room remained quiet as we changed to sweats and packed our bags. Lindsey and I were ready to go at the same time, but I stopped at a side door.

"I'm going out this door. I don't want to see my parents or Cassandra and be forced to talk about the game right now," I said.

She nodded as if she understood. "Did he say anything to you?" she asked.

"Just when I came out. Things like I let my person get a rebound, I made a bad pass, or missed a free throw."

Neither of us had the energy or interest to discuss it further. We were deflated from the loss and the frustration of not understanding what was happening.

In bed later that night, I could hear my parents talking in their bedroom.

"I just don't understand, Mark. You saw it." My mom sounded exasperated.

"We don't know the situation, Suzie. Maybe he explained it to her on the bench. Maybe it was his way of trying to teach the rest of his team some lesson." Unlike my mom's emotional tone, my dad's voice was dispassionate.

My mom's response came out as a sharp hiss. "Why do you always defend him?"

Always! How many times had they discussed this? And why was this something we never discussed together?

Thursday's game was away, and as I visualized different parts of the game all day, it was as if my body felt it happening. It was our next chance to win and erase some of the pain of losing our first two games. The pain from losing lingered long after the final buzzer. Winning was the only remedy I'd found.

Lindsey seemed a little more talkative, which lightened my spirits. We were on the same page right from the beginning of the game. Either Lindsey or I got a steal in our first three defensive possessions, leading the way for an easy transition score. On the offensive end, we read each other's movements and anticipated openings to make scoring appear easy. We kept up the attack in the second quarter, and our teammates fed off our energy. Everything was clicking and felt effortless. We dominated the other team and went in at halftime with a twenty-point lead.

During the halftime talk, a positive energy hummed through us. And in the brief warm-ups before starting the second half, it looked and sounded like we still had all the momentum on our side. Then, with no explanation, Coach Walters began the second half with me on the bench. There were looks of confusion on my teammates' faces. I cheered from the sideline, hoping to communicate that things were fine. They weren't.

My palms were sweaty, and my heart raced as I watched the other team become more aggressive and confident with each possession. Our team's reaction was the exact opposite. By the end of the third quarter, our lead had been cut to six points. Their team sprinted to the sideline, slapping hands and celebrating with each other, while our team shuffled off the court, looking like they'd rather keep walking straight to the bus.

Without explanation, I remained on the bench the rest of the game, watching helplessly as our lead continued to dwindle. By the time the final buzzer sounded, we'd lost by ten points—a thirty-point turnaround in the second half.

Anger boiled up to my throat, making it almost impossible to mumble "good game" as we marched through postgame handshakes. When their coach got to me, he paused, and with a perplexed look, he asked, "Did you get hurt? Why didn't you play in the second half?"

"I have no idea. Maybe you can talk to my coach and let me know," I said, my voice full of venom.

In the locker room, our team sat silently, staring at the floor, waiting for the coaches to join us. I glanced sideways to gauge Lindsey's mood. She'd played hard and had a great first half, but she had no help against the press in the second half. I knew that's what she would remember the most from this game. When our three coaches finally marched into the locker room for our postgame talk, Coach Walters just rambled on about turnovers and poor press handling making the difference in the game. He ended by saying, "We showed good fight and never gave up." I thought he must've been watching a different team because, from where I sat, it sure looked like resignation to me.

On our bus ride back to school, I thought about how relieved I was to be leaving for my campus visit to Boise State the next day. My mom would take me to the airport in the morning, and I was happy to focus on volleyball for the weekend rather than thinking about this game.

Before letting us off the bus, Coach Walters stood at the front to announce an additional practice on Saturday. Now I'd be missing two practices. Would he bench me for the entire game on Monday instead of the first half? Or would he bench me for both games, justifying it by saying two practices equals two games?

Trying to fall asleep that night, I turned from side to side, looking for a comfortable position, trying to calm myself. The one thought that helped was to remind myself that I had volleyball as my ticket out of there. That was my only solace.

The following week was a haze of mixed feelings. If my trip to Sacramento had felt like a first glimpse at freedom, the one to Boise went even better. The team and campus were great, and everyone raved about Coach Stevens. Boise had a great vibe; I could see myself living there for the next four or five years. It gave me more confidence that I could be happy playing college volleyball if I did not have basketball as a way to escape.

That buzz did not last. As I expected, Coach Walters did not play me in the next two games or explain why to the team or me.

Lindsey's level of discomfort became palpable. I became disengaged and listless in the two places that generally brought some joy into my life—my English class and my workouts with Ms. Collins. I was going through the motions in everything except basketball practices. I channeled my fury to excel—I was first in every conditioning sprint; I was the best at every drill and scrimmage situation—because I didn't want to give Coach Walters the satisfaction of getting to me.

In everything else, though, I was methodically wrapping myself in a cocoon of cling wrap. It was a gradual process, starting at my feet and moving up, sealing off all sensory input, hoping it would shield me from the constant pain and anger. What would happen when it finally reached my face? Would I pass out, suffocate, and die? Would I even care?

I would've preferred to be like Teflon rather than feeling trapped in Saran Wrap. Then the things Coach Walters said and did would simply slide off. But that was a level of control I didn't have. Things seemed to be spiraling out of control with basketball and within me, but I didn't know what to do about it. The silence and inaction of those around me only compounded my misery.

We took the court on Monday for our final game before Christmas break. We were playing at home, and despite how things had unfolded during the season, I still felt the competitive fire burning in my belly. We were playing our cross-town rival. Their star, Theresa Eastland, was probably the most hated player in our league—a cocky senior guard, not nearly as good as she thought she was. Her play bordered on dirty, and she tried to get underneath everyone's skin with snide comments, always delivered out of earshot of the referees. I couldn't imagine anyone enjoying being on the same team with her. As much as I wanted to win every game, no other win would feel as good as beating her team.

During the last week of practices, Coach Walters started teaching a new defense for the team and, more specifically, for Theresa. It was a box-and-one, with Lindsey glued to Theresa every minute of the game. The goal was for her to keep Theresa from touching the ball.

We got off to a fast, aggressive start. Lindsey and I played well together, reading each other and responding in tandem to allow us to force turnovers. But then, in the first opportunity to run their half-court offense, their pass found Theresa open on the baseline, and she nailed a 15-foot jumper. Before the end of the first quarter, Theresa had been able to take three more open shots, each time with Lindsey nowhere close to her. As we jogged to the bench between quarters, I slapped Lindsey on her back and said, "Hey, you got her, Linds. Those are the only shots she's getting for the rest of the game."

At the break, Coach Walters focused first on our offensive execution before turning to the box-and-one defense. Theresa was getting open too easily. "Stick to her like glue! Otherwise, we can't play this defense," he implored no one in particular.

Unfortunately, for most of the second quarter, Theresa continued getting the ball. Coach Walters called a timeout with two-and-a-half minutes left in the half. Frustrated, he barked out for us to move into a straight man-to-man defense. Since he didn't specify who should guard Theresa, I called out her name as we ran back on court. I held her scoreless the rest of the half, and we went into the locker room with a six-point lead.

Nothing could have prepared me for his half-time tirade. Coach Walters stormed into the locker room right behind us as we hustled to sit in front of the chalkboard. Standing directly in front of me, Coach Walters started yelling over and over how we had worked on this special defense, and I just "floated out there in my own world." His face was beet red, eyes bugged out, and a vein bulged in one of his temples. Spit spewed from his mouth as he continued, unabated, with the harshest criticism and condemnation of me as a defender, a basketball player, and seemingly, a human being. I quickly dropped my gaze to the floor. All around me, it was silent.

When he finished, he stormed out, panting and snorting like he'd just finished hill sprints. The other coaches followed him. No one in the locker room said a word. When I stood up, my eyes landed on the chalkboard. The pregame notes were still there, and next to box-and-one, Lindsey's name was written in all capital letters. Next to her name were #22 and the name Theresa Eastland.

Coach Walters kept me on the bench the entire second half. We lost by seven points. Coach Walters made what had become his usual post-game comments. No one acknowledged what had happened at halftime.

I left the gym through a side door, preferring a long walk to the parking lot over talking with anyone in the gym. Outside, it was a cold, rainy, and windy night with only a sliver of moon, a perfect match for my dark and stormy insides.

To my relief, no one was in the den when I got home. I quickly headed to my bedroom, not wanting to see anyone. I heard my mom's voice and stopped outside my parents' room. I could tell she was mad.

"What is it going to take, Mark? How long will you sit by and allow this man to destroy Sam's spirit?"

"What do you want me to do?" My dad's tone was pure exasperation. "You want me to tell him how he should be coaching his team? Do you think that will make things better for Sam? She's already undermining him by working with that middle-school teacher, and now you want her father to swoop in and tell her coach that he's not doing his job?"

"This has nothing to do with coaching; it's a stretch even to call that man a coach. I have no idea why he's doing this to her—if it's anger that she has these volleyball offers that Lindsey doesn't, or that she's better than Lindsey at basketball . . . I don't know." My mom's anger was making it hard for her to talk. I could tell her mind was working so fast that the words couldn't keep up.

After a long pause, my dad finally said, "Suzie, what do you want me to do?" His response focused on placating my mom more than validating anything she shared or expressing concern for my well-being.

"You could start by talking to your daughter."

I'd heard enough. I'm sure my dad was as excited as I was about the idea of having a conversation. Even if he bothered to ask any questions, it wasn't like I could answer them honestly. It was difficult enough dealing with Coach Walters's treatment, but it would be far worse to deal with more of my dad's trite explanations for Coach Walters's behavior: he should be coaching boys; I shouldn't be so sensitive or take things so personally; if I couldn't handle this, I wasn't ready to play at the college level. It would be much easier to deal with my anger toward Coach Walters than with the shame I would feel in the wake of my dad's lecture.

January 2007

Dear Rachel,

I don't know if I can top the beautiful things Whitney said the other day when she presented you with our team's first Cinnamon Award, so I won't try. Instead, I'll echo everything she said.

When faced with personal challenges, it's much easier to shrink, retreat, and disappear. True courage is looking around and asking ourselves how to use our pain to serve others. That's precisely what you've done this season.

I know watching your teammates compete without you can't be easy. But from my perspective, they haven't. They haven't played a single game this season that didn't reflect what you've brought to the team in one way or another. You were an integral part of our team before your injury, but you are the heart of our team today.

Coach Sam

CHAPTER 24

JANUARY 2007

Steph beat Fitz to our Thursday meeting and was discussing her plans for the weekend when he arrived. He sat down without taking off his coat. "Have you already talked about the game?" he asked, looking back and forth between Steph and me.

I laughed. "Nope. We were waiting for you."

"Oh good, because I wanted to start by complimenting Steph on another great game. Your consistency has been amazing."

She shrugged her shoulders. "I guess I wouldn't have considered it consistent. I only scored half of what I did in the previous game."

"Consistency is shown in more ways than points," he said, unzipping his coat. "It's your defense, hustle, talk, rebounding, and passing. I know this will sound paradoxical, but you set the tone for the whole team while letting the game come to you. That is a tricky balance, but you've been doing it beautifully."

"Wow, Fitz," I said. "That's a great way of describing it. I hadn't thought about it in quite those terms, but you're right."

"What's the date and time?" He glanced at the clock on the wall. "I better write this down because Coach rarely says I'm right." He winked at Steph like they were in on the joke together.

She smiled. "Well, thank you. It has felt pretty good in the games. I think we are gelling as a team."

"Have you been doing anything differently?" I asked.

"I've always thought I was focused for games. But now, with so much going on for me away from basketball, I think extra hard about not letting those distractions affect me when I'm on the court. Does that make sense?" She didn't wait for an answer. "Right now, basketball is the only place where the issue with my parents isn't on my mind, distracting me. Sitting in my classes or trying to study, my mind constantly wanders to my family."

I nodded and said, "Do you have other outlets besides basketball? Do you have people you can talk with?"

"I think going out to the animal sanctuary will help me. I don't have to worry about burdening a horse or a donkey if I vent to them," she said, chuckling. "And I'm going to try writing," she said, looking at me.

I nodded again and said, "You used the word 'burden' to describe venting or talking about what's bothering you. Would you be burdening a friend if you shared with them?"

There was more silence before she responded.

"Well, maybe 'burden' is too strong of a word. But I guess I feel like everybody has problems and stresses. They don't need mine too."

"Nikki shared with you about the pain of losing her grandmother. Did it feel like a burden to you?" I asked.

She furrowed her brows and shook her head. "Not at all. I'm glad she shared with me."

"How would you feel if she didn't share that with you? If she only shared the positive things?" I asked.

"I mean . . . I think . . . I'd feel like she was keeping me at a distance. I'd probably wonder if she trusts me."

"Hmmm . . ." I mumbled, wanting to give her time to sit with those thoughts before continuing. "It's hard to ask for help and share our pains and sorrows with someone. It lets others see our weaknesses and failures. I'm not saying you do this with everyone you meet, but when it's people we care about and are close to, it's the only way to know them and for them to know us. It's about trust and authenticity. . . . It's about love."

Steph held eye contact with me as I spoke. Then she said, "Who do you share things like that with?"

"I've got two wonderful friends that go back to my high school days. One started as a mentor but has become a friend. The other was a friend from school. And I have Fitz."

She tilted her head and looked at me. "Not your parents?"

I shook my head before answering, "No."

She frowned slightly and turned toward Fitz. "What about you?"

"Well, I'm lucky enough to say my wife is one. Just because people are married doesn't necessarily mean their spouse is that kind of a true friend, weird as that may sound. And I've got a great friend from my college days. He lives in Colorado, so we don't see each other much, but I know he'd always be there for me." He nodded toward me. "Coach and I have developed a strong friendship even in the short time we've known each other."

"Not your parents either?"

"Well, mine are gone now. But even before that, I wouldn't have put them on that list." After a pause, he continued. "It's not that I didn't love my parents. I did, and they loved me. I'm sure that's the same for Coach and her parents. That parent-child relationship changes over time. There's love, but people also play roles in families. Sometimes those roles become so entrenched they never change, even as someone has changed as an individual. Unfortunately, those roles can keep us from truly knowing each other."

I gave him a minute to see if he'd go on, but when he stayed quiet, I said, "That's one of the things I love about coaching at the college level. It's a big transition period with lots of changes. For most of us, college is the first time we're carving out room for ourselves, discovering and creating our identities separate from how our parents defined us in our younger years. That's a good thing, part of the natural growing up process."

Fitz nodded. "Definitely. But that transition can be hard for parents to embrace fully. When their kids no longer live at home, they feel they're losing control. They may worry about their kid's safety or no longer having a say in their decisions. While the kids often feel excited about the independence and possibilities of the future, sometimes parents feel sadness and loss for a time they won't get back."

Steph crossed her arms across her chest. "Hmmm . . . my parents are having that experience on steroids," she said.

"Well, I'm not sure I'd go that far," Fitz replied.

Steph said, "You know what I mean. If this change is hard for parents in general, then my telling them that I'm gay just made it infinitely harder for them."

"It might mean they'll need a little more time," Fitz said.

I quickly added, "But remember, you are still the same amazing, generous, loving person you've always been."

Steph gave me a small smile. "Next week is my sister's birthday. Since they return my mail and won't answer phone calls, I don't know how to tell her I'm thinking about her."

I leaned forward, resting my elbows on my knees. "You could keep showing the effort by still sending her a card. You never know when things will change on your parents' end or what might be the tipping point."

She pressed her lips together. "Maybe." Then she glanced at her phone and grabbed her bag. "Shoot! I've got to get to class. Thanks, you two. Door open or closed?"

"Closed, please," I said. "See you this afternoon, Steph."

When the door clicked behind her, I turned to Fitz. "So many times, I've wanted to pick up the phone to call her parents and read them the riot act."

That night, we faced off against Great Falls. Their new coach, Rob Jeffries, was the arrogant young coach I'd met at the preseason coaches' conference, when he'd been brazen enough to announce that he'd joined our conference as a way of "paying his dues" until he could get back to "real coaching" on the men's side. Not that I needed extra motivation to want to win, but I was planning on our team dominating Great Falls tonight as our way of welcoming him to Kalispell!

Our team delivered! Playing on our home court in front of our home crowd, the team charged out of the gate, firing on all cylinders. Defensively, we created havoc, completely disrupting their game plan, while our offense appeared unstoppable.

Coach Jefferies's team looked robotic on offense as he tried to call everything from the bench. I felt terrible for his point guard; she spent more time looking to him for directions than looking at her teammates and our defense. They all played tentatively, afraid of making mistakes, knowing their coach had a sub ready to check in at any moment.

With eight minutes left in the game, Coach Jeffries sat down and did not say another word to his team. He'd thrown in the towel.

In our postgame talk, we praised our team's effort, execution, and mental focus. When a game becomes lopsided, it's easy for a team to play down to the level of the opponent. But ours remained sharp till the buzzer.

Stepping back into the gym, I saw MJ with her parents and a young man. I walked over to say hi. MJ introduced me to her brother, and her parents gushed about how our team was playing. I appreciated that they focused on the team and complimented several players by name, not mentioning their daughter once.

"Your daughter continues to amaze me, and we couldn't be happier having her here with us." MJ's mom and dad wrapped arms around her, beaming with pride. "I think an area of MJ's game that goes largely unnoticed is how mentally tough she's had to be. From her first day, she's been our role model for competitiveness." I paused to look directly at her brother. "I bet she can thank you and your brothers for much of what she learned in that department," I said, smiling at him.

They all laughed, and I said, "Seriously, Maddie's teammates weren't always as appreciative of her competitiveness as Fitz and me. That's not an easy spot to be in. With a little time and MJ's perseverance, it has finally rubbed off on her teammates. We're proud of her—as I'm sure you are."

Mrs. Jenkins's eyes welled with tears. She shook her head and blinked several times to keep them from escaping.

"I can't believe I'm going to cry," she started, sounding embarrassed and apologetic at the same time. "We can't tell you how happy Maddie is here, playing for you and Coach Fitz. This is the first time she has ever played on a team where she's been allowed . . . no, more than allowed . . . encouraged and supported to play with that fire she has. In high school, she'd come home after every practice and every game, and it was like a little bit of that fire had been extinguished. It used to just about kill us." MJ looked embarrassed to be the center of so much attention.

Mr. Jenkins jumped in next. "Maddie is so happy here. Every time we talk on the phone, we can feel her excitement when she talks about basketball and her team. Thank you."

"Thank you for raising," I pointed at MJ, "this incredible daughter and sharing her with us. And now I'm going to let you have her all to yourselves. Have a safe trip home." They beamed at MJ and thanked me again as I turned to leave.

At the far end of the court, I saw Steph standing with Amy. Steph was adjusting Amy's shooting form as she stood near the hoop. Amy's mom smiled as she sat alone in the bleachers, watching Steph and Amy. I wondered how long they'd keep buying the stories Steph was telling to explain her family's absence. One last glance at Steph nudging Amy's right elbow to be directly in line under the ball brought a smile to my face before I headed to my office.

Late Sunday afternoon, I decided to call my parents. My mom answered but had me wait so she could get my dad on the phone. They asked about my recent games.

"We've been playing well since the turn of the year, scoring in the eighties and holding teams under fifty. Things are clicking on both ends of the court. Our game this Wednesday will finish our first round of playing everyone in the conference. It's against Lewis-Clark State, the perennial powerhouse of our league. We are both undefeated, so it should be an exciting one."

"Good luck," my dad said. "We'll be thinking about you."

"Thanks, Dad."

Neither asked any follow-up questions, so after a brief and awkward silence, I changed the subject to something I knew they both cared about—my dad's season.

Just one question from me and he talked nonstop for over twenty minutes before my mom finally broke into the conversation.

"Oh, Sam, I keep forgetting to ask. Have you gotten tickets yet for your Hall of Fame induction in April? I want to ensure I've got it on the calendar to pick you up. Are you just going to fly in for the ceremony, or do you have time to visit for a few days? We're both so excited to see you."

I sat up, shook my head, and took a deep breath before speaking. "Oh . . . well . . . I got the invitation. It's nice, but I don't know if I can make it. That's a busy time for recruiting, and Fitz and I are usually at two different tournaments. I don't know yet."

"Don't be silly. You must come. It's an honor, and you and your dad will be up on the stage together." I didn't respond.

"You heard about that, didn't you, Sam? Chris Daniels is being inducted too. It'll be so exciting. You remember Chris; he was a year behind you." My dad said this as if I might not remember the guy who strutted around the high school like he owned the campus.

"Yeah, I heard. I remember he was always one of your favorites, Dad. That should make it an especially exciting ceremony for you." I was tempted to say that Chris hadn't had much of a sports career after high school, but I didn't say that.

They had never mentioned the letter I'd sent them. I'd been hoping that they'd read it, taken it to heart, and were quietly trying on their end. However, this felt like proof that it was a pipe dream. This was the same communication pattern we'd always had—if I said something they didn't want to hear, it was like yelling into an abyss.

I leaned back against the pillows on the couch and let my head tilt back. Even after so many years had passed, this was a pain with deep roots and deep meaning. I found it ironic that my parents wanted to celebrate those past accomplishments now; they certainly hadn't at the time. What had made my goals, dreams, and ambitions so easy to dismiss back then? The deeper problem and more profound pain were that those goals, dreams, and ambitions *were* me—*I* had been dismissed.

The conversation ended with a discussion about clothes. "Maybe you could come in a day early, and we could go shopping for something for you to wear," my mom said cheerfully. She then launched into a story about a recent shopping trip she'd taken with Emily.

Once we were seated in the office on Monday morning, I asked Steph if she'd made it out to the animal sanctuary the day before. Instantly, her eyes lit up.

"I did. It was incredible, and Lauren is so nice. She loves those animals . . . and I think the feeling is mutual."

"I'm glad you enjoyed it. That was a great idea, so I'm glad you took the initiative with it," I said.

"Hey, what did you decide to do about your sister's birthday?" Fitz asked.

She sighed. "I put a card in the mail to her today."

"You can just keep trying to leave that door open for when they are ready," I said.

Fitz shifted gears. "You know, I was thinking about you on my ride in today, Steph."

She let out a small laugh. "Uh-oh. Why's that?"

Fitz turned toward his computer, then looked back at Steph over his shoulder. "Do you know who Cat Stevens is? If not, lie to me. Don't break my heart."

Steph and I both laughed out loud.

"Yeah, I know who Cat Stevens is," Steph said with a smile.

Fritz looked at me. "Coachie, do you know who Cat Stevens is?"

"A little before my time, Fitzy." I winked. "Yes, I know who Cat Stevens is."

"Anyway, this song came on the radio and made me think more about relationships with parents. I haven't heard it in years. It's called 'Father and Son.' Now, I know this will be a new music experience for you. Unlike today's music, the idea is that you listen to the lyrics. They're actually saying something." Steph grinned and shook her head at him. Then she looked at me and rolled her eyes. Fitz clicked something on his computer, and sounds of soft guitar strumming filled the office. As Cat Stevens's quiet voice joined the guitar, we sat motionless and silent, listening to every word.

"Have you heard that one before?" Fitz asked Steph.

She shook her head. "No. But I liked it. That line near the end about how he'd agree with his folks if they were right, but they don't know him. I felt that."

Fitz shrugged his shoulders. "I think we all probably recognize that feeling. We want our parents to know and love us, but sometimes they forget we're independent. We're not just miniature versions of them."

Steph paused and asked, "Was it like that for you guys too?" She looked back and forth between us.

Fitz answered first. "Absolutely. More with my dad than my mom. My dad couldn't understand why I wanted to go to college since he hadn't gone. It was almost like he took it as a personal insult. It was as if my decision to attend college was me saying I didn't think his job, life, or choices were good enough for me. The reality was it had nothing to do with him. It goes back to that idea—he knew himself, but not what made me tick."

Steph took that in for a minute before looking at me.

"Me, too," I said. "I could come up with many examples, but after hearing Fitz's, the one that instantly popped into my head was with my mom. My mom has done the same thing as Fitz's dad but around marriage and kids. She can't understand why I'm not married with a couple of kids because it's so different from her life. She interprets my choices as a judgment against her. She's afraid she must have been a terrible mother for me to make these life choices."

Steph's eyes widened. "Wow! Well . . . thank you for sharing something so personal with me. It gives me a lot to think about . . . the song, which I liked," she said, smiling at Fitz, "and how things can be with parents. Maybe something to journal about."

"Yeah, how's that going?" I asked.

"I've never really done any personal writing before, only assignments I had to do," she said with a sheepish grin. "But I'm finding that I kinda like it."

"I'm glad to hear that. There's no right or wrong way; try to find what works best for you," I said.

Steph thanked us again and stood to leave, but then I remembered a question. "I saw Amy and her mom here on Saturday again. Did they ask about your family?"

Her cheeks puffed out with the air she audibly exhaled. "Yeah, they did. I'll have to say more if they keep coming to our home games. I don't know what yet."

"How about any of your teammates?" Fitz asked.

"I talked to Whitney after our game Saturday. I just kept it vague, but she's the only one," she shrugged. "Anyway, see you at practice later."

I tried to return to work, but Ms. C's last email had my mind wandering. Our conversation with Steph and the expression on her face when Fitz and I shared some difficult personal experiences with our parents remained with me. It had me reflecting on the profound impact hearing about other people's challenging personal stories can have on others.

January 2007

To: Laurie Collins
From: Samantha Shuster

Dear Ms. C,

I can't thank you enough for your last email. Your thoughts and support are invaluable to me and much appreciated. I was incredibly touched by your willingness to share such a painful personal experience. I won't lie—the thought of you being treated that way broke my heart.

I apologize for not writing back sooner, especially with the personal nature of your message. I tried to write this email twice before but deleted both attempts because I just couldn't find the words to convey my sincere thoughts and emotions. I'm so sorry you had to experience such a painful injustice due to others' selfishness, ignorance, and intolerance. We all know that bad things happen to good people, but when it happens to someone close, we feel it.

I've always admired and respected you, and I feel so fortunate to have you as a mentor and friend. Because of that, though your email was painful to read, it was also filled with a positive message of strength and resilience. It's given me so much to think about, especially as I'm working with Steph. Your courage in sharing your story inspired me, and I thank you for trusting me.

You guided, supported, and inspired me throughout my challenging experiences in high school, and I fear that my spirit would have been crushed without that. I learned so much from you. Here you are again, teaching and inspiring

me through your wisdom, strength, compassion, and honesty. You are the kind of coach I strive to be every day, and, more important, you are the kind of person I strive to be every day. I thank you with all my heart.
Your friend,

Sam

CHAPTER 25

DECEMBER 1986

The next day at school, following our loss and Coach Walters's explosion, I realized there were positives to being invisible. As I walked through the hallways and sat in classes, no one said a word to me or looked my way. I didn't have to put on a happy face and act like everything was fine when I felt the opposite.

At practice that afternoon, it was the usual routine. There was no mention of the game, the box-and-one defense, or why I didn't play in the second half. My dad walked through our practice two different times. He didn't stay long, and he didn't talk with Coach Walters. Maybe he was checking up on me, ensuring I wasn't giving Coach Walters any reason to bench me.

After practice, Lindsey and I were at our lockers together. Lindsey seemed unusually quiet and drained, with dark circles under her eyes.

"Hey, are you all right, Linds? You look tired."

"I look that good, huh?" She gave me a small smile.

"You can pull it off. If you keep this up for a few days, you'll start a new fashion that all the girls at school will try to copy."

She rolled her eyes, which I took as a good sign.

"Just a sec," she said. She walked down the aisle, glancing into the next few rows of lockers. "No one's here." She still looked uncomfortable. "Can we talk out in my car? I don't want anyone to overhear us."

I nodded and grabbed my bag, a pit forming in my stomach.

When we got to her car, we threw our bags in the back seat and sat in the front. She took a couple of deep breaths before starting.

"I didn't sleep at all last night. I overheard my dad on the phone. I was debating whether I should tell you or not. And whenever I came down on the side of telling you, I'd ask myself what you could do with this information. I also tried to think about what I'd want you to do for me if our situations were reversed, but honestly, I went back and forth. I hope I'm making the right decision to share this."

The suspense was killing me, and I had to bite my tongue not to yell, "Spit it out!" But I could tell how difficult this was for Lindsey. I had to let her tell me in her way.

Rather than looking at me, she stared blankly through the windshield. She took a deep breath before continuing. "I didn't think much about the call until I heard him say your name. I could only hear my dad's side of the conversation, but putting two and two together was easy. It was a college basketball coach asking about you. I know he's been unfair to you at practices and games, but this shocked me. The other coach must've asked him a question because he said, 'No. I've seen your team play. I don't think Sam could play at that level.'" With that, she let out a muffled cry that she'd been holding back, and it was my turn to stop breathing.

"Oh my God, Sam. I am so sorry. I hate to tell you this, but I also couldn't stomach the idea of you not knowing." She was crying now, squeezing her words in between her sobs. I still hadn't said anything. I was speechless.

"It's so unfair. But I don't know if there is anything either of us can do to change it." There were more sobs and gasps before she was able to continue. "And I'm so ashamed I haven't stood up for you this season. I kept hoping one of his assistants would say something to him so I wouldn't have to. Like last night at halftime—how did they let him continue screaming at you like that? I was the one who didn't do the job in the box-and-one, and everyone in the locker room knew it. But no one said anything. Oh God, I am so sorry."

Her head slumped forward, her chin on her chest, and I could see the outline of her shoulders shuddering with each sob.

Tears began pouring down my cheeks. We had always managed to skate around the edges, keeping a safe distance from the thin ice. Now we were standing right on top of it, hearing the cracks forming under our skates, watching them branch out like an expanding spider web, and knowing they could engulf us. Our crying was the only sound in the car, the sound of shared pain neither of us knew how to handle. Layer upon layer of this injustice had built up over our high school years. We had both seen it and felt it but had never put it into words before.

In some ways, it eased my heart and mind to hear Lindsey acknowledge what her dad had been doing to me. It validated my struggle, but it also confused me. *Why* was he doing this to me? If Lindsey could see it, why couldn't the assistant coaches? Why didn't they do something?

And what about my dad? That thought was like a blow to the stomach and triggered a new round of sobs. Although still painful, I realized it was easier to deal with this situation when I faulted myself, when I kept telling myself that *when* I improved, *when* I made it so apparent that I was the best player, *when* I played as near a perfect game as could be played, *then* I would be worthy of another coach, or my dad, stepping in on my behalf. Then, someone would validate that what I was experiencing was real.

"Thank you for telling me, Linds. I'm sorry you're being put in the middle of all this. It's not fair to you either." I didn't know what else to say. We sat in the car together for ten minutes, each of us alone in our thoughts. Finally, I broke the silence. "I guess I better head home."

"What are you going to do?" Lindsey asked.

"I don't know. But I'd tell you before I did anything." Confront her dad, tell my parents, go to the athletic director—none seemed like reasonable options.

"I hope you know how sorry I am," she said as new tears streamed down her face. "You don't deserve this." She leaned in to hug me. I hugged her with both arms. Once I'd fought back the lump in my throat, I said, "You don't have anything to apologize for, Lindsey. Thank you for sharing this with me."

When I got home, a powerful feeling enveloped me somewhere between closing the front door and closing my bedroom door, and I began to shake. Even my breathing came out in shaky bursts.

In a blind frenzy, I ripped my Spud Webb poster off the closet doors, tearing it into strips. I shredded my goal cards, tossing the pieces on the floor. My eyes burned, and my vision blurred. I yanked my top desk drawer out with such force it came out entirely and landed with a thud at my feet. I grabbed my record-keeping sheets—timed runs, shots made and missed, free throws made and missed—and tore them into bits.

Just as I'd finished destroying all signs of my basketball ambitions, passion, and life, I heard a light knock on my door. Emily pushed it open just a crack. Her expression told me I must have looked like a deranged lunatic, a psychopath on the loose. She glanced around at the demolition.

"What happened? Are you okay?" Her voice was filled with genuine concern.

"Get out." The first time I said it was in a steady tone and volume. But when she continued to stand there, looking shocked, I went ballistic.

"Get out! Get out!" I screamed. I raced to the door; she stepped backward, unsure of what I'd do. I slammed the door so hard I was surprised the frame didn't collapse. "Leave me alone!" The scream scratched my throat raw.

I dropped to my knees, and the dam broke. What had previously been silent tears became full, gut-wrenching sobs. I slumped over to my side, lying with my back against the door, my whole body heaving with the weight of my sobs.

I don't know how long it took for my tears to end, but I stayed on the floor, curled up, motionless, spent. More than anything, I wanted to be swallowed up by the night so I wouldn't have to face the morning, another day at school, another practice. I wanted to disappear.

The next day at school, everything was a dull blur. My mind replayed parts of the conversation with Lindsey and me screaming at Emily. I wondered how much she'd told my mother. No one had said anything to me that morning.

During practice, I tried to act as I always did—outworking my teammates and treating every drill as a real game. I'd wondered if I'd have a hard time looking Coach Walters in the eye after what Lindsey told me, but my years of experience hiding my true feelings and living behind a mask allowed me to keep going. Lindsey was quieter than usual in the locker room, and I was also at a loss for words. When I walked by her, I patted her shoulder to say goodbye.

"See ya, Sam," she mumbled back.

I hustled out to my car, fired it up, and turned the heater and the fan on high, though the blowing air was not yet warm. I stared blankly through the windshield, thinking about Coach Walters—how he was making the basketball season so dismal for me, ruining my friendship with Lindsey, and likely limiting my college basketball opportunities. I felt anger, and even hate, lodged deep in my gut. I didn't know how to deal with those feelings. I had no outlet for them, so they morphed into intense feelings of shame.

Who was I to feel anger toward my coach? Who said I was even good enough to play Division I basketball? Would it be his fault if I didn't get a basketball scholarship? Maybe my goals had always been out of my reach, set unrealistically high.

I slammed my hand against the steering wheel. What was wrong with me? My emotions seemed to be on a teeter-totter, going up and down between anger and emptiness, anger and despair, and then back to anger. Now the anger was turned inward at my emotional fragility.

The thought that these hollowed-out feelings would be with me for the next two months of my senior basketball season was a daunting and depressing image of my near future.

"I can't believe nobody said anything!" Cassandra sat back, eyes wide and mouth open, in the red vinyl booth. It was the first time I'd told anyone the story about Coach Walters screaming at me and pulling me from the game, and her outrage felt comforting and validating.

She leaned forward and looked me in the eye. "Were the assistant coaches there? Even if they didn't feel they could correct him in front of the team, they could have said something once they were away. Or at the absolute minimum, they could've said something to him after the game, and then Coach Walters could've said something to you, maybe the next day at practice. But he didn't, did he?" She took a long gulp of iced tea, looking at me the whole time and shaking her head.

I was amazed at how empowering it felt to have my unspoken feelings acknowledged. At the heart of Cassandra's message was, "Of course you're angry." There was nothing wrong with *me*. It was normal for me to be angry about how I'd been treated. And I hadn't even told her about the conversation Lindsey had overheard.

"And when he didn't say anything to you the next day at practice, you didn't bring it up with him?"

I twisted the paper napkin in my hand. My answer came out in a snort—the idea was so unrealistic. Her facial expression softened to a look of concern.

"I don't know how you do it, Sam, how you can stuff your thoughts and feelings down like that. You are way too nice. I would've spoken my mind, and then some, a long time ago."

I wished I had some of her directness. My attention and worry focused more on the response of others. I was a keeper of the peace, although lately, it felt like everyone else's peace but not mine. Was there a way to do both?

I slumped back in the booth and finally said, "Speaking of speaking your mind, what is the update on your letter to the editor?"

Cassandra flashed a sly grin at me. "Nice try, Sam. You're not changing the subject that easily; we will return to basketball."

Our waitress brought salads and some warm garlic rolls to the table.

"It got rejected by our 'big boss,' Mr. Ellis. He said if someone felt that strongly about the issue, they should be willing to sign their name. But I think there's more to it than that because when I asked him if he'd publish it if the anonymous writer agreed to sign their name, he never really answered."

Cassandra paused to take a small bite of bread and then continued. "Eventually, he said that even if the letter was signed, he didn't think it was appropriate for our school newspaper because the tone was overly critical and could lead to negative responses and even confrontation at school. How lame is that?" She rolled her eyes. "It seems like our newspaper editor doesn't understand or support the idea of free speech."

"Well, I'm still glad you wrote it, and I have a copy." I felt terrible about Cassandra's rejection, but I was relieved that my teachers and classmates would not be reading her letter.

"So I came up with a backup plan. Instead of the school newspaper, I will make a few modifications and submit it to the local newspaper. I'll be able to sign my name to it then." She looked triumphant.

I was stunned. I took a sip of water to clear my throat.

"Aren't you worried that people might feel like you're criticizing our school?" I felt my anxiety rising.

"Well, I am being critical, to an extent. But I'm not calling anyone out by name. I'm just shining a light on how things are at our school, and I bet it's like that at many other schools. My goal isn't to make people mad; it's to raise awareness. That's the first step to change something."

Cassandra appeared comfortable about her approach and showed no doubt or hesitancy. Thinking about how my words or actions impacted the people around me usually paralyzed me. If there were even the slightest chance that something might boomerang back negatively, especially to my parents or family, I wouldn't do or say it. But now, listening to Cassandra's reasoning, I realized if everyone approached situations like me, nothing would be questioned, challenged, or changed. My drive was to try and make everyone else happy; Cassandra was driven by something else, something more significant.

Her voice broke through my thoughts. "Enough about the newspaper; let's get back to basketball. What are you going to do?"

I shrugged. "Let my actions do the talking. I will show him I'm tough enough to take whatever he says or does to me. I will show him I'm not too sensitive and don't take coaching personally." Even as the words came out of my mouth, I could hear how they mirrored all the pitfalls of coaching girls I'd heard my dad repeat over the years. Was I trying to prove myself to Coach Walters or my dad?

"Sam, you're already the best, hardest-working player on the team. What more could you possibly have to prove? Sometimes, when something is wrong, you must confront it head-on. I think you've tried your way long enough, and honestly, it doesn't look like it's worked very well."

I blew out a breath. "From the outside looking in, it's hard to understand. But I think this is just part of sports culture. It's not bad or good; it's just how things are done."

"Well . . . there are lots of things that happen due to 'culture,'" she made air quotes with her fingers, "but that doesn't mean they're right, or even that they're the best way to handle situations. And it certainly doesn't mean that they should just be accepted. When something is wrong, saying it's just the culture doesn't give it a free pass." Cassandra gave me a serious look. She made it sound personal to her, and I was touched.

"Thank you for your support, and I know who I can turn to if I need help taking a stand and making a case. Right now, though, I appreciate you listening to me and caring. I admire your spunkiness."

She laughed. "My spunkiness, huh? That's a nice way of calling me a loudmouth, but I'll take it." She got quieter, then said, "I don't know, Sam, but it's not right."

"Hey," I reached across the table and squeezed her forearm, "this is the last time we'll hang out for a few weeks. Let's not make it a downer."

She sighed and nodded.

Driving home, my mind replayed some of our conversation. My emotions about basketball and Coach Walters had alternated between silent, seething anger and demoralizing depression. Neither was constructive, and neither propelled me into action. I didn't know who to turn to, what to do, or if I could even change how I used to react. My style had always been about *not* rocking the boat. Cassandra was willing not only to rock the boat but also to tip the boat over to see who could swim.

Maybe what I had always seen as respectful behavior only masked my feelings of unworthiness—I was not worthy of being treated better; I was getting the treatment I deserved. I knew Cassandra wouldn't allow herself to be treated this way; she wasn't soft, sensitive, or weak. Until I could change my personality, I couldn't expect to be treated any differently than I was treated now.

January 2007

To: Laurie Collins
From: Samantha Shuster

Dear Ms. C,

It is late, so I'll keep this short. Fitz and I have been meeting with Stephanie twice a week. I feel good about how she's doing and how open she's been with us. Of course, I still have a broken heart for her, but at least I'm not in crisis mode, worrying about her for things like severe depression or worse.

Today she asked Fitz and me a more personal question about our relationships with our parents. She was amazed when we each shared a struggle (one struggle of many!). It made me go back and reread your email and remember the shock I felt at learning about the personal trauma you had to work through. This made me think about the irony that strength comes from sharing our weaknesses, struggles, and failures.

Because of the impact of your letter on me, I am considering sharing some of my struggles with Steph as we continue this journey together.

I'm sorry this is such a brief note, and I hope it doesn't seem too weird. Thank you, again, for all that you have taught me and continue to teach me. Your friendship means more to me than I could ever put into words.

Your friend,

Sam

CHAPTER 26
FEBRUARY 2007

Our team marched through early February with military precision. Usually, by this time in the season, Fitz and I had to fight against a lull, the kids sleepwalking through their days. The seemingly monotonous routine could create fatigue that settled in like a heavy winter snow. Seeing our team so internally motivated and driven was a brand-new experience. I loved it.

Our meetings with Steph continued to evolve. She now shared openly, without prompting, and I felt heartened by that shift. One Thursday meeting, she rushed through our office door a few minutes late, holding the journal I'd given her.

"I'm so sorry," she said, dropping her bag on the ground and sitting down. "I sat down in the union to write and lost track of time."

"No worries, Steph," I said. "When you get in the groove, it's hard to stop. I'm glad you're getting to that point."

"Oh, yeah. I've never done any writing, but when I pick up a pen, it's like the rest of the world goes quiet. I'm working on a poem.

Actually . . . I've written several poems, but most sound like I'm still in the second grade or something. Especially the ones about the dogs out at the sanctuary," she said with a grin.

Fitz leaned back in his chair and crossed his legs. "I don't know. I'd buy a book of poetry about dogs."

She shook her head and laughed. "You'll get the first copy, I promise. Anyway, this poem I'm working on now is one I want to share with you two. When it's ready."

I looked at Fitz, then back at her. "I'd love to hear it. But don't feel you need to share your writing with us. It's just for you. It's not an assignment."

She opened her bag and dropped the journal inside, saying, "Oh, I know. But this one is something I'm proud of, or I will be once I've worked on it a bit."

That made me smile. "It's one of the things I've always loved about writing. It doesn't have to be perfect the first time for it to be beautiful in the end. Poetry's a challenge, though. How'd you end up there?"

"I don't know. I've never really read a lot of poetry. But then I started writing things down in my journal, mostly words, phrases, and questions since my thoughts and emotions don't appear in my head in fully formed sentences. When I go back and read through some of it, the broken flow and choppiness just made me think about poems . . . Or maybe that shows how little I know about poetry. That kinda sounds insulting, huh? Broken flow and choppiness," she said with another chuckle.

"Well, I understand what you're saying, but maybe you should think of some different descriptors before sitting down with your lit professor," Fitz joked.

"Good call. It's not quite ready yet, but I'll let you know." She sat back and folded her arms. "I've also been waiting to tell you I talked with Amy's mom at this last home game. Amy had gone to the bathroom, so I brought it up quickly when it was just the two of us."

She said all this as if I knew exactly what she was saying. When she didn't continue, I asked, "You talked with her about what?"

"Well . . . you know . . . why they never see my family at games anymore. Being vague would be enough if Amy and her mom came to just one or two games. But they're coming to every home game, so it wasn't feeling right."

I felt panic rising from my gut, seizing my heart, and constricting my throat. It was hard to swallow. My mind instantly went to the worst-case scenario. I pictured Amy's mom making hurtful, derogatory comments and then never bringing Amy back to the gym. I imagined her calling Amy's teacher to say she didn't want Stephanie working with Amy anymore. After losing her connection with her entire family, working with Amy had been a positive reminder to Steph: It reminded her that she had a big heart, was generous, and a good person.

"And?" I asked, trying to mask my alarm.

"I thanked her for coming to all the games and told her how much I enjoyed my time with Amy . . . that I thought Amy was such a great kid. And then I said that because they were at all these games and asking about my family, I didn't want to lie to them directly or by omission. I told her I'd recently come out to my parents, and they'd disowned me . . . at least for now, and I wanted to share that with her first. You know, to see how she felt about it and what, if anything, she thought I should share with Amy."

I realized I'd been holding my breath when I tried to ask the next question. "What did she say?"

"She listened and said how sorry she was for me, that it must be difficult and painful. And then she said she wanted to think about it before deciding what to share with Amy because she's so young."

Steph shared this in such a matter-of-fact way that my initial panic started to wane.

"What made you want, or feel the need, to share with Amy's mom, and possibly Amy next, before sharing with any of your teammates?" Fitz asked.

"Well, I guess I started thinking about it after you two told me about some of the struggles you had with your parents. I realized that we don't talk about that stuff enough. And then we start to look at other people's lives, even those close to us, and think they have it easy or their families are perfect when they aren't. I know Amy's been struggling with her parents' divorce, and I thought maybe if she knew a little bit about what was happening in my family, she'd know that lots of families go through hard times. Just let her know she's not alone."

I felt tears forming in my eyes. I nodded, but a knot in my throat made speaking difficult.

"What's the matter, Coach?" Steph looked genuinely concerned.

I've never been a good crier—either I fight to hold it back, which makes my face look like I'm constipated, or I cry and have red, blotchy, swollen eyes and snot dripping from my nose. Trying to hold it back is the better of two bad options. But as soon as I began speaking, tears slipped down my cheeks.

"Oh, Steph! I've always known what an amazing person you are. But sharing your situation with Amy's mom and *why* you did this is incredible. Here you are, still going through such difficult times, and yet you reach out to Amy showing nothing but thoughtfulness, compassion, and a generosity of spirit well beyond your years."

Fitz started talking, and I used the opportunity to grab a Kleenex from my desk.

"I couldn't agree more," he said. "That instinct is amazing. And I would add another reason—courage. You were willing to take a huge risk, not knowing how Amy's mom would respond. You still don't. Knowing that she might respond the way your parents did and still sharing—that's bravery, that's strength of character. Regardless of how Amy's mom handles this, I'm proud of you, Steph."

Fitz stood up, motioning that he wanted to hug her. When he let her go, I wrapped her in a hug of my own and said, "I'm so proud of you too."

We had never been competitive with the top teams in our conference. But here we were, halfway through the season, and preparing to play the conference's only other undefeated team.

The game started with both teams playing at a high level. It was back and forth for the first ten minutes, evenly matched. When they got a defensive stop, we'd get a defensive stop. When they scored, we'd score. It was uncanny.

Then, with five minutes left in the first half, they made a small run, and we didn't score on three straight possessions. I called a thirty-second timeout to stop their momentum and refocus our team. We executed well in the final four-and-a-half minutes before halftime and were only down two to end the half. I stepped into the locker room, feeling a surge of adrenaline.

"Congratulations, ladies. You just played one of the most impressive halves of basketball I've ever seen. And what I love the most is that it's not one of those crazy nights where everything's just magically clicking. This is who we are!"

I nodded to Fitz, who talked about two key points on the defensive end, and then it was back to me for the offense.

"Keep attacking. Our transition offense gives us great early looks, whether we're coming up the left or right side. Olivia will call a set play if we don't score a few possessions in a row. Their defense can't stop us if you execute like you did to close that half."

I looked around the room to make eye contact with each player. I could feel the fire burning in my gut, and I was sure they could see it in my eyes.

"Hey, are you having fun?" I yelled.

They all nodded, and a few called back, "Yeah!" But it wasn't the kind of energy that shook the walls.

"Are you having fun?" I yelled again, this time cupping my hands behind my ears.

Everyone answered this time, but I wanted it louder. I cupped my hands behind my ears again.

"I can't hear you—are you having fun?!"

This time, they yelled back, almost rattling the walls. Then, they jumped up and formed a huddle, ready to go.

"Enjoy every minute of this game. I know I am. This is the best game you can play: two championship-level teams battling on every possession. We've got twenty minutes left. Leave it all on the court!"

The second half picked up right where both teams left off. The lead changed four times in the first ten minutes. Coming out of a timeout, we ran a set play, and it worked beautifully, with Steph knocking down a three. Our bench went wild. We continued to battle on every defensive possession and executed well on the offensive end. But when the final buzzer sounded, we'd lost the game 68–65. Our team had done everything I'd asked, and I could not have been prouder.

They trudged back to our locker room, spent from playing their hearts out yet coming up a few points short of a victory. Fitz and I gave them a few minutes to collect themselves before joining them.

"I know that in our win-loss record, this one goes down in the loss column. However, you just played the best game we've played all season against the best opponent we've seen. That was the most consistent forty minutes of focus, intensity, execution, and unity that I've seen from this team. You know how much I hate losing, but I can honestly say that tonight, it does not bother me. You know why?" I looked around the locker room, making eye contact with each young woman.

"Because of tonight's performance, you all know what this team can do. This was our best game so far, but we will follow this one up with even better games. We are that tough and that good, and we will keep improving."

"Oh no, they're not going to take no for an answer," I grumbled into the phone, rubbing my temple. "I'm running out of ways to say I'm not coming."

"Suzie and Mark will wait you out. They're playing the long game on this one, kid." Cassandra chuckled on the other end of the line, and I had to laugh too. My parents were tenacious, that was for sure. "Hey, all jokes aside, I'm not trying to dismiss you on this. It's incredibly disrespectful of them to keep ignoring this boundary. You told them this ceremony isn't something you want to participate in, which should be enough."

"Yeah. I mean, this is part of the whole problem in our relationship. They stop listening if I say something they don't want to hear. It's the entire reason I sent them that letter—so they had a chance to process everything on their terms, then, they could decide what, if anything, they wanted to do with what I shared."

"Girl, that took courage. You laid your heart out and were vulnerable with them. Reaching out like that, doing your part to shift those family dynamics. . . . I take it that means they haven't mentioned it."

"Not yet. But here's the weird thing. I keep asking myself if I'm doing the same thing they're doing to me. Just like they wish I were different as a daughter, I wish he was different as my dad." I shifted on my couch, tucking my legs up under me. "Think about it—just like I could never be the outgoing, pretty, social type he admires, I don't think he can be a good listener. Maybe he's not someone who can share about himself and try to get to know me at a deeper level. Is it fair to want another person to give you something they are incapable of giving or being someone they are incapable of being? So maybe I need to change my expectations as much as they do. We at least need to reach a truce, but how do you ever do that when the other person doesn't acknowledge what's happening?"

Cassandra sighed. "That's exactly what you're trying to help them do. I hope they'll make the tough choice to reach out and meet you halfway. You keep putting the ball back in their court." She gasped. "Look at me with the basketball references!"

I laughed and shook my head. "Pretty sure that's tennis. But a solid attempt."

She giggled. "I'm taking that as a win."

My talk with Cassandra had given me a sense of optimism, so that afternoon, after a workout and some lunch, I decided to call my parents. My mom answered and quickly shifted to speakerphone to include my dad. I listened as she described a few work-related things, and my dad told me about his team.

At a natural pause, I asked, "Hey, I mailed a letter to you guys a while back. Did you get it?"

There was an extended silence on their end, and I heard my dad clear his throat. Finally, my mom said, "Oh! We did, yes. . . . Hey, tell us about your team. Are you still on track to make the playoffs?"

I shook off my initial confusion and gave them an abbreviated update on my team, including that we were likely headed to postseason play. She followed up with several questions, a rare occurrence, which I answered.

"Is Dad still there?" He'd been unusually quiet, and I thought maybe he'd left the room. Their answers were choppy.

"Yeah, your dad's still here," my mom said.

"I'm here, Sam," my dad chimed in.

"Oh, good. I'm glad you received my letter. Have you had a chance to read it?"

My mom's voice was tentative as she said, "We did . . ."

I felt my heartbeat in my throat. *Just keep putting the ball back in their court.* Maybe all that I needed to do was ask. This time, the answer was both immediate and abrupt. My dad cleared his throat again, then said, "Thanks for calling, Sam, but we've got to run. We're meeting the Randalls for a late lunch."

Before I had a chance to respond, I heard the click of their phone being hung up. I sat motionless, stunned and confused. I closed my eyes and rested my head on the couch cushion. They'd gotten the letter. They'd read it. They had nothing to say. Maybe they were writing back, taking as much care with their response as I had with my original letter. But if that were the case, they could've just said so.

Once again, I had gotten my hopes up, only to have them squashed.

February 2007

Dear Steph,

Thank you for how open and honest you've been with Fitz and me and for trusting us to support you.

I recently received an email from a friend—a teacher and mentor in my youth. She confided in me about a painful experience she had earlier in life, one that took a long time to recover from. Initially, it shocked me to my core. I felt outraged and hurt for her. After reflecting further, I began thinking about what we can learn from the people we know and respect when they share their journeys through obstacles, setbacks, failures, and heartbreak.

So often, we only hear about the positive stories, and her email made me realize that sharing our challenges is just as important—maybe more critical—than sharing our victories. Sharing those stories gives the teller power over their own story and allows the listener to see that life isn't a success-only journey. This may help the receiver avoid blaming themselves and internalizing the confusion that comes with the pain from their struggles. I want to share some personal truths with you now, not because our situations are the same—everyone's situations and feelings are uniquely their own—but because I want you to know that you are not alone.

Ever since you asked Fitz and me about our difficulties with our parents, I've thought about the irony of sharing an example specific to my mom. Although I feel like neither of my parents genuinely knows me, in reality, it has always been the relationship with my dad that has caused me the most inner pain and turmoil.

You might know that my dad is also a basketball coach. When I was young, it was something that brought us closer. But starting around middle school, I felt like a different set of expectations suddenly emerged.

None of it was necessarily spoken out loud, at least not directly to me, but at some invisible juncture, it became more important for me to look a certain way—namely skinny, feminine, pretty—and act a certain way—specifically, social and well-liked with lots of friends. I didn't fit that mold at all. I mistakenly thought that if I excelled in sports and had more athletic accomplishments, I could gain my father's approval and make him proud of me as his daughter.

I'd see and hear him praise my sister for the characteristics he deemed worthy: her social charms and looks. That hurt, but the part that was even more confusing was how much pride he'd show over some of the boys he coached on the basketball team. These players always had the best work ethic and were disciplined and committed. I couldn't understand why all the characteristics he praised in his players were a source of pride for him in them but not me. I wanted to hear my dad say, "Sam, I'm so proud of you. You have worked so hard. Look at what you've accomplished."

I didn't necessarily have the words then, but I'd describe it now as feeling "less than" but not understanding why. It felt like a rejection from my dad. Unfortunately, some side effects of rejection are a sense of shame, unworthiness, and not being enough—not good enough, not pretty enough, not social enough. I've had to fight those feelings and the conflicting desires to meet my parents' needs over meeting my own by being true to myself and who I am.

Parents may define us first, but if those definitions don't match who we truly are and what we want at our core, those definitions can limit us. That becomes the challenge, fighting conformity and not hiding ourselves or living part of our lives in some fantasyland to make others happy. The closer our inner and outer lives match, the closer we'll be to experiencing genuine happiness and inner peace.

From the outside, you'd probably think that my dad and I have a normal relationship. Still, the truth is that neither of us has been brave enough to be honest and reveal ourselves to each other, and that keeps us from having a genuine relationship.

I want you to know how much I admire your courage in being fully honest with your parents about who you are. As painful as it feels now, it is the best thing you could do for your relationship going forward. But it takes both parties being willing to go there, talk openly, and listen without judgment.

You've shown them that you are willing to do that. With all my heart, I hope your parents can recognize your honesty for the gift it truly is.

Coach Sam

CHAPTER 27
JANUARY 1987

For the first time ever, Christmas break and Christmas itself hadn't felt festive. It seemed like the weather outside and the storms brewing within me were coordinated. I felt deflated, and I was sure it showed. Either I'd hidden it better than I thought, or my family was preoccupied with the social activities of the holidays, because no one seemed to notice. Outside of basketball practices, I spent most of those two weeks alone. Even practices, once the primary source of my happiness, had become like every sad day at school. But I still had intense feelings of anger driving me, like I had something to prove. I still won every sprint and was the best in every drill, every competition, and every scrimmage situation. But I noticed a difference.

The fire that fueled me on the court felt like it started deep and spread upward and outward, like it was always burning just beneath the surface. It had a natural outlet. However, this new fire inside me was deep and smoldering, with nowhere to go. Inside, I was burning with anger. Outside, I was resigned to putting on a happy face and acting like everything was fine for the benefit of those around me. That act fueled my fury. Wasn't giving in and going along, being accommodating rather than taking a stand, what I'd always done? I simmered in silent rage while worrying about the cost of my silence and inaction.

A couple of weeks after we'd returned to our regular schedules, I sat at the desk in my room, working through calculus problems. The front door opened, and I paused to listen to who it was. Just as I heard it bang closed, the phone rang. My mom yelled, "I'll get it!" and I went back to finishing the last problems for my assignment.

Suddenly, Mom was standing at my door. "Sam, it's for you. Why don't you take it in my room?"

I nodded my thanks, crossed the hall, and picked up the phone as I sat on the edge of my parents' bed.

"Hello. This is Sam." I heard Mom hang up the line in the kitchen.

"Hi, Sam. My name's Coach Dan Reid. I'm the women's basketball coach at the University of Montana. Do you have a few minutes to talk?"

I sat up straighter, twisting the phone cord around my fingers. "Yes. Thank you for calling me."

"Today is the first day college basketball coaches can call high school players directly. You're my first phone call."

Coach Reid started with questions about how school and our basketball season were going. Then he described his team's style of play. He'd seen game tape of me and thought I'd be an excellent fit for his team.

Coming out of my parents' bedroom twenty minutes later, I could hear that Emily and my dad were home. With my mom's voice added to the mix, the three were animatedly sharing stories of their day.

I went into my bedroom and shut the door quietly to avoid disturbing the family gathering. I lay on my bed to contemplate what Coach Reid had shared.

I heard a light knock on my door. Mom opened it a crack. "Can I come in?"

I sat up. "Of course."

She sat on the edge of my bed, nudging in next to my legs. "So now it's basketball too?"

I nodded. "He's seen game tape of me. Thinks I'd be a good fit for their team."

"Sam, that's great! What's with the frown? This is what you've been waiting for!" I grabbed my pillow and hugged it to my belly.

"He knew I'd had some volleyball offers and reminded me that the volleyball signing date was much earlier than the one for basketball. It's nothing I didn't know. All the volleyball coaches have said they can't wait until the end of basketball season for me to decide. But hearing him mention it, it feels more real now. You know, the time pressure."

"Well . . . now that you're into the basketball season, are you leaning toward one sport more than the other?"

"Basketball is still my favorite and my best sport, but—" I let a long pause hang between us as I worked through the thoughts running through my head.

"But what?" My mom asked.

"But we were much more successful in volleyball than basketball, and it's always more fun winning. Also, we were seen by more coaches since we went to districts and state, which we obviously won't do in basketball. It's feeling like the difference between a guaranteed versus a possible scholarship. Honestly, it's hard not to go with the sure thing," I said.

There was so much I'd left out, like I'd be spending so much time riding the bench that I couldn't be sure they'd see me play if a scout came. If they did, the level of play wouldn't be nearly the same as what we'd had this volleyball season; they might be unimpressed. They'd want to talk to my coach even if they liked the way I play. Every new layer made the possibility of a basketball scholarship seem more and more like a pipe dream.

Mom's voice cut through my thoughts. "I know this is so hard for you. I wish there were something I could do to help."

"You are, Mom, just doing this," I reassured her. She smiled and squeezed my knee, but her smile didn't reach her eyes. Her smile said everything would be fine; her eyes told a different story—one of worry. Most people read the smile more than the eyes. But the eyes are real. Had my parents never looked into my eyes?

"If you took the volleyball scholarship, could you be happy playing that sport for four years? I mean, since you said basketball is your favorite sport?"

I nodded. "Yeah, I think so. It would be fun if I like my teammates, especially if we're winning."

"Then maybe trying to see it as a win-win situation might make it less stressful. It'll be good, whatever you decide." She pulled me into a hug.

Her eyes roamed around my room, taking in everything. After a short pause, she said, "I can't believe how different your room looks with everything off your closet doors. Why the change?"

I didn't know if Emily had said anything about that afternoon.

"Just time, I guess." I tried to keep any sadness out of my voice. I was relieved when she didn't push it.

After she left I got into bed, though I knew I wouldn't fall asleep right away. Shortly after I cut off my light, I heard my parents enter their bedroom. My mom told my dad about my phone call and asked if he'd talked with me about my college decision lately. He must have entered their bathroom because I couldn't hear his answer.

I could hear the frustration in my mom's voice. "I wish you'd talk to her. You know a lot more about the recruiting process than I do."

Then I heard my Dad loud and clear. "Suzie, how many times do I have to tell you? She doesn't want to hear what I have to say, especially after the big volleyball coaches were here putting ideas into her head about playing Division I. She could simplify this by starting at the community college, where she could play both sports."

"How can you say that? They offered her a scholarship. They must believe in her abilities and potential. Do Sam's wishes fit into your equation? This transition to college, more independence, and being away from home need to be her decision. Sam has always been mature beyond her years. I trust her judgment. I wish you did, too, and you'd support her more. If you treated her more like the boys you coach, we'd be in a good place."

It was some relief knowing that my mom recognized that Dad wasn't supporting me like he did his own players—it wasn't just my imagination. I appreciated her recognizing this and trying to stand up for me, though it didn't seem to be helping.

I turned on my radio to help block out their voices. I didn't want to hear any more of this conversation. It seemed like it would make more sense for all three of us to sit down to talk about these issues instead of my mom playing messenger between my dad and me. But I guess that pattern had developed for a reason. Making new patterns might be too difficult, maybe impossible.

As I stepped onto the bus, I spotted Lindsey, but not in our usual spot in the back. She was leaning against a pillow, wearing headphones with her eyes closed. Without her, I felt alone, even among my teammates.

During the first half of the JV game, I sat next to her in the bleachers. We hadn't talked much, but I held out my right hand, pinky finger extended, and said, "We still have a deal, and we're still in this together." I breathed a sigh of relief when she gave me a weak smile, extended her pinky and shook on it.

We played tentatively on both ends of the court in the first half of our game. At halftime, Coach Walters told us that we weren't doing anything we'd been working on at practice, so he was done coaching for the night. He sat at the end of our bench with his arms crossed over his chest for the entire second half and said nothing. The two assistant coaches did a little subbing, called one timeout, and talked to us between the third and fourth quarters.

If Coach Walters thought his actions would fire us up, he was wrong. It had the exact opposite effect. Lindsey and I maintained our intensity, but no matter what we did or said, it was like we were playing two against five; the rest of the team was shell-shocked. We lost by 22 points.

After the game, Coach Walters didn't come into the locker room to talk to the team. The assistants told us to be ready to leave in five minutes since we had a long drive.

I was last off the bus, and everyone shuffled to cars, looking like a funeral procession. All three coaches stepped off shortly behind me, and I heard Coach Walters say goodnight to them.

Then he called my name. "Sam. Come here a minute." I turned and walked back to where he was standing. "Where were you tonight?"

"Where was I?" I slowly repeated, confused by his question.

"You think you're so good. Have you looked around you, Sam, or are you so caught up in your goals that you're blind to reality? We don't have much basketball talent on this team, which translates into you looking like a superstar. You parade around here like you're so much better than everyone, but if we had any basketball players, you wouldn't start, you wouldn't even play that much, and you certainly wouldn't score 20 points a game."

He stepped nearer to me, so that his face was close to mine. I maintained eye contact, though his glare indicated he'd prefer to shoot daggers at me instead of words.

"You are not a college basketball player, and that is exactly what I will tell any coach who calls me. You are all show and no substance, both on and off the court, and don't you forget it!" He spun around and strode away; I think I finally blinked and took my first breath when he was in his car.

His message was anger mixed with hate and contempt; all I could do was stand there, frozen in disbelief.

I watched him peel out of the parking lot before I walked to my car. I threw my bags in the back seat, turned the key in the ignition, and switched on my headlights. I was halfway home when I realized I was shaking.

The front door had been left unlocked for me. Instead of going to my room, I walked through the kitchen to our den. My legs were rubber, and I collapsed onto the couch. Sitting there in the darkness, I focused on slow, deep breathing. My mind was numb, but my body felt jumpy all over.

I must have been sitting like that for twenty minutes when the small kitchen light above the sink came on, and footsteps moved through the kitchen, stopping at the edge of the room.

"Sam, is that you?" It was my dad.

"Yeah, sorry if I woke you." I was relieved that he hadn't turned on more lights.

"Well, it's 12:30 a.m. Aren't you going to bed?"

"In a minute."

"Did you guys win?" He did not come any farther into the room.

"No."

"Well, did you at least have fun? Those long bus rides can be great for team camaraderie, even if you lose."

Fun? Long bus ride? Losing? Who did he think he was talking to—Emily? Would *he* ever feel that way or encourage his team to feel that way?

"Yeah, Dad. We had fun." Somehow, even though his question struck a raw nerve, my voice remained monotone, revealing nothing of what I was thinking or feeling.

After a pause, he said, "We can't lose sleep over our losses, so get to bed. It's late. Goodnight."

I wanted to tell him that if I lost sleep over losses, I wouldn't even bother going to bed during this basketball season.

The next day's practice went surprisingly well. Not only did my teammates seem to have more positive energy and talk throughout, but Coach Walters was also in a better mood. He seemed to want to be there.

After he dismissed us, I caught Lindsey.

"I was going to stay and do some shooting. Want to join me?" I held my breath, hopeful.

"No, sorry, I've got to go."

I exhaled and felt as deflated as her voice sounded. This distance between us felt like a form of torture. I didn't know what else I could do. I kept trying to clarify to Lindsey that none of her dad's actions affected my feelings toward her. I'd have to give her the time and space she needed and hope we could put this behind us before senior year ended.

I knew the boys' team would be in for practice in about thirty minutes. I jogged to the opposite end of the gym and started with my shooting routine. The repetition felt good. There was only the sound of the ball bouncing, my shoes squeaking, the net swishing, and my breathing—it felt like meditation.

Their shouts and laughter entered the gym before the boys did. That was my cue to leave. I changed into my running shoes and headed to the track.

After pushing myself to exhaustion, I began thinking again about my college decision. Volleyball or basketball? Sign now for a sure thing, or wait for an unknown? Would I ever grow to love volleyball as much as basketball if I focused only on volleyball?

But basketball had been a big part of my life for so long. And with basketball, I would get even better once surrounded by players who were better than me. It would be what I needed to propel me to reach my full potential. That inner desire to be great wouldn't disappear if I switched sports, but I questioned whether I could attain that same high standard in volleyball. The bottom line was that I knew I wouldn't be content reaching the end of my playing career only being average. No matter which sport I chose, average was unacceptable.

The phone rang on Sunday afternoon. Emily knocked and said it was for me. It had to be Coach Stevens. I'd already had a call the day before from Coach Braxton. She could give me one more week to make my decision. I'd assured her that I understood.

"Hi, Sam? This is Lori Stevens."

Our phone conversation went much like the one with Coach Braxton. She'd call in a week to see where I was with my decision. I assured her that I was aware and looked forward to her call. I hung up, trying not to think any longer about volleyball right now.

I heard Mom in the kitchen getting dinner ready. Wouldn't you know I would get this call right before one of the rare nights during basketball season when we would be eating as a family? I hurried into the kitchen to help my mom and was relieved when she asked about my classes and exams rather than my phone call.

After I set the table, she rounded up Emily and Dad, and we sat down to eat. We all took several bites in silence before my mom asked, "Sam, what about your phone call earlier?"

I was a bit surprised. It wasn't like her to put me on the spot like that, especially with my dad and Emily present.

"One of the college volleyball coaches called to see if I'd made any decisions. The other coach called yesterday. Both said they'd need a decision by next weekend."

"What if you're not ready to decide?" she asked.

"Then they'll have to offer the scholarship to the next person on their list, and they wouldn't be able to guarantee that they'll have a scholarship available for me."

"Have you decided on a sport?" My dad's question stunned me, not the question itself, but that he'd asked one.

"Not really," I said.

My mom started to ask a question, but my dad started talking simultaneously, so my mom quit midsentence.

"That's been my big message to Chris in all our talks about college. The sooner he can decide between football and basketball, the better. Then when he takes his campus visits, meets coaches and teams, that kind of thing, he'll be comparing apples to apples—" And he was off.

I glanced at my mom and Emily to see if I could read the response on their faces. Both were staring directly at him and listening with full attention. After his lengthy story, he paused for a sip of water, and Emily jumped into the quiet space.

"Are you guys in first place in the league, Dad?"

I sat back in my chair and slowly chewed my last bites of dinner. I could relax now, because we'd never get back to my college decision.

Dad continued his story of the season so far, needing no other questions to prompt him, as we all started grabbing our dishes and taking them to the kitchen.

"Dad will help me with the dishes tonight so you two can return to your schoolwork and still get to bed at a reasonable hour."

I marveled at the realization that the time my dad spent talking about Chris over a single meal exceeded the total time he'd spent helping me with my decision. I wondered if he had given Chris the idea of a community college. The thought made me laugh out loud.

February 2007

Dear MJ,

I recently came across a quote from the soccer star Mia Hamm that reminded me of you and of the conversations we've always had about embracing competition:

"Somewhere behind the athlete you've become, and the hours of practice, and the coaches who have pushed you, is a little girl who fell in love with the game and never looked back … play for her."

As little girls, we're often praised for our grit, tenacity, and drive because the adults in our lives love to see us giving our all and being unafraid to reach our goals. We don't do it for their praise but because it is innate.

As adult women, we must protect that little girl inside us as the world tells her she is too hard, aggressive, and bold. She's the source of our passion. She's the one who will push us to keep going. She's the one who wins championships.

Thank you for being you, even when the world tries to convince you to be someone else.

Coach Sam

CHAPTER 28

FEBRUARY 2007

Fitz and I were excited about how our team was coming together. They moved through the week like they were the only people around, and basketball was the only thing on their minds. Yet amid this mission-driven focus, our kids seemed to have more fun than ever. I credited this mainly to our extraordinary senior leadership—and to winning! Winning makes it easier to ignore things that might otherwise ruffle feathers, softens the blow of less playing time than a player wants, and adds fun to a demanding and repetitive schedule. For our seniors, I was delighted that their commitment through the previous three years was paying off.

Wednesday's game on the road was another solid 20-point win. On top of that, Stephanie had brought her book of Mad Libs and her crazy sense of humor along. Having that part of her personality return was like a breath of fresh air.

With our win on Wednesday, we secured a spot for the postseason tournament, something done only once in the women's program at our school. But Fitz and I weren't yet talking about that with the team. I chalked up our hesitancy to our own nerves or superstition because the team's focus all season made them more than capable of handling the added pressure.

We were on a roll with another large crowd for our next game. Before the game started, I stood on the sideline, looking up into the stands, in awe of the crowd's support and energy. Then my eyes locked on a familiar face. Kelsey sat in the top row, her eyes expectantly scanning the court until her gaze met mine. She gave me a shy smile and raised her hand in a small wave. I smiled, waved back, then turned to my players, waiting for final words before tip-off.

We did not disappoint. When team's win regularly, a coach's most significant concern often becomes complacency. Our kids showed none of that, and not because Fitz and I had cracked the whip. It was as if our team had taken on a collective personality with our seniors' focus and self-motivation, MJ's competitive fire, and Steph's lighthearted love of the game. I could not have created a better mixture if I'd been able to handpick the team like the ingredients of a recipe.

The following day, as I walked down the hall toward our office, I could hear Steph and Fitz bantering back and forth. I couldn't make out what they were saying, but the conversation was full of the gregarious energy that made them both special.

I rounded the corner, and Fitz gestured to me. "There she is! Sit, sit. Steph's got a story, but we were waiting for you."

"What's new, Steph?" I said as I rounded my desk and plopped down in my chair.

"Last night, Amy asked me when my parents would be at another game. My mom always brought snacks for her to eat in the stands, so I think she mostly wanted to know where the cookies were, right?" Steph laughed. "I froze because I still hadn't finished thinking about what to tell her. But when I looked at her mom, she just nodded at me, like it was okay to share with her."

"And? How did it go?" I asked.

Steph laughed again and put both hands on top of her head. "It was a nonevent. She was funny about it. I'd thought a lot about how I wanted to frame it to her once I got the okay from her mom. So I told her that I had recently shared with my parents that I was gay and that they were struggling with that. I told her they needed time away from me to deal with it. I tried to keep it simple and honest but didn't want to give her more information than necessary. I figured she'd ask questions if she wanted to know more."

"And did she?"

"Nope. She said something like: 'Well, that's silly. You can't get mad at someone for telling the truth. And they're missing a lot of great games.' It was just so matter of fact how she said it. Her mom and I both laughed."

Fitz and I broke out in laughter too.

"Kids are great, aren't they?" I said. "They're direct because they don't know any other way yet. And they're curious because they want to understand, not to judge and gossip. I don't know when that all changes, but it's too bad that it does."

It was the last weekend in February, and although we'd made it to postseason play, the momentum had been building toward our final home game against Lewis-Clark College, the only conference team that had beaten us that season. This was why our team hadn't celebrated the idea of making the conference tournament: they still had unfinished business to take care of that night.

The last home games were an opportunity to honor the seniors. This year was even more special; this senior class was the first one Fitz and I recruited together. They were willing to take a chance on us, new and unproven coaches, at a school where the women's basketball program finished in the bottom third of the conference every year. Olivia, Whitney, and Heather had given us nothing less than their best, on and off the court, for four years.

We announced each player and their parents and celebrated their contributions to the team. Fitz and I pulled them aside before sending them off to their teammates.

"Enjoy this special night and know that the three of you are the reason it's not the end of our season. Thanks to you, your play, and your leadership, we will compete in the conference tournament for only the second time in program history. Play your hearts out tonight, and enjoy every minute of it," I said.

Fitz added, "We are so proud of you!"

With that emotional start, we were ready for the game to begin. Much like our first meeting, the game was a back-and-forth battle. We came up short again, but I could only feel good about our performance.

In the team room, Fitz and I had nothing but praise. To wrap it up, I said, "You only have tomorrow to feel the disappointment for this loss. By Monday, we need you here wearing your warriors gear. Of course, we're excited about making it to the conference tournament, but just making it is not enough for us. We're going there to win, and I think there's a good chance we will play this team again before the season ends."

Fitz showed up to our office on Monday full of energy and excitement, like it was the first day of the school year and our first practice.

"So, did your parents call you yesterday to congratulate you? Are they coming to the tournament?"

It killed me to burst his energy bubble, but I also had to be honest. "Uhh . . . no . . . and no."

He stopped short, and his face changed from a smile to a blank expression, to confusion, and then to frustration, all in ten seconds.

It would've been impressive had it not been in response to a subject so close to my heart.

By the time Fitz asked, my heart was already shielded behind layers of steel. The day before, while I studied the game tape, I'd watched the clock, imagining what my parents were doing and wondering when they'd call. It didn't sink in until nine that they weren't going to, and I began raising my defenses to minimize my disappointment. I kept repeating to myself: "*I don't need your validation.*"

Fitz's irritation was evident as he blurted out, "They didn't even call you yesterday?!" His frustration and anger were on my behalf as he started pacing, but he could take only three steps in our small office before having to retrace his path. "You know, we've worked together for four years, and I've never even met your dad. He hasn't been out here, not one time."

I started to say something about his coaching schedule, but Fitz stuck his hand up to stop me. "I know he coaches basketball and our seasons overlap but *come on*. He could visit in the fall, see your house and where you work, meet the people you are close with, and watch the team with our fall workouts. Or he could come in the spring. He's made no effort, and I find it inexcusable."

"Look, Fitz, you're right on all counts. You are. And I appreciate your concern, but I'm trying to stay focused on what is happening now. I don't have space for what isn't." I sensed a blush rising on my neck and felt flustered. I felt an intense desire to defend my dad and explain it, but I couldn't. Instead, I gathered a stack of folders from my desk. "I've got a meeting across campus. I'll be back in a couple of hours."

The next day, Fitz got to the office early. I looked up to greet him and saw him holding a large bag. Even across the room, I knew the smell of peanut butter chocolate chunk cookies, my favorite. He gave me a sheepish look, placed the bag on the corner of my desk, and stood there with his hands clasped.

I chuckled. "Looks like somebody wants to do some buttering up. It'll take more than cookies, mister. What is it you want? Drive the new van? Get out of laundry duty?"

He ran his hand through his hair, then shook his head and started to take off his coat.

"No, it's more of an apology for yesterday. I feel bad about how I overreacted about your parents. And we don't know they're not coming just because they didn't call. I assumed and spoke before really thinking."

He pulled his chair close to mine and sat down.

"Oh, Fitzy. I told you yesterday that I understood where that came from, and there were no hard feelings. You didn't need to apologize. Really."

"I wanted a second chance to say something about that, and then I'll let it drop . . . at least until after the season. I promise."

"*Now* I understand the real reason for the cookies," I said as I reached into the bag and pulled one out. "You figured if I was eating one of my favorite treats, it would help soften the edges of what you wanted to tell me." I acted like I was looking inside the bag. "Hmm. I see many more in here. Is that a sign of how serious this topic is or how much you will talk about it before you drop it?"

I took the first bite and let it melt on my tongue, savoring the flavors of peanut butter and chocolate. "Mmm . . . okay, I think I'm ready now. Go ahead," I kidded him.

He smiled. "I sincerely hope your parents will be at the tournament and are intentionally staying quiet to surprise you. But if not, I hope they'll find a way to show their support and celebrate from a distance." I nodded at his thoughtful message.

"The second part is more about your relationship with your dad . . . or, more specifically, the one you *wish* you had. Sam, the relationship you had as a kid doesn't have to be the same one you have as an adult. Too many times, we think we know each other while we may only be looking at a snapshot in time. There's more to your dad than the parts you know from his role as you grew up in his house. Especially things from his childhood and earlier experiences, as well as inherited DNA from his parents. It's like that for all of us, tracing back to previous generations in ways we don't always see or understand and, therefore, don't discuss."

He leaned forward and looked into my eyes. "And there's more to *you* than what he knows from the eighteen years you were under his roof. But nothing will change unless you, and more important both of you, look for different ways of communicating and are willing to reach out to each other. Staying silent and hoping they'd get your message through your actions allowed them to continue the same patterns, blissfully unaware of the pain it was causing you. But now you've told them. Now it's their responsibility." I could hear Cassandra. *Just keep putting the ball in their court.* "Have they mentioned getting your letter?"

I'd finished my first cookie at this point. "Hmm . . . I might need a second cookie for that conversation."

"I brought a whole bag."

I shared my difficulty interpreting my parents' nonresponse response from our last phone call. "I guess it's like the saying: 'You can lead a horse to water, but you can't make it drink.' I'm trying not to jump to conclusions or make assumptions, but it's challenging. I thought maybe they were working on a letter to send to me. I didn't write mine in one day. Or maybe they'll surprise me at the tournament. I'm trying to be patient."

He took a deep breath before speaking. "I'm sorry to hear that. Getting that kind of response after putting yourself out there must be disappointing and painful. I'm glad you're trying to be patient and give them time. I sincerely hope they see this as an incredible opportunity to change the patterns and dynamics that have been established and change your relationship for the better. You were brave enough to extend your heart to them, and now it's their turn to do the work and extend their hearts to you."

I nodded and paused before continuing. "But what if my dad doesn't think anything is missing in our relationship? What if, in his mind, it's fine as is? What if we have very different definitions of what it means to be close to another person, to know them? What if sharing my truth and vulnerability is met with a lack of acknowledgment because he doesn't see it? Or what if it's met with outright denial? How do I move forward from there?"

Fitz sighed. "Those are great questions with no easy answers. Sometimes, you might move backward, stay in place, and then push forward again. It's complicated. At some point, we all must decide where our boundaries are, where we can find a healthy balance between accepting each other with all our flaws and feeling like we can fully be ourselves. And of course, always leaving open the possibility for those boundaries to move as people change, learn, and grow over time."

I smiled at him. "This is all great food for thought." I reached out and put my hand on his arm. "I appreciate you spending time thinking about this and sharing it with me. That's being a true friend. Thank you."

He patted my hand and said, "It is a lot to take in and process. Can I leave you with one more question to chew on?"

"Of course."

"Do you need an apology to reach forgiveness?"

February 2007

To: Laurie Collins
From: Samantha Shuster

Dear Ms. C,

It is now safe to say that we've made it to postseason play. I'm so excited for our kids; it couldn't happen to a better group. I feel lucky to have extended our season and gotten the chance to spend more time with them. Saturday, we had our last home game against the only conference team that's beaten us. It was another great game. We came up short again, but the game could easily have gone the other way.

Stephanie continues to do well as she works through her challenges. I mentioned that I was considering sharing some of my struggles with her, mainly to let her know she was not alone. I did, and she surprised me with how she took what I did and added to it. She's been working with a fourth-grade girl she met while volunteering in a classroom. It came at a good time because this little girl was struggling with her parents' recent divorce. The girl's teacher and mom raved about the difference Steph made in her life.

The girl and her mom have been coming to most of our home games and noticed the sudden absence of Steph's family in the bleachers. After talking with the girl's mom first, Steph decided she didn't want to continue being deceptive when asked about her parents. She wanted to be honest and thought it might help the girl realize she was not alone in her difficult time with her parents' divorce.

I'm telling you about this because your honest sharing with me was the catalyst for putting this into motion. Like in the movie Pay It Forward, your "gift" has been passed on to me and continues to expand outward.

Once again, I thank you for continuing to share with me. I couldn't have asked for a better teacher, coach, mentor, and friend for basketball and life itself.

Your friend,

Sam

CHAPTER 29

JANUARY 1987

After meeting with the referees at half court, Lindsey and I initiated our pinky finger shake. Looking me in the eye, she said, "Tonight is our night."

It was our night because we were getting the chance to prove ourselves against the number one team, Sehome High. It was our night because it was our final chance to beat them at home. It was our night because no matter what happened, Lindsey and I had committed to each other that nothing would come between us.

"Yes, it is," I responded with a smile, feeling the power in our unity.

Lindsey and I took control of the game at tip-off. Although she and I scored all but four of our team's points in the first quarter, our teammates played great defense and were aggressive on the boards. We challenged every shot, gave up no offensive rebounds, and forced five turnovers in the first quarter. When the buzzer sounded to end the first quarter, we were ahead 16–4. Even our bench was energized by the aggressive play on the court.

To start the second quarter, Coach Walters left the same five on the court; their coach put in five new players.

Lindsey and I stayed on a roll in the opening three minutes of the second quarter. With each basket we scored, our team played with more confidence. At halftime, we led 36–20.

During halftime, Coach Walters almost didn't know how to act or what to say. His main message was to be prepared for them to put more pressure on us, including a full-court press, and to continue playing in attack mode.

Both teams started the second half with the same starters that had begun the game. Their 6' 1" post player was dominating our smaller defenders. Coach Walters called a timeout, and he described a defensive change. He wanted me to guard the post. Unlike when he'd done this before when it felt like he was setting me up for failure, his intent seemed constructive this time. We were finally on the same page, with the same mission, and it felt good.

My eyes remained wide open, keeping eye contact with him, and I was hanging on every word. I nodded and said, "Got it."

Jogging to the baseline where we would inbound the ball, I felt light in my step and breathing. I could not remember the last time Coach Walters had made eye contact with me and communicated a plan, nor could I remember the last time he'd complimented me. Both things happened during one timeout, and I knew then and there that I could do exactly what he wanted.

Our defensive change worked and took them out of their offensive rhythm. With intense ball pressure on the perimeter and my full fronting in the post, we forced three straight turnovers. Their guards adjusted quickly and started attacking off the dribble. They were closing the gap in the score, and it was apparent they would fight until the final buzzer.

We were only up two points with one-and-a-half minutes left in the game. We traded baskets on a couple of quick possessions, and then our point guard turned the ball over for an easy score for them. The game was all tied up, with only 16 seconds left. Coach Walters called a timeout. He stayed surprisingly calm as he drew up our final play on his clipboard. His final words were, "We take the last shot. We win or go into overtime, so it's a no-lose situation. We win now, or we win later."

With the mindset to score or get fouled, I drove past one defender, which made two others step up to stop me. I jumped in the air to pass over the taller defender's hands and hit Lindsey on the left wing as she came off a screen. Without hesitation, she caught the pass and elevated into her jump shot. It was nothing but net as the final buzzer sounded.

Our teammates rushed onto the court from our bench, jumping up and down and screaming. Lindsey and I embraced each other and just held each other tight. She whispered into my ear: "We did it."

Once through the line, Lindsey and I draped our arms across each other's shoulders. As we walked toward the locker room, I saw Ms. Collins standing on the far side of the court. She was beaming and gave me an enthusiastic two thumbs up, then clapped her hands together. Walking off the court, arm in arm with Lindsey and with acknowledgment from Ms. Collins, I felt like I was floating. My smile was so big my cheeks hurt. All our success in volleyball now seemed in the distant past, and I could not think of a time that I felt happier than right then.

Most of our team had already left, but Lindsey and I stayed in the locker room longer, savoring the victory. Finally ready to go, we paused at the double doors leading outside and into the pouring rain.

"Hey, I know we'll be making a mad dash to our cars, but one last congratulations," I said, dropping my bag to hug her. "I'm so glad we get to share a moment like this in basketball. Our greatest moments have mostly been in volleyball, but this is equally good and maybe better because we've had to wait so long."

Lindsey smiled, but I thought I saw the hint of tears in her eyes. "Thanks, Sam, and not just for this game. Thanks for how you have been all season long. Not many people could do what you do." I knew she wasn't referring to my basketball abilities.

Before getting into bed, I opened the bottom drawer of my desk. Underneath a few magazines, a book, and an old sketchpad was a wadded-up bag. With only my bedside lamp on, I opened it and pulled out the papers and index cards one at a time. Many were wrinkled, and several were torn into pieces that I'd had to fit together like a jigsaw puzzle to read. Even after I'd yanked everything related to my basketball dreams off my closet doors, I couldn't part with them entirely.

This was the first time I'd touched them since that awful day. It was as if the power of our win, the change in Coach Walters, and the improved bond between Lindsey and me had planted the seed to pull these out tonight.

Rereading them, I wondered if tonight's game was a turning point. Maybe Lindsey playing so well and even hitting the winning basket would be enough to bring out the happiness we all saw in Coach Walters tonight for the rest of this season. Maybe he would treat me differently for the rest of the season. Perhaps I could still reach my goals and dreams. All these possibilities filled me with calm, contentment, and, most important, optimism.

The next afternoon, I sank into the couch cushions, enjoying the silence of being home alone. The last twenty-four hours had been such an emotional whirlwind that I needed the time and space to process it, but I had only twenty minutes before leaving for practice.

I realized that, at some level, I'd almost resigned myself to playing college volleyball without officially accepting any offer. But this abrupt change in basketball reopened the door to what had always been my number one passion.

The phone rang, startling me out of my thoughts.

"Hello?" I answered.

"Hello. Is Samantha there, please?"

"This is Sam."

"Oh, Sam. I'm calling on a whim, but figured you'd probably be at school or practice. This is Coach Eric Garrett. I'm the women's basketball coach at the University of Idaho. How are you?"

My heart skipped a beat with excitement. But as the conversation continued, it became a long monologue, and I started to feel anxious about the time. I glanced at the microwave; it was 3:30 p.m. I'd planned to leave ten minutes earlier and couldn't afford to be late to practice. I paced back and forth, waiting for Coach Garrett to take a breath so I could say something without rudely interrupting him. My breaths turned short and shallow with my deepening anxiety. I kept shifting the phone between my hands to wipe my sweaty palms.

I finally jumped in, forcing him to stop talking. "Coach Garrett, I'm sorry to interrupt and cut the call short, but I must run to practice. I'm pushing it to make it on time. I'm sorry."

He claimed he understood but then discussed setting up a campus visit once the state tournament was finished. I reminded him I needed to go and asked if we could finish the conversation later. As I thanked him and said goodbye, he apologized for holding me and said to have Coach Walters call him if I was late. It was his fault, and he'd take full responsibility. He laughed as if this was a lighthearted situation, easily explained to my coach. He did not know Coach Walters. I grabbed my keys and sprinted to my car. I didn't even stop to lock the front door behind me. It was now 3:50 p.m.

I sped on my short drive to school, fearing the wrath of Coach Walters far more than a potential speeding ticket. Squealing into the parking lot, I took the first open spot and sprinted to the locker room. I quickly changed into my practice gear and left everything on the bench in front of my locker. As I raced onto the floor and joined the full-court drills we did to start every practice, I glanced at the clock on the wall—4:07 p.m.

Coach Walters blew his whistle when I got to the front of the line. Everyone stopped and froze, ensuring no basketball bounced after the whistle. "Sam, anything you'd like to share with the group?" I looked up and locked eyes with him. "Care to tell us why attending practice isn't worth your time?"

I felt a sense of dread at his anger, but I didn't want to casually mention a call from a college coach in front of my teammates. We'd been working hard to mesh as a team this season, and I didn't want to affect that by sounding like I was bragging or making excuses. "I'm sorry for being late, Coach Walters. Could we talk about it after practice?"

"No! You're going to tell me right now!" he barked. I had never been late to a single practice in any sport, yet I was publicly shamed for being seven minutes late.

"I got a phone call from a college coach. I told him several times that I had to go because of practice, but he kept talking. I'm sorry."

Coach Walters's expression changed from anger to a contorted look of disgust. That disgust was evident in the words he spoke next.

"Oh. Aren't we special . . . ? Did you guys know you were teammates with a superstar? Doesn't it make you mad that she cares more about her personal goals and future team than our team?" He'd been getting louder with each rhetorical question he asked my teammates. He shouted his concluding comments. "Get out! Get out right now, and don't come back! Put all your gear in your bag and give it to someone else to turn in because *I don't want to see you again*!"

The last phrase was the staccato of machine-gun fire. I was speechless, in shock. My skin burned like I had been shot. He turned his back on us and said something to Coach Fox, who started walking toward me. No one had moved since the outburst, but I would not be further humiliated by having Coach Fox escort me off the court. I started walking away, keeping my eyes down. Coach Walters blew his whistle and yelled for the team to start again. I did not look back.

Once I was safely in the locker room, my wobbly legs practically collapsed as I bent to sit on the bench. I slumped forward, chin on my chest, and closed my eyes. My ears rang, my hands trembled, and my stomach burned. I felt like I was going to throw up.

I didn't know what to do. Should I stay in the locker room to talk with Coach Walters after practice? Maybe I should call him at home later that night or wait until the next day to let him calm down?

I kept telling myself this was a misunderstanding and we'd work it out. He'd see that by tomorrow. He'd find a more appropriate punishment, like extra running or benching me in Monday night's game. He'd dole it out, I would take it, and we'd move forward. I sat listening to the sounds of balls bouncing and the occasional whistle.

After thirty minutes, I pulled a sheet of notebook paper and a pen from my backpack. I wrote a note to Lindsey and slid it through the top slot of her locker. I knew she'd see it. I was relieved to be going home to an empty house. I wouldn't have to say anything about this to my parents. If I didn't talk about it, it wasn't final, and it wasn't real.

January 1987

Lindsey,

Please have your dad call Coach Garrett from the University of Idaho to explain the reason for my tardiness. When he gives your dad the specifics, maybe my penalty will be running or sitting out the next game rather than being kicked off the team.

Thanks. I'll look for you after school to see what he says.

Sam

CHAPTER 30

MARCH 2007

Driving to the conference tournament, we stopped for a break. I stepped out of my van and squinted in the sunlight. Then I heard hysterical laughter coming from the direction of Fitz's van. The kids tumbled out, wiping their eyes and smiling. As they headed into the hotel lobby, I caught up with Olivia.

"Hey—what's so funny? Am I missing another comedy hour by Fitz?"

"No," she managed to say through her laughter. "It's Steph. You know how she likes to do those Mad Lib things? She wrote her own, with the blanks and the part of speech needed, all about our team. It's hilarious. We told her she'd have to share this at our banquet."

A broad smile spread across my face. Without hearing the Cougar Mad Lib she created for her teammates, I shared their joy and exuberance, for slightly different reasons. To know that Steph was letting her guard down with teammates was a big step.

I caught Fitz before the hotel entrance and quietly asked him about it.

"It brought tears to my eyes," he said. "Luckily, because everyone was laughing so hard, they just figured they were tears from my laughing."

Our players started trickling into the conference room five minutes early and sat facing the TV. Fitz began by showing a few clips illustrating our opponent's offensive tactics and reviewing our defensive plan for both the on-ball and double screens they liked to use for their best three-point shooter. Then he showed a few defensive clips and quizzed the team about our plan to attack the weaknesses in their zone. To finish, I showed a montage of our plays, all showing hustle and extra effort. After the last scene, I pushed stop, and the screen went blank. I stood in front of them with all eyes on me.

"We've won many games this season because of plays like those," I pointed to the TV. "From day one, we've talked about controlling what's controllable, and on the court, that's our defense and hustle plays like those. Our offense is clicking some nights, and we're shooting lights out. That's fun. But other nights, we can't find our offensive rhythm, or maybe we can't hit the broad side of a barn. Those are the games that separate the champions from everyone else. We can always control our competitiveness and hustle. When we do that, regardless of the final score, we can walk off the court with no regrets."

I didn't want this to sound like our end-of-the-year banquet, with the message that we were just happy to be here. On the other hand, I wanted them to feel proud of this accomplishment regardless of the outcome this weekend.

"You've proven yourselves to every coach in the conference, and more important, you've proven yourselves to yourselves. That is where belief is born. And when you combine our team unity, commitment, focus, and competitiveness with our collective belief—that's a force to be reckoned with. *We* are a force to be reckoned with, and we'll let it all out on the court for these two games this weekend."

I saw the fire in their eyes as they listened and soaked up every ounce of energy I could put into each word. I made eye contact with each person before having the seniors take the floor. "Our seniors each wanted to share a few special thoughts with you." I nodded to Whit, Olivia, and Heather, then sat in the back.

Olivia started by thanking all her teammates for such a special season. She reminded them of our fast start, then hitting a roadblock with Rachel's injury and Kelsey leaving the team. She said that was a decisive turning point for our team—we could've either fragmented into smaller groups and just survived the rest of the season or united around a common goal and turned the obstacle into a launching pad. She finished by sharing her pride in everyone on the team for making their decisions at that crucial juncture.

She looked at her teammates and said, "Thank you! And we're not done yet." It was not a rah-rah, get-everyone-on-their-feet, jumping-around ending. Instead, it was heartfelt and full of a quiet intensity that fit Olivia's personality.

Heather went next, thanking her teammates and telling them how much they meant to her. She handed out sheets of decorative paper. She had typed a poem, and once everyone had a copy, she read it aloud. When she finished, she said, "And I second Olivia's motto—we're not done yet."

Finally, it was Whitney's turn. I had been so moved by what and how Olivia and Heather shared that I did not think it was possible to exceed that. But Whitney did.

She started with general congratulations and thanked the team for making the season memorable. She then described how each person, in their way, had impacted both her and the team. Whitney then read from typed notes, beginning with her fellow seniors and progressing to the freshmen in class order. She said each person's name and read a short paragraph specifying the strengths they brought to the team and something she'd learned from them. The room fell into a profound silence. A lump formed in my throat as I listened to her insightful compliments for each person.

Then she turned to Fitz and me. Whit had managed to stay poised until that moment. Her voice cracked, and she paused occasionally as she expressed her appreciation for our coaching. That was enough to push me over the edge, and without warning, tears cascaded down my cheeks.

She finished with: "And I third Olivia's motto—we're not done yet!" It was a rallying cry, and her teammates fed off that energy.

We took the court for the official twenty-minute warm-up with an air of collective determination. Our kids were talking and giving high-fives to each other throughout the lay in and shooting warm-ups. There was a good buzz of electricity humming through all of them. Although I sensed some pregame jitters, they disappeared when the referee tossed the ball into the air.

Olivia ran the show like a floor general, directing traffic on both offense and defense. She knew when to push the ball in attack mode or slow things down in a set play on offense. She was like a symphony conductor, each section coming in at the perfect time and with the ideal volume to create a harmonious masterpiece.

We were up 16 points at the half. In the locker room, I had only two messages for our team. First, don't let up. Second, be prepared for anything and everything they might throw at us. Desperate teams are dangerous teams. "Forget the score; it's zero–zero. Let's go dominate the next twenty minutes."

And we did. The closest Carroll College got to us was 12 points. We played our second group for the final six minutes, allowing everyone to play and winning by 19 points.

Back in the locker room, Fitz and I kept our comments brief. Our focus needed to shift to preparing for tomorrow night's championship game. We wanted our team to get their sweats on and sit in the bleachers together to watch the second game. The winner would be our next opponent.

As I followed the team into the gym, I saw Cassandra hugging Whitney. I walked over to join them.

"You made it! Thank you so much for coming this weekend." I embraced her in a full hug.

She started talking before we even pulled away. "Oh my God! I can't believe how great your team played."

"And what do you think of this star?" I looked over to Whit, who was still grinning.

"She's awesome! I mean, I always knew she was good, but wow! I'm a journalist who uses words for my job every day, and she's rendered me speechless."

I chuckled and put a hand on Whit's shoulder. "Not only is she awesome on the court, but she's also awesome off the court. Her leadership is a big reason why we're here."

Whit seemed bashful dealing with so many compliments. She mumbled a quiet thank you and then excused herself to find her parents.

As Whit walked away Cassandra said, "God, I just love that kid."

I smiled in agreement and turned to watch Whit walk into the stands. I saw her face light up with joy and recognition, and I followed her sightline up a few rows. Kelsey was walking down the aisle carrying three bouquets of yellow roses, a soft smile on her face. I saw her open her arms to Whit, then lost sight of them in the crowd.

Cassandra jumped right back to our team and our game. "Sam, I can't believe how good your team looks. I don't know much about the game itself or strategy, but what I could see from watching is how hard they played and how in sync they were with each other the whole time. It was like watching a machine." She was gushing, and all I could do was listen and smile.

"Did you see who else flew in? Hey!" she shouted and waved to someone behind me.

For a moment, hope filled my chest. Had my parents come after all? I turned, a smile spreading across my face. But I didn't see my parents anywhere in the crowd. I started to turn back to Cassandra. "Who—"

"Ms. Collins!" She waved to someone in the bleachers on the other side of the gym. Ms. C was standing and waving. When she saw me, she flashed two thumbs up.

"I can't believe this! Come on, let's go say hi before the next game starts," I said.

I jogged up the bleachers to Ms. C and wrapped her in a huge hug. Before I could even release her, she was already praising the team.

"Congratulations, Sam. Your team looks amazing."

I stepped back. "Wow—what a surprise! Thank you so much for coming this weekend." I looked back and forth between Ms. C and Cassandra and could feel tears building in my eyes.

"Oh . . . you guys," I said, stepping forward and reaching an arm around each of them. I pulled them into a loose group hug since we stood awkwardly in the bleachers.

"I can't even tell you what this means to me. Two of my most important people are here to share this special team moment. I don't know what to say . . . Thank you."

Ms. C said, "I wouldn't have missed it, Sam."

On the court, they were getting ready to announce the starters for the next game. I told them I needed to join our team for a quick postgame meeting but hoped they would join us for dinner afterward. They agreed.

Our team had to sit at various tables in the same large room. Once the team was settled and ready to order, Fitz and I joined Ms. C and Cassandra. Before sitting down, Fitz made both of them stand up so he could hug them.

"Thank you for making the trip to be with us for the tournament. It means a lot."

Everyone slid into the booth, and Ms. C and Cassandra spoke almost simultaneously.

"Congratulations on such an accomplishment." They wore their happiness like bright multicolored scarves waving in the breeze.

I felt so lucky to have these friends who celebrated our team's success like their own. And to have my three best friends together at once—I was moved beyond words. The smile on my face hurt my cheeks. It was a moment I wanted etched in my memory.

Ms. C said, "We want to hear more about your team, your season, the highs and lows. We want to feel like insiders."

Fitz and I shared all sorts of stories and fun memories. We didn't need any prompting, and a story he'd share would instantly trigger a different memory that I'd share. And the way Fitz could tell a story! Even though I'd had the experience with him, he had me cracking up just as hard as Ms. C and Cassandra. After being so keyed up and focused on this weekend, it was a powerful release to let loose with all the laughter.

There was a brief pause as Fitz took a bite of his food, and Ms. C asked, "So if you look back at each of the seasons leading up to this one, what do you think made the difference this year? Or what has been building over the previous seasons to make this year the breakout year?"

Fitz and I considered this, but he spoke first. He emphasized the team's cohesion at the low point in our season when Kelsey quit and Rachel was injured. I pointed out that the cohesion Fitz discussed came mainly from our senior leadership.

Fitz followed up. "As much as our seniors deserve so much praise, Coach Sam deserves a large chunk of the credit." He continued, "I think coaches . . . well, people in general, often don't reflect much on what *they're* doing, why *they're* doing it, or how *they* might do it better. Instead, they always ask for more from the team. I've seen so much growth in Sam over these past four years. Her first year she was so full of competitive fire, she thought she'd be able to make the team successful from her own sheer will and determination." He grinned at me.

"But when we weren't as successful as she wanted, she adjusted and looked at herself to see what she could do differently. Her ability to see and bring out the best in each player and then expand that to the whole team has steadily improved. Instead of coaching from her internal fire, she's coaching from her compassion. You'd think they'd be diametrically opposed, but she's shown how they feed one another. So to me, Sam's examples about our senior leadership are largely *because* of how she coached the team. She provides the environment conducive to these kids learning, growing, finding, and showing their best selves, and she does that by always trying to improve her own game."

"That does not surprise me at all," Ms. C said proudly.

I jumped in. "Actually, Coach Collins, I'm just paying forward what you gave me. You saw potential in me all those years ago and believed in me more than anyone else did. You showed this by giving me the gift of your time. You brought out the best in me. And through you, I saw a model of the kind of coach I wanted to be. So thank you."

The next morning when Fitz and I met up with our kids eating breakfast at the hotel, it was like déjà vu. They were all eating the same thing and sitting at the same tables with the same teammates as the day before. They even asked to eat at the same place for our pregame meal, as if doing the same things would give the same result.

Although we didn't sense any nerves during our shoot around, we could see subtle signs by the time we took the floor for pregame warm-ups. They weren't as talkative with one another, and they moved through the lay in and shooting lines more mechanically rather than with an extra skip in their steps.

Our final messages to the team were about game psychology and reminding them to enjoy the moment.

"Lewis-Clark has all the pressure on them. They went undefeated this season and finished number one again. They're playing in front of their home crowd, and everyone expects them to win. We are the underdogs. We've never been here before. Teams that have nothing to lose and everything to gain are dangerous. *We are a dangerous team*," I said.

Whitney led them in our final "We're not done yet!" cheer. But when our starting five took the court, those ideas may have been in their thoughts and words, but the message had not gotten through to their bodies.

We started tentatively, which unfortunately became a self-fulfilling negative loop. We tightened up even more each time we made a mistake or Lewis-Clark scored. By halftime, we'd dug ourselves into a sizable hole, down sixteen. More than the point differential, I was concerned about our attitude. When Fitz and I talked with our team in the locker room at halftime, we said nothing about strategy; we spoke entirely about how we played.

"I didn't recognize that team out there in the first half. I've never seen us play so tight, tentative, and fearful. What are you afraid of?" I waited a moment and then answered my own question. "You know what I'm afraid of? I'm afraid that if we go out and play that way in the second half, this will be your lingering memory of this incredible season. Instead of remembering the obstacles we overcame, the competitive fire we developed, and our growth together, we'll remember this game where we played more like scared individuals instead of the relentless fighting group we are."

I paused for a moment to let that sink in before going on. "I want you to forget about the score and compete together on every single possession. Lift each other with your words and actions because that's when we're at our best. Right now, it's not about winning or losing this game. It's all about ensuring we have no regrets when that final buzzer sounds and we walk off this court. Win or lose, it's about what we have right here," I said, waving my arm across the room, including everyone. "Compete together. No regrets."

They charged out of the gate to start the second half like they'd all had an IV infusion of extra-strength caffeine. Their feet, their hands, and their mouths were all moving. In our first four defensive possessions, we got one steal that led to a breakaway lay in, forced two turnovers, and took a charge. We followed those defensive stops with scores at the other end, narrowing the lead to single digits. Suddenly, Lewis-Clark was calling a timeout.

It was a thirty-second timeout, so I made my point quickly. "Now that's the team I know! Keep it up, one possession at a time." The same five raced back onto the floor before the buzzer sounded, collectively looking like a boxer charging from his corner to the center of the ring, ready to deliver a knockout punch.

It was back-and-forth for the rest of the game, evenly matched, but our eight-point deficit didn't budge. The kids on the bench were hoarse from cheering teammates and celebrating each little success. We tried everything from full-court press, half-court trapping, zone defense, man defense, and more, but we could not disrupt them enough to close the gap. In the end, it was a classic case of expending so much effort to get the score within striking distance that we didn't have enough energy to put us over the hump. We ran out of time and fell short.

As the final horn sounded, Lewis-Clark started jumping around in celebration. Our five players on the floor stopped right where they were, bent over at the waist with hands on their knees in exhaustion and defeat. The kids on the bench stood, staring at their teammates, frozen in place. Their faces said it all—shock and disappointment.

March 2007

To: Samantha Shuster
From: Laurie Collins

Dear Sam,

Thank you for making me feel like a genuine member of your Cougar family this weekend. It was an absolute joy to meet all your players in person finally, and I was so proud of how they played.

More than that, I was in awe of the coach you have become. I could look at each of your players and know that you have become a true mentor. What you've taught them will last far beyond their years on your team.

We never know who will come into our lives, when, or for how long, and yet they can make such a lasting impact. If we approach people and situations with integrity, compassion, and love, then at least we know the ripples moving outward will be positive. The positive ripples can create waves to help push the person forward, rather than storm waves causing a person to drown.

Big CONGRATULATIONS on making it to the postseason tourney. I am confident that postseason play will become a regular occurrence for your teams.

Your friend,

Ms. C

CHAPTER 31

JANUARY 1987

When I got home that night, I paced the house, walking from my bedroom to the den and back. I wanted to know if Lindsey had shared the note I left for her with her dad. Why had I ever answered that phone call? If I'd just let Coach Garrett leave a message, none of this would be happening.

My pacing wasn't helping. I didn't feel calmer and wasn't getting closer to a solution. Although it was dark outside, I decided to go running. Physical exhaustion was the surest way to quiet my mind and calm my nerves. My eyes adjusted to the night sky as I jogged to the park. The light from the full moon was enough to see the dips on the trail. I was running like a mountain lion was chasing me, and my life depended on it.

I had not planned to tell Ms. Collins anything about Coach Walters throwing me off the team since I still hoped it would be worked out. However, as soon as she opened her office door and congratulated me on our Monday night win, emotions engulfed me like a tidal wave. The tears started, and I knew there was no holding back. I covered my face with both hands, leaned against the wall, and slid down until I sat on the ground. I didn't make much noise as I cried, but I knew my shaking shoulders told Ms. Collins everything. Luckily, she didn't start asking questions immediately.

I don't know how long it took for my sobbing to stop and my jagged breathing to slow. I still hadn't raised my face from my hands and didn't want to. I hated crying in front of anyone, and now I felt embarrassed and ashamed.

Finally, I heard Ms. Collins's soothing voice. "What happened, Sam?" Her tone was full of concern and support, everything I needed in those three words.

Still trying to recover from my breakdown, I took a few deep breaths before speaking. "Coach Walters kicked me off the team yesterday." That was all I could get out.

Without betraying any emotion, Ms. Collins asked, "Can you tell me what happened?"

How do you put into words your heart being ripped out? How do you describe a pain so great that the mere act of breathing seems impossible? Slowly, without looking up at her, I gave her a condensed version of what happened.

Her chair squeaked as she stood up. Standing before me, she offered her hand to help me up and embraced me with both arms. I hugged her back, appreciative beyond words for her support. She let me go and leaned back against the edge of her desk while I sat back down.

"I'm sorry to dump all of this on you. I'm so embarrassed." The second part came out under my breath, meant for myself, but Ms. Collins heard it in the confines of her tiny office.

"You have nothing to apologize for and nothing to be embarrassed about. Do you hear me?"

I was looking at my feet, avoiding eye contact, but I nodded.

"Of course, you feel this way and don't let anyone try to tell you that you should feel otherwise. Your emotions are yours to feel. You don't have to explain or justify and certainly don't need to be embarrassed."

"Well . . . I shouldn't be acting like it's the end of the world. I mean, how can I sit here and cry, be angry and hurt when other people have serious issues like parents getting divorced, parents dying, car crashes, and homes burning to the ground? Those are real problems."

"Whoa, whoa," Ms. Collins chuckled. "I'm sorry, Sam. I'm not laughing at you at all. But by that line of reasoning, maybe only one person, one family, or one group of people could ever let themselves feel bad or experience grief. Where does it end, and who decides what is the worst? It's not a competition. Pain, suffering, and grief are not comparative."

Although my words had made sense in my head, when Ms. Collins said it like that, I realized it did sound a little irrational. I still couldn't look at her. It was difficult enough to *hear* her support, but I worried if I *saw* the kindness in her face, I'd start crying all over again.

"What did your parents say?"

"I haven't told them yet. My dad's team had an away game last night, so they got home late. I was hoping that today I could work out something more reasonable with Coach Walters, and then I wouldn't even have to bother them with this."

Even though it was the story I'd been telling myself since last night, deep down, I knew Coach Walters would not change his mind. He had been waiting for an excuse to do something more drastic than just benching me.

"Sam. I am so sorry that you must go through this. I know you need to head to school, but I'm not letting you leave here until you've heard a few things. I need you to look at me, though."

When I looked up, she gave me a small smile full of compassion. I tried to blink back the tears in my eyes.

"This is not about you; it is about Coach Walters. What he said and did cannot, for a second, have you doubt yourself—not your commitment, work ethic, or attitude. This does not reflect who you are as an athlete or as a person. You can't absorb the poison in his words or actions; don't let him kill your inner spirit. Remember, this is not about you. It's about him."

She paused. "And the second thing I think you already know is that I'm always here for you. I'm here to provide help and support in any way I can, and I want you to know how much I believe in you."

"Thank you." I had to swallow the lump in my throat, fighting back a new set of tears threatening to spill over.

"Will you tell me how it goes with Coach Walters and your parents?"

"Yeah. I wish it were as easy to talk with all of them as with you."

We both stood up, and she wrapped me in a tight embrace. It felt like she was trying to pass all her strength to me with a hug. I wished it were that simple to be as strong as her.

I sat through my classes like a zombie the next day. A heavy sense of fatigue and dread had drained all my energy. During my last period of the day, I went down to the locker room once I knew the PE students would be in the gym. I lay down on the bench in front of my locker. The image that came to mind was being on trial, waiting for the verdict. Coach Walters was the judge, jury, and executioner, holding my future in his hands. There was still a sliver of hope as long as I didn't know the final verdict.

Suddenly, it dawned on me—would I be ready for practice if Lindsey had good news for me? Should I change into my practice gear? I hadn't eaten lunch, which would make it difficult to get through practice. I sat up and rummaged through my bag for a granola bar but found nothing. I berated myself for being so distracted that I hadn't come prepared.

The bell rang, and I heard Coach Nelson congratulate Lindsey moments later. "I'm just sick about having to miss your game Monday night. Sounds like you and Sam were unstoppable."

"Thanks, Coach," Lindsey said.

Then Lindsey was standing next to me, opening her locker. I didn't look directly at her but watched out of my peripheral vision for clues. She changed quickly and then sat beside me, bending over to lace up her shoes. I waited.

Lindsey finished tying her shoes and stood up. She turned to close her locker. She moved slowly, like she was trying to buy herself time. I turned to look at her for the first time. She looked like a mess. Dark circles under her eyes, the whites streaked with red; it looked like she'd been crying. She turned slightly toward me, but her eyes never reached my face. The movement of her head was so slight that if someone else had been watching, they would have denied that any communication had taken place. But I saw it, a slight shake of the head. Her head was still hanging, and I felt bad for her too. I knew she'd tried to do what she could at home, yet we were both powerless.

I made it out to my car unseen. Racing home, I went straight to my bedroom, closed the door behind me, and collapsed onto my bed. Grabbing my pillow, I buried my face and began to wail. Even though no one was home to hide the sound from, I didn't want to hear it myself.

I allowed myself to cry until there were no tears left. My voice was hoarse, and I had a pounding headache. I wanted to climb into bed for the night, but I needed to call Coach Braxton and Coach Stevens. I wanted to resolve this issue before my parents got home to avoid any drawn-out conversation about college options and decisions. It would be hard enough explaining what had happened with basketball; I did not need two monumental issues to deal with that night.

I dragged myself off the bed and into the bathroom. The cold water was a shocking relief to my hot, tear-stained face. I drank a glass of water, trying to soothe my raw throat.

My first phone call was to Boise State. Coach Stevens had given me until this weekend to decide, but I was ready. I missed her, but I spoke with her assistant coach and told her I'd like to sign my letter of intent to be on their volleyball team next year.

"That is fantastic. I know Coach Stevens will be thrilled! We'll get the papers in the mail to you tomorrow and call Coach Nelson to set up things like PR in your local paper and the paper here." She shared a few more details before congratulating me again. I hung up, relieved to have phone call number one behind me.

Unfortunately, my next call would be more difficult. Coach Braxton answered on the second ring, surprised to hear from me. When I shared with her that I would not attend her school next year, she asked, "You decided to wait and go the basketball route?"

"Um . . . no. I decided on volleyball at Boise State."

There was an awkward silence before she responded. "Oh . . . well, I'm glad to hear you chose volleyball but disappointed that you chose someone else. Can I ask you what the difference was? Why Boise State over us?" She was friendly about it, which I appreciated, but I had not considered possible questions and answers in my rush to make the calls. My brain wasn't working.

"It's kinda hard to put into words. It was just a feeling. I guess the campus at Boise State and the city felt like a better fit. But I liked you and your team and appreciated all your time and interest. I'm sorry to have wasted your time."

"Sam, it was not a waste of time at all. I appreciate your phone call with your decision and wish you the best of luck."

Coach Braxton's question got me thinking. I'd better prepare a better response for my parents tonight. Otherwise, I could hear my dad's comments—*Typical female reactions based on emotion rather than logic.* Of course, it would be tinged with plenty of disdain.

I decided to wait until after dinner so Emily wouldn't be there, and it would seem more informal. As we carried our dishes into the kitchen, I broached the subject.

"I wanted to tell you guys something that happened yesterday."

My dad set his dishes on the counter, and as he walked out of the kitchen, he said, "It's getting late, and I need to call Mike. He scouted a game and will give me a verbal rundown before I get the full written one. I need that to help with my practice planning. Gotta be ready for a big game Friday night!"

"Mark. Sam said she had something to share with *us*."

"That's okay, Mom. You can retell the story to Dad at a better time." He smiled, winked at me, and was gone before my mom could press the issue.

She started rinsing the dishes and handed them to me to put in the dishwasher.

"What's your big news, honey?"

As much as I thought it would be easier to tell just my mom, I still felt emotional. Even if I started with the so-called good news—that I'd verbally committed to Boise State—that would not explain the reason for not finishing the basketball season. I wondered if I should make up an excuse, like maybe I was worried about getting hurt and didn't want to risk it now that I'd decided to go with volleyball.

"I decided on Boise State volleyball, and I won't be finishing the basketball season." I tried to make my voice sound cheery like it was all good news, but I was glad to have my back to her as I loaded dinner plates in the dishwasher.

"Excuse me?" she said, turning off the faucet. Without the running water, the silence was unnerving. "I don't think I heard you right." She'd stopped handing dishes to me, so I couldn't keep my back turned. As I faced her, I avoided eye contact. She had a brown smudge on her cheek that looked like the gravy from our dinner. I looked at that instead of her eyes, and it somehow lessened my sense of dread.

"Well, you know I had to give the volleyball coaches an answer by this weekend. And if I said I wanted to wait, they'd already told me they'd have to offer my scholarship to the next person on their list. Maybe I'm just not that much of a risk-taker. When I thought about the potential scenarios, I decided I couldn't live with the idea of losing a guaranteed scholarship while I waited for an unknown one in basketball." The last sentence sounded like I was trying to convince both of us.

My mom's eyebrows furrowed. "Okaaaay," she said with hesitancy. "And what was the part about basketball?"

I licked my thumb and reached to wipe the gravy off her face. I exaggerated my movements and facial expressions so she knew I was joking. Whenever she used to do that to me as a young kid, it always grossed me out so bad it would trigger my gag reflex. That would make her laugh and try to wipe more spit on my face in the name of cleaning. She didn't take the bait. "Sam. What did you say about basketball?"

Don't cry. Don't cry. Look and sound like you're talking about an everyday thing, like your homework. "I'm done." It was only two words, but I got my message out and kept repeating to myself: *Don't cry, don't cry.*

"I don't understand."

I wanted to shout, "*Me neither!*" but obviously, that would blow my cover. *Don't cry . . . don't cry.* "Yeah. Well, I was seven minutes late to practice yesterday, which made Coach Walters mad. I guess that was my third strike, so I'm out." I saw concern, confusion, anger, and compassion in her eyes. If I was going to maintain my composure, I had to avoid her gaze, so I shifted my vision around—her eyes, then the refrigerator, the floor, and back to her eyes.

"Why were you late? You've never been late for anything. And how was that strike three?" Although she remained calm, her voice was starting to betray her impatience.

I summarized why I was late and skipped her question about this being my third strike. I stayed stoic.

"This cannot be right. We need to set up a meeting since you told him why you were late and he wouldn't consider that. Either all three of us could meet with him, or you and Dad could meet with him at school if that would be faster to schedule. But it needs to happen now." This was a demand.

"Mom, I appreciate your support, but nothing will change. Coach Walters is not the type to back down because it would make him look weak. Honestly, it'll just make things worse."

"Worse? How can they get any worse? You've been kicked off the team! Your senior season is done, just like that?" She'd hidden her Mama Bear response for awhile but reached the end of her restraint.

I paused before responding because I didn't want to sound like I disregarded her thoughts. "Things function differently within a team, and rules maybe aren't so clear-cut as they are at work. Maybe you can run it by Dad later tonight to see what he thinks. I've got some homework I need to get done."

She slowly and audibly exhaled. "All right, Sam, for now. But I am sharing this with your father. You may miss the game tomorrow, but there will be a meeting by Friday at the latest."

"Well, let's wait and see what Dad thinks." I stepped forward to hug her. "Thanks, Mom."

It hit me that if I had been able to only involve my mom, I would've shared and gotten help much earlier. My mom's willingness to listen and acknowledge starkly contrasted with my dad's responses. And the pain of my dad's minimization just added to the pain caused by Coach Walters. At the time, silence had seemed the best solution.

"Mom—thank you."

Closing the bedroom door behind me, I sat at my desk with my English papers in front of me. I needed to revise two pieces, but I'd be midsentence, and my eyes would stop moving. They glazed over, turning the paper into a white blur. I was getting nowhere. Crawling into bed was the only thing that sounded appealing.

After sitting at my desk for twenty minutes and accomplishing nothing, I pulled out my journal. Thoughts raced through my mind but had nothing to do with my homework assignment. Writing in my journal might clear my head so I could focus on what I needed to do. Words and phrases flew from pen to paper. I didn't try to filter or shape the ideas. I was simply the scribe, recording the whirlwind of feelings in my head.

When I had written myself to exhaustion, I paused. It was like coming up out of water for air. I gasped. I was drained. Rereading my words, my raw emotions expressed in such a visible fashion felt like blood being drained from my body one vial at a time until there was no more to give. Numbness washed over me. Would there be a transfusion? Would it come in time?

March 2007

Dear Steph,

The last time we met, I noticed your journal had gotten full. Nothing is worse than sitting down to write and realizing you've run out of space, so this is to ensure you keep writing.

An exceptional coach once told me something I'd like to pass on to you: The most important thing you can do is be the author of your own life. Make every chapter count, even the painful ones. One day, you can share your story with someone who needs the perspective only you can provide.

There's a danger to ourselves when we feel like a specific part of us is so shameful that it needs to stay a secret. There's a liberating power when we shine a light in the darkness.

Keep shining your light; never let anyone convince you to dim it.

Coach Sam

CHAPTER 32
MARCH–APRIL 2007

Fitz and I paused outside the locker room door before going in. I felt a pit in my stomach and a vise squeezing my heart. This wasn't a regular postgame talk, where we'd try to focus on what we did well and what we could learn going forward. This wasn't a pep talk. This was about acknowledging the finality of the end of a season, a season I did not want to end. There were no words for this kind of pain. Our seniors knew they would never wear that uniform or be part of the same incredible team again. What we had this year was exceptional, and our returners knew that next year would be different. Losing Olivia, Heather, and Whitney would require them to step into leadership positions and build a new team dynamic.

The locker room was silent when I walked through the door, except for a few cries and sniffles. Every player sat with her face buried in her hands or arms. Seeing them like this took my breath away. I had to fight back my own tears.

Without verbalizing our plan, Fitz and I knew we needed to console each player individually. As I went around the locker room, I asked each one to stand up so I could embrace them and whisper the same message: "I'm so proud of you. And thank you."

After Fitz and I hugged every team member, we pushed back the benches to create an open space on the floor. "Let's make a circle here on the floor," I said.

Most of the crying had stopped. There was an occasional sniffle, and as I looked around the circle, there were many red eyes and splotchy faces. I did not want to rush this sacred moment. I knew something would change as soon as we walked out of that locker room, and we could never return. I took a deep breath and hoped to find words fitting for this moment together.

"You know, any time we throw our whole heart into something that means so much to us—whether a relationship, a personal goal, or a professional goal—we take the risk of feeling unbelievable pain. Think about that range of emotions we discussed at the beginning of the season—the higher the highs, the lower the lows. The two go together. But although I feel deep sorrow and pain right now, I wouldn't change a thing. We've had incredible high points together, and now we share this low point. Sometimes, especially in times of immense sorrow and grief, the best gift we can offer someone is to just sit with them in the pain. Right now, that's what we are doing for each other. We're not trying to deny, ignore, minimize, or laugh it away. We are feeling it together."

I paused, letting my eyes slowly make the rounds of our team circle, trying to memorize each precious face. I was ten years older than them when I was introduced to this concept, or maybe that was the first time I could understand it. Before then, the idea of letting myself fully feel, experience, and acknowledge deep pain felt like being overly sensitive and weak. Exposed and vulnerable were the last things I wanted to be. That memory brought the final thought I wished to share.

"So many times, we are taught that showing emotions, especially around sadness, is a sign of weakness. I want you to reject that notion wholeheartedly. It is not true. Expressing emotion is the opposite of weakness. It is courage. It takes courage first to take the risk of giving your full heart and commitment, and then second, to let yourself feel the disappointment when things don't turn out how you wanted them to. Thank you for showing such courage. If you hadn't taken that risk, we wouldn't have had this amazing team and remarkable season."

After sitting with the team longer, soaking in the emotions surrounding our final game, Fitz and I left the locker room to take care of a few postgame details. Our kids emerged about thirty minutes later. They probably weren't ready emotionally, but their hunger had won out. Fitz and I caught the three seniors to ask where they wanted to eat.

"We thought a pizza place would work best because they usually have a back room so we can all sit together."

I walked over to where Ms. C and Cassandra were standing. Cassandra was more subdued than usual, showing her respect for the moment. But it was Ms. C's facial expression that said it all. "Oh, Sam. I'm so sorry, and I don't envy you for that last locker room talk." I could tell she spoke from experience.

I hugged them both. "It's heart-wrenching to see kids you care so much about feeling such disappointment. It's a helpless feeling . . . but I hope we shined at least a small ray of light into the darkness. They have so much to be proud of, and I believe, with time, that this team and this season will live on in their memories in the best way."

"I believe it will too," Ms. C said.

"I don't know when you're planning to head back home, but if it works, I'd love it if you both joined us for dinner tonight." I looked between Ms. C and Cassandra, waiting for their answer.

They agreed, and as I started apologizing for not spending more time with them, Ms. C held up her hand to stop me. "Don't even say it. I wanted to support you and your team and celebrate this accomplishment. You've been generous with your time, and I'm happy to be here."

"Thank you again, and I'm so glad you'll join us." Then, looking directly at Ms. C, added, "Especially because your fingerprints are all over this team." She smiled, a hint of tears glistening in her eyes.

It was Thursday afternoon after our big weekend, and Fitz and I were in the office. There was a knock on our door. When Fitz opened it, I was pleasantly surprised to see Steph. She was holding a large plastic bag. "Come in, Ms. Stephanie," Fitz said, with a slight bow at the waist.

"Great to see you, Steph. To what do we owe this pleasure?" I asked.

"Well . . . I wanted to check with you guys about our meetings. I didn't come in on Monday, but I didn't know if we would still meet even though the season is finished?"

"It's up to you. We'd still like to meet, but it's about you and your schedule. We could always change to days or times that work better for you." I hoped she would want to continue. I was concerned that with a slower basketball schedule and less time with her teammates, she might start dwelling on her family problems again.

Steph jumped right in. "I'd still like to get together. I appreciate how much you've helped me, and I don't think I would've gotten through that tunnel without you." She looked at both of us before continuing.

"There was a second thing I wanted to talk with you about," she said, grabbing the plastic bag at her feet. "I made something for you. It's just a little gift to thank you for all your support. I didn't want to wait until the banquet because it's more private." She pulled two wrapped packages from her bag and handed one to each of us.

"Thank you, Steph. You didn't need to do this," I said.

Fitz asked, "Would you like us to open it now?"

"Yeah, you can. It's nothing fancy . . . just a little something I made."

Fitz and I started unwrapping at the same time. It was a framed piece of writing, and before I read the piece, I scanned to the bottom, where she had signed her name. "You wrote this?" She nodded. I looked back at the gift in my lap and started reading. It was a poem titled "Layer Upon Layer." I read it twice, the first time quickly and the second more slowly, appreciating specific words and phrases.

When we finished, Fitz and I looked at each other with wide-eyed amazement. Fitz shook his head in disbelief for a few seconds, then said, "I'm speechless."

"This is the nicest gift anyone has ever given me," I said.

She grinned, but her gaze dropped to the floor as if she were embarrassed. The office remained quiet. I still couldn't find the words to convey how touched I was, and I was sure Fitz felt the same.

"Well, I better go," she said. "I'm glad I caught you both here and thank you again for all you've done."

Fitz and I jumped to our feet and embraced her in a group hug, which made her laugh. "You guys are funny. You're like the parents who put their kindergartner's artwork on the fridge, even though they can't tell whether the blobs are people, dogs, trees, or maybe an airplane," Steph said with a chuckle.

"I'd hardly compare this to kindergarten artwork. And I will find a place better than my fridge to display it. It is amazing. Thank you, Steph," I said.

When I picked up the mail, there was a large packet from Cassandra. She had told me that she mailed a DVD of the Hall of Fame ceremony I'd missed. We'd had a strange conversation the night after the event. Rather than being excited and wanting to share stories like usual, she was surprisingly lukewarm about it. Even when I asked her questions, she was vague or had little to say, "You'll see for yourself when you watch it," she said.

While Cassandra wouldn't share any details with me, my parents had been more talkative. My mom described the ceremony, the different speakers, what a great job Cassandra did as the emcee, and her pleasant visit with Coach Nelson and Lindsey. She said she'd saved the newspaper article and program for me and wished I could've been there to receive my award, and it seemed like she meant it.

My dad had let her talk longer than usual before cutting in to share his stories. But when he did, it was all about—Chris Daniels! It was like a reunion, seeing Chris and several teammates. The closest he got to acknowledging my award, the same award that Chris had received, was when he said, "You missed a great evening."

The DVD could trigger some of my worst memories from high school or bring some positive closure to a hurtful chapter in my life. When I told Fitz it had arrived, he asked if I wanted to watch it with him, but I told him I'd rather watch it myself first.

"I understand. But I hope you'll let me watch it sometime when you're finished. No rush." He paused, still looking at me and continued, "I know you have mixed feelings about all of that, and I'm sorry that so many negative memories overshadowed such a big award and accomplishment. I hope you'll watch the DVD however many times it takes for you to feel the pride you deserve to feel. I, for one, am very proud of you." Then he made me stand up so he could hug me.

On my way home, I stopped at my favorite Thai restaurant to pick up dinner. I gave myself the entire evening to experience the ceremony without distractions. When I finally pushed play on my remote, I smiled, seeing Cassandra standing behind a podium in front of a room full of people. She radiated confidence and professionalism, balanced with warmth and sincerity. Her transitions were seamless and natural, and I couldn't help but think what a great TV journalist she would be.

She introduced the four Hall of Fame inductees, beginning with the oldest and progressing to the most recent graduate. This placed me as the third inductee and Chris Daniels as the last. She called the first two athletes to the podium and talked about their accomplishments before handing them their plaque. When it was time for my introduction, she'd had to do something different, since I was the only inductee not in attendance.

"Could I have Samantha's coaches join me up here?" I saw Cassandra look out at the crowd and smile before going on. She shared a few statistics from volleyball, even though I was being inducted for basketball. She even mentioned that I started my college career on a full-ride scholarship for volleyball at Boise State. Transitioning to basketball, she read off a list of my compiled stats and some of the records I'd set.

"Unfortunately, Sam couldn't be with us this evening. She's deep in recruiting season for her team. Go Cougars!" She beamed, and the crowd laughed. I couldn't help but laugh too. "And though we wish Coach Walters could've been here as well, we're sending our best wishes for his health."

Then, two familiar figures appeared from the corner of the screen. Lindsey and Coach Nelson stood tentatively at the bottom of the stairs to the stage as Cassandra motioned for them to join her, a smile on her face as she continued. "But our fabulous committee has invited two women who I know Sam would feel represent all of the best experiences she had as a high school athlete."

"Lindsey Walters was Sam's teammate in both volleyball and basketball. Coach Walters is also her father. Lindsey, I hope you'll pass on all our well-wishes to your dad." Lindsey smiled and nodded. "Kathy Nelson coached Sam and her teammates to the 1986 state volleyball championship." Cassandra hugged both women as they approached the podium. "Even though Sam couldn't make it, she sent a note of thanks, and the committee has asked Lindsey to read it tonight."

I had not seen or kept in touch with Lindsey over the years. However, as I watched her read my letter to the committee, my mind wandered back to some of the fun memories we'd shared despite how her father treated me. I hoped that she could remember many of those good times too.

When she had finished reading my letter, she went on in her own words, complimenting me for my athleticism and strong work ethic. She also shared some fun times as teammates, which made me smile. But then her face shifted, and I held my breath, waiting to see what would come next.

Transfixed on my TV screen, I watched as Lindsey paused and cleared her throat before going on. "My dad is a good man and coach, but I think he made mistakes in coaching Sam. I believe, subconsciously, it stemmed from him not wanting someone else to outshine his daughter. But the reasons don't matter or make it right. Sam had to suffer through that, and I know it impacted her decisions about college. I think most people in that situation would have been angry, and they would've transferred all their bad feelings about my dad onto me. But Sam could always separate that, and we were very close. Our friendship and time together as teammates remain among my most cherished memories from high school. I wish Sam could be here tonight to congratulate her and express my gratitude. The wonderful moments we shared and the valuable lessons she taught me have become even more evident over the years."

I paused the DVD, reminding myself to breathe. Lindsey had acknowledged some of this to me in high school, but sharing it publicly was different. I whispered a thank you.

I restarted the DVD. Coach Nelson talked mostly about volleyball and how proud she was of my accomplishments, especially since I hadn't started playing until my sophomore year. Looking a bit choked up, she paused before resuming.

"I didn't know all the specifics of what was happening at basketball practices, in the locker room, or at halftime of games during high school, but I sensed something wasn't right. As coaches, we hold critical roles with power and influence over the athletes we mentor. It pains me to hear stories about coaches misusing that privilege and causing emotional harm to their athletes. Despite feeling positive about Sam's experience on our volleyball team, I recognize that I should have inquired further into what was happening with basketball. Even if it hadn't changed anything on the court, I believe acknowledgment and support from others might have prevented Sam from temporarily halting her pursuit of the sport she loved most. I'm glad Sam ultimately found her way back to basketball and played collegiately and internationally, but I'm most proud of her for transforming those negative experiences from her past into something positive in her collegiate coaching. Still, it doesn't erase the fact that she should never have had to endure those experiences as a high school kid."

I paused the DVD again as tears streamed down my face. After all this time, these memories were an old, deep wound that I rarely felt anymore. But bringing them to the surface stirred emotions within me as if they had just happened last week. While I heard Coach Nelson's words, I imagined a text scrolling across the bottom of the screen, saying: *"Sam, you were not imagining things. You were not being overly sensitive. You were not crazy. It was real, and your feelings about it were justified."*

I pushed play again. There was a small bit of pomp, officially inducting me into the Hall of Fame, and then it was all over. Coach Nelson and Lindsey left the stage, and Cassandra reclaimed the podium.

She smiled, took a deep breath, and then called my dad's name. "Coach Shuster, could I have you join me up on the stage?"

March 2007

To: Kelsey Jones
From: Samantha Shuster

Hi Kelsey,

Thanks for making the trip and supporting the seniors and all your teammates. I was so happy to see you in the stands.

I know it's a busy semester, but what does your schedule look like next week? Let's find a time for you to come by the office so that you, Coach Fitz, and I can discuss your plans for next year.

Coach Sam

CHAPTER 33

JANUARY–JUNE 1987

Getting thrown off the team had turned my world upside down. I felt like I had a clothespin pinching my nose shut while I breathed through a straw. There was not enough oxygen, whether I was inside or outside. And if Thursday at school seemed strange, knowing there was a game that night and I would not be there made it even more surreal.

Our girls' basketball team never got the same attention that the boys' team did, but I had expected that someone would at least have heard what had happened and asked me about it. No one did. The whole school seemed focused on Chris's ankle sprain and the fact he was missing games. I guess I couldn't entirely blame them. Besides the greater importance given to the boys' team, Chris's use of crutches made his injury visible to everyone, his crutches a symbol of healing. An injured ankle would heal, but I did not know if a broken heart could.

Things at home weren't any better. My mom continued to press my dad for action. Mostly, this happened behind closed doors. Late Thursday night, when I should've been at my basketball game, my mom forced the issue by having the three of us sit together and discuss things—a first. My mom announced that there would be a meeting with Coach Walters tomorrow, and the only question was whether it would be just my dad and me or all three of us.

"Suzie, we have a game tomorrow and Coach Walters has practice. When is this meeting supposed to happen?" He sounded exasperated.

"What do you think, Dad?" I asked quietly.

His head was bent forward, and he was pinching the bridge of his nose, his eyes shut. "Did you say something, Sam?"

"What do you think about this situation? As a coach?" I hoped he picked up on the rational side of my question instead of the emotional element.

"Well, it's complicated, Sam, as I think you understand better than your mom." He was looking at me now.

My heart sank. My dad knew my personality. He knew that I would always stay quiet and go along with the adult in charge, even when my insides were screaming and my heart was breaking. I was never one to make waves, question, or challenge any authority figure. I was the good girl, the pleaser. Because of all that, the only thing I could do at that moment was nod and stare blankly at the coffee table.

He took several deep breaths and continued, "But I'll sit down and have a conversation with him, coach to coach." My eyes immediately flicked up. Was he agreeing to this? "We'll sit down with him and talk it through," he motioned between us.

He looked at my mom, who patted him on the arm and smiled. "That's all I'm asking. Just talk to him and sort it out." My dad nodded and then looked at me. And I felt a tiny flicker of something I hadn't felt in weeks—hope.

The following day, my dad left early for school, leaving me a note to meet him in his classroom as soon as I arrived. I popped my head into his room at 7:40 a.m.

"Your mom has no clue how difficult it will be to meet with Coach Walters today with all our different schedules. If she had said this weekend was soon enough, we could've done something more involved, but since it had to be today, I think calling him at lunchtime would be the best way to talk with him. I'll see what I can learn about his perspective on what happened and where he is with his decision. Does that sound okay with you?"

My stomach sank, realizing his heart wasn't in this. All this was about placating my mom, and I could already see where this was going.

"Yeah, that's fine."

Although he had not asked questions about the incident, I decided to share one thing, knowing this was my last shot.

"Coach Walters has told college coaches I'm not good enough to play for them." My heart rate doubled just by saying those words out loud. He'd been shuffling papers on his desk but paused to look at me for the first time. That pause felt like an eternity.

For all the ways my dad had let me down, I knew this one thing about him: he was a good coach. He cared about his players and would do anything to help them succeed. I knew there was no way he could imagine purposely shooting down the hopes of a kid playing at the college level. That just wasn't the kind of coach he was, and maybe, just maybe, this was the thing that would finally get through to him.

"Okay. Swing by my class right after school so I can tell you how it went. We'll need to be on the same page with details for your mom tonight, or she still won't be satisfied."

I swallowed hard. Was he doing this to appease my mom and end the conversation at home? Or was there a chance that I'd finally made him understand how bad things had been? Even if he didn't care that my chances of playing college basketball were slipping through my fingers, maybe the coach in him was outraged enough to stand in my corner for once.

The school day felt endless. I couldn't focus during my classes, with my brain racing through endless questions. *What was my dad going to say? Would he stick up for me with Coach Walters? Would Coach Walters listen to him and put me back on the team? Would he treat me better if he did, knowing that my dad was watching?*

After the final bell rang, I raced to his classroom and waited patiently as all his students filed out.

"Hey, Sam, come on in." He was organizing papers into files and placing them into his school bag. "I had a good visit with Coach Walters at lunch."

I could feel relief rising in my chest, knowing this would all work out. I began searching my brain, trying to remember if my sneakers were still in the trunk of my car so that I could go straight to practice.

The harsh buzz of the school intercom shook me out of my thoughts. A voice came over the speaker in his classroom. "Coach Shuster, please come to the office. You have a call from a parent."

My dad sighed as he stood up from his chair. "I'll be right back."

I barely squeaked out a response. "Okay, Dad."

I watched him walk into the hallway and head for the office. I looked at the clock on his classroom wall. Okay, I still had time to get home to get my gear if needed. I dropped my bag and slumped into one of the front-row desks. I closed my eyes, rubbing my hands back and forth across the desk's smooth surface, trying to calm my nerves.

Five minutes later, my dad strode back through the door, his brow furrowed. I sat quietly, waiting for him to come back to our conversation. He opened the top drawer in his green metal filing cabinet and shoved open a hanging folder, thumbing through papers.

Finally, I couldn't take it anymore. "Dad?"

He pulled out a packet of papers and laid them on his desk.

"Hmm?" He closed the top drawer and slid open the middle one, squinting at the labels on top of the files.

"Dad, the meeting? With Coach Walters?"

He looked at me for a second before crossing his arms.

"Right, Coach Walters." My dad cleared his throat. "The bottom line is he feels like he can't change the punishment now because of the message it would send to the team. He reminded me of the practices you missed for the volleyball visits, and even though they were excused, they were still disruptive. He said that he's seen more cohesion in the team over the last two days and that it's probably better for the team, which guides coaches' decisions in situations like this."

My stomach sank. *Situations like this*—like I was just a run-of-the-mill player on the team, there to socialize, who had finally caused too many problems for the coach. My dad's eyes met mine briefly before turning back to his files.

"He said he was sorry for you but knew things would still work out fine whether you chose volleyball, basketball, or both sports at a junior college."

It was hard not to roll my eyes in disgust. Coach Walters was not sorry for me. But I kept my face neutral, recalling when I'd heard my dad say how relieved he was that he didn't have to coach girls because they were always so emotional. I was determined to show him that I could handle this blow without the emotional response that fit his stereotype about females. If I couldn't gain his pride through my sports accomplishments, maybe this might make him proud.

"Wish I had better news for you. I thought he might come around, but no luck. Your mom's going to ask. You fine with the details?"

"Yeah, but what about how she wanted us to do it together?"

"Uh . . . we'll just say we had the phone call together at lunch. I did the talking, but at least Coach Walters knew that you were with me, hearing what he said."

"Okay, Dad." I stood up and grabbed my bag. "Good luck tonight."

"Thanks, Sam."

He changed gears effortlessly back to his files without acknowledging how the world had just shifted underneath my feet.

For the next week and a half, my only focus was getting through each school day. In the back of my mind, I'd already devised a plan to keep me busy and out of the house—a part-time job. At this point, all I cared about was finishing the school year so I could have a fresh start in college. Between school, a job, my workouts, and periodic meetings with Ms. Collins, I could see the light at the end of the tunnel.

I had always been on the quiet side, but going through this personal trauma, I became more withdrawn. Without practice, I didn't see Lindsey at all, and I was unsure what an interaction with her would be like. I just kept busy and to myself. I hadn't seen much of Cassandra outside of English class either. We still talked, but not as regularly. Instead, I focused on my volleyball workouts in preparation for next year and worked as many hours as possible at a drug store to save money for school.

As much as I had always used writing to process my emotions, I couldn't find any words during this difficult time. It was too big and too painful. There was a silent gaping hole, a void, inside of me. Maybe the edges of the hole had become less jagged, a little smoother, as the weeks went on. I couldn't be sure because my day-to-day life was on autopilot, both physically and emotionally. I would not allow myself to peer into the abyss.

Over the next few weeks, my mom expressed occasional concerns about my behavior to either my dad or me. One night, I overheard her ask him if he'd noticed anything different about me. He said he thought I was going through a moody phase, typical of most high school girls, and he just hoped Emily wouldn't go through it too.

Moodiness. If only it were a moody phase. At least then, I'd know it would end. Every day, I wondered if my pain would subside. My busy schedule masked it well during the day, but I carried it around with me always.

In addition to school and a job, I had my workouts from Boise State. Given the unexpected change in my schedule, I convinced Coach Stevens that I'd like to start the conditioning program early. I saw this as trying to turn a negative situation into a positive one. I knew that every other player on the team would have more experience and game knowledge than me, and I couldn't do much about that. But from the first day together in August, I could be the team's strongest, fastest, and best-conditioned athlete. At least, that was my goal, and I attacked these workouts as if my life depended on it; in many ways, it did.

I tried to block out the past and focus only on my future, but a feeling of heaviness descended upon me. It was like wearing a robe made of steel. Coach Walters, the basketball season, my friendship with Lindsey, my outcast status at school, and never being "enough" for my dad all wove that robe. But rather than collapsing under the weight of the robe and never getting up, I pictured the added weight as a way of increasing the intensity of my workouts. That robe was making me stronger, improving my endurance and explosiveness. I imagined what I'd be able to do when I got to college and shed this heavy burden—I would be able to fly.

For four months, every night before going to bed, I'd drawn an X through the day, alternating royal blue and orange pens, the colors of Boise State. It was my secret countdown to the day I'd finally leave my high school, home, and family. I hung on to the hope that college would provide my first opportunity to be myself instead of always trying to be the person others wanted me to be.

I continued to meet with Ms. Collins once every two weeks in the morning before school. If I had feared my dad's response to working with her earlier in the year in preparation for basketball, this would be seen more like treason, worthy of execution. I never understood why he'd felt that way, but I knew it to be true. Although I would have liked to meet with Ms. Collins more frequently, a meeting every week would have shown up on my dad's radar.

Instead of basketball, Ms. Collins and I worked on the mental aspects of competition. She continued to challenge me with new and unusual activities, forcing me to become more comfortable with mistakes and failures. Her messages at the end were always the same: failing at something was neither a statement about me as a person nor final. I just hadn't mastered what I was trying to learn *yet*.

Ms. Collins prepared just as thoroughly for our meetings as she did for her regular classes. I knew she spent significant time reading and researching in preparation, judging from the depth of our discussions and the up-to-date study materials she provided. To say her generosity and support touched me would be a vast understatement. Her belief in me empowered me more than any of the skills and lessons she taught directly. Although our meetings focused on lessons to develop mental toughness, her most valuable gift was her complete acceptance of me and her unshakeable belief that I could accomplish anything I set my mind to. Her acceptance and belief set me on my path to self-acceptance and self-belief.

The last few months of my senior year were uneventful and not filled with typical teenage rebellion. Quietly, I went about being the dutiful daughter, always smiling on the outside. But inside, I kept my feelings of anger, frustration, and hurt locked away. I knew my parents did not want to see that, and it was something they would never understand.

Even graduation day was just another colored X on my calendar—orange. My parents were shocked that I did not want a graduation party and had no intention of attending our senior class party. I was shocked at their shock. Had they been paying attention? How often had I told them directly and indirectly that my high school years were not enjoyable? How many times had my actions shown them that I was essentially alone—if they were paying attention? It amazed me to realize they could not see what was right before them. What *did* they see, I wondered.

Although I felt like I had disappointed my parents with my social shortcomings, I left high school with a light heart and my sense of self-worth intact. The source of the solid and positive closure to my high school years came to me in the form of a letter I would cherish for life.

At our last meeting, Ms. Collins handed me a small package with a card affixed to the top with a gold sticker. "You don't have to open it here," she'd said, smiling. "When it feels like the right time to you."

The right time came two days after graduation. The sun was out, showing a hint of the summer weather still to come, so I packed a bag and visited the park where I'd spent many hours working to become the best athlete I could be. The sun's warmth felt good, but I soon realized there was nowhere private for me to sit and open Ms. C's present. It all looked and felt too exposed, but I finally decided on the baseball dugout.

I sat on the bench, leaned against the back wall, and stared through the chain-link fence separating the dugout from the dirt infield. I felt like I was about to start something new, a whole new beginning.

Even before I opened it, Ms. Collins's gift had become something meaningful. She knew better than anyone the anger and pain I'd experienced. She'd taught me so much about basketball and things bigger than basketball. She'd been a teacher, coach, counselor, and mentor all rolled into one. Holding her gift and realizing we'd no longer have workouts or much time to talk hit me hard. It felt like a final goodbye.

I opened the small package first. It was a book of inspirational quotes. I rubbed my hand over the cover and smiled. Next, I opened the pale blue envelope containing her card. The front had a brightly colored painting of a water scene with a sailboat, identical to the postcard in her office. It reflected her passion for art, but more important, it reminded me of the important lessons she had shared. Inside, both sides of the card were filled with a note in her small, neat handwriting.

As I read, hot tears streamed down my cheeks.

I sat in the dugout for a long time, waiting for the tears to stop. When they finally did, instead of feeling drained and numb, I experienced an overwhelming sense of gratitude like I'd never felt. I had known simple gratitude for things like Christmas presents, recovering from injuries, and meeting my basic needs, but this felt different. This gratitude was deep, layered, and struck at my core, radiating outward and infusing my entire being with warmth, light, and energy. Ms. Collins' gift of words, expressing both empathy and support, was a gift that would keep on giving. It was a heartfelt gift that would change my life forever.

When I finally felt strong enough to stand, I slowly made my way out of the dugout. On my way home, I took the long route around the park, letting the sunshine and gratitude wash over me. It was both soothing and energizing at the same time.

Throughout the summer, before leaving for college, I was reminded again and again of the power of friendships and the weight of words. One thing I realized was how much I wanted my parents' acknowledgment and acceptance of how I felt, with no judgment or effort to convince me I should feel something different. Although I did not have the words at the time to express it, I yearned for an acknowledgment of my reality. I did not get that at home, but luckily, I had gotten it from Ms. Collins.

As I struggled through dark moments of seemingly bottomless despair, slowly climbing step by step out of the deep canyon and finally believing I could see the light ahead, it was not my family that gave me strength and support. It was rereading the card from Ms. Collins. I didn't blame my parents; they couldn't understand me. Our parents often see us as who they think we are, who they want us to be, and how we reflect upon them. Having a mentor who truly sees us can make all the difference. I hoped that one day, I could give that same gift to others.

June 1987

Dear Sam,

I tried to show empathy and support for what you were expe-riencing with basketball this year, and I hope you felt that. I have also had a similar painful experience. It took some time, but I recovered and learned much from that experience. I didn't want to share this with you earlier because I did not want you to think that I was somehow minimizing your pain by sending an unintended message that "everyone suffers." Because pain and grief are unique to every individual, I thought it best to give you the time and space to work through your own in your way. Remember that hardships are not evaluated and ranked somehow, allowing only those who've suffered "the worst" to grieve.

As you embark on your journey for independence, I hope you will listen to and trust your inner voice because you possess a reservoir of strength and wisdom well beyond your years. Up to this point, many external forces have directed your life. The chance to draw guidance from within is one of the most exciting things about heading to college, and you are more prepared than any young person I've ever met.

Don't let anyone label you based on conforming to their social norms. Don't allow others' words or beliefs to drown out your voice; never let anyone take away your passion—these are yours and yours alone. It's worth standing up and fight-ing for! Don't give up, and never fear failure. Keep fighting because YOU are worth the effort.

Congratulations on your high school graduation. I wish you the best of luck as you begin this next exciting chapter in your life. Keep listening to your inner voice, keep believing, and KEEP DARING GREATLY!

Warmest wishes,

Ms. C

CHAPTER 34

I paused the Hall of Fame DVD again, not quite ready to hear what my dad had to say. I got up to take my dishes into the kitchen and make myself a cup of tea. By the time I returned to the couch with my steaming mug in hand, it occurred to me that the words from Lindsey and Coach Nelson were just as powerful as Ms. Collins's words had been so many years earlier. They were like a salve for a deep wound that had never completely healed. But while their kind and encouraging words helped lighten the scar, they were still no substitute for encouraging words from the one I wanted to hear them from the most—my dad.

I wrapped a blanket around my legs and pushed play. Cassandra read a list of stats and awards Chris had won in high school as my dad looked on with a wide smile. Then, as applause filled the room, Cassandra called Chris to speak. Even as he read his speech, my eyes remained fixed on my dad.

When Chris had finished, he passed the microphone to my dad. Full of charisma and passion and relishing the spotlight, he praised Chris for the records he'd set and what he'd meant to the program. When Dad finished, he beamed with pride and embraced Chris in a big hug, draping his arm over Chris's shoulder as they walked off the stage together.

I was stunned. During his ten-minute speech, my dad did not mention or acknowledge that he'd raised and coached another of the night's honorees. He gave no indication he was even proud of his daughter. It felt as if my accomplishments meant nothing to him.

I ejected the DVD and put it back in its case. I checked to ensure my doors were locked and turned off all the lights. Then I went into the study and sat down at my desk.

I grabbed a stack of blank printer paper to start getting some thoughts out of my head and onto the page. I didn't even want the lines of notebook paper somehow confining my writing; I needed blank pages.

Putting pen to paper, my hand desperately tried to keep up with my thoughts as writing blanketed the pages in jumbled phrases, bullet points, circled words, and arrows linking ideas.

I reached a stopping point after three pages. As I stared down at the final words I'd written, I was surprised to see drops hitting the page, darkening the words I'd written. Once again, my tears had come without warning.

I read through these pages once, folded them, and put them in an envelope with a printed copy of the letter I'd mailed to my parents months earlier. I would give Fitz the envelope and the DVD. By sharing my most difficult burdens, just like I'd suggested to Steph and Kelsey, I thought I would be unloading part of the weight I'd been carrying by myself for years. I was turning the page. I was starting a new chapter.

The next day, I gave the DVD and envelope to Fitz. He thanked me several times and seemed touched. Later, he called and, without explanation, said that he would pick me up at my house at 8:30 a.m. Saturday morning, and that I should be dressed for a hike in cold weather.

Saturday, we drove to the trailhead in silence. April was still cold, and as we started hiking, our breath blew in front of our faces in large plumes. We hiked the three miles in silence. I listened to the water as it churned within its banks. I listened to the birds chirping and singing, music to my ears. I listened to the occasional gusts of wind blowing through the trees, making the branches sway and the new leaves of spring rustle as they rubbed against each other. Spring was a time for new growth.

With the towering trees framing our meandering trail, I paid attention to the light and dark, the shadows cast by the sun's angle. Fitz hiked ten yards ahead, unaware I had stopped in a shaded area. Although surrounded by the beauty of nature, my parents came to mind. I felt like I'd walked in the shadows of their unmet expectations and quiet disappointment for too long.

Standing in the shady woods, I realized I didn't need an apology from my dad to reach forgiveness. The more important step was forgiving myself for abandoning myself all those years ago and waiting for validation from my dad.

I took slow and steady steps forward toward the end of the shadow and the beginning of the light. To any outside observer, my next step probably looked like any other. But to me, that step was momentous.

Stepping out of the shadow, I knew I could now paint with bold and vibrant colors. Stepping out of the shadow, I could now paint with wild, unrestrained brush strokes. Stepping out of the shadow, I could now paint outside the lines. I could create new lines, my own lines, my own picture, and my own masterpiece. I finally felt willing and able to step out of the shadow, to live out of the shadow, and to begin again.

EPILOGUE
TWELVE YEARS LATER
JANUARY 2019

The clock read 4:45 a.m. when I awakened to two of my favorite smells. I realized I wasn't dreaming when Joel entered the room carrying a tray holding our usual: two steaming hot mochas and heavily buttered homemade pumpkin bread, one with a lit candle. I faked sleep as he leaned over, gently kissing my neck.

"Wake up, my love. Enjoying these treats together will be worth missing our usual morning snuggle." I blew out the candle as he continued, "I got up early to be the first to wish you a happy birthday. I know Cassandra always wants to be the first, but not this year!"

Watching the sun slowly rise over the mountains, we began the day with our usual ritual, toasting each other with mochas. I felt lucky to have found a life companion who loved nature, meaningful conversations, and the small things that made life beautiful. I had found someone who understood and loved me, just as I am.

Opening my computer, my inbox had more emails than usual, full of birthday wishes. Cassandra had sent hers at 12:01 a.m. Her brief note said she'd call me today and included a video of her daughters dancing wildly to the Beatles' "Birthday" song.

The next note was from Kelsey, wishing me a happy birthday and giving me an update on her team. She'd added a P.S.: "I'll forgive you for taking your birthday off, but I'm looking forward to your feedback on that game tape I sent. Thanks for being my extra set of eyes."

Steph had also sent an email wishing me happy birthday and including two photographs. The first was a family photo with the Christmas gift we'd sent for her one-year-old, June—a Little Tykes basketball hoop. June stared at the net with wide brown eyes as Steph and her wife, Sasha, beamed on either side. The second showed Steph and Amy sitting together at a coffee shop. Amy, dressed in her medical school sweatshirt, smiled while Steph grinned from ear to ear, toasting her with a mug that read, "Relax, the school counselor can fix it!"

I continued to scroll, reading each email in turn. I was thankful for the birthday wishes, but more than that, I reveled in the updates from each person. I was honored that many people felt comfortable sharing their successes and failures and occasionally asked for my guidance as a mentor and trusted friend.

I gazed at the photo of Ms. Collins and me, taken years before at a tournament. Losing her to cancer had been difficult, but I felt her presence in those moments when I saw the difference that her coaching and mentoring had made in my life and when I tried to pass that gift forward.

After spending the morning reading emails and sending brief notes of thanks to my friends, I turned my attention to a large manila envelope I'd received from Fitz. He usually sent an e-card for my birthday, so I was curious about its contents but waited to open it, imagining it might contain birthday wishes.

The large envelope contained two smaller ones. Fitz had written *Open First* on a sunny yellow envelope in his barely legible script. Inside was a corny birthday card with a handwritten message:

Happy birthday, Sam!

Finding the right card is hard, but I knew you would get my humor!

I paused briefly before opening the second envelope, a small manila mailer, and slowly unwound the string holding it closed. Inside, there was another note from Fitz:

Dear Sam,

I was sorting through our attic and found this. It belongs to you.

I know this is a painful time with your mom being sick. You should read this on occasion as a reminder that you extended a sincere invitation to share a loving relationship with your parents. I'm so sorry they never responded to you. I know that had to hurt more than you showed, and I'm proud of you for staying in close contact with them anyway and being there for them, especially now. Maybe for reasons we will never know, they were not capable of accepting your gift.

Count my family as part of the "chosen family" you have worked hard to create. We all love you and always will.

Love,

Fitz

I paused again, remembering when I'd mailed my parents the original of this letter over a decade ago and never received an answer. They had kept me at arm's length, and our relationship never changed. Instead, I created a family of people who loved, supported, and knew me for who I was.

Looking at the letter in my hand, I was uncertain if I was ready to reopen this old wound. I wished I could tell my younger self who wrote that letter that so many beautiful things were waiting for her in life. I wished I could tell her how proud I was that she'd had the courage to write this letter. I couldn't do that, but I could honor her strength by reading it now. I unfolded the white paper and read.

Dear Mom and Dad,

I want to share some thoughts and feelings that have been on my mind and heavy on my heart for a long time. Some of these things may be difficult to hear, but I hope you will read this with an open mind and heart, recognizing that what I share and why I share it comes from a place of love.

You both know that I have always loved basketball. At first, it may have been the chance to share time with Dad, doing something together that we both loved and enjoyed. Remember in the sixth grade when Dad had me playing on the boys' basketball team in a tournament at the Tacoma Dome? I scored the most points in the game! It made us all so happy, and I felt you both had a sense of pride in my accomplishments.

Many things suddenly changed in middle school. Not only did my schoolmates begin treating me differently, but

Dad also began discouraging my passion for sports, instead emphasizing the importance of me looking a certain way (skinny, feminine, pretty), and acting a certain way (more social, having lots of friends). And Mom, though you supported me during high school by religiously attending my sporting events and helping me to secure a college scholarship, that also changed after I graduated. It feels like your "support" transformed into pressuring me to get married and have children rather than encouraging me to continue pursuing my passion for sports through then playing and now coaching and mentoring young female athletes.

I have probably never fit the mold of who you think I should be, either when I was a young woman or today, as an adult. Though you love me, it feels like there are conditions on that love, many of which center on image, what others think, and, maybe unconsciously, focusing on meeting your needs and goals. I mistakenly thought that if I continued to follow my passions and excel at my life choices, you would both finally be proud of me. Because you have continued to discourage me, it feels like that will never happen—like I will never be enough.

Feeling like I've had to choose between following my passion or making my parents happy is a no-win situation. I've always known that sports, particularly basketball, are my passion. Sports have been my way of standing on my own two feet, leaving home, attending college, and pursuing a career in service to others doing something I love.

I know you love and care about me, just like I love and care about you, but it has always seemed like you don't *listen to me, see me, or want to know me. Even now, it feels like you fear knowing me better. It's as if it might make you even more disappointed or unhappy about how I am reflecting on you.*

I take responsibility for my role in how our relationship got to where it is. Trying to make everyone happy always seemed so important that I often didn't tell you what I thought or felt. The result was that I carried around hurt feelings and anger like rocks in a backpack. As an adult, I now realize that I have been expecting you to observe my actions and read my mind, hoping that you would remove some of those rocks for me rather than me doing it myself.

I want to see and hear you so our relationship can be better. I desire a relationship where we truly know one another—not playing roles expected or needed, but striving for an authentic relationship based on mutual respect, acceptance, support, and curiosity in each other's journeys—a relationship that is full of patience and love. Our relationship in the past does not have to be our relationship in the future, but we must actively address the obstacles in our path.

This process starts by being honest about what we need from each other, being vulnerable, and sharing who we are—becoming a true family and showing genuine love. I know this can be done because I have experienced it with close friends who have become my "chosen family." I long for the same deep connection with you. It will take time, patience, and, most of all, courage. I love you both, and that is why I am reaching out. I hope that you will both join me on this journey.

Sam

Tears streamed down my face, but not tears of sorrow or pain. They were tears of pure love and deep gratitude for my incredible, beautiful, and loving "chosen family." We had built it together, layer upon layer.

READING GROUP GUIDE
DISCUSSION QUESTIONS

1. In Chapter 1, Sam describes her concerns—going back to her youth—about disappointing others. She shares that she internalized the injustices she felt and believed she could prove her worth through her actions. Is others' approval essential to you? Do you feel like more importance is placed on "external validation" by females in society? If so, what effects might this have on women in the long run?

2. In Ch. 3, Coach Sam says building trust to ensure a strong team foundation is based on communicating honestly and regularly, showing genuine interest, and being consistent in word and action. Do these factors apply to all relationships? What characteristics do you feel are essential for building trusting relationships?

3. Throughout the book, Sam describes mentoring as vital to her coaching. Name instances in which mentorship played an invaluable role

in this novel. Has a mentor played a crucial role in your life? If so, did you pass on the lessons you learned to others?

4. In Ch. 4, Ms. Collins coaches Sam on her challenges with perfectionism. She suggests Sam can't realize her full potential until she becomes comfortable with feeling uncomfortable. Does Ms. C's advice resonate with you? Is one gender more prone to perfectionism? If so, why and what effect does that have on their lives?

5. *Layer Upon Layer* presents the perspective that females are commonly discouraged from being as competitive as males. What's your reaction to this? Does it seem like women often have to "act like men" to be successful in many roles? Why is this, and can you share how this affects women in sports, politics, the workplace, and home?

6. In Ch. 9, Coach Sam observes that her players accept compliments with seeming embarrassment. She adds that the confidence generated from compliments seems short-lived, while a single criticism or failure can become toxic and long-lasting. Do most females you know accept compliments with grace? Are females more sensitive to criticism than males? If so, why?

7. Coach Sam shares this James Baldwin quote with her team: *Not everything that is faced can be changed, but nothing can be changed until it is faced.* How does this quote relate to Sam's journey? Does it relate to yours? Would embracing this shift in viewpoint affect how you deal with family, friends, and coworkers?

8. After receiving Ms. C's revelatory letter about her painful experiences as a high school coach, Sam reflects on the positive impact of hearing others' personal stories. Knowing that people we admire

and respect have had similar problems can make us recognize that burdens are universal and that experiencing them doesn't mean something is wrong with us. What's your take on this? Have you found that sharing deep pain with others has given you power over that experience? How can being vulnerable build deeper connections with the important people in your life?

9. After learning Coach Walters has sabotaged her basketball opportunities, Sam's hate and anger morph into "strong feelings of shame." She begins to realize her silence in the face of poor treatment may not be coming from "respectful behavior" but feelings of unworthiness. Would a male be likely to experience these feelings of shame and unworthiness in the same situation? What effects can a sense of unworthiness have on male-female relationships?

10. In Ch. 26, Sam explores her feelings about receiving no response to the letter she sent her parents. Is it unreasonable to need others to be someone they are incapable of being? How can you reconcile with someone who refuses to validate your perspective about what's happening? Is a "real relationship" possible with that person?

11. In Ch. 32, Coach Sam shares her players' pain and grief after losing their championship game. What profound lessons does Sam teach about grief? How do you deal with grief? Is showing emotions courageous? Can you sit with others in grief, and how does this help?

12. Steph is surprised to learn her coaches work through their worries and sorrows with nonfamily members. Fitz says the roles we play in our families can become entrenched, and as we change, those roles can keep us from truly knowing one another. Do you play a "role" in your family? Does that role affect your ability to be authentic

with family members? Who helps you most through your worries and sorrows?

13. In the letter to her parents, Sam describes having found deep love from her chosen family. Can "chosen family" fulfill our deep need for unconditional love and acceptance? How do you define "family"?

14. At the end of *Layer Upon Layer,* once again disappointed by her father, Sam has an epiphany: She doesn't need an apology from her dad to reach forgiveness, but instead needs to forgive herself for abandoning herself by waiting for his validation. How might this self-discovery affect Sam's future? Have you ever experienced a moment of great self-discovery? Can you share how it changed your life?

For other questions and quotations to consider for discussion, please visit layeruponlayer.com.

ACKNOWLEDGMENTS

The ten-year path to publishing this novel involved many "layers," most notably the support of many generous, patient, intelligent, kind people along the way. Given the tragedy of losing DeeDee, there may be contributors I have forgotten or am unaware of. If so, I ask for their forgiveness and understanding.

One vital layer was female authors who have modeled vulnerability and courage in their insightful stories of self-realization. Works by Brené Brown, Glennon Doyle, and Mary Pipher impacted DeeDee and me by stimulating deep discussions and further strengthening our connection. Drawing inspiration from their writing, DeeDee hoped her book might support others on their journeys to self-discovery.

But the most critical layer in creating this heartfelt novel was DeeDee herself, and her six years of steadfast commitment and creativity. She wrote two narratives totaling one thousand handwritten pages before combining them into the story she wished to tell. I often marveled at DeeDee's dedication. I'd tell her, "They say everyone has a book in them, but you're the only person I know who's written it." With her usual humility, she'd laugh and remind me that she felt no pressure because she had already sold "nickel novels" from the back of her red wagon as a kid. DeeDee! Oh, how I miss her!

After completing the original story, DeeDee sought early guidance from Marla Daniels at NY Book Editors on shortening her work to a publishable length. Using what she learned from Marla's critique, DeeDee made serial edits and successfully cut over 55 percent of her manuscript. Sadly, she became ill while beginning what was planned as the final edit before seeking publication.

Another support layer came from early readers: Joe DeBruyne (DeeDee's real-life Fitz), Carrie Gueller, Leslie Horton, and Lou Webb. Their suggestions and encouragement motivated further edits, after which prepublication readers grew: Laurie and Greg Creighton, Linda Frady (DeeDee's aunt), Laurie Kennelly, Lois Kussman (DeeDee's grandmother), Kathy Savatini, and Anina Winters. DeeDee said she was "humbled and grateful for your belief, support, and most of all, your love and friendship."

After DeeDee passed, editing support for *Layer Upon Layer* also arrived in layers. Rea Frey and Jacqueline Hritz from Writeway provided developmental and structural editing. Due to Rea's recent book tour (congratulations, Rea), I managed the line editing via numerous self-reads and reader suggestions. Many thanks to Diana Douglas, Janet Horton, and Bill and Martha Wittgow for their multiple reads and helpful recommendations. Thanks especially to Ken Horton for his patience and skill in the final line edits.

Fortune next led me to Michele DeFilippo at 1106 Design. Michele and her phenomenal team efficiently coordinated the final editing and book design in preparation for publication. I also wish to thank 1106 Design's copyeditor and proofreader for their meticulous work, which made for a smoother read.

Thanks to Jessica Zweig and her fantastic team at SimplyBe for providing marketing guidance for getting *Layer Upon Layer* in front of readers: Hollie Boodram, Julie Girsch, Kendall McKinven, and Meenal Rahatkar. You each brought unique skills to the task and were patient with someone new to marketing and social media!

Special thanks for loving support found in unexpected places: Liz Wittgow-Styles, whose enthusiastic response to reading *Layer Upon Layer* spurred me to discuss completing the road to publication with DeeDee—after agreeing to protect its "heart and soul." Much love to Mark Freret and Laurel Gauthier, whose appreciation for DeeDee's writing further encouraged belief in publishing this novel. Thank you to Suzanne and Reina at Olympia Copy and Printing, who expedited printing a bound copy of *Layer Upon Layer* for DeeDee to see and hold before her passing, which brought us great joy.

We will be forever indebted to Anina Winters, who lived with us for almost eight months when not working as a flight attendant in order to assist in DeeDee's end-of-life passage. And Laurie and Greg Creighton, who canceled their winter vacation to remain "alert and available" to help care for DeeDee. You are not only the ideal of true and special friends but also gave us the greatest gift we could ever receive, allowing us to share innumerable incredible moments during DeeDee's final journey.

Thanks to our "chosen family" who steadfastly supported honoring DeeDee in pursuing the publication of *Layer Upon Layer*. You all made us believe that this book would be a gift to readers. You know who you are!

Finally, thanks to some special family members for their love and support. Joel Horton for being more like a brother than an uncle. Janet Horton for being like a sister. Ken Horton, a brother most people only dream of—the world would be better if everyone had a loving sibling like you! And finally, Bonnie Lacey Horton, our wonderful, caring cousin, for seeing beauty in DeeDee's writing and generously providing her steadfast expertise, energy, love, and endless support and guidance to make this publication a reality. We did it together—layer upon layer!

To infinity . . . DeeDee & David

ABOUT THE AUTHOR

DeeDee (Bailey) Horton had a passion for writing since youth. She grew up a gifted athlete who alternated between collegiate volleyball and basketball—as does her protagonist in *Layer Upon Layer*. After teaching middle school, where she especially enjoyed teaching writing, DeeDee returned to her love of sports as a college basketball coach for more than a decade. After retirement, she wrote *Layer Upon Layer,* pulling from her athletic experience to shed light  on the importance of mentors and positive female narratives that bring constructive change to women.

While beginning final edits, DeeDee was diagnosed with an inoperable brain tumor. She entrusted her husband, David, with the completion of *Layer Upon Layer* while prioritizing the writing of two "Love Books" to carry him through the grief ahead.

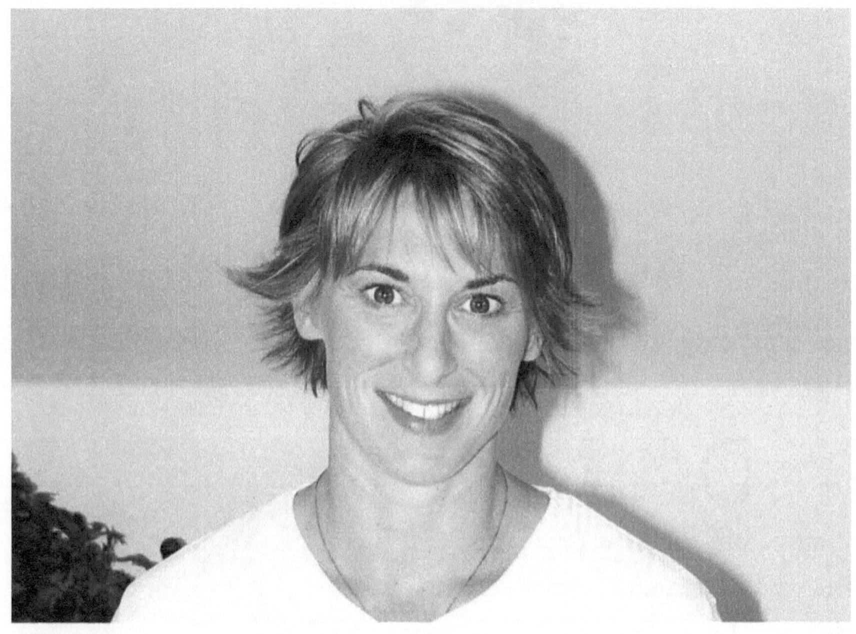